Stewards
of the Flame

Sylvia Engdahl

✳ *Ad* ✳
Stellae

Eugene, Oregon

This is a work of fiction, set in the distant
future. The opinions expressed are those
of the author and are not intended to
apply to personal healthcare decisions of
individuals living today.

Book design and layout by Sylvia Engdahl
Cover photo © by Pklimenko / Dreamstime.com

ISBN-10: 0-615-31487-2
ISBN-13: 978-0-615-31487-7

Contents

Preface

This is one of five novels—a duology and a trilogy—that are tied together by the concept of a flame as the symbol of the evolving "paranormal" powers of the mind and by their setting in an imaginary future in which those powers are developed first by a small group of people, and later by their successors' influence on human civilization. But the books are separate stories that can be read independently, and this one, in particular, is quite different from the others. It is focused on an additional theme: the tyranny that could result from a society's excessive devotion to healthcare.

Because my portrayal of a medically-based dystopia is controversial, readers tend to either like the book a lot or not like it at all. If you are reading this far, you probably have seen descriptions of the story and decided it's something you'll find interesting. But if it turns out that you don't, please don't assume that the other four "Flame" novels will be similar. They don't deal with healthcare issues, and none of them depend on having read this one. They center on more typical science fiction themes such as space colonization and alien contact. I probably made a mistake in giving them such similar titles, because readers who dislike one often avoid others they would enjoy.

Each of the "Flame" novels can stand alone. When I wrote them, one at a time, I had no intention of writing another; the idea for the succeeding story didn't come to me until months, or years, later. They can be read in any order, except that each includes enough backstory to affect the suspense of the preceding one. Please note that unlike my earlier books these are adult novels and contain some material inappropriate for readers below high school age.

Sylvia Engdahl, June 2021

Formerly, people rushed to embrace totalitarian states. Now they rush to embrace the therapeutic state. When they discover that the therapeutic state is about tyranny, not therapy, it will be too late.

—Thomas Szasz, *Pharmacracy*, 2001

Of all tyrannies a tyranny sincerely exercised for the good of its victims may be the most oppressive.

—C.S. Lewis, *God in the Dock*, 1970

Experience should teach us to be most on our guard to protect liberty when the government's purposes are beneficent.

—Louis Brandeis, *Olmstead v. United States*, 1928

Part One

1

WHEN HE OPENED his eyes he could not recall what world he was on. There had been so many. But he wasn't on a starship, Jesse realized, and . . . and he must return to the ship, right now. Memory flooded back. This was the colony planet Undine, and his ship was due to break orbit. He sat up, his face in his hands—and caught sight of the white-jacketed medic at the foot of the bed.

"I guess it's stupid to ask where I am," Jesse said, revising his assumptions. It was obviously a hospital, and he did not remember entering it. He did not remember being ill, even; this felt more like one hell of a hangover. It was a familiar feeling. He'd waked with hangovers on all too many worlds in recent years. Never before, though, had they required hospitalization.

The medic said nothing. "Was there an accident?" Jesse inquired.

"No. You were lucky. We got to you before you tried to leave the bar."

Puzzled, Jesse groped for recollection. Yes, he'd been in a bar. That was about the only place there was to go, onworld. He had not drunk enough to pass out, however. Besides, if he'd passed out in the bar, there would have been no question of his trying to leave it, and if he hadn't passed out, why would anyone have called the medics? He wasn't licensed to drive a ground vehicle, so why would they even have detained him?

"Exactly where did I collapse?" he demanded.

"You weren't quite that bad," the man said. "You were out for only a minute or two, then came around. We sedated you in the ambulance. You wouldn't remember."

"But why was the ambulance there?" Jesse persisted. He was beginning to lose patience. What he'd seen of this colony so far, he had not liked, and his opinion of it wasn't improving.

"Just cruising," said the medic. "The guy next to you saw you had a problem and pushed his flag-stop button. It would have been better to come in sooner, on your own, you know. You'd need less treatment if you'd reported to admissions long ago."

"Treatment for what?" There was some serious misunderstanding here. Perhaps he'd not yet been seen by a doctor.

"Alcohol abuse, what else?" A second medic had appeared in the doorway; the first one turned and said, "Denial. Typical. Why do they hide from care when they know the law?"

"This one's from offworld," said the second man. "Technically he's not subject to health laws until he's in custody."

"Now, hold on!" said Jesse, rising. "I don't know what kind of second-rate facilities you've got here, but diagnosis doesn't seem to be your strong point. I am not an alcoholic. I am Jesse Sanders, Captain of the Unified Colonial Fleet star freighter *Eureka*—"

"Not anymore, you're not," the second medic told him. "The *Eureka* broke orbit yesterday, with the first mate in command. Did you think they'd lose a window while you were incapacitating yourself?"

Jesse's knees buckled; he slipped back to the edge of the bunk. "God," he said in shock. "Oh, God. What the hell have you people done to me?"

He was not an alcoholic. He never drank on shipboard, or excessively while onworld in the company of his crew. On shore leave, alone and without duties, he sometimes got drunk on purpose; but he had never lost track of time. He hadn't passed out even briefly before, and had drunk no more than usual on this occasion. He'd have been awake to board the shuttle the next day, and the *Eureka*'s cargo wouldn't have been fully loaded until nightfall. The window for the latest departure required to keep the ship on schedule had lasted another thirty-five hours after that. They had sedated him for two days and three nights while his ship went on without him.

Why? What possible motive could anyone have for it? He knew no one on Undine. It had no political entanglements with other colonies. He had no enemies on the *Eureka*; it was a small, contented crew. He had no enemies in Fleet, either, as far as he knew. What did anyone have to gain by ending his career?

He would never get another command. The best he could hope for would be a mate's billet on the next freighter to touch here. The worst . . . well, if he couldn't get the record straightened out, he might not even get transport out of the colony. If it was entered as AWOL due to drunkenness, he would be on this outlying world for the rest of his life.

"I want to see the man in charge," he declared grimly.

"I'm your doctor," replied the second medic. "I can help you."

"Not you. The man, or woman, over you. The one who can tell me who authorized the sedation."

"Authorized? It's routine. The ambulance crew starts it; it's maintained until you're detoxified."

"I didn't need detox, and you know it. Somebody was paid."

The medics looked at each other meaningfully. "Paranoia?" asked the first one.

"We'd better check it out," agreed the doctor. "I'll send him up to Psych later today."

Perhaps, Jesse thought, he really had tied one on and was hallucinating. This could not be happening.

"I'll admit," the doctor said to him, "that you haven't damaged your body much with alcohol yet. You are very, very fortunate that this has been caught early. I know you may not feel you have a problem, but drinking to the point of intoxication is a danger sign. On Earth they don't treat everyone who's in danger. We do, here. We have the finest medical facility in the galaxy, and we take just pride in it. Don't worry about anything, Jesse. We can make you well."

"Sanders, to you," Jesse said grimly. "Captain Sanders."

"This isn't a social occasion," said the doctor. "We're here to care for you. We call all our patients by their first names—"

"And do they call you by yours?" Jesse snapped. "I see a nametag there that says Dr. Yasir. I'll not use that title unless you reciprocate."

"Hostile," said the other medic, as if Jesse were deaf. "Should I wait for the psych report before I schedule him for aversion therapy?"

Aversion therapy. God! But it was the standard treatment, of course; he knew that. He had never liked the idea of it, even in the case of people who really were substance abusers. Not that any spacer liked any medic much; there was antagonism of long standing between the two professions. There were, however, degrees of distastefulness.

"We're not scheduling anything," he said. "I'm checking myself out, right now."

They started at him blankly. "I'm not drunk now," he said, wondering if they were stupid as well as officious. "You can't hold me here. I won't sign the consent form."

The younger medic, looking blanker still, asked, "What consent form?"

2

THEY SENT HIM up to Psych. Jesse, dazed though he was, attempted to be cooperative; psych therapies were, after all, an even less inviting prospect than forced treatment for non-existent alcoholism. He took endless tests, answered endless questions. He lied only with regard to the most offensive ones.

He was put to bed in a cubicle which was, surprisingly, private. He hoped it was not part of the psych ward. He hoped he was there only for lights out.

He lay looking out the small window at the strip of dark sky visible over a vast complex of well-lit buildings. The sky, the only home he had known for the past twenty-odd years—he had no ties left on Earth, though he had grown up there. He'd gone into space young. He'd been eager then, excited. He'd had dreams of exploring the universe. It had not turned out like that, of course. Things never did. You knew, after ten years or so, that they never would.

But you didn't expect them to take a turn like this, either.

It was not that he couldn't face the idea of being worldbound. Space actually didn't mean that much anymore. He was not exploring; he was on a milk run between colonized solar systems. There was little if anything to be seen from the bridge of a freighter, and one freighter was pretty much like another. One port was like another, too. You saw more of what went on in vids than through sightseeing.

But he enjoyed freighter command as much as he could enjoy any job, and it was the only work he knew. He was considered good at it. The very routine of it was insulation against . . . other things. Things you once believed in, cared about, and then stopped caring about. That was the worst: you stopped caring. You stopped thinking you'd someday find a meaning.

Would it have helped if he'd had a family? That had been a dream, once, too. It wasn't practical for a spacer to have a home base, but couples in mixed crews did marry. Fleet took pains to keep them together. They got free care and schooling for their kids. But an arrangement like that was very, very permanent. It lacked the flexibility of an onworld marriage; if it didn't work out, there you were. He'd had short-term relationships with crew women, but never one worth a binding commitment.

It was just as well he didn't have a family now. God, if he'd been involved with anyone aboard the *Eureka*—!

Yet if he had been, he wouldn't have been drinking alone. He wouldn't have tried to get drunk, and in any case would not have been taken into custody. No crew woman would have let an ambulance team misjudge his condition. At the worst, if they'd persisted, she'd have lodged a protest with the local authorities long before the end of the departure window.

As things were, the crew hadn't guessed the true cause of his disappearance. The fact that he'd been abandoned proved that. He might have no close friends aboard—the Captain always kept apart, except from lovers—but he was respected. His habit of drinking on leave had never affected his duties; the mate wouldn't have believed a report of substance abuse. The *Eureka*, if told he'd been hospitalized, must have assumed a true medical emergency. The diagnosis would bypass them, be sent to Fleet headquarters without the chance for his crew to contest it.

Jesse's body ached with tension, and his heart constricted. What would happen to him, stuck on a world like this? What if the aversion therapy took? He would then lose the small solace drink could offer, and what else, in a port, was there to do?

Work? He was not qualified for onworld work, at least not in terms of official credentials, which on just about any world were all that mattered. Yet for any job not demanding credentials, he'd be called overqualified. There was small chance that anyone would hire him. He would not need to work; his credit was good, and his back pay had accumulated for years. It was enough to retire on. Jesse did not want to retire.

He turned onto his stomach and lay, for hours, in mute agony. There would be no sleep, he knew, after two days and three nights of sedation. Who had engineered that? He could see, on reflection, that no one had. The doctor had been honest. They did it here to all drunks. He was the victim not of foul play but of fate. It occurred to him suddenly to wonder how many other victims were imprisoned in this hellish excuse for a hospital. Not just drunks; if they knew nothing of consent forms here, they must treat everything else by force too. What had the doctor said, that as an offworlder he wasn't subject to the health laws until taken into custody?

This was not the kind of colony he wished to join as a citizen. And without transport, he might not have any choice.

Eventually, the room began to grow light. He looked back at the sky and saw the sun rising, a yellow sun much like Earth's. Buildings, of identical stark design and interconnected by elevated walkways, spread out in every direction; he was in one of the tallest. Were they all part of the hospital? The colony's population wasn't large enough to support such huge one. It seemed odd, now that he thought of it, that it dared claim "the finest medical facility in the galaxy."

The cubicle's curtain parted and a nurse came in. She was tall, dark-haired and slender; somehow the white uniform she wore didn't suit her. There was something a bit familiar about her. "Hello, Jesse," she said to him. "My name is Carla."

Jesse sat up. "Well, we're on an equal basis with names, anyway," he said, "even if you're my jailer."

Carla looked straight at him with green eyes that seemed almost luminous. "Your record says you're an alcoholic," she said. "Are you?"

"No."

"Why do you abuse alcohol, then?"

"I don't, as I'm sure you know." He remembered, now, where he had seen her before. She'd been present during the psych testing. He'd assumed she was a technician, but evidently she must be one of the therapists. They were cross-checking. They wanted to see if he would remain stubborn in his "denial of the problem."

"Jesse," she said. "You do drink—maybe not to the point of abuse, that's a subjective term, but you get drunk sometimes. I want to know why."

"Because I haven't anything better to do when I'm not on duty," he said honestly. And then, wondering why he felt compelled to confess to her, he added, "Because it helps me forget the emptiness."

She held his gaze for a long, long moment. Then she said quietly, "Thank you for telling me, Jesse." She started to leave the room, but turned back. "Don't tell anyone else," she advised. "If you do, you'll be put on antidepressants. And my guess is that you'd rather keep your brain intact."

But the psych tests would have revealed his underlying dissatisfaction with life, he realized in dismay. Why had he not already been drugged?

A few hours later, orderlies came for him. Hope, aroused against reason by Carla's presence, died at the sight of them. Jesse struggled to his feet and tried to regain the bearing of a starship captain. He had never been a coward, and he'd be damned if he'd let a bunch of frigging medics on a backwater world turn him into one.

"Therapy, I suppose," he said resignedly. "Don't you at least issue bathrobes?"

"Where you're going, you won't need one." And without it, wearing only the skimpy gown in which he'd slept, he could hardly make for the exit, Jesse realized. Not that these burly escorts would let him escape in any case.

They took him to an examining room large enough for an operating theater, where, unceremoniously, he was stripped naked and strapped to a table. White-garbed technicians clustered round. Equipment carts were pushed toward him, closing in. He was conscious of more tubes and electronics than there were on the bridge of a starship.

Above the other voices, one stood out. Carla's voice. "There's been a mistake," she was saying. "This man isn't scheduled for a full workup. He's under Psych's jurisdiction."

"Psych ordered it," someone replied. "Dr. Kelstrom."

"No! That couldn't have happened. A computer error, maybe."

"See for yourself. Kelstrom's signature. You're from his office, aren't you? You'll recognize it."

Evidently Carla did recognize it. Jesse heard no more from her as they turned up the lights and plunged a large needle into his hip.

3

CARLA FRANCESCO HURRIED down the corridor from the stairwell, her face flushed as she strode into the office of the one man in the Hospital she fully trusted. "There's been some sort of snafu," she declared with anger. "Since when have you been signing orders without reading them?"

He was calm, composed, as always—yet strangely distant. "I do read them."

"Not this morning, apparently, unless somebody's learned to forge your seal. They have Jesse Sanders in the demonstration room; they're about to do a full workup with student techs."

"I know that. In this case, I'm allowing it."

She couldn't believe what she was hearing. Upon finding Jesse's bed empty, she'd run a computer trace; the result had been so surprising—so unlike Kelstrom—that it hadn't occurred to her it could be anything but an error. "There's nothing wrong with the man, no possible reason to subject him to that," she protested. "It would be hell for him even if he were used to such things."

"Anybody who works for Fleet is used to medical workups, I imagine." He turned to his computer, not looking at her.

"Not like ours. Offworld they're not like ours, not unless there are symptoms serious enough to warrant the stress. *You* told me that." Furious, confused because he was holding back in a way not at all characteristic of him, Carla paused. Her heart was pounding, and not just from rushing upstairs.

"Carla. They wanted a subject on whom there were no recent records; the computer tagged Sanders. The official view's that we're doing him a favor. He's getting tests that would cost twice his annual pay on worlds like Earth where preventative care's not free."

His voice was level; none of the irony she'd have expected came through. "That's not *your* view," she insisted, baffled. "We spend half our time knocking ourselves out to protect patients assigned to you from that sort of thinking."

Still not meeting her gaze, Kelstrom agreed, "I don't order physical workups often enough to suit my colleagues. Well, for once I saw a chance to display orthodoxy. My position here will be strengthened by it."

Incredulous, Carla could only stare. He had never been so cold before. He'd shown no lack of feeling even yesterday—when she'd shown him the results of Jesse's initial psych tests, he'd shared her outrage at the injustice already done. "We'll get the man out of here," he'd assured her. "Action's clearly called for, from what I can see at first glance. He's not a true substance abuser, and certainly not paranoid. There'll be no problem with a quick discharge."

And then, about to close the file, he had taken a closer look at its biographical section. "Carla," he'd said in a low voice, tinged with excitement. "This man is a *starship captain*."

She had known what lay beneath his reaction. The responsibilities he bore obscured boyish enthusiasms, at least within Hospital walls—but like herself and most of her friends, he was stirred by the mere thought of starships. Not that offworld travel would ever be possible for any of them, but space was a symbol. It meant freedom from the problems they faced on Undine.

Their eyes met, and as usual, their emotions; voicing

them wasn't necessary. "I'll call up his chart at home to-night, and review it carefully," he'd said, clearing the screen. "Meanwhile, he does have a drinking problem—not one that warrants intervention, but a problem nonetheless. Find out what's back of it."

"Frustration, don't you think? If his case had gone to anyone but you, I'd have tweaked the test results." By most staff doctors, Jesse's underlying discontent would have been labeled "illness" and antidepressants would have been or-dered in high enough doses to distort his natural response to what was happening to him. "How can I learn anything more specific?"

"Try asking him. He'll reveal more than he says in words, to you. I don't want to talk to him myself—he won't trust me in this setting."

"He'd be a fool if he did," she'd agreed. Now she won-dered if her own trust had been misplaced. Yet it couldn't have been. The grounds for it had been unquestionable. How could anyone, let alone this man, change so totally?

"I believe what Jesse told me this morning," Carla said, "as I reported in the first place. He was open with me, and our minds—touched." The moment was vivid in her memory: an ordinary-looking man, light brown hair, skin pale from a life spent aboard starships . . . and yet his grey-blue eyes had met hers in a way that was not ordinary. "I think he's more of a workaholic than an alcoholic," she added. "He drinks to fill the hours away from his job. That's not the kind of problem we should mess with here. How can you use him like a lab animal, let him be tortured, his body exposed and probed without regard for his human dignity—"

She broke off, aware with dismay of her sensations. She had seen Jesse's nakedness in the examining room, and unlike the others present, had been embarrassed by it. She was a psych technician, not a medical nurse. Her attitude toward bodies was not clinical. In view of her longstanding hatred of Hospital policy, she had taken pride in that. Now, unaccountably, she felt vulnerable and a little afraid. Remembering, she saw not just a helpless patient, but a man. She had never reacted to a man's body before, except one, her former husband's; though he was dead, such feelings had been reserved for him. . . .

"Carla." The man across the desk stretched out his hand, then quickly withdrew it. It was as if on the verge of reassurance, he drew back from the bond of friendship that they normally shared. "Is it possible that you're feeling what I think you are—and for an offworlder?" he asked softly.

"And why shouldn't I? Is an offworlder less than we are? Is that why you're violating all your own rules?"

"My rules have always permitted ruthlessness. People I work with do suffer at times, as you know."

"Not without their consent. That's how your rules differ from the Hospital's, isn't it? Jesse Sanders has not consented to *anything*, let alone to a three-day invasive workup that serves no purpose except to train tech personnel and produce a standard file on him! Or to aversion therapy. Are you going to allow that, too?"

Kelstrom nodded. "Yes, I think so. It will be expected by the staff. There's an experimental protocol they've been wanting to try, but most patients aren't in shape for it. I see no reason to deprive them of this one."

"Experimental?" Appalled, Carla felt her knees weaken. She was up-to-date on the research discussed in the department, though much of it was repugnant to her. The idea she'd heard advanced with regard to aversion therapy was so repellent that she'd assumed not even the Administration took it seriously.

"I'm sorry," Kelstrom told her, not showing any genuine regret. "My goal here is to help as many patients as possible. That means sparing the weak ones, not the strong. Sanders can handle himself—or if he can't, I want to know. I think under these circumstances it's justifiable to ignore his not having consented."

Bitterly, Carla burst out, "I never thought I'd see you compromise your ideals on an end-justifies-the-means basis. And I won't stand by and let it happen, either! If you're expecting me to go along with you, you'll be surprised."

"I doubt it," the psychiatrist declared. "I was surprised a moment ago, I'll admit. I've watched you a long time, wondering when you'd let your sexual awareness resurface. Perhaps you wouldn't have dropped your guard if this man were one of us. In a way it's too bad it happened. Personal feelings may make the case tough for you; I want you to go on visiting him, keep me informed of his reactions. But I don't think you can surprise me further, Carla."

We'll see about that, she thought grimly. There were ways around Hospital orders. She'd find opportunity to intervene, as she had many times in the past. But without her supervisor on her side, the risk was going to be a great deal bigger.

4

JESSE LAY FLAT, not daring to move, wondering if there was any portion of his anatomy not sore from internal probing. Local anesthetic had, of course, been used for the most traumatic flesh punctures. With that added to repeated blood samplings, he'd felt more needles than he could count. The feeling of sensitive inner parts, however, had not been dulled. His stomach hurt. His throat hurt, though the apparatus thrust into his windpipe had long since been withdrawn. His ass and a good portion of his gut hurt—what he'd once thought a mere vulgar expression had been carried out all too literally.

Wearily he forced his eyes open, sensing someone's approach. To his relief, it was Carla who stood beside him. "Keep your spirits up," she said gently, straightening the sheet with which he'd at last, mercifully, been covered. "This phase lasts just one more day."

"What will they do to me tomorrow?" he asked, feeling that there was little left they could do. In addition to getting a variety of scans, they had directly examined every nook and cranny of his body's interior; not only all orifices, but arteries had been explored. They had inserted miles of tubing. They had injected dyes, taken tissue samples. They had probed the very marrow of his bones.

Now, for the night anyway, he had been granted respite, perhaps only because the supervising doctors were tired. There seemed to be an endless succession of technicians and interns. Last night he had been left alone, but hardly at peace; he'd undergone violent purging in preparation for this morning's intestinal studies. Tonight the only procedure in progress appeared to be IV feeding, necessitated by the past two days' required fast and the fact that his stomach was too badly abused from inner inspection to hold liquid nourishment. Tomorrow . . .

"What will they do tomorrow?" he repeated, for Carla's face was averted; she seemed reluctant to reply.

"You don't want to know."

"Yes, I do. Nothing's worse than trying to guess." This woman would be honest, he felt. She would not resort to stock, patronizing phrases. Perhaps she might even offer *reasons*.

She pressed his hand with cool, smooth fingers. "Biopsies of internal organs to start with, I think. The ones they couldn't reach with endoscopy. Liver, kidney and so forth."

"You're kidding. Needles in my *liver*? But there's nothing to look for, no symptoms that would suggest—"

"They don't wait for symptoms. There might be something wrong, you see, that could be found long before symptoms showed up."

"But there isn't. I'm healthy! At least I assume so—they haven't by any chance discovered a problem, have they?" Dismaying as that thought was, it was almost better than the idea of so much invasive work having being done by mistake.

"No!" Carla exclaimed. "Don't start thinking that way, Jesse! There is nothing wrong with your body. The problem

is with the system we've got here. It can't tolerate an in-
complete file."

"You mean all this is done to every patient who's admitted for some minor complaint?" She wasn't a psychologist
after all, he realized, for she didn't speak as a member of
the system's hierarchy.

"To every citizen of this colony," Carla replied. "Not all
at once like this, of course. And not so many invasive tests
for young people. Besides telemetry of data from our
homes, we have scheduled checks and rechecks according
to age."

"Oh, my God, Carla. That's carrying annual physicals
too far."

She said slowly, "Not really—it's the logical extension
of the concept." She paused, almost as if waiting for a retort.

"Well, it's a tradeoff between stress and benefit," Jesse
said, trying to be tactful. "Not to mention economics. The
chances of finding anything serious enough to warrant such
tests on a routine basis must be pretty small."

"That's not the point. The theory is that preventing illness is worth *any* cost, either in discomfort or in resources."

"I'm not sure I feel up to arguing with you, but there's a
flaw in that logic. If you subject people to this much regular
stress, and make them worry enough about their health to
put up with it, they're going to get problems that might
never have developed otherwise."

"Exactly," Carla said, her eyes lighting. "That's one reason statistics support the testing. It does turn up potential
problems. Sometimes it actually creates problems, because
none of these things are wholly risk-free."

Jesse grimaced. "Instruments poked into bladders, you
mean? Catheters shoved up arteries into hearts? I tried to
tell myself they couldn't really slip, but—"

"They can and do, especially in the hands of student
medics. It's not dangerous, you understand. We're skilled
here in repairing damage." She sounded bitter.

"You mean I needn't be afraid they'll kill me."

Carla turned white. "No," she declared with strange intensity. "That's the one thing they will *never* do."

He frowned. Something was wrong in this place, something more than the hospital's gung-ho policies and its obvious violations of patients' rights and privacy. "You seem to share my skepticism," he said to Carla. "Yet you said 'we' as if you get checked like everyone else."

"We aren't given a choice."

"God! Is that what's meant by the health laws someone mentioned?"

"That's part of it."

"I guess maybe I don't want to know the other part," Jesse admitted, wishing only to be light-years away.

"Believe me, you don't. You've got enough to face right now."

He saw she was really troubled. "Don't worry, I can stand another day of this, Carla," he said with such cheerfulness as he could muster. "Internal organ biopsies can't hurt more than the spinal tap and the bone marrow sampling."

"That's not what I'm thinking about. I wish—I wish I could get you out of here before they start the treatment phase."

"What? Oh, you mean the aversion therapy. I can stand that too," he declared grimly. "They can't keep me nauseous all the time, after all; I'm supposed to associate it with drinking." Presumably, he thought sardonically, I will forget all about associating it with having my guts turned inside out for the inspection of assembled interns. "So it won't be bad compared to this—just brief episodes."

"Do you know anything about the theory behind aversion therapy, Jesse?" Carla asked, seeming reluctant. She drew a chair to his bedside, sat close to him; he was aware of the sweet, fresh scent of her hair.

"Well, it's a standard conditioning technique, I guess. Behavior modification. They make you drink and then punish you, so you'll connect suffering with the act of drinking."

"No. The induced nausea isn't punishment; it works on the principle that makes animals reject poisonous foods. We have a built-in genetic mechanism for avoiding things that make us sick when we ingest them. Ordinary aversive conditioning, using shocks, isn't nearly as effective."

"But it doesn't always work, at least not permanently."

"Because we have minds that override associations. Humans know, underneath, that alcohol doesn't produce nausea. A person has to be awfully suggestible to be fooled subconsciously, even for a little while."

"That's some comfort," Jesse remarked, trying to make light of it. "I don't think I'm the suggestible sort."

"Definitely not. Your psych tests show you're not. And the Meds know that, of course. Aversion therapy's standard procedure, but they're aware that it has a worse record here than on worlds where submission to it's voluntary. That's a problem they've been trying to get around."

"Well, they might try eliminating the force."

"The Meds? Never; that's contrary to their goal of curing everyone."

"Much as I'd like to prove them wrong, Carla, I want to get out of here—and *stay* out. So I'll pretend to be 'cured.'"

"Never getting drunk again would be wise, certainly. But are you ready to give up social drinking, too?"

"Well, temporarily—in public, anyway. But I'm not an addict, after all. I can drink small amounts with meals."

"I'm sure you can. But the authorities here won't recognize that. Being drunk just once is interpreted as susceptibility to addiction; they don't rely on DNA data, which has proven unreliable for predicting behavior."

"Then why isn't liquor banned entirely?" This had been puzzling him; it seemed the kind of world where prohibitions would flourish.

"There's no need for a ban. Alcohol really isn't a problem here. Anyone drunk enough to cause trouble is treated, and that's the end of it—except there's a small amount of recidivism. Medical science hopes to eliminate that." Carla paused, then added painfully, "You've been chosen as the guinea pig, Jesse."

That figured. He was stranded, friendless, and strong enough to withstand unlimited therapy—no wonder they were verifying his health. "Tell me what they'll try," he urged, steeling himself.

"You'll be given drugs that cause real sickness when combined with alcohol. Not just nausea—heart symptoms, difficulty breathing, and so forth."

"But that's an ancient technique! They were doing that on Earth as far back as the twentieth century. It doesn't work on anyone who won't keep taking the stuff."

"You won't have to take it. They'll implant an internal device for timed release, just as they do to treat chronic diseases—a much more sophisticated one, of course, than the cheap near-surface implants used on most worlds."

"It's *permanent*?" He swallowed, repelled not so much by the loss of drinking pleasure as by the thought of unauthorized tampering with his body's reactions.

"Effectively so, unless you leave this world and have it removed. They'll bring you in for frequent maintenance checks."

He might not get a chance to leave, Jesse thought grimly. Not soon, anyway. "What's experimental about this?" he asked, thinking the pieces didn't quite fit. Implants were not experimental. Besides their medical uses such devices were routinely used for contraception; he'd had one since adolescence, though unlike female contraceptive implants it was not of the drug-dispensing type. He'd always wondered how women put up with those.

"The dosage," Carla informed him. "It's been tried with low, safe doses, but some addicts become inured to them and drink anyway. You will be made seriously ill, to a degree that would be risky if ambulances weren't constantly on patrol. There'll be an implanted microchip transmitting heart and tracking data constantly so that they can find you anywhere, just like anybody else on the planet who's not in perfect health. One taste of wine and you'll truly need to be hospitalized."

"Isn't that overkill, even in the case of real alcoholics?" he protested, knowing as he said it that protest was useless. Overkill was the name of the game here. The hospital seemed to run the entire colony.

"It is," Carla agreed, "and so it's controversial. All sickness is considered evil here, to an extent you probably can't imagine. It is rooted out. No natural form of discomfort is left untreated. But side effects of treatment aren't counted as bad; they're tolerated to minimize future risks."

"I've always doubted the reasoning behind that practice. Better a small risk of illness than a lifetime of sure misery."

"The authorities don't see it that way. They claim the right to decide what's 'minor' compared to the reduced risk. In this case, though, the effects can't be called minor by anybody's standards, so it's taken a while for the substance abuse people to get the go-ahead."

Jesse frowned. "Politics, maybe? Eliminate drunkenness at any cost before somebody gets the idea of banning liquor after all?"

"That's about the size of it," Carla said, "though the main political consideration is the points they'll score by proving it can be done. In any case, the Administration has agreed to stamp out substance abuse at the risk of more serious illness. The hope, of course, is that it won't come to that; the implant is supposed to act as a deterrent."

"I expect it will," Jesse said dryly. "I'm not going to chance getting picked up by an ambulance again. I wouldn't, even without the implant."

"A real alcoholic might, though. Even apart from craving liquor, he wouldn't mind the Hospital itself. Your view—and mine—isn't typical; most people view this as a place of refuge. The Meds' policies aren't widely opposed."

"If that's the case, why do they expect any deterrent effect?"

"Because the illness itself is so awful—and you will experience it repeatedly before you're released. They'll make you drink while they adjust dosage, and then more after the implant's in place."

Jesse tried not to let his feelings show. "I guess I'll survive that," he assured her. "It doesn't worry me as much as the implant does—and a heart monitor implant, too? Broadcasting my location day and night?" Perplexed by the strength of his repugnance he went on, "I'm not sure why I mind so much. It's not the end of the world if I can't drink socially. I could give it up easily if I chose, so why does the idea of having to seem so bad?"

"It doesn't," Carla said with conviction. "You mind losing your privacy to a tracking device, of course. But more than that, it's the manipulation of your body that's horrible. The violation. It's—obscene."

"Some of the tests were," he agreed, surprised that he felt able to speak of them to this charming young woman. "I never before asked myself why white coats on the assailants should change anyone's perception of what's otherwise classed as rape."

"It's custom, not logic. People who submit by choice tune out their natural feelings toward such things."

"I suppose it's medically necessary, sometimes."

"That's a matter of opinion. Where it's warranted by serious symptoms, the choice may be wise—but even then, tuning out's a mistake. Doing that leads, step by step, to what we've got here."

He looked quickly at her, seeing how grave she was. It was more than a matter of sympathy for him. Something deeper was involved. She evidently had not tuned out her own feelings, and they matched his, not her society's. "You're not a medical professional," he said, sure of this.

"No, I'm a data technician, though I assist with some kinds of psych therapy."

"Why do you work in this place?"

Carla hesitated. Finally she said, "The world is the

world. One way or another, we've got to live in it. Here, I'm useful, if only to victims like you."

"Worse things are done to some of them," Jesse observed.

"Yes."

"Electroshock, psychosurgery—things like that?"

"Yes, sometimes. And various drug protocols that are comparable."

"Am I in danger, Carla?"

"Not because of alcoholism. If you should be diagnosed as hostile—"

"Oh, God. Either I submit or they make me submissive, is that it?"

Carla nodded. "In theory, yes. There are sometimes—alternatives."

Again Jesse looked at her, taking in the attractiveness not only of her body—though that did attract him—but of her face, her whole manner. She was poised, serene, yet at the same time warmth glowed in her. Warmth toward him, and heat too, against a system she clearly disliked. She was involved, caring—he *knew*.

"You said you wished you could get me out," he reflected. "Is that possible?"

"Maybe. I have friends. It's been done before."

"I don't want you to run risks on my account." He realized that this was true. He was not in any serious danger; Carla might be. She could lose her job, or worse, she might be judged unstable. . . .

"I've never been caught," she assured him, smiling, "and I've done worse things, by Hospital standards, then restore clothes to a diagnosed substance abuser. I've gotten people out who were doomed to the Vaults."

"The Vaults?" Jesse was chilled, not merely by the ominous-sounding term but by the tone in which Carla spoke it.

"Forget I said that," she said hastily. "We've got to leave now, if you want to. The shift's about to change." She rose to retrieve a sack that she had set by the curtained entrance to his cubicle.

It contained his Fleet uniform. Jesse sat up; she was already committed, had come prepared, and he certainly did want to get out of the place. "What happens to you if we do get caught?" he asked.

"Never mind about me. Attempted escape will count against *you*," Carla said soberly. "You're under Dr. Kelstrom's care, so normally I wouldn't worry—but he's not himself right now. I can't predict. All the same, I've got strong reasons to trust him. I'm sure the worst that can happen is that the implants will proceed as scheduled."

Jesse pulled himself out of bed and dressed quickly, ignoring his various aches, which seemed to have lessened considerably during the past half hour. Attempted escape, she'd said, as if this were a true prison—did Carla herself view the hospital that way? Why had the colonists here given it so much autonomous power?

They ventured into the corridor. Carla gripped his arm, steadying him. "Walk normally, head up," she said. "We won't be noticed until we reach the checkpoint at the lobby entrance. The security officer coming on duty there is my friend."

As she'd said, the shift was changing; the hallways and elevators were crowded. Uniformed hospital personnel mingled with people in street clothes. A black silver-trimmed Fleet uniform was a bit conspicuous, Jesse felt, yet no one paid any attention to him. Probably there were hospital visitors mixed with the employees. Like colonists everywhere, they seemed healthy, and neither happier or unhappier than average. They didn't have the look of citizens repressed by force.

As they left the elevator at ground level, Carla held back, waiting for the tall redheaded security officer to take her seat. People were thumbing a plate at the exit barrier; there was an ID check! Jesse, fighting panic, glanced at Carla in dismay. Surely she must have known . . .

"Put in your thumbprint as if you expected the computer to pass it," she said, in a low but calm voice. "Anne will hit the alarm override. She knows what to do."

Carla moved forward and joined the line, Jesse close behind her. She smiled at the redhead. "Hello, Anne," she said. "Will we be seeing you on the Island next offshift?"

"Wait just a minute, will you, Carla?" Anne replied, motioning Carla back. The man in front of her had gone through. Jesse had no choice but to press his thumb firmly against the plate, holding his breath while the computer scanned its print.

The alarm began to scream.

The gate locked. Jesse stumbled back, almost colliding with the people in line behind him. Carla, beside the desk, had frozen in shock. If for an instant he'd thought she had betrayed him, he knew better when he saw her face. It was pale with dismay and bewilderment. Anne was evidently not as good a friend as she'd believed.

"I'm sorry, Carla," Anne said smoothly. "Dr. Kelstrom called me. He warned me to watch for you two. You're to report to his office now, before you leave for the night."

"Both of us?" Carla asked, as if doubting what she heard.

"Of course not. The patient will be taken back to his ward."

Orderlies were waiting; they must have been called in advance. Despairingly, Jesse left Carla to her fate and went with them.

5

THE FIRST TIME he was made sick, they used low dosage. His heart raced, but did not falter, and his breathing wasn't seriously impaired. All the same, it was worse than Jesse had expected. He had somehow thought that youthful experience with spacesickness would make induced nausea easier to bear. He remained in anguish for a long time afterward, and eventually he perceived that this had something to do with his general situation. He was unable to muster much optimism.

The memory of Carla tore him in two. It was a light in the darkness; he closed his eyes and recalled her scent, her touch, and it seemed that no world she lived in could be all bad. Yet at the same time, he worried.

How would they punish her? She'd violated rules, not law—surely no more than her job had been at stake. She'd be better off without it unless jobs were hard to come by in the colony. He didn't know, and in his blacker moments imagined her destitute, forced to seek welfare because she had risked herself for him. The local authorities weren't the sort she'd want to appeal to. Nor, perhaps, were her friends, if Anne was a sample! If only he were free. . . .

To his impatience for release was now added a burning wish to see Carla again. He knew this was more than desire to repay her kindness.

They moved him to another floor. He was given pajamas, but no robe; the rooms and corridors were kept at an even temperature. Nobody displayed any antagonism toward him, and he was forced to concede that they meant no cruelty. They really believed themselves to be helping a sick man. They behaved with uniform cheerfulness, even as they administered injections that—combined with the drinks they forced on him—would send him into agonizing, uncontrollable spasms of retching, followed by hours of lingering nausea combined with ever-more severe headache, palpitations, and labored breathing.

After several sessions of this, during one of his brief periods of relative calm, new orderlies appeared with a gurney. "You're going back to Psych for a while," they announced. He was not given the option of walking there under his own power.

Jesse's spirits rose momentarily; Psych was where Carla worked—or had worked. But he was not taken to the same area as before. After an endless trip through the grid of corridors they wheeled him into a small room filled with ominous electrical equipment and proceeded to strap him into a reclining chair, over which hovered an elaborate metal headpiece bristling with wires.

Electroshock? Undoubtedly, Jesse thought, striving to conceal his terror as they lowered the headpiece, encasing his scalp, and attached electrodes to his temples. Or something else that would even more disastrously alter his brain. . . . Carla had admitted that such things went on here. He was not sure what he had done to provoke it; perhaps it was merely that the initial psych testing had revealed too much of his personality for him to be judged on the basis of behavior alone. Dr. Kelstrom, or whoever else had looked at the records, must have realized that it would take more than "friendly health advice" to subdue his inner rebellion.

The room dimmed and various lights on the instrument board beside him began to glow, accompanied by a nerve-jarring electronic hum. The technicians had disappeared; whatever was going to happen to him was evidently remotely controlled. He waited . . . and waited. Nothing seemed to have happened yet; he could still think clearly—but perhaps the shock was yet to come. There was no way to judge time; it seemed as if hours had passed. At length he heard the door open and someone outside saying, "All right, now inject him. Kelstrom said to use truth serum."

Jesse was past the capacity for protest. He lay mute while the technician inserted an IV into his arm. After that things got hazy.

He knew, later, that he had been extensively and repeatedly interrogated, probably for psychiatric reasons rather than as any sort of conspiracy suspect—although the latter, he felt, would have been preferable. The voice of the unseen interviewer was absolutely emotionless, devoid even of supercilious courtesy. Having nothing to hide, he had not tried to resist the questioning. They'd already known he hated them. They'd known Carla had helped him, and that he found her attractive. What had they possibly hoped to gain?

When he woke he was back in the substance abuse unit,

with his brain intact, as far as he could tell. Emotionally, however, he was deeply shaken. He felt stripped, violated, now that the last vestige of personal privacy had been taken from him. The physical indignities paled beside the callous probing of his inmost thoughts. It scarcely mattered that within minutes he was called for another session of aversion therapy, one of many to which he was subjected during the next few days.

Though normally, these sessions would have been held in a room outfitted as a bar, the experimenters dispensed with that in favor of one with a gallery from which medical students could watch. "We're not trying to condition you," he was told. "This is simply what will happen if you drink, from now on, for the rest of your life. Awareness of it is necessary for your future safety."

For the rest of his life, then, his decisions were to be based on their standards of well-being instead of his own? No one suggested that he might ever leave the planet, and indeed Jesse had begun to doubt it. If they'd believed him still in the employ of Fleet, they would not have chosen him as a guinea pig. They planned to turn him into a healthy colonial citizen. That was acknowledged, in fact; several people remarked on how lucky he was not to be deported. They seemed genuinely unable to conceive of anyone's not appreciating the protection of the galaxy's finest medical facility.

As the drug dosage was increased, each drinking session made him sicker than the previous one. The goal was to find, then stop short of, the point at which he'd pass out before feeling distress. By the third day, Jesse feared struggling for breath more than he feared the nausea. Still, he drained the glass given him without protest, for it had been made plain that if he refused, the liquor would be poured down his throat. The less indignity, the better. He had few enough chances to avoid it.

The seriousness of the attacks was now such that they were terminated by antidote, leaving him with no worse than residual nausea and weakness. He could thus have multiple "treatments" per day, which was desirable, one nurse said, because hospital beds were in demand. This news was halfway welcome; it meant that he might get out soon. On the other hand, he'd have the implants before he got out. That would be soon, too. It was too final for his liking: a symbol of permanent subjugation to this world's medical authorities.

During the last session of the fifth day, just before he drank the proffered whiskey, Jesse looked into the observers' gallery and saw Carla.

She wasn't in her own uniform; instead, she wore the gown of an intern. She was holding a mask, briefly removed so that he could recognize her. He nodded quickly, almost imperceptibly; she caught the gesture almost before he knew what he was doing. When he looked again, her face was covered.

Yet he felt as if she had spoken to him. He had never met anyone before from whom he got such a feeling. He knew, as positively as if he'd been told, that she would come to his room. The knowledge sustained him. He found he hardly minded getting ill. He did not even react to the announcement, made by the night nurse, that he was scheduled to receive the implants in the morning.

Carla didn't appear until past midnight, when the corridor was quiet. She still wore the intern's gown. "Oh, God, Carla," Jesse said, torn between relief and fear for her. "You shouldn't be here. If you've got to wear a disguise—"

"I'm all right," she said calmly. "I got only a reprimand, and that not even from Dr. Kelstrom. He hadn't time to see me and left it to a subordinate. But I was ordered to stop visiting you, so someone might report me if I were noticed—" She stared at him, frowning. "When did they shave that patch of your hair?"

He told her about it, futilely attempting to hide what he felt at the memory of interrogation under truth serum. "I still don't know what the aim was. If it was meant to change me somehow, I don't think it worked."

"The machine only records brain activity. It's an experimental protocol of Dr. Kelstrom's; he's into research of that kind. I've—assisted with it, sometimes." Carla's frown deepened. "It should have been explained to you! He should have been there personally to oversee! To deliberately terrify you that way—it just doesn't add up. And as for the truth serum, Dr. Kelstrom *couldn't* have ordered that! Not for an unconsenting subject. Whoever mentioned his name must have misread your chart."

"I heard 'Kelstrom said,' Carla, not anything about charted orders."

She shook her head. "There had to have been miscommunication somewhere. But we haven't time to wonder about it. There's just one chance left now to prevent the implants."

"To escape, you mean? We can't try the front door again."

"No, right now there's nobody I can trust, since Anne—" She broke off, obviously deeply concerned; the implications of Anne's betrayal, he guessed, went further than this one incident. Bending down, searching his face, she went on, "Jesse, how badly do you want to get out with your body unaltered?"

"You don't have to ask, do you?" He was sure, somehow, that the strong rapport between them made discussion unnecessary.

"Just checking," Carla acknowledged. "We can manage it, but you'll have to run some risk. That is, you'll have to trust *me*. There'll be no real danger, but it will take nerve."

Jesse's heart stirred. Action, even dangerous action, would be welcome at this point, and the thought that Carla cared enough for him to initiate it was even more welcome. He trusted her completely, without asking himself why he should.

She drew a small flask from under her gown. Measuring him, she said, "This is brandy. Are you willing to drink it?"

"Carla, I don't suppose I can. They give the injections

on a regular schedule, simulating the implant, I think. I had one just a couple of hours ago; I doubt if it's worn off."

"It hasn't. That's the point. They won't guess, of course, that any liquor could have been smuggled to you, or that you'd have touched it if it had. So if you have an attack now—if you are unconscious, an emergency case—they will assume continued high dosage has unpredictable side effects."

He nodded, seeing the strategy. "Then what? Will they release me?"

"Maybe, after a standard course of aversion therapy. We won't wait to see; there are other routes of escape—but none that can be used before tomorrow morning."

Drawing breath, Jesse said, "Okay. Why not? They'll do it to me again anyway; I've nothing to lose." She had watched from the gallery, he realized, to learn what to expect of the attacks, so she could judge when to call for help. He would be a real emergency case, and there was no heart monitor in place yet. He could die if Carla waited too long. . . .

It did not worry him. With her, he was utterly safe. He seized the flask from her hands and took several swallows.

The illness hit fast. Before he had time to gasp for breath, his heart lurched wildly, erratically; he clutched at his chest, for once in too much pain to vomit. It passed quickly—her hands touched his and for an instant he knew a strange sense of peace, even well-being. Then he felt himself seized by convulsions. Carla screamed, whether in terror or by plan he was not sure. As people rushed into the room, he blacked out.

When he opened his eyes, it was morning. Carla was gone.

That day they repeated much of the physical exam, omitting only the most invasive portions. A succession of frowning doctors shook their heads over him. "Observation," one of them declared finally. "Start with light dosage tomorrow, then work up again—and get a video cam in here to watch for symptoms."

In the early evening the familiar pair of orderlies appeared, this time with a wheelchair. God, Jesse thought, is there to be no respite? So far, when allowed, he'd been able to walk. No doubt the chair was deemed necessary for return from whatever horror they now would subject him to. He bit his lip and put on as brave a face as he could manage.

They took him not to the treatment room but to the front desk of the substance abuse unit. "There's been a mix-up," the clerk announced. "Somebody in Psych ordered your discharge this morning. We weren't told here."

They gave him a bag containing his possessions. In a small dressing room, Jesse donned the Fleet uniform, not daring to let himself feel joy. He wasn't out yet. The wheelchair waited, standard transport for dischargees—he must be kept helpless, he judged, as long as he remained within the walls.

Not until they were at the security checkpoint did they release him. He entered his thumbprint gingerly, but the computer raised no alarm.

Dazed, unbelieving, Jesse found himself free on the sidewalk. It was dark. He had no idea what to do beyond getting as far away from the hospital complex as possible. The colony's city was unknown to him; he'd seen only the bar near the spaceport, into which he'd not venture again, and at the spaceport itself his welcome might not be too warm.

A cab pulled up. The door opened and someone waved to him, beckoning. Even before he saw her face, he knew it was Carla.

6

THEY WENT TO a restaurant on a side branch near the island's main waterway. Undine was a water world, and canals permeated the seaward areas of the city. "Like Venice," Carla said, "on ancient Earth."

He wanted little to do with food, but Carla ordered for

him anyway. She also ordered wine, and poured him some. Jesse accepted the glass gingerly. "You're offering me this?" he asked in amazement.

"The drug they gave you wore off hours ago. I checked the file on it to be sure."

"But all the same—"

"I believed you when you said you're not an alcoholic," she said. "I want to know."

"Whether I can stop with one or two, you mean? Carla, I'm not going to want any of this for quite a long time."

"Yes, you are. To hell with their goddamned aversion games! A few days of treatment can't affect you unless you let it. Don't."

Impressed, he took up the glass and sipped it. Her eyes were on him. Presently he began to eat, and found he was hungry.

Carla seemed radiant, even elated, as if it were she who had escaped from prison. Her color was high. "You won!" she said. "It's good to see you able to celebrate."

"With wine, you mean?" He raised his glass. "It's nice, but not worth the price. Was it for this I let you risk your job, and God knows what else?"

"Not for this. For a principle. And in the end, there wasn't much risk."

"You managed an official discharge," he agreed. "How?"

She averted her gaze. "I've got a close friend on the staff. He—does favors for me sometimes."

"Then I was not really cleared for release."

"No. The substance abuse unit would never have let you go. Psych had to override, which required some hacking. That part was easy, but without the staff signature seal you wouldn't have got past the door."

He frowned; hacking could be a criminal offense. "Why should you stick your neck out for me, Carla? Before you brought my clothes the first time, you'd only talked to me for five minutes."

"Sometimes that's enough." She smiled at him. "I do

what I can, Jesse, and you're from offworld. It's bad enough for the rest of us, but when they start in on offworlders—"

"Medics are a pain everywhere," he said, trying to be fair. "I suppose they mean well. Here, they seem to have got hold of all the funds they want, and I'd judge that makes them even more arrogant than on Earth." That was the root of it, of course. Compulsory treatment couldn't have been established without unlimited funding. He knew, without wanting to know, that the thing itself would not be hard to get people to vote for. Ongoing medical care was a blessing; most people would believe anything they were told about the need to force it on those who didn't want to be blessed.

"They mean well," Carla agreed. "So did the Verquistas, I'm told."

"It's not quite as bad as that," Jesse said. "The Verquistas were a political party. They had the citizens of New America so thoroughly sold on their platform that there was no opposition to them; bit by bit, people on that planet voted away their own freedom."

"And how do you think it is here?" she demanded, with some bitterness.

"Well, I guess the majority supports the medical lobby," he said, "since they do seem to get the funding. I must say I don't see how they get so much in a colony as small as this, though my ship's cargo manifest showed that it's a rich colony. But they're not the government, after all."

"But Jesse," Carla said, "they are. Didn't you know that?"

"Know what?"

"That the Meds are the government here, literally. There is no colonial administrator other than the Hospital Administrator. There is no legislative body other than the Medical Review Board. There's no police force apart from the ambulance officers; all crime is classed as illness, and untreated illness is considered crime. That's why they picked you up."

"God!" Jesse said, staring at her. For the moment he couldn't think of anything more to say.

"It's one reason the Hospital's so large," Carla went on. "All our government offices are in it. As for funding, the Board levies taxes and skims health care costs off the top. They say all treatment's free, of course, but we pay through the highest tax rates of any colony in the League."

Horrified, Jesse protested, "All colonies have free elections now; that's Colonial League law."

"Oh, the Board is elected. The Administrator's elected, too. We have campaigns just like anyplace else; there are lots of candidates and the vote's close sometimes. But they are all Meds. It's in our constitution—you can't run for office without a medical degree."

He sat for a moment, toying with his wine, absorbing all this. "How did it get into the constitution?" he asked finally.

Carla said, "It was approved by vote, of course. People thought it would be a waste of money to duplicate too much in a new colony. Obviously medical judgment had top priority. The history books say we have a unique arrangement that eliminates unnecessary bureaucracy."

"And nobody pushes for constitutional change?"

"Oh, no. Almost everyone's happy with this system. People feel secure with it; they know their health is being protected. Those who've grown up here don't object to forced treatment even for themselves. But I—well, I knew that you, being from offworld, probably would."

"Carla," he said shakily, "I haven't even said thanks."

"It's not necessary," she told him, her green eyes glowing. Changing the subject abruptly, she went on, "Tell me about your ship."

Jesse told her. He spoke of all the things that had been in his mind the past few days: the monotony, the hopelessness, the frustration. She was a good listener. They talked a long time, until the restaurant was empty and the waiter had dimmed the lamps. When they rose to go, he felt that Carla understood him better than anyone else ever had, anywhere.

"It's late," he said. "I've got to find a hotel somewhere."

"You can come home with me for tonight," Carla said easily.

He drew breath, his heart beating fast, but stepped back and let go of her hand. They had shared only a few hours. He hadn't thought of her as a woman who would say that.

Carla gave him a smile, the clear, guileless yet knowing smile he had come to look forward to. "It's not what you think," she told him. "You'll sleep on the couch. What I'm saying is that I trust you, Jesse."

They went to her apartment, said goodnight. Carla went into her room and closed the door. Jesse stood for a while watching boats pass beneath the window, then settled himself with a blanket on the couch. He slept soundly. He felt more at home than he ever had before onworld.

7

IN THE MORNING, Carla sparkled with energy. "Today's the start of my offshift," she told Jesse. "We have a ten-day week here, five days work and five off, though lately I've done some trading. Now I relax. Some friends may show up soon; we have plans."

"I'll get out of your way," Jesse said, wishing for plans of his own.

"No," she told him. "Please stay awhile, Jesse. I want you to meet them."

When he got out of the shower, she was talking on the phone. "Absolutely. A-OK," he heard her say. "Come on over; I'm fixing breakfast."

He stood watching her, wondering how to bring up the question that was puzzling him. Finally he came right out with it. "What's all that electronic stuff in the bathroom for? I looked in the mirror and got my retina scanned, as if I were entering a high security site."

Carla sighed. "Required telemetry to the Hospital, what

else? A lot of medical data can be obtained from scanning people's eyes."

"Telemetry—even from the *toilet?*"

"Of course. The content is analyzed, and the armrest attachment checks your blood pressure. They had toilets like that on Earth as far back as the early twenty-first century; the idea was to help sick people keep track of their medication level. Here, everybody's health is monitored from infancy on."

"But what about families living together? And guests like me who use the facilities?"

"The computer checks the DNA."

"God, Carla!" It was bad enough in the Hospital, but constant surveillance of private functions in people's own homes . . .

"Some of the outlying islands don't have satellite uplinks, so we're allowed to be away for five days," she explained. "But if we're not signed out and the data doesn't get through some morning, the Net generates an alarm and a repair technician shows up."

Before he could comment, the first of her friends arrived, soon followed by the others. There were two women and two men, all about her own age, all with that serene yet vibrant air that was so characteristic of Carla, but in no other respect alike. Ingrid, Liz, Kwame . . . Jesse could not see what bound them together. Something did. They were all outgoing, seemingly free of worries or antagonisms, and he sensed a depth, a special intimacy between them.

While he was pondering this with the first three, Carla called to him from the door. "Jesse," she said, as if making an announcement. "This is Peter."

He was a tall man of slender build, light-skinned with tawny hair. What was most striking about him, Jesse thought as they gripped hands, was his self-possession. It was hard to guess his age. He was certainly far younger than Jesse himself, and his hazel eyes had an almost boyish sparkle and vitality—yet at the same time they were knowing eyes. Whatever caused him to seem young was not inexperience. He would not have looked out of place in a Fleet uniform. He was the kind of man you would trust your life to.

Well, thought Jesse, so much for any hope that Carla was free of attachments. He had best be on his way.

They insisted that he stay for breakfast. He found himself talking a lot while they ate; it was some time before he realized that all five of them were deliberately drawing him out. Were they really that interested in star freighters, or did they just feel sorry for his bad luck? Jesse wondered. Immediately he regretted the thought. An inner sense told that they were simply, and somewhat mysteriously, the most friendly strangers he had ever encountered. He felt comfortable with them.

"I watched your ship come in," Kwame said, his black face alight with enthusiasm. "The first shuttle, I mean, from your mother ship—I work at the power plant and from our lunchroom, there's a view of the spaceport. Were you aboard?"

"Not the one you saw. Till the cargo's unloaded, I stay on the bridge, so I didn't come down here before dark." Ruefully he added, "This time I'd have been better off skipping my shore leave."

"Maybe not," Carla said, "if Fleet hasn't everything. That is, you did escape the local equivalent of jail. And now you're free."

Free to do what? Jesse thought sadly. Wouldn't he have been better off in space, dull though it often was, than at loose ends in a colony like this one? Then for the first time, looking at her, it occurred to him, *maybe not. . . .*

"Perhaps Jesse's aware that freedom's limited here," Peter remarked.

"I can't say I like the kinds of laws you've got," Jesse agreed. "But no doubt they do provide excellent care for people with real medical problems."

"Well, that's a matter of opinion," Peter said slowly. All

the others were watching him, Jesse noted. "Don't feel you should hide yours out of courtesy to the natives."

"Carla said most people like this system."

"Yes," Carla agreed, "but I didn't say I choose my friends from the majority."

Of course not, he realized. Independent by nature, she would not find docile sheep congenial. He smiled. "Frankly, I think there's too much focus on health care even on Earth—and making it compulsory no doubt magnifies the problems that causes. Yet hating the Hospital's no answer. Nobody likes being hospitalized on any world, after all."

"That's why people deny their feelings," Ingrid said. "Dislike is normal, so they tell themselves to ignore it."

"Sure. When we know it's for our good, we do that."

"Even where it's a matter of indoctrination rather than compulsion," Peter declared.

"I never looked at it that way—but yes, I guess you're right. We are indoctrinated, or else we wouldn't put up with half of what the medics advise. But how else could we nip illness in the bud?"

"You've seen where that sort of reasoning leads," Carla murmured.

He stared at her, bewildered. Put that way, the colony's laws were no worse than extensions of medical standards existing everywhere—to which, after all, there was little alternative. Yet he *had* seen, and wasn't sure he could now face even Fleet checkups gladly.

Looking around at the group, he observed, "We're all healthy. We're not qualified, I guess, to judge what's best for those not so lucky. It's a matter of attitude, maybe—if some get sick because they're taught to worry about sickness, others like us keep healthy to stay out of the clutches of the medics. I, for one, don't plan to get caught with anything treatable."

He was speaking lightly, but nobody laughed. Peter in particular lit up with unmistakable pleasure, as if he had just recognized an old acquaintance whose companionship he valued highly. Finally, out of a silence less uneasy than solemn, Carla rose and said, "It's late. We'd better get going."

Jesse rose too, ready to take his leave, but Peter stopped him. "Jess, we're headed for an island where we spend offshifts," he said. "We'd like you to come." The welcome in his words was unmistakably genuine.

"Thanks, but I won't intrude," Jesse said, returning the smile. "It's time I found myself someplace to live."

"You're not intruding," said Carla. "Please come." Then, as often happened with her, it seemed she picked up what he had not voiced. "I'm sorry," she said hastily. "I didn't think. There's nothing special between Peter and me, Jesse. A lot of friends gather at this place we're going, more than a dozen this shift, probably. We'd really like to have you. I'd have invited you sooner, but—" She paused for an instant, then concluded, "I wasn't sure there'd be room in Peter's plane."

It was a six-place seaplane, moored in a basin that they reached by water taxi. At sight of it Jesse began revising his estimate of these people's place in the colony. Peter, at least, must be wealthy. Perhaps inherited wealth—he was surely too young to have accumulated it, rich in diamonds though Undine was said to be.

"The government's monetary laws are complicated," Peter told him, answering his unspoken question. "All of us here have assets apart from our jobs, assets that are . . . uncommon, elsewhere. But we're limited in how we can spend what's left after taxes. We can buy goods through importers—and since flying's the only practical way to get to most of the islands during an offshift, many of us own planes, just as people own cars on worlds where there are roads."

"Apart from import transactions, though, we can't spend our funds offworld," Liz added. "Not for passage, not for living expenses. So we don't have the option of leaving the planet."

"Which is why we envy you for having traveled in space,"

Kwame said. "If I'm lucky, I might someday get into orbit to work on our power satellites. Most people can't hope to go even that far."

No wonder Fleet's installation here was a small one, Jesse thought, if there was no passenger traffic. Like most colonies, this one was dependent on solar power satellites and thus on a permanently-based shuttle to service them; it had no source of fuel, and due to its limited land area, no means of generating hydroelectric power. But since its moon wasn't used and there were no other habitable planets in its solar system, there was little else for Fleet personnel to do when no freighter was in orbit. Undine was an isolated, backwater outpost compared to others he had visited.

Yet as the seaplane took off and rose over the vast expanse of water surrounding the island city, Jesse decided that if he must be worldbound, this particular world was not such a bad one to be stuck on. It was a cool blue world— blue ocean and blue sky, with only small blotches of green. There were farms and small settlements on some of the larger islands, too widely separated for frequent boat traffic, but no other cities yet. Colonies tended to centralize things.

Very soon he was wholly confused as to directions. They couldn't be navigating by sight without landmarks of any kind; they must be on instruments. "Got a chart?" he asked casually, his voice easily heard over the hum of the plane's high-powered electric engine. "I'd be interested in getting my bearings."

Nobody answered; they seemed to be waiting for each other to speak. Finally Peter said, "There's no use telling a space pilot we haven't got a chart aboard. The fact is, Jess, our offshift retreat is privately owned. The management doesn't want crowds, so our use of it's conditional on not giving out the location. Okay?"

"Okay," Jesse agreed. "My feelings aren't hurt." Am I crazy? he thought suddenly. I don't know these people; even Carla, I've known outside the Hospital for less than a day.

They could be taking me anywhere. I could never get back on my own. For the first time since meeting them, he felt on edge.

He could not doubt Carla. But how reliable was her trust in the others? She'd trusted Anne, too—and he recalled, now, that she'd mentioned seeing Anne "on the Island." Anne's betrayal had evidently troubled her. He'd sensed concern beneath her elation during dinner last night. Perhaps the hacking she'd done might still be uncovered—even today, she wasn't being quite open with him.

Something was hidden. Something she knew of this group had not been mentioned. Yet to be with her, he'd blocked that out; he'd noticed only their friendliness. How odd, when he did not even know their full names. . . .

It was still odder that no one had been introduced by a full name. He looked at Carla, her dark hair resting against a window, half-covering a face that was by now, to him, unforgettable. She had not even told him hers!

She turned and smiled at him. "We're very informal," she said. "A lot of us like to escape from the city; we hate to think of the world outside during offshifts. So we've made a sort of rule about conversation, the opposite of what we'd follow at home—we don't ask questions about what people do. Am I making any sense?"

"Maybe I'd better get it straight before we land," Jesse said forthrightly. "We don't know where in the world we are. We don't know each other's full names. We don't know what anyone does in the city. And yet we're all close friends."

"You've got it," said Carla, not elaborating.

And do we know who's married and who's not? Jesse wondered. Probably we don't. Okay, that should be clear enough. He had never been a swinger, and had not taken Carla for one; but there was something going between these people beyond mere friendship. He could feel a tension between them even now. It was hardly cause for suspecting anything sinister. What the hell, this could be a fun offshift—though with Carla, he'd hoped for more.

After several hours they touched water and taxied across the wide bay of an island that seemed deserted. It had rocky outcroppings, with thick trees down to the shore, willowy green trees he knew had been planted by the terraforming team that originally prepared Undine for settlement. There was a long dock with a pole from which a windsock flew alongside a bright red pennant. Other seaplanes and some small boats were tied up there. Only one building was visible, a sprawling stone structure backed by more trees. It seemed too large for a private house; it looked more like a hotel of some kind.

He followed them up the path to the wide porch. It was a rustic place, built partially of natural wood. Jesse had never seen its like; onworld, he'd known only cities. "Does this place have a name?" he asked, as they mounted the steps.

"Officially it's Maclairn Lodge, after the owner," said Carla. "But we just call it the Lodge. Sometimes there are lots of people here, but it will be quite empty this time. We'll have to fix our own meals."

The heavy wooden door led into a spacious room occupied by nine or ten more attractive young people who were introduced to him. It had no furniture except a few tables with benches, but in the center, large comfortable floor cushions surrounded a huge circular stone fireplace, above which was suspended a hammered-metal hood and chimney. Sunlight streamed in through tall windows. Nobody seemed to be doing anything in particular. They were simply relaxing. They looked as if they felt at home.

"I'll find you a bed," said Peter, "and some clothes. That Fleet outfit you're wearing can't be comfortable."

It was, by Fleet standards, but it was warm; everyone else wore bright, flimsy shirts outside casual pants. Jesse went with Peter into a hallway. The rooms opening off it were, to his astonishment, bunkrooms, with two double-tiered bunks in each. Peter followed his glance and said, "We have cottages, but since no couples are here today, we've not bothered to open them. I suppose starship captains rate private quarters, but I take it you don't mind?"

"Of course not," said Jesse, somewhat stunned. God, he thought, do we not even pair off? Is it going to turn into some sort of orgy out in the common room?

They fixed lunch. Nobody seemed to organize it, but after changing clothes Jesse found himself making sandwiches. People clustered in small groups on the wide porch and ate casually. There was a lot of laughing and joking, and it seemed happy laughter, not the sort you heard in a bar. The food was good, too, much better than last night's tasteless restaurant fare, which, Carla had said, was legally required to meet the standards set by nutrition inspectors—as were all edibles offered by city markets. It appeared that only on this secluded island was it okay to enjoy eating.

Pretty soon people started taking their shirts off to lie in the sun. They were not at all self-conscious about it, though even the women wore nothing beneath. Jesse looked at Carla, looked away, and then looked back, realizing that he was not supposed to react. Colonial customs would take getting used to, he decided.

"Hey, guys," said Peter. "Let's go swimming."

Everyone headed toward the waterfront. Carla grabbed Jesse's hand. "I'll race you," she cried, with enthusiasm.

Jesse froze inside. "I guess I'll pass," he said. "I'm not a swimmer."

"Oh, come on, Jesse. Nobody cares how good you are."

"No," he confessed, "I mean I never learned to swim. Most spacers don't; there's no opportunity."

"But you were born on Earth. Didn't you ever swim as a child?"

"No," he said shortly. It was the first lie he had told her. This was not something he liked to think about—splashing happily at the beach with other kids, then the pier, the fall into deep water, the undercurrent dragging him down. His uncle had rescued him, though he had no memory of that part. He'd been only about four then, and had avoided water thereafter. But he still had dreams from time to time.

In space training, the issue hadn't arisen; there were no pools on the spartan orbiting stations that housed Fleet cadets. The phobia was on his record, however. You could not lie about such things in psych evaluation—if you denied every fear on their list, they knew you were lying and probed. For that reason he had not lied about it even on the Hospital questionnaires here. God, had Carla seen? She was, after all, a psych technician, though readouts normally showed profiles rather than answers to specific questions.

"Come with us anyway and watch," said Carla. "Please, Jesse."

Relief swept over him. She could not have seen; if she had, she wouldn't be urging him to come. It was not in Carla to do anything unkind. Nor would she scorn him—he'd feared not that from her, but pity. Better to make excuses than to have her offer them for him, and watching wouldn't be bad.

"Okay," he said evenly, and followed.

8

A CLUSTER OF people gathered on the rocky shore, some distance from the dock. The water was calm and deep there; the cliffs dropped off sharply beneath the water and there was no surf. Peter stood on a tall rock, sunlight illuminating his hair. He dove, cutting the water with effortless grace. Jesse stared at the spreading ripples, wondering how long he would stay down.

"It's safe at high tide," said Carla, noting Jesse's indrawn breath. "We know these waters. There aren't any rocks beneath the surface."

She took off her long pants, revealing swimwear beneath, and plunged in from ground level. Soon they were all in, laughing and shouting, having a glorious time, like children. Peter dove repeatedly, and others followed. Jesse sat on a flat rock away from the edge, realizing with dismay that he envied them.

After a while Peter came and sat beside him, drying his bright hair with a towel. "You should try it," he said. "Carla says you never learned, but we wouldn't let you drown, you know."

Jesse forced a smile. "No, thanks. I'll leave it to you young folks." For the first time the fact that he was older than the rest struck home. He had never thought much about age. In space, he was a Captain. Everybody looked up to a Captain. Here . . .

"Really," persisted Peter. "You might surprise yourself."

"I'd look like a fool, floundering around out there."

"I'll tell you how to make real fun of it, and not flounder," Peter said, with a rather cryptic smile. "Jump off the high rock there. You'll sink, of course. The trick is to relax completely as you come up. Don't try to swim. Just let yourself rise to the surface and float—"

He broke off in response to what Jesse had hoped was an impassive face. "Yes, I can imagine how it might feel to do it that way if you've never been in deep water before. But that's the fun part, you see. Isn't it? I mean, why do people ride roller coasters? Why do they jump out of planes? God, Jess, what do spacers do for that kind of fun?"

Well, nothing, thought Jesse, which was one of the things you learned about the difference between what you thought space would be, and what it turned out to be after you got there. Peter's argument was unassailable. The difficulty was that Peter wasn't in a position to imagine how it would feel in his case. He didn't know about the phobia, and even if he had known, it was unlikely that this man had ever feared anything in his life.

"Come on," said Peter, standing up. "I dare you, Jess."

He seemed eager—too eager, Jesse thought suddenly. It was irrational for a grown man to play with dares. Yet wasn't it even less rational to see hidden menace in this?

There could be no conceivable motive. His own nerves were playing tricks on him, surely.

Carla approached them. "He's a trained lifeguard," she remarked, her eyes sparkling. "There's no way you can drown."

She smiled brightly at him, not in a taunting way, but with genuine enthusiasm. She too was much younger than he was, which was a thought he did not relish.

Jesse rose and stripped to his briefs. What the hell, he thought sardonically. How you felt scarcely mattered; you upheld the honor of Fleet. Not Fleet as it really was—God, what a travesty—but as these young people on an isolated world believed it to be.

He climbed to the rim of the rock and jumped.

He had known he would sink far below the surface; he had not realized quite how far, or how fast. He had the presence of mind to keep his mouth closed, but his lungs were bursting—he hadn't stopped to think of filling them beforehand. That was the only real discomfort. In airlock emergency drill you learned to deal with such things. Somewhere along the way it dawned on him that the plunging sensation itself was not much after zero-g, a condition he hadn't yet experienced at the age of four.

As he rose, he made a conscious effort not to struggle. He surfaced, throwing himself onto his back to breathe free air. Peter was in the water with him. So was Carla. They were laughing, but not in ridicule—it was sheer exuberance and playfulness. He found himself laughing with them. He wasn't really floating, they were holding him up; but he knew that by tomorrow he could float.

"We'll have you scuba diving before the offshift's over," Peter remarked as they climbed out onto the low rocks. Jesse perceived that this had been meant quite seriously.

The afternoon passed, then the evening. Everyone sat on the porch to watch the sun go down, dipping toward the western horizon to stripe now-grey water with orange. As dark came on the air turned cool; lightweight sweaters covered the thin shirts. People talked. They drank wine. They shared the intimacy of mutual trust. But nothing more than that happened.

It was unnatural, Jesse thought, perplexed. They were not what he'd first assumed, that was evident—but they weren't strangers to each other, either. It was not as if they lacked sexual feelings. The undercurrents between them were unmistakable. Why should they behave as if in public, when their Lodge was so evidently a loved home?

They went indoors and built a fire, gathering in a circle around it, quiet, not even speaking. Carla put her arm around him. She moved close, with warmth but without provocation. Well, this was how we were last night, he thought, and it's too soon to go further in any case . . . and all the rest are acting the same way. And then suddenly he thought, do they know? Is that why? Have they that much regard for my feelings, that they avoid what I can't yet share?

What a strange thing to guess. If it was true, he'd been given no sign, and certainly other colonies had no such custom. Why did he want so much to believe the best of them? They were concealing something vital, something bigger than mere motives; why did all suspicion vanish easily in their presence?

Someone turned on music—surging, soaring electronic music, not hard, yet more exciting than tranquil. His spine tingled with it. He forgot Fleet, forgot the drab years, felt he had never belonged anywhere but here, in an island lodge on an obscure planet among people who somehow already mattered to him.

"Would you mind giving up space for this?" Carla asked softly. "Is it the end of your life if you're marooned here?"

"No," Jesse said. "It feels more like the beginning, right now."

9

THE DAYS PASSED too quickly. They swam again; they cooked food over an outdoor fire; they climbed the hill above the Lodge to view a dazzling jeweled chain of green islands. The group's camaraderie remained strong. After a while, Jesse's liking for its members overshadowed his clear sense of something concealed.

They did go scuba diving. Apparently it was a sport popular among them, for a storeroom in the Lodge contained a wide variety of gear. The breathing apparatus was simple to manage and not intimidating, considering his experience with spacesuits. Only the swimming involved proved challenging. Jesse felt strangely calm about it, and he found that under Peter's direction it was possible to learn fast. The man was a born instructor, just as he seemed born to do everything else he tried with casual ease. The others all seemed to look up to him, young though he appeared to be. He was wasted on a world like this—in Fleet, he could in time become Captain not of a mere freighter but of a liner or even a colonizer. Yet Peter never spoke of ambition, never mentioned any longing for the space travel his colony's laws denied him. What did he do for a living? Jesse wondered. But that was one of the questions that had been declared taboo.

Families were another, and it was strange that all present seemed to be without them. Most were not so young as never to have married, not unless the colony's customs in that regard were unusual. They were healthy. They valued closeness and caring. Yet while behaving as if at home, relaxed, they did not live or act as couples. There were no private exchanges between them even to the extent of those that took place between him and Carla. It was like one big happy family, Jesse thought rather wistfully—yet would that always be enough, without relationships, without kids?

Evenings, they sat around the fire, and again Carla nestled close to him with casual warmth that on the surface was almost childlike. Beneath the surface was something Jesse couldn't define. It was not mere submerged sexuality; he sensed that in some indescribable way she was holding back more than that, some central facet of her personal life. He had no choice but to accept her wish. It was obvious to him that she wasn't involved with anyone else present, equally obvious that she was as eager for him as he for her. They knew each other well enough now; in ordinary circumstances he wouldn't have hesitated. But there was something here that was not ordinary.

It was not just Carla, Jesse realized, and not just the specifics of their lives these people were hiding. There was a restraint among them he couldn't explain. It was if they were all on guard against revealing their true selves, even while they enjoyed life with wholehearted, innocent abandon. They seemed untouched by the world outside—a term they used as one might speak of another planet—and yet connected to everything that mattered in it. Despite their strange reticence he felt he knew them, liked them, better than any people he had shipped with. God, he thought, have I missed out on life by staying in Fleet? Will they ever truly accept me as one of them?

On the last night of the offshift, they gathered in the Lodge for a more formal meal than the buffet arrangement used so far. Jesse was not sure whether it had been prearranged—he was somehow never sure of anything in the interactions between these people—but there seemed to be enough of a planned menu for everyone to sit down at the same time. They pushed the tables together. When they'd finished eating, they brought out more wine.

He looked around at their faces. Peter, Kwame, Bernie, Ingrid, Liz, Nathan . . . more than a dozen, and he knew them all now as friends. All so different, and yet they had something in common, something other people did not have. It was a kind of balance, poise. He'd sensed that in every one of them, from the start. Even in Carla! It wasn't just the interaction of the group; they interacted as they did only because they were what they were. How, he wondered, had they ever found each other?

"Back to reality tomorrow," Peter remarked, more as simple fact than with regret. Turning to Jesse, he said, "You're not lost in the land of the lotus-eaters, you know."

"I wondered," Jesse said lightly. Privately, he had not only wondered but worried. He should be thinking of contacting Fleet, not hiding out among friends with no practical cares to concern them.

Carla, on his right, looked up at him and smiled her special smile. "Do we puzzle you, Jesse?" she asked.

He was startled; it had not occurred to him that this would be brought out into the open. He was at a loss for words. "I like what I see," he said finally, "but it's beyond me where you get it. I don't know what you do elsewhere, but here you are all so—alive."

"Perhaps," Nathan suggested, "we want to take advantage of the opportunity."

"To live before you die, you mean? We all try that, I guess. We don't all succeed so well."

"The pressures aren't the same everywhere," Ingrid said. "Jesse, have you ever been on a ship that was in danger?"

"I've had a few close calls. Nothing spectacular." He did not say that like any officer who'd served on freighters, he had on rare occasions been obliged to defend his cargo against piracy; not only were guns illegal on Undine, but there was a strong taboo against mentioning them.

"Nothing where the people aboard were living under threat of imminent disaster, then."

"Not for more than about five minutes, no." Jesse thought about it. Such things did happen in Fleet; there were ships low on life support that made it home after more extended periods of peril. The experience did tend to create a bond between people. He had never yearned for quite that sort of bond.

"You're not in any danger here," he said, puzzled.

"Not mortal danger," Bernie agreed, "but under this

world's laws—" He broke off, seeing Peter frown. There was a sudden silence, broken only by the sound of a plane. They were all alert to it. Undine's moon, larger than Earth's and with greater albedo, was full; there should be plenty of moonlight for landing on water.

"It's Anne, probably," Liz said. "Tonight of all nights—"

Carla froze, staring at her. Liz, seemingly embarrassed, murmured, "Perhaps not."

"I'll turn on the dock lights," Peter said. He rose and went to the door, looked out, finally let it swing shut behind him.

Carla said, "Jesse, we're all tired. Let's turn in early."

But they had just poured another round of wine, Jesse thought; their glasses stood untouched on the table. The fire had not even been lighted. Puzzled, he watched them head for the bunkrooms. "I'm tired," Carla repeated. "We'll clean up tomorrow."

She didn't expect him to be fooled, he realized. She thought he would be tactful enough to retire. There seemed to be little choice; he was a guest, and at the moment, obviously an unwelcome one. He was not meant to meet whoever had come in the plane. Anne? Anne's friendship had proven false. Perhaps they didn't want him to watch the inevitable showdown.

He followed Kwame into the bunkroom they shared with Peter. As he expected, Kwame didn't stay long; he disappeared as soon as Jesse was in bed. But there were no voices from the common room. Nor did the plane take off again, and indeed, it was too late to fly back to the city before moonset. Jesse got up and stood by the window. There was no ocean view, since unlike most of the bunkrooms it was on the back of the building. It was strange, he thought suddenly, that a guest wouldn't have been offered a room with a view.

He was torn. Carla did not think him dense enough to believe they'd all gone to bed; therefore she trusted him. Whatever was going on was none of his business. Yet more and more he felt that it meant trouble. Her worry about Anne had been more than disappointment. In her face just now, in all their faces, there'd been tenseness not usually visible. And they had started to speak of danger. . . .

What threat did Anne hold over Carla, perhaps over them all?

Carla didn't want him to know. She was aware that if he knew, he might make some effort to protect her. And if he did that—if Hospital politics were involved, as they must be—his case might be reopened. It was vital to his continued freedom for the Hospital to forget about him. Hacking, she'd said . . . she had altered Hospital records. Disclosure of this would mean trouble not only for her, but for him; his name might be restored to the pickup list. She wouldn't risk that, nor would she allow the group to chance it. They would make some sort of deal with Anne, one she did not want him to know about.

Quickly, decisively, Jesse put his clothes back on and went outside.

The Lodge was deserted. Even the illuminated dock was empty. Some distance away across the water, beyond the rocky area used for swimming, he saw a dim cluster of bobbing lights.

They were in the boats, then. He'd heard no powerboats tonight, but the ones from which scuba diving was done also had oars. What point was there in rowing? They couldn't go far, and indeed, as he watched the lights, he saw they were going nowhere. It was almost as if they were anchored.

He didn't know how to manage a boat, and in any case, an approach by boat would be seen. But if he followed the shore trail beyond the swimming beach, he could stay hidden by trees. There was a chance that from there he could learn more.

It was dark; the moon was by now below the horizon. Jesse wasn't used to trails or wild growth—his sole experiences with them had come in the past four days. Several times he stumbled, and as he passed the swimming area, sticking to cover, branches lashed across his face. The cluster of boats, on the opposite side of a boulder-strewn point from where they'd swum, was close now. He did his best to move soundlessly. Voices carried to him on the breeze.

Jesse couldn't make out words. But there was a woman's voice—not Carla's—and then Peter's. And then, astonishingly, the group spoke in unison. The cadence sounded like poetry.

Abruptly, the lights rose higher, and he could see that they were candles. Held by raised arms, their flicker illuminated the center boat. Peter and Bernie were standing up, between the seats, and lifting something. The boat rocked; he could hear it bump against the others, though people in each were holding on to its gunwales.

The lifted object was long and evidently heavy. It seemed to be a bag of some kind, a stiff sack that retained its shape as they pushed it over the stern. It was about the size of a person's body. Jesse stepped onto the rocks and leaned forward through willowy branches in order to see better.

Oh, God. It *was* a body—it could be nothing else. The sack splashed and sank, sending out small waves that broke on the rocks at his feet. Incredulous, not wanting to accept the implications, Jesse knew that he'd witnessed a burial.

The wet rocks were slippery. His mind was far from them. As his feet slid out from under him, he grabbed at a branch; it gave way. With an involuntary cry, he fell, and black water closed over his head.

10

THE WATER WAS deep at this point. Deep enough even at low tide to hide bodies, Jesse realized, fighting panic. He sank through darkness, trying desperately to move as he'd learned while scuba diving, though he had too little swimming experience to get far without fins. There was no bottom. Nor was there any sensation of rising; having no sunlight above made a difference, perhaps. Ultimately he floundered, aware that his arms were breaking the surface. Then a spotlight hit, and Peter was pulling him toward the boats.

He gulped air, gratefully. He should still be afraid, he thought. His suspicion of trouble had not been mere imagination; on no world could it be routine to dump a body overboard under cover of darkness. The mysteries here were a good deal more ominous than he had guessed.

Carla had tried to keep him from learning them. Had her wish been to protect him? Was she herself in danger from what she knew? It was a reasonable speculation. Yet he could not bring himself to fear the others; Peter's grip was, inexplicably, comforting. In spite of everything, he found he felt safe with Peter.

Oars were stretched out to him. Strong hands helped him aboard. As he watched, the candles—fixed to buoyant bases—were put over the side to float away, evidently as part of the planned ceremony. Wet and shivering, dazed, Jesse huddled on a seat, wondering what he could possibly say to Carla.

"Well, we didn't suppose you lacked initiative," Bernie told him, without anger. "But it was only fair to give you a choice about getting involved."

"What did you see, Jess?" asked Peter gravely.

"You know, I think," Jesse told him. "If I'm wrong—if it wasn't the burial of a body—then set me straight. I know it's not my business, but under the circumstances—"

"You're entitled to an explanation," Peter agreed. "My guess is that you'll find it easier to understand than our fellow-citizens would. I doubt if you're a man to be unduly worried by the legalities of the situation."

"Maybe, maybe not." And yet, Jesse thought, he was ready to believe any explanation that would let him keep trusting these people. He was as drawn to them as ever. It would take more than he'd seen tonight to make him doubt them.

The boat carrying Carla had come alongside. It was too

dark to see her face, but her voice was soft, steady. "Jesse, one of our friends died in her bed this morning. She was ninety-seven, and knew she was dying; she didn't want the ambulance. Would you want to spend your last hours in this world's Hospital?"

"No," Jesse admitted. "But why bury her here instead of in a cemetery?"

"If the authorities knew she was dead, they'd wonder why no ambulance got to her," Liz said.

"That figures. I suppose if one wasn't called, her family and friends could be accused of some crime." As he spoke, it dawned on Jesse that what elsewhere would be ironic exaggeration was here, no doubt, the literal truth.

The boats separated; people took up paddles. "You don't have to keep so quiet now that I'm here," he pointed out.

"It's best to be on the safe side," Peter said. "We can never be sure outsiders' boats won't pass by—we're within range of the mining camp on Verge Island."

Back at the Lodge, he and Peter changed to dry clothes in silence. When they returned to the common room, people had gathered as usual around the fire. But there was no music, no casual chatter. They all seemed to be waiting.

Jesse looked for Carla, then froze. Anne was sitting beside her. Anne had indeed brought the plane, then, and the body. . . .

"Forget your first meeting with Anne," Carla said easily. "She couldn't tell me in public, but she knew there'd be a way to get you out—a better way, one with a legal signature."

Days beforehand? Jesse thought, puzzled. Well, if Carla was satisfied, he would be too; he returned Anne's friendly greeting. Still, he felt something had been held back.

"Okay, people, we need to talk," Peter said. "Jess needs to know the truth about this world. Now that he's seen what went on tonight, that's more urgent than ever."

Carla said, "We were going to tell you tonight, anyway. It's a hard thing to speak of casually. Bear with us."

Jesse nodded. "All right. I'm listening." The truth about the world? he thought, with foreboding. Not just what he'd seen of its dictatorial health laws?

"I'll ask you a hard question, straight out, Jess," Peter said in a tone uncharacteristically serious. "What's the worst thing you can imagine happening to you, that really could happen? I don't mean some freak accident. What do you really fear about your own eventual end?"

Jesse froze. This was a taboo subject in any society he had ever known. You simply did not ask that question. Everybody already knew the answer to it, anyway.

"Don't back away from it, Jesse," Carla said. "We are not going to be shocked by what you say."

All right, they wanted honesty. "Old age," he confessed. "Outliving my capabilities. Being helpless, dependent on strangers, even on—" He broke off, unable to carry it through.

"On machines," Bernie finished for him. "Or being mentally incapacitated, senile. Physical dependence might be tolerable, but disintegration of the mind's harder to contemplate."

Jesse bent his head. "Yes," he agreed. He was older than they were; he had not supposed they'd even ventured to think about it yet. Still, the friend they'd buried had been elderly. "Do you think I'd question your not calling an ambulance for an old woman?" he asked. "Stop worrying—you don't need to justify yourselves to me."

"The issue goes deeper than that," Kwame said. "Earlier, we mentioned shared fear—"

"And we have to explain the reasons for it," Ingrid said. "Jesse, you may have to live out your life here. The Hospital provides custodial care. Does the idea frighten you?"

They were all looking at him very intently, and he perceived that he was being tested in some obscure way. With them, there was no end to the surprises. The only clear thing was that they did not like timidity—not in any form whatsoever. If you shrank from something, then that was the very thing they contrived to make you do.

"Yes, I fear that," he repeated forthrightly. "I guess we all hope to go quickly when our time comes. But it doesn't happen often nowadays, after all—not as it used to before all fatal disease except aging became curable. I'm not likely to have much choice."

"On some worlds I hear they do," Nathan said pointedly.

"Assisted suicide, you mean? Yes, it's legal on Earth, in fact. But—" Jesse paused, guessing now why they'd hidden the death and hesitant to risk offending. They sat silent, not letting him off the hook. Hell, he thought, if anyone takes this as an insult, they asked for it! "It's not my business to judge others," he said, "but that's not the choice I'd make for myself. It's always struck me as cheating, somehow. I mean, where does it stop and start, if you believe in that? Where do you draw the line? Certainly not at mere inability to function well; plenty of disabled people stick it out and find life worthwhile. Not at pain—in my book, that's simple cowardice. So where, then?"

"You can't say," Ingrid agreed. "So what will you do when you are old and feel your time has come, if you don't believe in cheating?"

"Well," said Jesse, "if you want frankness on this subject, I'll do what people who don't talk about it do. They refrain from doing anything. They don't try to prolong the natural process. That's how my great-granddad went, and nobody questioned it, and what he didn't tell the doctors was left unsaid." God, he thought, does it have to be spelled out for them? Are they all too young to have figured it out for themselves?

But they *had* figured it out—they had, perhaps, acted on that basis. Were they looking to him for validation?

"In other words," said Carla, "you believe there are times not to seek treatment."

"Sure I do. I'd even go so far as to refuse advised treatment—" He broke off, aghast at the implications of what he was saying. He knew where they were leading him, now.

"You'd refuse just as you refused treatment for alcoholism," Peter agreed. "But that's an option we don't have here."

"Oh, God," Jesse said. "You're saying it wasn't a matter of whether to call the ambulance. Your friend had to be hidden from one already after her." It had become all too clear. The city's ambulances, after all, had police powers.

"She was due for a mandatory checkup," Anne said, "and this time, she'd have been held permanently. Even if her condition had stabilized."

"You mean everyone—everyone on this world who's not killed outright—dies slowly in that damned hospital, hooked to machines?" Jesse persisted. "You all know that's what you're facing? It's not even a matter of odds?"

"I wish that were what we meant," Bernie said. There was an uneasy silence. Then, with irony, he went on, "But you see, we have the galaxy's finest medical facility in this colony—"

"So I've been told. That's not quite how I'd describe it."

"And," Kwame declared, "the galaxy's finest medical facility can't let people die."

"Till they've disintegrated from old age, you mean." God. It might take years, with unlimited forced treatment. . . .

"No, Jesse. It can't let them die at all. At least not according to the Meds' criteria."

He stared at Kwame. "I guess I don't quite see."

"You wouldn't," Carla said gently, "and yet you have to, in order to live here even for a while. It's better that you hear the facts from us than by chance, from strangers. You're not going to like what you hear."

Jesse was silent.

"Our medical facility," Bernie told him, "really is an advanced one. From the technological standpoint it's superb. It has developed sophisticated techniques not common elsewhere, and as you know, its funds are unlimited. The law says everyone must be treated for everything. So you see, bodies are just—maintained. Indefinitely."

"Even after they're brain-dead?" Jesse asked in a low voice.

"Yes—like bodies from which organs for transplant were taken, back in the days before cloned organs were perfected. Sometimes there's minimal brain stem activity, but no possibility of subconscious mental functioning."

"Surely the goal must be to restore the mind, or perhaps someday transplant it."

"No. We're not talking about coma. People in comas have an interior life, some form of consciousness, whether or not they show evidence of it. But even in principle, technology can't restore or transplant a mind that no longer physically exists."

"The law holds that personhood resides in mere flesh," Liz said. "The general public perceives maintenance as eternal life. But though some religions once held that only if a soul were still present could bodily functions be made to continue, that can hardly be said now that our technology's so advanced."

"The Meds are fully aware that they're dealing with bodies that would be pronounced dead on any other world," Ingrid added. "And they aren't maintaining them for religious reasons. On the contrary, they reject any concept of soul. To them the body alone is central, the definition of human life and therefore sacred. So the aim is to preserve its biological operation."

"You're right that I don't like it," Jesse said, knowing no way to strengthen the understatement. "But aren't they going to run out of bed space someday?"

"Well, they don't use regular rooms," Carla said painfully. "The bodies are kept in stasis units, like those that were once used on slow starships. Besides the treatment floors there are maintenance floors. That's a euphemism. The more accurate term is vaults. It's another reason the Hospital is so large."

"Carla," Jesse protested. "You work in that place! You mean all the time, while you're working there, you know these stasis vaults are around ... and that someday—"

They all stared at him in clear dismay. Carla averted her face, stricken, suddenly, by feeling too deep for words. With chagrin he saw that his outburst had hurt her, touched some sensitive point that the others knew to avoid. He longed to comfort her, but he didn't know what he could say.

"Let's drop it," Peter put in quickly. "We've got other issues to clear up now. For one thing, Jess, we need you to be aware that what you saw tonight was a crime involving all of us—even you, should it ever become known that you witnessed it. That's why we gave you a chance to stay out. According to the law you're now an accessory to murder."

"Murder? All I got a glimpse of was a wrapped body, already dead. That's all any of you saw, except maybe Anne."

"But officially, you see, there is no death from natural causes here. This world has no cemeteries. To bury a body is murder, unless it's been in an accident and is not intact."

"We could all be arrested for this? Imprisoned?" There were no prisons, Jesse recalled in horror. There was only the Hospital, which no doubt had methods for dealing with murderers. How could they have dared to take such a chance? The whole group—a formal ceremony—when a single boat with two men would have been sufficient. . . .

Peter nodded. He leaned across the table, held Jesse with his eyes. "Jess, I'd guess that at this point you've got some serious doubts in your mind about the wisdom of our legal system. Am I right?"

"Damned right," Jesse declared grimly. "I wouldn't ordinarily mix in colonial politics, but this—"

"This is not a political issue, except in the sense that any government, anywhere, seeks to reinforce and extend its own power. The Meds are in control because they're supported by the public. No form of political action could help matters."

"Why not? If enough others were willing to confront reality as you people do, the law or the constitution or whatever could be changed. You do have free elections—"

"And if we held one, even after raising the public's consciousness, the vast majority would vote against change. People don't want to die. They may not like to discuss the Vaults, still they see them as a form of immortality."

"You don't. I don't."

"But we are exceptions. Our particular group of friends is composed of exceptions. Would you have us impose our view on the public by force? Should we be trying to run the government in the name of what we think is good for people, instead of what the Meds think is good for them?"

Jesse shook his head. "That would be self-defeating," he conceded, "if you're for freedom. But there should be individual choice."

"There should be, but again, people will not vote for that. Not on a matter of health policy."

True enough, thought Jesse. He'd seen that himself, even before hearing of this far more disturbing issue. Not to be treated might be crime here; elsewhere, it was sin. People would not vote to permit what they'd been taught to feel guilty about, whatever they might do privately by themselves.

"Furthermore," Kwame said, "they won't vote to cut off their income. The people in the Vaults, you see, are legally alive. Their accounts in offworld banks still earn interest. That's why we're all relatively wealthy here—though we can't touch the principal, we get steady income on money inherited from our forebears, generations back, starting with those who got rich on homesteaders' diamond-mining rights. The government takes most of it in taxes, but it knows better than to confiscate it all. It won't risk jeopardizing a system that not only pays the cost of preserving bodies, but fills the treasury as well."

"I'd think the banks would have caught on by now," Jesse protested.

"Banks don't turn away depositors," Ingrid pointed out, "not without official death certificates, which they'll never receive from Undine."

"The banks are heavily invested in the pharmaceutical companies," Nathan added, "and for obvious reasons, Undine is the pharmaceutical companies' model of heaven. No way will its policies ever be criticized."

Jesse clenched his fingers. "There's got to be some answer," he insisted. "Laws aren't like this everywhere. This is just one colony."

"But it's an advanced colony," Peter said. "We here are forerunners, Jess. You know in your heart that when our technological advances spread, so will the system derived from them: first to more colonies and ultimately, perhaps, to Earth itself. It would not make any difference if we changed our laws. The trend will be in favor of more like them."

"Oh, God, Peter!" Jesse burst out. "The way you're putting it, we'd end up with a galaxy full of vaults. Life can't be meant to end that way. There has to be a better goal than that."

"We think so, too," Peter said. To Jesse's amazement, he smiled as he said it. Suddenly they were all smiling—in dead earnest, untouched by fear or despair. It was if the meaning that had always eluded him were not an illusion, as if they somehow had an inside track on it.

Carla, her normal spirits restored, caught his hand and squeezed it. "We go in for this sort of discussion," she said. "It's a bit like jumping in over your head—you develop a taste for it. We're alive, as you said, Jesse! We don't worry about the future. We're living."

Was it simply courage he saw in them, then? Jesse wondered. They had a form of it he'd never encountered—they'd led him to an impassable abyss and stopped just short of the edge. They had stopped on his account; he sensed there had been more to say. He found himself wishing that he were fit to follow them.

11

LATE THE NEXT afternoon Carla sought Jesse on the porch, where he sat reveling in onworld sunlight. "I'm going now," she said, "in Bernie's plane. You can wait for Peter."

"I'd rather come with you," he said, torn between desire to prolong what might end soon in any case, and an irrational wish to stay at the Lodge until the last possible moment.

"Bernie hasn't room. We will see each other again, Jesse —at least I hope so." She smiled, but it seemed a struggle.

Jesse rose and put his arms around her. "Carla, you know I want to see you. You know I want more than that. Is there any good reason why we have to wait for more?"

"Yes," she said gravely. "You'll know soon enough, one way or the other. Oh, Jesse, I—" She pulled away, to his dismay blinking back tears. "Please don't ever hate me, however things turn out." Before he recovered enough to answer her, she was running down the path toward the dock.

Jesse followed slowly. The plane took off, circling the Lodge and disappearing into a cloudless sky. One by one others went; he sat at the water's edge and watched them. It was like being aboard a flagship, he thought, when all the shuttles were leaving: there were people you'd served with, been close to, and they were going separate ways now; you would probably never see them again. You did not yet know where you yourself would be sent. And there was a centeredness to the base, simply because it was a base, and you clung to that. You clung to what it stood for, and to the memories.

It was almost dusk; evidently Peter planned to fly by moonlight. When Jesse saw him on the path, he started toward the dock. But Peter came to him instead. "I'm not leaving till tomorrow," he said, sitting down on a flat rock beside him. "I can get you transport, but I was wondering if you might want to stay on for a while."

Reprieve, Jesse thought, amused by his own surge of gladness. "Overnight, you mean?" he asked.

"Longer than that. Maybe quite a bit longer."

Jesse shook his head. "I can't impose on your hospitality," he said with reluctance. "Or somebody's hospitality—I'm still not clear about who owns this place. What is it, a co-op of some sort?" He wondered, suddenly, whether he might be allowed to buy in; it would be worth it even for a short stay onworld.

Peter hesitated, searching for words. "Does the term 'safe house' mean anything to you?" he asked slowly. "That's the closest thing I can think of that you might have come across in bigger colonies."

Turning, Jesse stared at Peter in sheer astonishment. "Maybe we don't have the same vocabulary," he said. "If this were what I know of as a safe house, I wouldn't have been invited here."

"You might. I'm a quick judge of character. So is Carla."

"Would it be out of line to ask who you need to be safe from?" It was just not possible, he thought, that they were on the same wavelength. A safe house would imply covert operations of some sort. This colony had no nations, no political conflicts; its government was monolithic, unopposed, and in the eyes of virtually all citizens, benevolent.

"We like to explore ideas, as you know," Peter said. "We have more such ideas than you've yet heard. Some of them are—unpopular. Some might even be considered irrational."

"But League law guarantees freedom of speech," Jesse protested.

"Does it? Or does that apply only to mentally competent citizens, those not in need of help from Med therapists?"

Jesse went cold. He should have known, perhaps, considering his own experience; but he'd assumed his view of the Hospital was biased. "I've heard of places where psychiatry's abused, where hospitals are used as political prisons," he acknowledged. "But you said the problem here's not political."

"Well, Jess, it works a little differently here," Peter said. "It's true there are no political uprisings, and we've no wish to start one. What I'm getting at is a bit more subtle. The Med government isn't corrupt. The worst thing about the authorities is that they're sincere. They really believe they're helping everybody. Some of us happen to disagree."

"And this is the only sort of place you can talk about it?" Good lord, he thought, were there microphones in restaurants? Was that why Carla had switched subjects so abruptly the first night?

"We can talk anywhere, except on phones, with reasonable caution. But we often do more than talk, you see." Peter's gaze was suddenly very penetrating. Jesse knew the key point had been made.

"God," he said. "Are you—recruiting me, Peter?"

"Yes, as a matter of fact," Peter admitted. "One of the things I do in the world outside is keep my eyes open for people who might be interested."

Jesse stared out across the bay, letting the shock settle. Despite all the speculation he'd done about these people, despite even their acceptance of criminal liability for the burial of a friend, such a thing as this had never entered his mind. Now . . . well, yes, the fire was there, the intensity; he could see them as ideological fanatics. But activists? Undercover operatives? They weren't hard enough, not unless they were new at the game. "Interested in what?" he asked slowly.

"In the power of the individual human mind. In the primacy of that, not only over oppression but over all the well-meant limits society imposes on it. And in a future Med policy can't dominate."

"I'm for that," Jesse declared. "I'd be interested if I were free to make a commitment. But Peter, if Fleet will take me back I've got to go."

"We don't ask for a commitment that would interfere," Peter said. "You'd make binding pledges, yes, but you wouldn't be bound to this planet. As I explained last night, the real problem affects the whole galaxy."

"I'd be expected to act—elsewhere, you mean? As an agent, a courier?"

"Not exactly. Our offworld contacts deal mostly with getting around this colony's monetary restrictions—hacking and so forth; I doubt if that's your thing. You wouldn't be taking on any specific responsibilities by coming in with us, at least not now. If later you were asked to assume one, you'd be free to say no."

"But I'd be committed as long as I'm here."

"Not in the sense you mean, except with regard to secrecy. We aren't quite the sort of group you see in the average action vid." Peter spoke slowly, with deliberation. "We don't expect anyone to renounce loyalties or attachments, except to this planet's government, which you have no allegiance to in any case. It's more a matter of outlook. There are certain premises you'd find yourself questioning, possibly some you've not questioned before. Some might prove hard to give up. The alternatives we offer might prove frightening. All we'd ask of you is willingness to learn."

"It's just philosophy, then? Reshaping of minds?"

"More than that. We act on our beliefs, develop skills outsiders don't have."

"What sort of skills?"

"For one, controlling our bodies to the extent that medical intervention's rarely necessary."

"Through fitness, you mean." This didn't ring true; the assortment of food eaten at the Lodge, unlike what he'd been served in the city, was hardly the fare of health fanatics.

"No," Peter said. "We control our bodies' reactions with our minds, consciously, just as you control your legs with your mind when you decide to walk."

"That's not possible," Jesse objected.

"So the Meds tell you. Need I point out that they've got a vested interest in making you believe it?"

"You—you boycott them, then?"

"Insofar as we can without getting caught. There are physicians among us, and whatever real treatment we need, short of limb or organ replacement, is given in covert healing houses. We take steps to escape the medication we'd otherwise receive for emotional reactions, alleged risk factors, and other conditions that interfere less with living than therapy would."

"I'm happy to hear it. What I've seen so far in this colony makes me think the priority given to health precautions over enjoyment of life has been carried to ridiculous lengths."

"The public's sense of values is distorted," Peter agreed. "It's true everywhere; historically, whenever health authorities succeed in overcoming some actual problem, such as contagion, they are left with a bureaucracy that must justify its existence by medicalizing more and more aspects of simply being human. Here, where it's combined with the natural tendency of government to encroach on personal liberty, that process has been unrestrained. We can't combat it directly. We've developed other ways of ensuring our own well-being. There's a price—the initial training's not a pleasant process. But I think you can see we're none the worse for it."

Jesse nodded. Their self-possession, their vitality, their enviable ability to have fun—whatever they'd been through must be worth experiencing. He'd give a lot to learn their secrets. "I guess you know it's a tempting proposition," he said. "But when it comes to activism, well, I'd have to know more of the specifics."

"You don't expect me to tell you, do you?"

"No. Of course you can't; I see that. But then we're at an impasse, aren't we? Because there are limits to what I'll do, even in a good cause."

"We don't plan to turn you into a hit man, if that's what you mean," Peter said. "You've seen too many of those vids, Jess."

"Not just vids. On Earth—on many worlds—such things happen. I'm not wholly ignorant of undercover work. Sooner or later, there's a line to be crossed. I'm not saying no one ever needs to cross it. I just don't see myself in that role."

"Do you see us in it?" Peter asked quietly.

No, of course he didn't; that was the absurd element in the whole business. He simply could not conceive of Peter, or any of them, turning to violence. According to reason, he could not judge; he'd known them only five days, after all—but through some uncanny sixth sense, he knew.

If not the usual sort of operatives, then, what were they? Jesse pondered it, chilled by the suspicion that came to him. Not assassins, but angels of mercy; the burial must not have been an isolated incident. He'd given them the benefit of the doubt last night, but as a general rule they could hardly beat the ambulance to unscheduled deaths.

"I suppose I do see part of what you're doing," he said with genuine regret, "and I can't go along with it. I respect your conviction—but as I said last night, I don't favor assisted suicide. Not even in the extreme situation you've got here."

"Suicide?" For an instant Peter seemed puzzled; then he smiled. "We don't favor that either, Jesse. Is that how it looks, that we save people from the stasis vaults by dumping them prematurely into the bay?"

"It would be logical. I'm not sure I wouldn't prefer the bay to the Hospital, if I were a terminal case. But I don't think rushing death's any more justifiable than prolonging it."

"If you'd argued otherwise last night, we wouldn't be inviting you to join us." Peter paused briefly before admitting, "As you've guessed, burials at sea are quite frequent. One of our jobs is to facilitate natural death for people who are already dying. Wholly natural—no drugs, no intervention. Nothing you'll find objectionable, at least not in the ethical sense."

"In what other sense might I object? Not the legal one," Jesse declared.

"No. But there are other aspects that may be upsetting. Nursing the dying isn't fun. What's more, sometimes people

argue for natural death in principle while insulating themselves from the reality of it. We don't let you do that."

It fit. They were absolutely uncompromising; in their
work as in their discussion, they'd permit no self-delusion.
"I'd actually tend dying patients? But I'm not skilled. It's
not my field."

"You're looking at it as Med-dominated culture does—
putting death off in a corner to be dealt with by professionals, as if it were some sort of abnormality. If you believe it
shouldn't be denied or abolished, you must back up what
you say."

"I could have a go at that, but I've got no aptitude—for
comforting the sick, I mean."

"You'd be adequately trained. That's a small part of what
you'd learn, of course. Caregiving's not our main focus and
no one has to keep on participating, though many of us do
from time to time."

Peter didn't seem bothered by it. Yet he was a man sensitive to others' feelings, and presumably to their suffering.
That issue hadn't been mentioned, Jesse realized. "No drugs—
not even painkillers? Or are you in the drug business, too?"

"I'd rather not answer that right now. It gets into some
areas I'm not free to discuss."

Well, yes, Jesse thought. It would. He already had far
more information than an outsider should be given. Were
they that sure of him, or merely imprudent?

"You'd never be asked to go against your conscience,"
Peter said, "because that's the whole point, after all. We're
for individual conscience. Individual decisions, even where
some might say they're not in a person's best interests. And
something else I can't explain yet—the full empowerment
of the individual mind."

A cold breeze drifted in from the water. Peter was silent, considering, then went on, "I can tell you a little more,
things that should be obvious to you anyway. You don't think
you're the only victim we've sprung from the Hospital, do
you? Most cases aren't as easy as yours. If we can't get an

official discharge, we have to hide people. That means other safe houses, some of which are used as hospices." He eyed Jesse. "In terms of the law this is more than conspiracy, remember. When someone dies naturally in our care, it's technically homicide. And all crime here—"

"Is considered illness," Jesse said. "You don't have to spell it out. The risks aren't what I'm worrying about."

"Of course not. You want to know the long-range goal, and that's what I can't go into yet. I'll warn you, though, that it's not anything like what you might imagine. Enormous demands would be made of you. My guess is that you'd like that, but the choice has to be yours."

Jesse drew breath, knowing that no amount of practical good sense could prevail over his feelings. Hell, he was stuck on this world, for a while if not forever. "All right," he said with mounting enthusiasm. "If you want me, count me in."

Peter's eyes met his. "It's not as simple as that," he declared. "There are formalities."

"You mean initiations, passwords, all that?"

"Yes, ultimately. Training in mind/body control comes first, but before that we have to verify your aptitude for it." Peter hesitated. "This is hard to explain. You're not the first person I've brought in, but I still don't know any good way to present it without making it sound like second-rate melodrama. We test you, Jess. It's a very challenging test, and you won't see the necessity for it. What's done may seem excessive, even sadistic, and at this stage I can't tell you why it's designed that way."

Jesse shrugged. There was no question of his refusing such a challenge; both Peter and Carla were aware of that. Looking back, he saw they'd taken pains to find out. "I've no objections," he told Peter. "You've got to be careful who you accept."

"That's not the issue. We already trust you, or you wouldn't be hearing this much. The test measures how far you trust *us,* among other things. Usually people know us a good deal longer before undertaking it. You don't have to commit now; you can go back to the city, wait, if you like."

"Maybe I'm a quick judge of character too," Jesse said slowly. "I'm not sure why, but I trust you as much or more than crews I've worked with for years. There's something— unique in you. I can't say just what it is, but I wouldn't hesitate to sign you on as shipmates. That's the only criterion I know."

"You'll see another side of us. I hope you won't lose faith in your own intuition." He paused, then went on, "I can set things up for tonight, if you want me to. You can't stay here any longer as a guest."

"Let's get on with it," Jesse said.

"Okay, then." Peter's smile was a bit forced; Jesse perceived that it took effort for him to proceed. "I've mentioned the power of the human mind. We do a good deal of experimentation with that, much of it in a lab setting with some fairly elaborate equipment. You're being asked to volunteer."

Jesse laughed. "Is that all? Evidently you've never heard what a person goes through to qualify for a starship crew, or you wouldn't find it so hard to broach the subject."

"Stress testing? Endurance of pain?"

"Certainly, when I was a Fleet cadet. It's not that big of a deal." But it had been then, he remembered. There'd been a spice to it then; there was, when you still thought your life was leading somewhere.

"I was afraid you'd say that," Peter told him. "Your biggest hurdle's going to be complacency. I've read a lot of what's been published on human endurance. Fleet knows little or nothing about it."

"I'm ready to learn more."

"That's fortunate," Peter said dryly.

"You're trying to scare me. That's an old game too, but since reason tells me I won't be harmed in research experiments, there's only so far you can go." Which, he thought, might be anticlimactic after a medical workup that had approached the point of injury more than once.

"What we do won't harm you," Peter agreed, with surprising intensity, "although it will scare you more than you think. There are reasons why it has to, but we can't share them with you yet. These particular endurance studies require naive subjects." He appraised Jesse thoughtfully. "That's a technical term; are you familiar with it?"

"Sure—subjects who don't know what to expect."

"Yes, so you won't be informed even of the aim. Nothing unprecedented will be done to you; the rest of us have been through the same protocol."

"Where is this lab?" Jesse asked, realizing that Peter had stayed after the others in order to escort him there.

"Downstairs." Peter pointed to the Lodge, silhouetted now against the darkening sky.

"Here?" The place was more than a safe house, then; it was a cover. For what, exactly? An underground lab with elaborate equipment would be difficult and expensive to install anywhere, let alone on a wild island; the group obviously had vast resources. Affluent as colonial citizens might be, its members could not all be carefree young people. Those he had met perplexed him more than ever, now. Peter's informed remarks on endurance studies were out of character, however much activism he might be involved in. Jesse remembered him on the rock, laughing, seemingly unburdened by worries; now he was indeed revealing another side.

Yet still he was drawn. Besides, there was Carla, who evidently had planned all along to recruit him. "I guess I've underestimated a lot of things," he reflected.

"Yes. You can back out—'volunteer' means exactly what it says. It's up to you to decide if you want to proceed."

"I think you know that decision's already made. I—I get the feeling you knew before you approached me." It was as if Peter had read his mind, his feelings, right from the first. . . .

"We know a lot about people," Peter agreed. "I would not bring you into this without believing you won't be sorry." He looked, Jesse thought, as if it were he who had just taken on a hard trial.

Part Two

12

IN THE PLANE, Carla looked down at the fading expanse of water, wishing the coming workweek behind her. When she next saw Jesse, she'd know the outcome . . . but before then, she would hear it from Peter. He had not allowed her to stay. She hadn't argued; she wouldn't want to watch, couldn't bear that, though for Jesse's sake she had offered. But her presence could not help Jesse. Only her love might help. She sent it out across the distance, a desperate, inner surge, wondering if she'd be equal to the days and weeks to come.

Her own ordeal had begun during Jesse's hospitalization, when she'd tried desperately to free him, not guessing the true situation. Now, aware of it, she knew harder times were ahead of them. And this night would not be the least of them. Jesse would suffer terribly—more terribly than was usual, Peter had admitted. It would not harm him. He would not regret the experience. Unless . . . unless he failed to complete the full test. Unless she'd failed to give him reason enough to see it through. . . .

She thought back to the point of decision, the moment when she had burst into Peter Kelstrom's hospital office, frantic, ready to fight fiercely once more for Jesse's release—only to find that he'd already signed the discharge order. "Tell me why you waited so long," she'd demanded. "Tell me you didn't order the truth serum."

"Carla, the stakes are very high here. I did what was necessary. Jesse Sanders wasn't damaged by it."

"Like hell he wasn't! You, a therapist, are saying that a man like Jesse is not damaged by forced extraction of God knows what thoughts are buried deep in his mind—by fearing he's revealed more than he actually has, believing he will never again have any shred of privacy? By knowing it's in his file?"

"It's not in his file. I did it by keyboard, using a synthesized voice he couldn't recognize later, and I wiped it immediately. In due course I'll tell him that."

"*You'll* tell him? Peter, you surely don't think he'll be picked up again?"

Astonishingly, Peter broke into a radiant smile, the smile reserved for exciting ideas far removed from his somber job setting. "Forgive me for not leveling with you about Jesse's case," he said. "But it worked, didn't it?"

"Worked?" At first, she was too confused to grasp what he meant. Peter sometimes played ruthless games; he was very clever at it, and they were always effective. But whatever he'd meant to accomplish, he would not have involved an innocent bystander. Members of the Group could and did volunteer for unpleasant roles in schemes designed to protect Peter's cover. To use a real patient that way would be unthinkable.

"He has to hate the Hospital, and yet trust *you*," Peter explained. "If I'd told you ahead of time why I was stressing him, you'd have given too much away. You're not well enough trained to hide your thoughts."

"But Peter, he already hated it, and anyway, why does it matter? He'll be leaving soon."

"No. That's one of the things I found out the night I viewed his chart at home. He's listed as an alcoholic; the report had already gone to Fleet—for which I was grateful, since I was spared the anguish of feeling I ought to correct it. He won't be able to get transport, not without undercover intervention, anyway."

"You don't plan to intervene?" It seemed an odd lapse of Peter's empathy.

"Not by sending him offworld. I got the impression that you'd be happy to keep seeing him."

"Yes . . . but you know it can't come to anything between us." How, Carla thought, could this be troubling her? Her life was defined by the powers she'd gained, by what she had become; and she did not in any sense regret that, though it did limit future relationships. "I can't love that way outside the Group, after all."

"Carla, we're not going to leave him outside."

She drew breath. "You mean—make him one of us? Is that possible?"

"It should be. He has the potential. If I had no other evidence, your attraction to him would be proof enough. And we need him. We—we need to see how our way of life will work for an offworlder."

"You turned him against the Meds just to recruit him!" she accused, suddenly understanding. "It wasn't fair." Despite her outrage, Carla's heart beat faster. Perhaps, after all . . .

"Certainly it was fair. He had to learn first hand what we're up against. He hated the authorities here on grounds of his arrest, but had no strong reason to distrust medics in general. Not having seen the logical conclusion of their policies, he might have remained under the impression that maximum medical care is a good thing."

"The recapture, days of brutal therapy . . . was all that really warranted?"

"It was harsh," Peter admitted. "I would not, of course, have let it go far enough for a tracking chip to be implanted; that's a handicap the Group can't cope with. But I did have to know how he'd react to stress, Carla."

"How do we know he'll want to come in? He hasn't any of the special talents we usually look for. Even with those who do have, it takes weeks of observation, weeks of interaction with us, before you're ready to recruit—" She broke off, frowning, "Is *that* why you used truth serum? To find out if our powers are latent in him?"

"And to judge whether he's susceptible to the dangers they involve."

"You don't drug other trainees. It's against all our principles—"

"There are rare cases where it's justified, just as there are in medical situations. I need to be absolutely sure of him." Reluctantly he added, "Not only for his safety, but for another reason I can't explain to you right now."

On the verge of asking why not, Carla stopped. Something strange was going on here. Peter's mind had been closed to her for days; it still was, despite his admissions about past tactics. Within the Group that was not normal.

"Jesse won't even begin to suspect what we are," she protested. "You can't be candid when you talk him into the initial testing. Will keeping him in the dark about us be justified, too?"

"You know why I can't reveal all he stands to gain."

"I didn't mean everything. Not the bonus that would attract the wrong people, for the wrong reasons. But recruits from our front group have at least some idea of what they're getting into. Jesse may not even *want* all our skills."

"Not at first," Peter agreed. "He'll find them frightening, unconsciously if not consciously. With our help he can overcome that. The rewards are very great, after all, even apart from the potential bonus."

"He won't know that when he's asked to endure pain," she said unhappily. "It will seem arbitrary, as if we were just testing his commitment."

Peter rose from his desk and came to her. "Carla, here is a strong, capable man who's been nearly ruined by years of insufficient challenge. Was he happy in Fleet? Will he be less happy after undergoing an ordeal that will open doors for him? Have any of us been sorry we went through it?"

No, of course not. But while it was happening, inherent benefits were inconceivable. "What if he won't consent?" she asked. "If you tell him it's for his own good, it will sound just like what the Meds say."

"Which is precisely why I can't tell him. He must have better grounds for submitting to it than that—he must sense that it's been good for *us*. That accepting it will promote what he values in us. That's why we present it as scientific research, so that the decision won't be based on the wrong sort of trust."

"Calling it research isn't quite accurate."

"A half-truth, the first of many. But still truth. If we hope to spread our ways to more people—perhaps someday to more worlds—we need data from a wide variety of subjects." Peter went on, a bit hesitantly, "There'll be some new data in this case. Jesse's background isn't typical. He'll have more than one kind of conditioning to overcome."

"You're troubled," she observed. "Peter, I want this. I know *he* would want it—to control his body and mind fully, to live free of the stress that wears people down in the world outside! But if there's risk—"

"There's none for a person whose mind is stable."

"That's not what Ian says when he prepares trainees for the Ritual."

"At that stage, specific dangers do arise. Warnings are given. By then, it's an informed choice, and we don't let anyone make it who's not qualified." Peter frowned. "The risk I worry about isn't that, Carla. It's the issue of motivation. This man now has reasons to join us, but will they be powerful enough to sustain him? If he feels no compelling need to see it through, he may back out. And if he does, life in this colony will be hell for him, all the more so because he'll hate himself for what he'll perceive as cowardice."

"Could he—really become an alcoholic?" She shivered, thinking of it.

"Yes. The seeds are there. That's probably why Fleet didn't promote him; stupidly, they allowed them to develop by not making full use of his ability. Here, with no family, no way to get a job, what else could he turn to? Eventually, he'd face both the problem and the cure, and it's questionable as to which would be worse."

"Peter, we *can't* let that happen! You've got to adjust the pressure, make sure it's not too extreme—"

"I'll have no choice as to how extreme it gets. Once the test is started, for me to stop it short of completion would be as harmful to him, psychologically, as for him to quit. And it's more than a test, remember—it's a phase of training that can't be bypassed."

"Then surely you'll give enough subtle encouragement to get him through it. You've never lost anybody before."

"No, because I am careful who I choose. I don't know Jesse Sanders. Since he's at loose ends here, we must move fast; I may have only a few days to get acquainted with him before I act. From his psych profile, I know that he has the capacity. The trust . . . at first, that worried me. I'm not sure of my ability to inspire that in such a short time. But when I saw you were attracted to him—"

"You manipulated us to make him trust me." And perhaps vice versa, she realized. "Okay, I won't argue; it was done to help him. But I can't give him a motive for enduring the test."

"No?" Peter asked quietly. "I rather hoped you could, Carla." He'd looked at her, meaningfully, and had not had to put it into words.

So she had set out to make Jesse want her, which had not been hard to do when her own feelings were so genuine. If they had not been, she would still have done it, and would have delivered on her promises. No member of the Group would do less to save someone worth saving. And yet, she might not have been capable of following through, Carla thought; she'd been frozen inside until love for Jesse warmed her. . . .

At the Lodge, things had gone well. Peter had liked Jesse; he'd been impressed. The rapport was there, he'd told her. If it could be established for mere scuba diving, it would be a great deal stronger during more difficult types of instruction. Yet he'd remained concerned. Though to the inexperienced eye it wouldn't be evident, his confidence was feigned. Finally, this morning, she had cornered him and demanded truth. "Is there any doubt left?" she'd asked, terrified by the thought that Jesse might not truly care for her, that he might, after all, not prove willing to pay the price.

Forcing a smile, Peter had assured her, "None. He's an even better man than I had hoped. And he wants desperately to stay with us—with you."

"I know you, Peter. You're dreading what's going to happen tonight. Why?"

"It's never easy. You've never worked as an instructor, Carla. You haven't been present during a test session since Ian conducted your own. But you're aware that I'll share Jesse's pain—"

"You're worrying about what it will do to *you!*" she perceived, astonished. Ian was an old man, now; for a long time Peter had borne much of the responsibility. He was trained, experienced, and very skilled. Still, while he'd seemed okay these past few days on the Island, he had appeared to be troubled lately. He'd been carrying far too heavy a load since Ramón's death . . . Ramón, who'd been among Ian's protégés, who would have taken on part of the work that had fallen to Peter. Ramón, her husband, who was now in the Vaults. . . .

The marriage was officially dissolved, of course. Though people in the stasis vaults were classed as living, their spouses weren't legally bound. Carla had nevertheless felt bound. She still loved Ramón, and it was not like the clean break of normal death. Daily, she walked beneath a ceiling above which the body of her husband was preserved. That's not life, she told herself. He's not there, not really. But he might not be wherever the dead go, either.

Could she really love another man while Ramón's heart beat, while his breathing continued, while his mind . . .

Where was his mind? Not in the stasis unit, surely. Brain-dead, he was not conscious on any level, not even those about which the Group knew more than orthodox science. The semblance of life maintained in corpses was illusion.

With dismay, she'd jerked back to the moment. She loved Ramón, but now she loved Jesse too. And she sensed that he was in danger. If the calm, self-possessed Peter feared for his own strength . . .

Peter took her hand, pressed it. "I'll be honest," he said. "You're better off knowing than wondering. It's going to be very rough for Jesse. He has the wrong kind of background; he'll try to be stoic and succeed too well. Ian told me what happens in such cases, but I've never witnessed one. I know what I've got to do, but I'm not looking forward to it."

"If—if it would help for me to be present—if I could support him—"

"No. You'd give too much support; you haven't the training to hold back. Besides, he would want to be a hero in your eyes, which would only make things worse for him— and damned hellish for *you*. It will be bad enough for the instruction team; the people who'll be on hand tonight aren't equipped for what they'll see."

She cringed. It had not occurred to her that Jesse would experience more severe pain during the test than she herself had, although she could now see why it would turn out that way. And it was because of her that he would have to. Yet he might otherwise choose to quit, and to quit would destroy him. . . .

Now, as the plane droned on above the water, Carla shared Peter's burden: the caring, the responsibility . . . and also the undercurrent of fear.

13

PETER APPEARED AT the door of the bunkroom late that night, still wearing the bright blue sport shirt he'd had on earlier. "I'll take you downstairs now," he said, as casually as he might have proposed another swim party.

With relief, Jesse accompanied him. He'd been told to skip dinner, to be in his room until contacted; then he had waited hours. He'd expected an escort from the lab, either a technician or ... what? Sheepishly, he admitted to himself that he'd pictured some sinister-looking professorial type. His imagination had been overworked by the wait, which he now realized might have been calculated. He'd felt foolish apprehension about pain he knew perfectly well he could cope with! He wondered why a group with serious purpose bothered with such charades, which seemed rather sophomoric. Secret labs, human experimentation, trial by ordeal—what did they take him for? If these people were as perceptive as they seemed to be, surely they knew he would not be deterred by melodramatic stage trappings.

The Lodge was quiet. Though the people he'd met had gone back to the city, there must be lab personnel present. Either they'd arrived during his wait, or they had been underground all along.

Peter led the way to a cramped elevator, inconspicuous within one of the storerooms that separated the kitchen from the common room. They entered; its door closed, but it did not move.

"We need a pledge at this point," Peter said with sudden seriousness.

"All right," Jesse said. "What do you want me to pledge?"

Peter spoke slowly, giving weight to the words. "That you freely consent to testing of your potential. That you agree to training that may prove disturbing. And that what happens from now on, what you learn of what we are, will not be revealed to anyone outside the Group. Not on any world, ever, whether you're in with us or not, no matter how you may feel about us then. Give me your hand on it."

They gripped hands silently, and it was as if more than a handshake passed between them; Jesse felt something he couldn't define. We'd be sealing this with blood if it ran true to form, he thought. Underneath, he knew he was making light of it only because its gravity embarrassed him. "This is all?" he asked. "Not even witnessed?"

"If you weren't sincere, I'd know," Peter said. "Don't ask me how. The others trust my evaluation."

The elevator descended. Below was another storeroom; boxes and bins of provisions were piled against the walls, leaving room only for the narrow door to a walk-in freezer. They entered it, the cold piercing Jesse's thin shirt. The hatch swung shut behind them. Peter swung a rack of frozen poultry aside. Behind it was a second door, and beyond that a short, dimly-lit hallway with rough stone walls.

They paused before what Jesse assumed must be the lab entrance. "We have an infirmary and hospice facilities down here," Peter said. "I'll show you around someday, but tonight we'll use just one room."

"You're involved in this lab business personally," Jesse perceived with surprise. Of all the occupations he could have guessed for Peter, this seemed the least likely, although he supposed it was natural that Carla would have friends among other psych technicians. "I'm not quite clear on what your position is here, Peter."

"I'm in charge," Peter said. "By profession I'm a psychiatrist, though I don't see the job in quite the same light as the Meds do." At Jesse's look he went on, "Yes, I work at the Hospital in the world outside. It's unpleasant work, since I despise many of their methods, but it gives me a chance to salvage some good people. I ordered your discharge. The power to do that is worth compromises."

So that was it. No doubt Peter had read his file; they were more thorough than he'd supposed.

Yet why the lengthy delay, if Peter and Carla had been working together from the beginning? If even Anne had known then that Peter could discharge him legally? Jesse frowned. "I owe you thanks," he said. "It must not have been easy; I was officially under the care of a Dr. Kelstrom, I think, though he never saw me."

"I did see you," Peter admitted, "via a camera."

Outraged, Jesse protested, "*You're* Kelstrom? But then—"

"I could have released you sooner, spared you the worst of what was done to you. Would you have had grounds for the decision you made tonight if I had?"

As Jesse pondered this, Peter added, "Carla wasn't told what I was planning; it put a great strain on her faith in me. There was no lack of candor on her part."

"I'm glad. It's not that I don't forgive you, Peter—still I'm not sure I like being manipulated."

"It will never be done to your disadvantage. But I warn you that sometimes during our training, similar tactics are necessary. And since the training can be disorienting, I'll need to relate to you as therapist as well as instructor. Okay?"

"Okay," Jesse conceded, wondering why he felt so convinced that it *was* okay, that Peter's tactics would always turn out well—as well, perhaps, as his bold advice on learning to swim and to scuba dive. "You act in your professional capacity, then, within the Group?"

"I'm head of our research and of training. I'm also a member of our Council; we're informal about it, but you should know."

Startled, Jesse began further rearrangement of assumptions. Peter looked far too young for such a role. For him to be a practicing psychiatrist was one thing, out of character though it seemed—but head of research? A policymaker in a clandestine organization, when he'd seemed so boyish and carefree?

No, not carefree. It went deeper than that. Any dissident in this society faced big problems, Jesse reflected; it had been hard to believe the Lodge offered escape even before he'd learned its true nature. There was something more special in these people than he'd seen at first. Whether or not they could control their bodies, they did have control of their feelings—not forced, artificial control, but the ability to turn off worry at times when nothing could be gained by it . . . to live the present moment fully despite real concern for the future. That was why they seemed so alive to him.

Strange that so many such people could turn up in one small colony; strange too that they would accept a misfit. Had they mistaken him for one of their own kind? he wondered. Had he put on as good a facade as that, and if so, could he keep it up indefinitely?

Very grave now, Peter turned and said, "I've had to move fast with you, Jess. I'd seen enough psych data to skip long evaluation on our part—"

Oh, God, Jesse thought. The truth serum interview . . .

"It didn't go into your file," Peter told him. "I conducted it alone; the voice you heard was synthesized. We respect our people's privacy." In his relief, Jesse didn't notice at first that this remark was specifically focused on a concern he had not mentioned aloud.

"It's a bit of a gamble," Peter went on, "to go ahead with this procedure without giving you more time to judge us. It will be impossible for you to get through it without wanting to very badly. You need to know that what we have is worth wanting."

An odd way to put it. He'd have expected them to focus on what was worth *doing*. For him, it was enough to want Carla, who would be unlikely to enter a relationship with an outsider. Yet apart from that . . . had it not been mere foolishness, the longing this place had aroused in him? Did Peter anticipate some such reaction? On the verge of affirming it, Jesse stopped, suddenly terrified by the thought of admitting wishes he had not fully acknowledged in himself. There was surely no chance that he, a Fleet officer, would fail in a trial of the nature described, yet still . . .

The door before them had a keypad, seeming out of place in the rustic-looking hall. Peter punched in a code, adding, "I've got to be rough as hell on you, Jess. Be aware that you have a great deal to gain."

Or to lose, Jesse thought. There could be no going back now, not even if Fleet would accept him. He could never again teeter between empty routine and the release of off-duty drinking—he'd seen too much to be satisfied by either.

Feeling himself flush, he resolved that he'd be damned if he'd let any test they presented faze him. Quite literally damned. There would be no hope left in his life.

He stepped forward. The room they entered was small, bare, and featureless except for two well-padded contour chairs, fixed to the floor. They were equipped with ominous-looking headpieces similar to the one that had been attached to him in the Hospital, Jesse noted, cursing himself for a nervousness he had thought he'd outgrown years ago. The green-tinted walls were glaringly blank except for a high interior window above a door in the one to their left. There was a light behind it.

"Sit down, Jess," Peter directed, indicating the closest chair. It was an order—accustomed to command, Jesse instantly sensed the change in tone. This man was in command here. It was as if he had stepped onto the bridge of a ship.

Jesse sat without comment. The chair was low and quite soft, with wide armrests. "Take your shirt off before you lean back," Peter said. "We'll be using sensors, and we need the sleeve out of the way too."

Obeying, Jesse glanced around the room, puzzled by its lack of lab-type equipment. Peter followed his gaze. "There's a control booth behind you," he said. "You'll find the neurofeedback facilities impressive. First, though, we've got to deal with the less pleasant part."

He sat on the edge of the second chair, holding Jesse's eyes with his own. There was none of his usual sparkle in them, the high spirits with which he'd proposed that jumping into deep water might be fun. Abruptly Jesse became aware that tonight would not be fun. Whatever was going on here, it wasn't a charade.

"The mind has far greater capability than Med science recognizes," Peter said. "Our Group's committed to exploring its limits. We do things you'd call impossible if I were to describe them to you, good things—though most members of this culture would find them . . . upsetting." His voice was sober, but at the same time reassuring. "The payoff's bigger than you've been told, for you personally as well as in terms of our goal. But the training is difficult. Not everyone is able to benefit. I believe you will be, but before you get in too deep I have to find out for sure."

"Okay," Jesse agreed, intrigued. This was no contrived ordeal. Whatever was done to him would be purposeful, and his experience with Peter told him that it would be managed with consummate skill.

"The protocol's more complex than it seems on the surface," Peter said. "It reveals a lot, both about the mind in general and about the subject's personal aptitudes. But it does involve pain, and I can't yet tell you all the reasons why it has to. For one, that's the only safe stressor we can use to get data about certain reactions. The stresses our proven people meet are hazardous. Pain isn't. With pain, we can reach limits fast, and more importantly, we can put a fast end to the stimulus. There's no risk of harmful after-effects."

An outright tolerance test, then, Jesse thought, finding the idea not wholly unwelcome. In this he could compete with the young colonials, probably surpass them; it would be worth a few bad moments to prove that to them and to himself. Himself? God, he thought, had it been as long as that since he'd met any real challenge? Had Fleet stifled even his inner confidence?

"It will be worse than you think," Peter said, as if reading his mind. He rose and moved behind the chairs, returning with a small cart full of electronic gear. "I can tell you're discounting warnings, and since I'm a believer in informed consent, I need you to take them seriously."

"Hell, Peter, you can't make me afraid of you," Jesse said. "Not as I would be of someone who meant me harm."

"No," Peter agreed frankly, "but I can make you afraid of your own reactions, which is what most fears boil down to in any case."

Not wanting to follow the thought, Jesse declared,

"Whatever you do will be anticlimactic after the buildup you're giving it."

"There's not much danger of that," Peter said. "There are twists you can't anticipate. Lean back, now, and take deep breaths while I set things up."

It was a more complicated arrangement than Jesse had been expecting. He knew various lab methods for testing pain tolerance that did not involve all this, certainly not the bulky, tight-fitting headpiece, much less the heart monitor he glimpsed beside him. He followed Peter's instructions silently, determined not to betray what he was beginning to feel.

"No questions?" A smile broke through Peter's composure, incongruous now, yet without any trace of cruelty or coldness. It was as if some tremendous, glorious secret lay just under the surface . . . and it had always been that way, Jesse realized. With all of them, even before he'd begun to trust them consciously. He wanted to share that secret. Whatever stress they might subject him to would be trivial beside the prospect of doing so.

"Tell me what I need to know," he said.

"The control booth is back of you, behind the window," Peter said. "There are two staff people there. I'll stay with you and communicate with them by arm signals; I'll have a handheld data readout."

The most unnerving thing about it all, Jesse thought, was that it wasn't arranged merely to unnerve him. Peter's own feelings seemed genuinely mixed. That was odd; procedures of this kind were fairly routine in psych labs.

"These are sensors," Peter continued calmly, proceeding to attach electrodes to his chest and fingers. "The wireless brain scan data from the headpiece goes to a machine like the one in the Hospital, from which I got a baseline— but the programming of ours is much more sophisticated."

"What's the heart monitor for?" Jesse eyed the machine with growing apprehension.

"Just a standard safety precaution. Needless to say, if a

monitor with a tracking chip had been implanted in you, we couldn't be doing this at all."

"Was I ever in real danger of that?"

"No. I was on top of the scheduling; I wouldn't have allowed it to happen. Tracking would be a serious hindrance to our way of life." Peter seemed suddenly troubled, as if struck by a thought he would rather not have recalled.

The most obvious question had not yet been answered. Jesse knew that Peter knew he had too much pride to ask it. He sat impassively, allowing straps to be buckled around his body.

"All right, now, Jess," Peter said at last, fastening an odd-looking metal device to the chair's left armrest. "Put your arm into the cradle, way in. Let me adjust it. It's got to make contact at the right points." The underside of the forearm, Jesse perceived, feeling the cold steel. The elbow. Thick pads were placed over his arm; he realized this was so the metal bands holding it immobile could not cut flesh, however much strain was placed upon them.

"You've had some experience," continued Peter, "so I don't have to explain to you that the size of the area stimulated makes no difference in the severity of pain. Many subjects assume that using one arm will hurt only half as much as using both would. You know better. This is very fine-tuned; it affects specific nerves. It's a constant stimulus, not intermittent. I have full control over the intensity."

Jesse nodded. There was a clear-cut limit to the intensity of pain; that had been defined long ago. It could not get worse than that, and volunteers had experienced it. Briefly, to be sure ... anything not brief would have been considered torture rather than psych testing. Despite himself, he felt fear rise in him. This elaborate setup had not been designed for brief experiments.

"It's harmless," Peter said matter-of-factly. "You'll think your arm is burned through or perhaps broken, but that's illusion. There will be no tissue damage."

He stepped back, glanced toward the control booth.

Jesse's resolve not to question broke down. He burst out, "What's the criterion for ending this?"

"Certain characteristics of the sensor data," Peter replied. "I can't tell you what they mean. If I did, you'd no longer be a naive subject."

"It's an objective test, then—not just a way of measuring motivation?"

"Yes. You can stop it at any time, of course. But if you choose to quit, that's a final choice, as far as the Group's concerned."

Jesse swallowed. In a standard tolerance test, he'd be asked to say when he'd had enough. It should not really matter, since Peter was surely competent to judge—but the psychological difference was immense.

"We're evaluating response to extreme stress," Peter said. "It would not be truly extreme if there weren't a high price for quitting, nor would we get valid results from a second trial. Once we start the process, we have to see it through step by step, letting each phase build on the one before."

"Damn it, Peter, it would help if I knew what the steps are."

"I know that. I've been through this as a subject, remember. Both of the people in the control booth have been subjects. So has Carla. You have to take it as it comes." Peter bent over him, pierced him with his eyes. "Jess," he said fervently. "This is *necessary*, necessary for reasons beyond anything you can guess. It's not a mere trial of courage. It does demand courage, but it involves much, much more. Believe that."

He stood and raised his hand toward the lighted window. The room lights dimmed.

Pain blazed through Jesse's arm. He gasped at the shock of it, but recovered quickly. Grimly, he told himself that he'd been making too much of the entire business. It would be a sorry state of affairs if an experienced Fleet officer let himself be thrown off balance by a little pain.

The arm began to burn. Jesse closed his eyes and held on, stoically. There was no real threat, after all. If a whole group of untrained people on a colony world had been through this, there was no possible question about his own ability to withstand it.

What aim could there be, if not just to verify that? As the intensity mounted, he found himself struggling for breath. He knew that if he were able to feel anything besides pain, he would feel the accelerated beat of his heart. If this were a vid that beat would be audible, he thought, trying to keep seeing it as melodrama. It was a game, a challenge—he had wanted challenge, hadn't he? Well, maybe not quite this much. . . .

Definitely not this much. Swift sickness struck him; his stomach heaved as his body rebelled against the sustained neural assault. He was engulfed by a wave of agony, suddenly aware that he had never felt anything like this, never imagined anything like it. You heard about pain, you experienced tastes of it, but there were things you did not know beforehand.

Jesse fought for clarity, compelled to open his eyes by the abrupt conviction that his arm had indeed been burned away. Sweat poured into them, but he could see enough to make out that it was still there. Something was there, under the padding, anyway. He found himself grateful for the straps; he knew he would not be able to sit still, much less hold the arm still, without them. His body strained against them of its own accord. He clenched his teeth, for the first time afraid that he might scream.

He stared at the wall ahead of him. The light from the control booth window threw a shadow against it: Peter's rising arm. God, Jesse thought, he's upping it again . . . he can't! No one can take more than this. He lied to me, they couldn't all have come through something like this. . . .

The pain surged, molten steel penetrating bone. Time passed, but he could not measure it; it could not really be a matter of hours. Relativity, he thought crazily. Like a rela-

tivistic ship, the time distortion . . . but no, that's backwards
. . . it's slowing for me, not speeding. . . . He could not reason
it out. His mind was getting muddled, and that realization
was more terrifying than any of the rest of it. He wasn't
blacking out. He would lose sanity before he lost consciousness. He would crack up.

Peter's blue shirt blurred above him, seeming dim and
far away. The pain was a huge, tangible thing. All other
perceptions shrank. Against his will, Jesse forced out words.
"Peter . . . I—I'm coming apart . . . how much longer?" There
had to be an end point. It could not go on all night. . . .

"Do you want to stop here?"

"Not—for good, but—"

"It has to be yes or no, Jesse."

"No." He was lying, and he was sure Peter knew it. What
point was there in forcing him to surrender verbally? He'd
had enough; the wish that had brought him this far no longer
seemed so urgent . . . yet to withdraw would mean losing
Carla. After one more breath, surely, Peter would relent. . . .

But what if he didn't? *Twists you can't anticipate,* Peter
had said, and those were yet to come. Was suffering in itself the object of the study? Could these people be perverts
. . . or alien beings in disguise, maybe, they were *different,*
certainly. . . . He knew this thought was ludicrous, that he
would have laughed aloud at it even ten minutes ago. Trust,
he remembered suddenly. Peter had warned that they would
test his trust in them, and he'd been sure it would remain
unshaken.

What did they really want of him? A surrender, perhaps, not of his commitment but merely of his pride?

"I've . . . had it," he whispered. "I won't tell you to stop,
but—but if you're looking for my limit . . . you've found it."

"Is that a plea for mercy, Jess?"

"Yes, if I have to admit it."

Peter shook his head. "You haven't reached your limit.
There are objective criteria apart from what you tell me. Unless you choose to stop short of it, we have to go all the way."

"What if I ... pass out?" Jesse asked, hoping for it to happen.

"I'll revive you and go on. I get data only while you're conscious."

But I'll crack up, Jesse thought in desperation. I'm being driven past sanity! What will they gain by destroying my mind?

They were admittedly experimenting with the mind's limits. It was obvious what they stood to gain.

Jesse felt himself sinking, falling through infinite depths of black water, unable to breathe, unable to fight free. He must already be insane to want any part in this ... to trust Peter, who was all cold scientist now, without emotion or compassion. It was no longer a matter of pride; he'd already abandoned that, abandoned even the determination not to scream. Dimly, he became aware that he was already screaming; he had not known it until the sound struck him as if from some outside source.

Carla ... she couldn't have been subjected to this! The claim that she had was surely a lie. Oh, God, perhaps it had been *all* lies; perhaps Peter *would not stop* even if told to! Black terror seized Jesse as in the grip of the restraints, he became conscious of total helplessness. Might he really have misjudged this man? Carla's image loomed before him, her green eyes brilliant. *He's a trained lifeguard,* she was saying, *there's no way you can drown.* . . . She too had been deceived . . . it would go on forever unless he gave in. . . .

Peter straightened, hand poised to raise. "Sorry, Jess," he said softly. Pain became a crescendo, blinding him, cutting off all thought, all vestige of will. Jesse made no conscious decision, but suddenly all pain ceased, and he knew, despairingly, that he had cried out for it to stop.

14

HE COULD NOT stand without help; Peter half-carried him into a small room of the infirmary and got him onto a cot. Dazed, Jesse stared unbelievingly at his left arm, in which he felt no trace of lingering pain. It looked perfectly normal.

"You're okay," Peter told him, resting a gentle hand on his forehead. "What you need now is some sleep."

To his own surprise, he did sleep, slipping gratefully into the oblivion it offered. But a few hours later, on waking, he found he needed a great deal more than that. His body was undamaged, but his mind's scars would take healing. He was not sure that they would ever heal. Why the Lodge still seemed a refuge, he didn't know, but whether it was truly one or not, he would be required to leave it. He wished there were a way to get back to the city without confronting Peter.

That, of course, was impossible. Peter appeared in the doorway before he'd even got his shirt fastened. He raised the lighting level, removing all shadows in which to hide. "We have to talk," he said, seating himself on the narrow cot beside Jesse.

"We've already talked too much." And I've heard too much I'll have to forget, Jesse added silently.

"If you hate me, say so and I'll go," Peter said. "But if you still trust me at all, Jesse, consider how I feel. Did you think last night was easy for me?"

"I wish to God I could hate you." If I could, he thought, maybe I wouldn't hate myself so much. "I believe you were honest with me," he admitted, wondering why he had become surer than ever of this. "I believe you and all the rest got through something that I just wasn't up to. I sensed the difference in you right from the beginning, only I couldn't put my finger on it. Now I see. You're—supermen, aren't you? Psych research, power of human minds . . . you are literally sifting out the supermen, the human race to come."

"Not in the way you mean. The aptitude we look for isn't new, and genetics plays little part in it—none at all in this particular test."

"Then I can't even blame my genes, can I? There's nothing I can blame but some weakness of my own that I never knew existed."

"You were far from weak. Most self-reliant people will do *anything* rather than let themselves lose control. You knew it was happening to you, yet you wouldn't say the word beforehand—"

"You knew, too, Peter."

"Yes, even before you did. I had access to sensor data. There are very strong reasons why I had to let it go that far, Jess. I can't explain them to you now, but I'm going to tell you some other things you have a right to know."

Jesse searched Peter's face. It was unreadable, yet at the same time he felt utterly convinced that this man was trustworthy. He said slowly, "The stakes here are higher than I thought."

"Higher, and more complicated. You're right that we're thinking in terms of human evolution. But not genetic evolution—evolution in humans now is mostly extragenetic, cultural, you know. We are not supermen, but we're finding ways to develop what some would call superhuman powers. There's nothing abnormal about them. We're simply taking a different approach to some very old ideas. We hope it may, in the long run, reverse the trend that's culminated in what goes on in this colony—may in fact lead to major advances in understanding what it means to be human. That won't happen in our lifetime, but somebody has to be the vanguard."

He faced Jesse, his eyes shining under the harsh overhead lights, no longer boyish, but no sense cold. "We're a vanguard," he continued, "but we are also stewards of something in humankind that our civilization no longer fosters: the awareness that we are more than our bodies, that the human mind and spirit is a tangible force that is no less real for being nonphysical. This awareness is a flame that must not be allowed to die. The policy of the Meds here is only a symptom. We resist not because there's anything wrong with medical treatment where it's truly needed, but because the right to free choice is denied us—and even that isn't the main thing we're fighting against. The underlying issue is that our culture's attitude toward health is based on a distorted view of life."

"And of death," Jesse said, shuddering at the horror of permanent stasis.

"Yes," Peter said, "the Meds' philosophy says preserve the body, brain-dead or not, because to them, mind is a function of body, life is a function of body, save that and by definition you've saved everything. But that's backwards. The whole infrastructure of medicine for centuries has been built on that, and it is false. It always has been, but until we saw where it led, our eyes weren't open."

"Yet the idea of spiritual power has been kept alive, surely, by religious believers on Earth if no one else, even though they've lost political influence."

"It has, both by major religions and by a variety of esoteric traditions. But they are powerless to counter society's body worship. They've usually tried to argue on the basis of mind surviving body, and you can't prove that—it may not even be true. Even if it is true, it's irrelevant to the evolution of human civilization. What we have to prove is that the mind rules the body here and now."

"By superhuman endurance? Peter, I don't see what good that does."

"Not by endurance—by committing ourselves to the full use of our minds' capabilities."

Whatever that meant, members of the Group evidently were thriving on it. There was some deep secret, just as he'd always felt, Jesse realized. Something *good,* something that justified the seeming brutality of the test he had failed. And he had lost his chance to learn it. . . .

"Jess, opposing Med control of government is futile without striking at its roots," Peter declared. "As I've told you, it's not just a local problem. It has arisen here because the funds and the technology happen to be available; eventually, when that's true elsewhere, Med dominance will spread. Never in human history has majority opinion given medical care less than top priority after immediate survival needs. Freedom has always run second to the dictates of medical advice."

"I suppose it has. Can anything change that?"

Peter eyed Jesse. "People give the Meds power over their lives because they believe they'll suffer if they don't—not physical pain alone, you understand, but all effects of stress that they can't cope with."

"Are you saying the only answer is to suffer, then?" Jesse protested. "I can't go along with that even in principle."

"Of course not," Peter agreed. "Our aim is to end suffering. But not by tinkering with bodies, or pouring drugs into them. There are better ways, ways involving conscious volition. We in the Group *do not suffer.* Not physically, that is, after we've had training. We don't have to endure pain; we simply adjust our perception of it."

"Just by thinking, you mean—mind over matter? Oh, Peter, you don't expect me to believe that. I heard plenty of that metaphysical crap back on Earth when I was a kid; my older sister was into it. As far as I could see it didn't accomplish much."

"For the few with the right preparation, it accomplished more than you realize," Peter told him. "Your sister may have been just a wannabe. With us, however, it's more than mere metaphysics. It involves specific, measurable activity of the brain that can be voluntarily controlled."

Jesse stared at him. "Let me get this straight. You control your own brains in such a way that you don't suffer pain."

"Yes. The ability to do this is every human's birthright. Pain is a biological alarm, you see, built in by nature to protect the bodies of animals that can't judge danger. But adult human beings judge danger consciously. We no longer need an ongoing alarm. In every era a few individuals have learned to turn it off. It's time the rest of our species grew up."

"Forgive me if I'm skeptical, Peter, but even if that were true, how about the less exalted beings in your hospices? Are they expected to suffer bravely until they grow up, as you put it?"

"No. Once we've mastered the skill ourselves, we can relieve others' pain as well as our own. That's one of our caregivers' responsibilities."

With just their minds? He must have misunderstood, Jesse thought. What he seemed to be hearing didn't make sense.

"I could have done it for you without lessening the physical stimulus," Peter continued. "It was very hard not to, since I'm an experienced healer. If Carla had been here she wouldn't have been able to refrain from it. But the aim was to see if you could be taught to do it for yourself."

"You actually believed I might develop such a talent if you pushed me hard enough?"

"Not immediately. I was testing for aptitude, not skill. The skill must be acquired through specific help and instruction. A person who gets all the way through the test can learn it, can gain the power to turn off suffering. And that opens doors to greater powers, beside which the issue of physical pain is insignificant."

This *was* true, Jesse perceived in wonder. These people could banish pain as well as worry. "I suppose it takes years of self-discipline," he reflected. "I'm not cut out to be an ascetic, Peter." It seemed incredible that any of them were. They enjoyed life too much.

Peter smiled. "It's not like that. Our methods are harsh, but they're fast. A matter of weeks, sometimes mere days, as far as immunity to pain goes."

"Some form of hypnosis, then."

"No, though the fact that hypnosis can block pain proves

human minds are capable of it. With us, there's full conscious control. What defeated you last night was your fear
of losing control, not the pain itself—isn't that true?"

Bowing his head, Jesse mumbled, "Yes."

"There's nothing to be ashamed of. It's a normal, healthy
reaction."

"But you hoped I'd turn out to be more than normal."

"I believed you had that potential." Peter didn't meet
his eyes as he said this, Jesse noticed.

"And if I had, in time I'd no longer feel pain?" He had
lost more than the Group's companionship, Jesse thought
despairingly.

"You'd feel the physical sensation without minding it;
you'd be in charge of your mental reactions. What's more,
that skill once learned can be applied to other things. People
can control a great many more of their own internal processes than the Meds will admit."

"I guess I should feel honored that you let me try out
for your team. But it's an empty honor now, isn't it?" Like
all the rest, Jesse thought bitterly. Everything turned out
to be empty if you traveled far enough, whether you stayed
in space or thought you'd found a world. Even the stasis
vaults were no worse a trap than the limits set within you.

"One more thing," Peter went on. "We can heal illness
in others through mind alone, too, Jess. Apply the concept
far enough, and the political power of the Meds fades away,
you see. Personal power moves into the foreground. The
implications are far-reaching. Think about them."

"You don't need to go on justifying yourself to me," Jesse
said. "God, Peter! Do you think I'd count the cost if there
were a chance of becoming like the rest of you? I'd give anything to have made the grade."

Peter lowered his gaze, seeming unsure of how to proceed. "What would you be willing to contribute without the
satisfaction of having made it?"

"Anything I can." Jesse drew breath, abruptly aware
that it had not been a rhetorical question. Obviously, few

could meet the standards of this very exclusive organization, yet he knew too much, now, to be dismissed. Was there work that needn't be done by actual Group members? It went against his grain to accept a support role, yet what choice had he?

"I believe you mean that," Peter declared. "If not, now's the time to say so. You know me well enough now to realize that I ask a lot of my people."

"I made a commitment I couldn't fulfill. If I'm any use to you, I'll stick by the spirit of it."

Again, Peter hesitated. "How much do you know about the experimental method?"

"Just what anybody in Fleet knows. You collect data from at least two groups, sometimes three, and run comparisons."

"Is that how we're working it here?"

"I guess you can't. You only have data from the people in your Group, who I'll continue to call supermen—" He broke off, spotting the fallacy in his assumptions. "No. You have data from me and others like me, who couldn't fulfill your expectations."

"We don't have enough," Peter said. "More detail about reactions of people who lose control under stress would be invaluable, to say the least. But of course, it would be very hard to find such volunteers."

There was silence. After a while Jesse realized that Peter would not say more, that they both knew it did not have to be spelled out further. If he walked out now, Peter wouldn't pursue him. He could go back to the spaceport and get drunk again, and sooner or later, whether he got off this planet or not, he would end up grounded in a bar somewhere—underneath he'd known that, even as he first denied to Carla that it had happened already. It was due to happen someday, however much he now gave to a cause he did not fully understand.

Would it be any worse, then, remembering more hours of hell than the one already burned into him?

Carla . . . Jesse saw, now, why she had held back. She'd known he might not qualify to become one of them. He would not see her again, for she, superhuman, would hardly choose a lover who was less. Yet Carla had wanted his love. *Don't ever hate me,* she'd said, *no matter how things turn out.* Had she feared he would blame her for the pain he could not bear?

If so, there was but one gesture he could make to show her that he did not.

15

TURNING TO PETER, Jesse stood erect. "All right," he said wearily. "Let's get it over before I have time to change my mind. How long do you need to set it up?"

To his relief, Peter had the sense not to belabor the issue. "Maybe half an hour," he replied matter-of-factly. "Can you walk, Jess? If you're still shaky, that's normal. You haven't eaten since yesterday noon."

"I can walk. If I'm shaky that's low blood sugar, but I can't say I have an appetite."

"It's best to skip breakfast," Peter agreed. "After you use the bathroom you can wait in the lab."

On the verge of protest, Jesse bit his lip and complied, finding his legs weaker than he'd expected. Peter surely knew that the lab would be the worst place to wait. As before, evidently, the protocol called for maximizing fear. Okay, if he was going to do this, he'd play along with the whole of it. The preliminaries hardly mattered when he already knew what it would ultimately come to.

He took his shirt off again and sat down in the lab chair, unconsciously drawing away from the innocent-looking steel cradle that was still attached to the armrest. Peter had disappeared. Minutes passed. After a while Jesse noticed that his hands were clenched together, their knuckles white. By force of will he unclasped them, laid his left arm in the cradle, and let it rest there, his empty stomach lurching as the metal touched his skin.

The light in the control booth came on, throwing a bright square on the wall opposite. Jesse could hear faint voices, one of them a woman's. More time passed, a long time. He began to get jumpy; his nerves were scraped raw. Then all of a sudden panic surged through him, rising, scorching his heart and then his face. He *could not* go through with this thing! Yet neither could he run. Though still unstrapped, he was paralyzed, perhaps truly so; there was no strength in his legs. . . .

Agony assailed him in waves. Whenever he managed to quell terror for an instant, it lashed back with renewed force. Each time he was sure it would prove unendurable—he would scream, convulse, lose his grip on himself. . . .

After well over an hour had gone by, Peter returned and without comment, moved the headpiece into place and began to attach the sensors.

The room seemed very cold. Jesse's skin was wet, and he was trembling. All at once his gut cramped painfully, adding a new dimension to fear. He was glad he'd been required to fast. God, would he prove lacking not only in will-power, but in control over bodily functions?

He couldn't help shrinking as Peter buckled the body straps. "Let go, Jess," Peter advised, laying a steadying hand on his arm. "Tensing up won't help, you know. This will be easier for you if you relax."

"You don't want it to be easy. You made me wait a hell of a lot longer than half an hour, Peter, and that wasn't by accident."

"No," Peter admitted. "I gave you time to reconsider, and you're still here. So stop worrying about how you'll re-act. Don't fight your fear—lower your defenses and let it flood you. There's no shame in it. The more frightened you are, the more we'll gain."

Though the words were spoken impassively, there was something else back of them. Not heartlessness. Jesse could not perceive Peter as cold, much less opportunistic, despite his readiness to let an outsider suffer for the Group's cause. Strangely, he began to feel better.

He was, after all, here by choice. He had volunteered not for the sake of the cause, but merely to convince himself—and Carla—that his crackup hadn't been total. Peter knew this! He had, perhaps, intended it. Abruptly, Jesse realized that Peter had brought him back not so much for the research as to restore what could be salvaged from the remnants of a failure's self-esteem.

Resolutely he tried to relax, realizing that the advice had been sincere. Peter smiled. "Visualize yourself on the rock, just before you jumped," he said. "Remember how it felt to commit yourself to that."

"You—*knew!* Knew when you dared me—" As he spoke, Jesse realized that of course Peter had studied his psych profile thoroughly, had known of his fear of water even before they met—and had somehow known that he would jump, too. There was a certain symbolism, which had just now been deliberately revealed.

"I'll never ask more than you can deliver," Peter said, standing back, "but neither will I let you off with less. Right now, I'll go as far as I must to get the data we need."

Jesse fought off renewed giddiness. "Further than before?"

"Yes." Peter paused, then went on, "There's no danger of killing you, you know. That's what the heart monitor's for; it's linked to a computer programmed to cut at any sign of trouble. In certain situations we'd lay our lives on the line. Lab research isn't one of them."

"I wasn't worried on that score." He hadn't been; instinctively he'd trusted them so far that it had not even occurred to him. But short of killing him, how much further was there to go? He'd already been taken past his breaking point. To continue the stimulus beyond that stage would either kill him or drive him insane; the former would almost be preferable....

"Your sanity's not at risk," Peter said, with genuine warmth. "If you didn't know that underneath, you wouldn't have volunteered. You're going to be okay when this is over."

The reassurance, oddly enough, was convincing. No, Jesse knew, he would not be driven insane! He was still entirely sane despite having been sure, last night, that sanity was slipping from him. Things could not get any worse. What lay beyond would be pain, nothing more. He recalled Peter's words: *What defeated you was fear of losing control, not pain itself.* He couldn't stay in control; he now knew that. In any case, the data useful to them could be obtained only after he had lost it. That loss wasn't going to destroy him.

"Don't try to prove anything, to me or to yourself," Peter went on. "Just stay conscious as long as you can. Okay, Jess?"

Nodding, Jesse once again willed his muscles to relax, discovering that they would now obey him. *Let it happen,* he told himself. A peculiar sort of calm spread through his body. He hadn't imagined how it would feel to pass beyond terror.

The pain began more gradually than before. For what seemed many minutes it wasn't hard to cope with; though his heart raced and his breathing grew labored, Jesse felt, ironically, in full command of himself. Why was Peter waiting? What point was there in drawing it out so long, when no valuable data would emerge at this stage?

Peter stood where his face was visible from the chair. It was tired, drawn; his vitality and forcefulness had drained away. He did not look like a superman. The impassiveness of his bearing was a pose, Jesse saw. However driven he might be by ideals, Peter was a compassionate man who suffered, in the emotional sense, as much as the subjects with whom he dealt. All at once Jesse grasped what this was costing him, what last night had surely cost.

"Peter," he breathed. "I'm . . . okay. I don't mind. Do . . . what you have to do, and don't worry about me."

Turning, Peter asked levelly, "Are you telling me to raise the intensity?"

"Yes. You've held off longer . . . than you needed to."

Peter moved behind him, adjusting the headpiece slightly. "First, I want you to see some of the data."

"Never mind. I'll take your word that it's worth getting."

"I have to show you. Evaluating your ability to think under stress is part of the protocol." He raised his voice, commanding, "Give us the visual, now."

Blindingly, astonishingly, the entire wall across from them lit up. There was a huge pattern, strange shapes and bright colors. Jesse's head spun. The effort of examining data struck him as one demand too many. Though he wasn't close to cracking, the pain swamped him with dizziness and nausea. It was hard to focus his eyes on the display.

"It's not just an EEG or brain scan image," Peter was saying. "There's more sophisticated input, and computer conversions have been done on it. But it shows brain functioning."

"It's . . . static. Unchanging."

"This one's from last night. We'll go to real-time neurofeedback once you learn to interpret the format. See anything significant?"

"Well . . . it's plain where I cracked up." It was; the shapes of the pattern broke into fragments near the top of the wall. "The y-axis is time?"

"Yes, in this case. It's not a graph, though; two dimensions are used in the pattern itself. We need another dimension for intensity of stimulus; that's done with color. Spectrum sequence, in reverse because to most people red means maximum."

Jesse grimaced. He had never gotten near the red zone; the image showed green shapes blending into yellow and ultimately, in the crisis area, into light orange. "It's . . . straightforward," he said. "Not much thought's needed."

"What I want you to do is predict the real-time data before you see it. What type of pattern?"

"Like the lower section ... the regular pattern, before those breaks start."

"And the color, Jess?"

"Green."

"That's where you're wrong. You've been steady on red for the past five minutes."

"That's not possible! What did you do, drug me?" It could have been done while he slept, he supposed.

"Of course not. What would we gain by that?"

"I'm not sure," Jesse declared, "what you're gaining by any of this."

"Right now I'm getting routine confirmation of well-known fact: the human mind doesn't perceive pain in terms of raw intensity. There are components of resistance and fear." Again he called out to the control booth. "Let's have real-time."

The real-time display was centered, with no time dimension. It was indeed clear red. The pattern was alive, moving, and drew him in somehow, as if it were a tunnel through which he was passing. As Jesse watched, the color of the shapes began to deepen. He found himself gasping again. His arm was on fire and he didn't need the feedback to be aware of the intensity surge. And yet, Peter was right. It wasn't just that he could take more when he wasn't fighting it—his perception was drastically altered.

"Keep your eyes on the pattern," Peter said.

"How soon will it ... break up?"

"Probably it won't. That's up to you."

"It wasn't up to me last night."

"You were given no feedback last night. What's more, you were in a different frame of mind. You panicked."

"That's all the breaks mean—panic? God, Peter ... it's really rubbing it in to show me this stuff. "

"Hardly that," Peter said. "Initial feedback's meant to be encouraging."

"I don't follow," Jesse protested, anger giving him strength to speak out forcefully. "It was bad enough believing that everyone has a limit and mine simply wasn't high enough to meet the standard. But now, to see I didn't come close to my limit and blew my chance through loss of nerve—" He broke off as the red deepened further. The shapes shifted, wavered.

"Keep your eyes on it!" Peter repeated. "You have control over your mind's response. There is no personal limit. It's a matter of acquired skill."

"The skill I'm . . . unqualified to learn." The skill that let them feel this *without suffering,* Jesse thought, gripped by an anguish not merely physical. Whatever Peter might say, anyone who could do that was superhuman! There was an unbridgeable gulf between him and such people, between him and Carla. . . .

"Did I tell you that you're unqualified?" Peter asked.

"Why—why not in so many words . . . but what am I here for if . . . if not to provide data from a washout?"

"You're here to learn, like the rest of us. Your potential is exceptionally high, as a matter of fact."

Stunned, Jesse jerked forward against the straps. "All right, Peter—stop!" he burst out in rage. "I mean it. Stop right now."

Without hesitation Peter raised his hand toward the control booth, fingers clenched into a fist. The pain stopped instantly, so fast that its absence felt like zero-g. Disoriented momentarily, Jesse found himself still staring at the feedback pattern, frozen on the wall before him. It was dark red, with no trace of irregularity.

He turned to Peter. "I've taken a lot," he said. "I was willing to take as much as you asked for. But not this—not to be told I could have learned if I'd been stronger, or even that I can learn now as a guinea pig instead of as part of the Group."

Incredibly, Peter smiled, the sparkling smile that Jesse had always found so disarming. "You weren't listening," he said, bending to unfasten the strap buckles. "Which isn't surprising, since you're too new at this to be fully alert under that much stimulus; I'd have cut anyway in another minute or two. I said you can learn *like the rest of us.* As one of us. You're progressing very, very fast."

"No," Jesse declared. "Not as a reward for volunteering, when I can't pass the normal aptitude test."

"Pass it? God, Jess, you're so far above the norm that the people in the control booth scarcely believe what they're seeing. I hold some trainees' hands for days while they develop to the level you've reached in one morning."

As he removed the sensors Peter went on, "What you've just been through is a necessary step in the training. It's hell, but it's worth it—the skill once acquired is permanent. We don't do this to anyone we don't plan to take that far. You've been in the Group since you pledged, conditional only on your own willingness to stick with it."

"Despite having cracked up last night?" Jesse mumbled, not bothering to hide bitterness.

"Everybody cracks the first time. The session can't end until it happens. The fear of it has to be gotten out of the way."

Jesse stared at him, outraged and bewildered. "Everybody . . . Peter, you knew ahead of time? You deliberately broke me?"

"I had to. You made it damned hard for me to do, too. For a while there, I was afraid I'd have to use intensities high enough to spoil today's demonstration."

"But then you were lying when you told me it meant I'd be out. God damn you, Peter—you were just trying to motivate me." The deception was the worst of it, Jesse realized. How could he have so misjudged this man's sincerity?

"You needed stronger motivation than pride," Peter agreed. "But I didn't lie to you. I told you that if you chose to quit you'd be out. There was no choice involved in what you screamed at me after you lost control." Peter waved a hand toward the still-illuminated wall. "We go by objective measurements. The mind-patterns in the data. You refused to quit before the pattern changed."

"Then for God's sake, why did you let me believe I hadn't made the grade?"

"For one thing, to put you into a mood that would make this demonstration work. If you hadn't been resigned to cracking up again, you couldn't have stopped fighting."

That was true, perhaps. But there had been more to the deception. "What was the point of all the rigamarole about the good of science? Even that bit about needing naive subjects was a lie—"

"No," Peter said. "The effectiveness of the protocol depends on not telling you what we're testing for, or what stressors we're going to employ."

Stressors—beyond the overt stimulus? Oh, God. *Psychological* stresses. Tolerance of fear, failure, despair; the physical suffering had been a mere instrument. "You weren't judging me last night," Jesse realized. "The test was *today*."

"The only thing that counted last night was your refusal to quit," Peter agreed. "Beyond that, the first session shows nothing about aptitude or commitment. What matters is how you get along the second time."

"Expecting to fail, you mean." Jesse frowned. He'd been warned about manipulation, and he had agreed; but that did not make him like it.

"It's not an arbitrary test," Peter explained. "It is built in, a principle behind this kind of learning. Willpower is counterproductive. In order to gain true volitional control, you must be wholly, unreservedly willing to lose control— to let what comes, come, with full consent to the consequences. That's true with lots of skills, and the others are harder to acquire than this one. We have to be sure you won't get in over your head."

"I don't understand—"

"Not yet. But you've had the first lesson under circumstances designed to make it indelible. You now know what doesn't work, and what does."

"What about that data you claimed to need from people who can't learn?"

"It would be invaluable, as I told you," Peter said. "But we're never going to get any, since by definition it would have to come from unconsenting victims. Anyone without aptitude to learn volitional control would be incapable of volunteering to come back in here. That's why I knew from the start just now that you'd be all right."

Jesse didn't reply. He was a long way from not minding pain, or even comprehending such a state. Yet he'd begun to believe that he might attain it.

16

AFTER SHOWERING, THEY went upstairs. Jesse had lost track of time below ground. When they left the elevator, the noon-day sun was pouring in through the windows of the deserted Lodge kitchen. Voices came from the common room, happy voices, laughter. New people had arrived to enjoy their time off from work.

"We have more skills than you've heard about," Peter told him, pausing before heading in to join them, "and some will come as a shock to you. Much of what you meet will be confusing at first. Bear with us."

Jesse nodded. With his hand on the door, Peter stopped. "You have no ties in the city," he said reflectively. "So you can live here full time if you want, unlike the rest of us, who can only come during offshifts."

"I'd like to, but I'll pay my way," Jesse said. So far, clean clothes had been regularly provided for him as well as his meals. "Can I log onto the local Net from here? I'll transfer my account to a colonial bank."

Peter shook his head. "That's the last thing we want you to do! You've got legal access to funds that can be spent offworld—don't let Undine's government find out about them. Save your money for when we need it."

"I thought you were allowed to import goods."

"Those we're supposed to have, yes. But the Hospital has a monopoly on medical supplies; stuff for our hospices and infirmaries has to be smuggled in. That gets expensive. And later—" Peter broke off, not finishing the thought. "To get back to the point," he said, "most people we bring into the Group have jobs. Training must be gradual, spread over many weeks, not only because of their limited time at the Lodge but because it's—disorientating, sometimes. Too much so to get up and go to work the next day as if nothing had changed. With you I'd like to try something different. Faster, more intensive."

Again Jesse nodded. The sooner he could learn what was really going on here, the better.

"There'll be pressure," Peter went on, "but I think you're up to it. Okay, Jess?"

"Okay." Then, seeing no reason to wait, he asked directly, "Will I be seeing Carla?"

"Yes." Peter hesitated. "Jess, you may feel it's none of my business, but am I right in believing you want a serious relationship with Carla?"

"I guess it was obvious."

"To me it was, so I'm obliged to speak of it. Carla is a very dear friend, and I don't want to see her hurt more than is necessary."

"God, Peter, I'd never hurt her—except, I suppose, if I eventually leave this world."

"Not just that," Peter said. "There are . . . factors you're not aware of. You may sometimes hurt her without meaning to, and she may hurt you. If you're not sure you want a relationship on those terms, the time to back off is now."

Jesse frowned. "It's up to her, isn't it?"

"Of course. But she is fully informed, and you're not. If she chooses to be involved emotionally, she'll do it knowing there'll be problems, and she'll expect you to stick by her in spite of them."

"I don't suppose you can be more specific."

"Not right now," Peter said. "When you're ready to understand, I will have to be. That's part of what goes with being the professional therapist here."

"You're speaking professionally, then, not just as a friend."

Peter nodded. "It's a matter of your adjustment to our ways. Newcomers find some of them . . . disturbing. Don't worry now, but never hesitate to come to me. Am I making myself clear?"

After a short pause Jesse said, "Yes." It had been plain from the beginning that the sexual customs of the Group were somewhat out of the ordinary. Was that among the things he'd been warned would confuse him—*sex*? To the extent of needing to consult a therapist?

"One more thing," Peter added in a low voice as they went on into the common room. "Don't eat anything yet. I know you're hungry, but stick to water for now."

Nearly a dozen people were gathered near a spread buffet table. All eyes were on him, Jesse saw to his dismay. Peter threw his arm around Jesse's shoulders, needing no words to convey what they'd obviously been waiting to know. Nor did the others need words—the strange sense of intimacy that had so impressed him during the past days was magnified tenfold. The air seemed charged with it.

A slender, white-haired woman, the first older person he'd seen, clasped his hand. "Welcome, Jesse," she said, and then hugged him. Somehow it seemed natural and right, as if she were family.

"This is Kira Tarinov," said Peter. "She's a Council member, and she's in charge when I'm not here."

Others came forward, were introduced, embraced him in turn. Gradually Jesse became aware that these strangers *were* family, more in tune with him now than his own had ever been. He'd felt close to crewmates on shipboard sometimes, but never like this. Never in a way that made him feel the connection would be lasting.

A bearded man approached him, accompanied by a blonde named Michelle. "Jesse! I—I'm so happy to see you looking great," she said, gripping his hand tightly. Her eyes glistened.

"Greg and Michelle were in the control booth," Peter said. "Michelle's only part way through instructor's training. I wouldn't have brought her in if there'd been anybody else available last night who knew the software. I spent half the time you were asleep consoling her."

Surprised, Jesse said, "I had the impression you people are used to this sort of thing. If you do it to everyone—"

"Yes, but we don't get seasoned Fleet officers, Jess. We rarely see anyone we have to start at high intensities. The average citizen of this world panics on green. It's psychologically equivalent; the brain response, which we call a mind-pattern, is the same—but the effects aren't. The pain is not really bad at that point. Typically we reduce people to tears, not screams. I meant it when I said you gave me a hell of a hard time."

"Believe him," Greg said. "He's a gifted telepath; he felt what you felt, *all* of it. The sensor data doesn't show everything."

Speechless, Jesse could only stand and gape.

"Peter said it would turn out all right, but I couldn't stop doubting," Michelle told him. "With me, it took five feedback sessions to get to red."

"But why, if the psychology works with less pain than that—"

"It has to be maximized for the breakthrough," Peter said, "the moment in which you grasp the skill of not suffering. Such powers don't emerge without a major shock to the mind."

"There's a mind-pattern you haven't seen yet," Greg added. "You have to be pushed into it. After the first time, it's easier. Once you gain full volitional control, that equips you to handle any level of pain, in yourself and ultimately in others."

"Equips *me*? Are you saying that I, personally, will be able to ease suffering in other people?"

"Oh, yes. There are degrees of talent; we can't yet tell how much you have. At the least, you'll be fit to assist in emergencies."

"But—but how can *my* mind-patterns affect anyone else?" Jesse protested, puzzled. "It would have to be their own brains controlling their perceptions—" This logical flaw had existed in what Peter had told him earlier, though he'd been in no condition to spot it then. Hearing that Carla could have eased his pain, he had been quick to believe—but that was crazy. There was no way it could happen, no mechanism for it.

Yet there had been a moment, in the Hospital, just after he'd drunk the brandy. She had touched his hand. The effect of the drug had hit him, he'd been in agony—and then for an instant before he passed out, the pain had receded.

Was Carla, too, a telepath? Was ESP what enabled them to ease pain in people who lacked their skills? No, that didn't fit. He himself had no such weird gift, would certainly not want it. . . .

They moved to the floor cushions where people were settling, plates and glasses in hand; one was given to him before he could refuse. Though shaky with hunger, Jesse set it down beside him. Peter's instructions, he'd found, were never without purpose.

No one had answered his question. Wanting to change the subject, he said, "There's a lot more I've been wondering. Such as how you get away with hiding people the authorities want kept in the Hospital—even dead people. I mean, doesn't anybody miss them? And what about the daily telemetry from their bathrooms?"

"The files are all electronic," Greg answered. "And according to the Net, dead or dying people we've helped are in the stasis vaults. Nobody's going to go in and visually check."

"But how can the Net— Oh. Hacking, you mean."

"Of course. Carla's one of our experts."

"She'll enter fake telemetry data for you, since you'll be here longer than the legal maximum without transmission," Peter told him. "She doctors it on a regular basis for members who have conditions they don't want treated."

"That's why she works in the Hospital as a data technician," Michelle explained. "Actually she's a talented programmer—she wrote some of our neurofeedback software."

Well, Jesse thought, that explained the mystery of why an intelligent woman like Carla hadn't sought a better job. But the danger . . . "What would happen if she got caught?" he asked.

"She'd be medicated for mental illness—be hospitalized awhile, then on probation for life—and her inherited income would be confiscated."

"Provided her examination was handled by Peter," Greg added. "Any other doctor might give her truth serum, and then our whole operation would be exposed. That's why none of us with illegal city activities can let it be known that we're Peter's friends. He wouldn't be allowed to treat a criminal he knew personally; it would be conflict of interest."

"But you're Carla's supervisor at work," Jesse protested to Peter.

"Yes, so I treat her as a mere employee when outsiders are around to overhear. Not that I'm expecting trouble on account of her hacking. There's a low level of security here; this world doesn't have hackers who do it for thrills, as Earth still does. And the reason *we* do it wouldn't occur to the authorities."

"I thought there were kids into hacking on every world. Just because some kids are rebels."

"You're forgetting the mandatory health checks in this colony," Kira said. "They begin at birth, and medication takes care of the potential troublemakers."

"Psychoactive drugs. By force." Jesse cringed.

"Force really isn't needed. Parents welcome the advice of the medical authorities. They want their children to have the best possible care. Forced drugging of kids isn't new, you know—it's been done on Earth ever since such drugs were developed. It's just more systematic here."

"How did you people escape it, then?"

"Most of us weren't born rebels," Michelle told him. "We came into the Group for other reasons."

"Reasons?" Jesse looked around at them, puzzled.

"Jesse isn't yet aware of the reasons," said Kira. "His route to us has been the reverse of the usual one. I'm told he had cause to hate the Hospital to start with. He's rebelling, not seeking, so far."

Seeking what? he wondered. These people all seemed to *have* something, something he still couldn't define. It was more than the ability to control their perception of pain. And it was not something mere training was likely to give him.

17

"PETER," KIRA SAID as Peter sat down, "I visited Ian this week, as you asked me to. He thinks he can make the flight once more. But personally, I am not so sure. It will soon be time for us to move him to a hospice."

Peter's eyes darkened. "Not yet! Not just when—" He broke off, bowing his head.

"Death comes when it comes, Peter."

"Surely, if that's imminent, he would rather be here. He loves the Lodge. He built it." To Jesse, Peter explained, "Ian Maclairn is our founder, the head of our Council. He is a very old man now and hasn't long to live. We will be with him, of course, at the end."

"It's not a matter of where he'd rather die," Kira said sadly. "It now depends on whether he's strong enough for the journey. I think not. We must face the fact what comes home to us here will be his body—and even that may not be easy to arrange."

"Kira! To fail in that would be unthinkable—"

Everyone else stopped talking, stopped eating. It was very quiet. Jesse sensed their dismay as plainly as, before, he'd sensed their elation. The Group's founder, he thought, near death—in danger, perhaps, of being found by an ambulance before they could retrieve his body for burial? Of ending up in the stasis vaults, the symbol of all they abhorred?

To fill the silence Michelle said, "Peter was hoping you could meet Ian. We have a ceremony of commitment for new people, at which he's normally present."

"Is that the formal initiation?"

"Well, we don't use that term," Greg said. "It's been devalued by silly connotations. Every occult or pseudo-occult organization for centuries has had an initiation, along with a lot of mere social groups. Ours is the real thing."

"What do you mean by real?" Jesse asked, curious.

"A rite of true transformation. Actually we have two. What you've just been through was an initiatory rite in the classic anthropological sense of the word: you felt you were being destroyed and awoke to new life. The Ritual's a more formal occasion. We don't use the metaphors traditional rites on Earth did; metaphor wouldn't work here, as on this planet we lack the long-established psychic environment that would unconsciously validate it for us. But the ceremony Ian created for us serves the same purpose. Words, symbolism—all very uplifting. The climax is a bit of a shocker, but plenty of Group members will be on hand to support you."

"Metaphors? Psychic environment? You've lost me," Jesse admitted. "What has that got to do with what planet we're on?"

"Have you ever wondered why Earth's religious and spiritual groups don't thrive on other worlds, except for the few they colonize themselves?" Michelle asked.

"I assume it's because people who choose to emigrate aren't inclined that way, and don't teach their kids to be.

They're too aware of scientific facts to cling to incompatible superstition."

"No," said Greg. "The human impulse toward spirituality is universal and the proportion of people strongly drawn to it is the same everywhere. What the rest call superstition is something else entirely—it is metaphor, a way of expressing abstract, inexplicable ideas in concrete terms. Whether metaphors are believed literally or not doesn't matter. Even in primitive societies—and certainly in modern ones—adherents of traditional religions don't all believe in the literal existence of gods or goddesses, for instance. Yet the language they use, in and out of ritual, has deep meaning for them."

"Well, that's always puzzled me. Long before interstellar travel existed, nearly everybody knew enough about the universe to write off myths based on ancient descriptions of it. Yet my sister hung out with people who talked about Earth, and particular locations on Earth, being sacred in some mystical way. Some of them even believed in astrology, as if the position of stars relative to one planet could influence individual lives when people are being born on dozens of worlds, not to mention starships. I used to argue with her about it, but she couldn't come up with answers that made sense, any more than Christian fundamentalists could."

"It's not a matter for logical argument, Jesse," Michelle said. "Metaphorical statements stand for concepts, not facts, and the underlying concepts they reflect are often true. Specific metaphors are associated with those concepts through unconscious transmission from the minds of thousands, often millions, of people, one generation to the next, over long periods of time."

"How can transmission of concepts be unconscious?"

"Telepathically, of course. Most telepathy is unconscious, after all."

"Oh, come on—" It was one thing to say that Peter and perhaps others were telepaths ... but millions of people, unconsciously....

"Jesse, you haven't enough background to understand this yet," Kira said. "But it's why the old metaphors are not viable except on Earth. Though in principle telepathy is not limited by space or time, human minds can link only at close range. Even unconscious influences don't extend over interplanetary distances. And deliberately-chosen metaphor is not nearly as powerful as that which rises from an unconscious source. So in our own Ritual, we don't use metaphor at all; we communicate concepts directly and emotionally reinforce them through one awesome concrete symbol."

"You're making it sound like the sort of staged production I've learned you don't employ," Jesse said, dubious.

"Oh, but we do," Michelle said. "For pragmatic reasons. This particular event needs a dramatic setting for buildup or else it won't come off. We'll see that you're psyched up to it—you'll be high, and the rest of us will get high, too. It's a peak for us all."

"High?" This, Jesse had not expected. It didn't seem quite their style.

Greg, seeing his face, laughed aloud. "This talk is premature, people. Jesse just finished his first feedback session, remember? He hasn't experienced any high at all yet. He's got no idea what we mean." To Jesse he said, "Not drugs. Among ourselves we don't even use legal drugs. We don't have to."

"Illegality wasn't what bothered me," Jesse said. "I've shipped my share of contraband. I don't know why I reacted."

"You should," Greg said. "The premises underlying drug use come from Med culture. We reject those premises and everything that follows from them."

Beginning with anesthetics, Jesse thought, awestricken. But that meant . . . healing! They could not reject all drugs unless they possessed the power to heal by mind. Peter had claimed that they did possess it. At least a few of them were telepaths. His head swam. What else did they have? He had not interpreted mind power in quite such broad terms, even while calling them supermen.

God, what had he gotten into? "From what Peter said, I assumed I'd be taught to control my perceptions, perhaps my own health," he said. "Now what I'm hearing suggests something—paranormal."

"That's a relative term," Greg said gravely.

Peter, his dark mood overcome, faced Jesse. "I couldn't warn you yesterday," he said. "This secret has to stay within the Group. Our so-called paranormal powers are a threat to the Meds and would be viewed as unhealthy. We'd be labeled mentally unbalanced—even delusional—in the world outside, and we'd be medicated to suppress the very capabilities that represent an advance in human evolution. You're a true experiment for us, because you're not the type usually attracted to such things."

"I always thought people interested in that stuff were kooks," Jesse confessed.

"Many are," Kira said. "But there are sincere seekers mixed in with them. We run a front group. We play harmless games that show us whom to approach."

"This is why we make sure of your trust in us," Peter said, "not only when it's talk, but under pressure. There will be pressure later when without the trust, there would be danger. You might truly—drown." He watched Jesse's face. "Yes, I sense thoughts as well as feelings. I can't do it against your will, but when there's emotion behind them I get the gist. You've known that underneath for quite a while, haven't you?"

He hadn't wanted to know it. He hadn't let himself think of what Peter's uncanny ability to answer unspoken thoughts might imply.

"It works both ways," Peter continued. "I can project my own feelings. You'd have been a fool to take what you did from me on the basis of talk alone."

"You . . . *made* me trust you? With *telepathy*?"

"Not forcibly. They have to be genuine feelings, and you're free to shut me out. One of the things I was checking this past week was whether you'd be receptive. You'll need to be, to learn our skills."

Near the end last night, Jesse realized, he *had* shut Peter out. His trust in him had evaporated, only to return with puzzling intensity this morning.

"That's what panic does," Peter agreed, "which we make sure you learn from day one. There will be times when your future well-being, even your safety, depend on that kind of receptivity."

"We have objective proof of the usefulness of psi powers," Greg declared. "The Meds won't ever accept it. Our premises conflict with theirs, and when has presence of anomalous data ever interfered with Establishment science's premises? But the future belongs to us. In time, our ways will spread."

"That would scare the hell out of some people," Jesse said. "I—I'm not sure it doesn't scare me."

"Of course it does. It will scare you more and more as you get in deeper. That's one of the things we're preparing you for by subjecting you to what may have seemed an unnecessarily harsh ordeal."

"Fear of physical pain is normal and unavoidable," Peter pointed out. "You can acknowledge it in yourself, confront it, because you know that. Learning to deal with it will give you the skills and confidence you'll need to face other fears you can't even put a name to."

Jesse sat silent, not knowing how to respond. Things were moving too fast.

Michelle stood up, saying, "Forget this serious stuff—let's celebrate! I'm going to get some wine. Jesse, you haven't drunk yours, you're not even eating—"

"Peter said I shouldn't."

They all looked at him in astonishment. Kira said, "You must have misunderstood. There's no reason now not to eat. You need to—you're depleted."

"No," said Peter, with some reluctance. "Jesse got it right."

"But Peter, why? As Michelle says, this is an occasion to celebrate. Jesse's earned a chance to relax and enjoy himself."

"It will be a bigger occasion later this evening," Peter said, "and a better celebration than we could have now. Wait and see."

"But why?" Kira repeated.

"Because," Peter announced, "Jesse and I are going back downstairs in a little while, and we're going to aim for breakthrough. He's capable of it, and now is as good a time as any."

Greg stared at him in disbelief. "Breakthrough? Peter, are you insane?"

Jesse found himself holding his breath. *Breakthrough . . . the moment when you grasp the skill of not suffering.* He had not thought this would be tried so soon. And evidently nobody else had thought so, either.

Kira was shaking her head. "Peter, did what I said about Ian have anything to do with this? Because if it did—"

"It did not, Kira. I told Jesse not to eat before we even came in here."

"All the same, are you sure—"

"There are valid reasons for speeding up Jesse's training. Not the least of them is that he's had no taste of our skills, no grounds for believing that they can be awakened in him—or for that matter in anyone—other than my word. He won't feel like celebrating until it has been proven to him. Isn't that right, Jess?"

"Yes," Jesse affirmed, glad that it had been stated openly. He had not felt like celebrating, warm though the Group's welcome had been. And yet . . . "I may not be up to this," he said. "Frankly, I'm wiped out. I'm not sure I can hold myself together."

"That's all to the good," Peter reminded him, "when what you need to do is *let go*. Besides, I've got to work in the city tonight, and I don't want to put it off until my next offshift. We'd have to build up the stress level all over again."

"I'll have no part in this," Michelle declared.

"I won't ask you to. Kira is here now, and she's better qualified as backup."

"She's also in better shape than you are," Greg said to Peter, in whom the toll of a stressful, sleepless night had become evident. "Is it wise for you to go on dual?"

"Yes," Peter said shortly. "To hand this over might prolong it, and Jess deserves a fast breakthrough."

"Surely there's no need to push it," Greg persisted, evidently troubled. "You wouldn't need to hand it over, your next offshift would be soon enough. Nobody's ever moved ahead this fast. What's the point in setting a record?" To Jesse he said, "You can refuse, you know. I advise you to call time out, if Peter won't."

Peter turned away from him, meeting Jesse's eyes. "Jess, there's no risk in this for you," he said. "That's not why Greg is objecting. Of course you're free to wait till next week, or even longer—but I hope you won't do that."

Jesse felt lightheaded, reckless. "What the hell," he heard himself saying. "Let's give it a try."

18

THE FEELING OF unreality that had carried Jesse through the past few hours gave way to terror as they reentered the lab. What in God's name had he been thinking of, assenting to this? Less than a day ago he had sat by the shore, enjoying the peace and quiet of a Lodge he believed to be a restful haven. Now, weakened both by trauma and by fasting, he was letting himself in for what promised to be an even more agonizing experience—culminating in the acquisition of superhuman powers? Perhaps, he thought, he had lost his sanity after all. Perhaps the whole thing had been a hallucination.

"Don't try to hide your fear of this," Peter said. "It's not only normal, but beneficial. Skills of this kind can be learned only under the influence of strong emotion. Later, for some of the other skills, we'll use pleasant emotions, but for obvious reasons we don't mix those with pain. So the more fear you feel, the better—just so you remember what you learned this morning. If you shrink from it, fight it, you'll be back to square one."

Kira had come into the lab with them; it was she who attached the sensors with quiet efficiency. It seemed incongruous. Kira, white-haired, probably retired, who'd welcomed him like a grandmother—well-qualified, it had been said, to take part in sessions of this kind? Looking up at her, Jesse wondered how old she was. Her eyes were wise, but her skin, her body, her stance showed no more aging than those of anyone in the Group. For the first time, he began to wonder if he'd misjudged their ages. With women, after all, you couldn't always tell.

He liked Kira, felt comfortable with her. Was she doing something to him telepathically, as Peter had, to bring that about? He didn't relish the thought. Yet Peter had maintained that projected feelings must be genuine. . . .

"From here on out we do this a bit differently," Peter said. "So far Greg's been handling the controls on my commands, but I'm taking over now with a dual hookup." To Jesse's astonishment, he sat down in the second contour chair and allowed Kira to attach an all-too-familiar metal device, twin to Jesse's, to its left armrest. Deftly, he placed his arm into the cradle and fastened the bands with his right hand, not bothering with padding.

"The stimulators are cross-connected," he explained, as Kira fitted a headpiece onto his head. "I'll control the intensity directly, using a remote. We'll see both sets of feedback. The aim is for you to match yours to mine."

Jesse stared at him. "I'd think there'd be too wide a gap for that, if your mind perceives pain in some new way."

"There would be, if I were not a trained instructor. There's an art to it; I'll stay close enough for you to follow."

"But that means—" Jesse pressed his lips together, recognizing what it did mean. Peter was relaxed, unafraid; he'd assumed this was because there would be literally no suffering for Peter. Yet if the state of not suffering produced a different pattern in the feedback . . . "Can't the computer generate model mind-patterns?" he protested.

"No," Peter told him. "It's been tried, but it doesn't work. A novice can't match with a computerized model or even a recording. There has to be a live mind behind it in real time."

"For—thought transference?" Jesse ventured. Good God, he thought, this was *real!* They used ESP systematically.

"Not on a level you'll be aware of," replied Peter, "but yes, that's involved." He smiled. "It was involved this morning, too. You'll always have support to draw on, Jess. This is the good part of instructing, the part that makes sessions like last night's worth going through."

Kira had left them, closing the control room door behind her; the lights dimmed. Peter reached over with his free hand, touched Jesse's shoulder. "Hey, Jess, loosen up! We're heading for a high this time. It's going to take a while. I may have to bring you close to panic more than once. But when it comes, I'll get it too, using the dual—and I don't anymore when I go straight into a mind-pattern and stay there unconsciously."

Jesse pondered this, suddenly uneasy in a way not stemming from fear. Something in that remark didn't seem quite right, though he shrank from defining what bothered him about it.

"Don't misunderstand," Peter said quickly, answering unspoken feelings. "The high isn't derived from pain. It comes from reaching an altered state of consciousness through deliberate, volitional choice. Other skills of the mind can produce it too."

"An altered state?" This raised new doubts. What Jesse had heard in the past of altered states was not inviting.

Peter said, "You may associate that term with being spaced out on drugs. But there are many altered states, of which those produced by drugs are among the least useful.

That is what the visual patterns mean—they're graphic, symbolic representations of different states of consciousness. It used to be that only a few individuals could enter such states at will, and those few generally spent years meditating before they learned how. Our sensing technology and our software, combined with the telepathic help we provide, make it possible to learn fast."

He called out, "Let's have the visuals, Kira." The wall lit up with side-by-side displays, alive now with a dot of violet at the lower left corner of each. Jesse hadn't even felt that; he found it took concentration to feel it as the pattern began to form.

"You might think," Peter told him, "that it would be easiest to learn the new mind-pattern at low intensities. That's not how it works. You can't learn it at all until your mind's pushed to it; otherwise this skill would have become commonplace centuries ago. If primitive man got pushed to the extent necessary, he was usually near death, or in any case occupied with the threat of death."

The violet patterns brightened toward blue. There was now no question about feeling the stimulus. Jesse drew in his breath and forced his mind to focus on Peter's voice.

"Pain is the most effective push for a novice," Peter was saying, "because there's no ambiguity in your mind about wanting the skill you're aiming for. Your thoughts aren't going to wander, and you're not going to have unconscious conflicts over it. You want, wholeheartedly, to stop suffering. And this overrides the deep-seated fear most people have of abandoning the 'normal' state of consciousness in which they've spent their waking lives."

Yes, Jesse thought dizzily. If you were supposed to admit your fears—which within the Group you obviously were—he would be obliged to confess to that one. Piecing together things said earlier, he began to see what they implied.

"Some cultures on ancient Earth did use stresses like fasting and pain to reach altered states of consciousness,"

Peter went on, "but their goal was different from ours. Most of us aren't pursuing mystical enlightenment. What we learn to do is of practical value in our daily lives."

The pattern of the displays was in the green range now, swirling, drawing him in, and it was getting hard to think of anything beyond pain. He wasn't supposed to resist it, Jesse told himself. He must let it envelop him.

"I'll keep talking," Peter continued. "Don't try to carry on a conversation. Just listen. You must watch the feedback too, of course, but that has to become automatic. You can't control it by giving your full attention to fine details any more than you can steer a car that way. Since you grew up on Earth, I assume you learned to drive. Imagine I'm beside you in a car. You have to steer; you'll crash over a cliff if you don't. But if you thought of that every instant, you'd start weaving. It would be more normal to hear what I'm saying, and steer with another level of your mind."

The analogy opened windows. "I don't think," Jesse said, "that primitive man would have been able to drive a car."

"Exactly! Nor would you, if you'd been born into a culture that had never even seen one; at least not in heavy, fast traffic. Yet before the end of the twentieth century, virtually every kid in Earth's industrialized nations could drive sixty miles an hour a car's length from death, with rock music blaring full blast."

It's in what you learn to take for granted, Jesse thought. The shapes of the feedback were now yellow, warming into orange. He realized with awe that he was close to the level that had, last night, been unendurable. The difference lay in his control over the feedback pattern, but was that from matching or only steadiness? So far the two displays were virtually identical. Glancing at the other chair, he saw that Peter's face, like his own, was glistening with sweat and that his fingers gripping the armrests were white.

"The intensity's still too low to try it," Peter said, sounding only a little breathless. "I have to prolong this until you get into the swing of following. Don't analyze the patterns.

You can't alter yours by force of will. Watch, visualize the two as connected, but keep your conscious mind on what I say.

"We'll never know how many humans developed this skill in the past," he went on. "Some did, such as yogis and shamans. There are also recorded cases of spontaneous occurrence, but few seem to have involved volition—and that's what's important, not the brain activity itself. Shutting off suffering in a brief crisis is one thing, but to do it deliberately, sustain it over long periods, is another matter. Conditions in the world outside aren't right for learning that. For one thing, pain usually can't be isolated from harm. Injury, torture, almost always involve the fear of bodily damage. Only in rare circumstances can an untrained person deal with both fears at once. Here, we take them in sequence—"

Without warning, Jesse's heart seemed to burst in him. He choked, stricken by terror so agonizing that he almost cried out. The pain of his arm increased a hundredfold; it was burned through again; he could not stand it one more second.... "Peter!" he gasped. "Cut it—something's gone haywire—"

It did not stop. "Watch the patterns!" Peter commanded sharply.

His vision was so blurred that he could scarcely see. Dimly, he made out the breaks characteristic of last night's panic; but Peter's feedback steadied almost immediately. He imagined his matching it, and let that slowly happen. The pain receded somewhat, though the pattern's color did not change. Jesse found he was able to speak.

"God ... I thought I was past cracking up. What did I do wrong?"

"Nothing. I led you into that, and you followed me both in and out," Peter told him. "You couldn't have done it if you'd had to stop and think. You couldn't have done it even unconsciously with an unfamiliar mind-pattern, so I had to use one you knew. Also, Jess, I had to make sure you're still able to risk losing control. It's easy to slip back toward reliance on willpower, and if you try to manage states of consciousness that way, you'll fail."

"Did you *feel* that break?"

"Yes. Panic is an altered state, just like the other mind-patterns."

"And for you, feeling it's—okay?"

"Well, not when I had to bring you down with me. And even for me, a small taste of panic under stimulus goes a long way. But yes, it's okay for me, because it takes a lot of self-control to initiate the switch, and that kind of control— the kind *not* achieved through willpower—is exhilarating. Just now, when you found you had the control to recover, didn't you feel something more than relief?"

Yes, he realized, he had. Just a brief spark, but it was something new, a feeling he hadn't had before except perhaps in shuttles sometimes, back in the early days when piloting had challenged him.

"That's akin to a high," Peter informed him. "It wasn't a true high because you were in pain, which overwhelms less urgent feelings. But what we're aiming for is breakthrough into a mind-pattern where the pain will no longer affect you. You will feel it in your body, but it won't bother you. That's a state unlike any you know. Think of it as like—well, like breaking the sound barrier. Have you ever flown an old-time jet aircraft, Jess? Twentieth-century Earth vintage?"

"No, just ground-to-orbit birds, mostly VTOL ones. But I've seen vids."

"In the early days, test pilots really feared that barrier, you know. When they hit Mach one they almost broke up. But on the other side—"

Peter's voice caught. How long could he keep it up? Jesse wondered. Peter was suffering agony that he could end mentally, by a simple act of volition from which he somehow managed to refrain, while at the same time talking calmly on like a professor. His feedback was beginning to show a slight, very slight, waver.

God, Jesse thought. We have to go through the barrier. The shapes glowed dark red now. Despite control over the feedback pattern, Jesse felt nausea. The perceived pain was worse than any he'd experienced outside panic; he wasn't sure how long he could hold on. Yet ... he wasn't supposed to hold on, for that would be willpower, and counterproductive ... he must risk losing control in order to gain it. He must commit himself fully to that risk. Determinedly, he ignored rising fear and listened to Peter. The voice seemed faint, distant....

"... have to push you. You will reach a point when your mind won't tolerate any more. Several things can happen. You can dissociate, which I'd have to ... deal with. You can lose consciousness, but I think you have too much stamina for that. Or slide back into panic ... if you feel it happening, watch the patterns ... watch the patterns. ..."

"Jess! Watch the patterns, Jess! Match with mine, *now!*"

He was cracking up again. He could see the breaks starting, and he could no longer get the rhythm back. He had to stop this! Nothing else mattered. He could not think; the need for escape dominated his mind completely. . . .

"... the patterns, Jess! Watch *mine!*" Peter's voice had become strong, commanding. Red shapes loomed in front of Jesse. The display on the left stood out, magnified, in clear focus. It was not broken, nor was the rhythm regular. It was slowly changing shape. Below, his own was changing with it.

The pain was still there, but it didn't seem important. Why had he thought he couldn't take more of it? Jesse stared at the feedback in silence. Suddenly, incongruously, he became aware that he was very hungry.

"That was a close call," Peter said. "I almost had to cut. I do, sometimes, when a person can't follow the first time we try. Then we have to go through the buildup all over again."

He was keeping something back. Jesse turned to see Peter's face; it shone. His eyes were alight with unspoken elation. It was more than absence of suffering—it was more as if there had never been any suffering in the universe, as if Peter had forgotten the very concept. There was a new gulf between them, and Jesse wanted to bridge it more than he had ever wanted anything.

The patterns of the feedback had stabilized. "How do you feel?" Peter asked, in a voice that made plain that he knew.

"Good. Great. Like nothing I've imagined, only—"

"Only I'm high and you're not. I hoped it would be both of us, but achieving that on a first try is a bit too much to expect."

"Why didn't I make it?"

"You didn't get here by your own volition. Your control was too good in the normal mind-pattern; you held it so long you nearly passed out, and then followed me at the unconscious level."

"Would it be hard on you if we gave it another shot?"

"Now? No, but you're overtired. It might be hard on *you*."

"Hell, Peter!"

"I'm a fool to let you try it," Peter said. "Still, you've already come further in three sessions than most people do in six. I'd hate for you to miss the chance—a shared high's more intense than what you'll feel spontaneously during practice."

"How much practice will I need to gain full control?" Jesse asked, beginning to realize that it would be grueling. Already, in these few minutes, he'd perceived that holding his mind to a new pattern took considerable effort, more than he'd be able to exert without the built-in incentive.

"A good deal, but most of it will be with other skills. Pain is a spur needed only till you've learned the knack of matching mind-patterns."

"What sort of skills?" He supposed this was what had been meant by the claim that health could be ensured by mind training, but he still couldn't imagine how that was accomplished.

"You'll learn to control the neurological processes you were born with—processes that in time would damage your body, as they do most people's," Peter explained. "The key to such control is the ability to consciously choose your brain's response to stress instead of being limited to instinctive reactions. Which you've now proven that you possess." He said this last with evident elation, more profound elation than could be accounted for by the high he was experiencing. Jesse perceived that for some reason his success was terribly important to Peter, as if he had some personal stake in it beyond the satisfaction an instructor might naturally take in the performance of a trainee.

Grasping the remote in his right hand, Peter continued, "Okay. I'm going to cut, then come back in the normal pattern. Be ready to follow, and we'll make this brief."

"Can't I follow you without a cut?"

"No. Dropping back into suffering is too advanced to attempt at this stage—you want to practice shifting up, not down. We'll do it on orange; the hard push isn't necessary after the new mind-pattern's familiar."

"I don't think I even notice intensity now. It's become—irrelevant."

"You'll notice in the normal mind-pattern, and you can't take any more of that on red today. You would pass out this time."

Jesse struggled with the concepts. "You're saying that right now, I'm still receiving enough stimulus to knock me out, and only my brain pattern is preventing it?"

"What does control level of consciousness, if not the brain? The high you feel will be produced by brain chemistry, too. The breakthrough here is that you, by volition, can control what your brain does."

"I don't see how. I thought only physical factors influence brain functioning."

"That's what Med science says," Peter agreed. "Now you are getting into deep waters, Jess. We could sit here all night discussing this, and some of us frequently do. But as to operating premises, which one pulled you out of trouble just now?"

Jesse didn't bother to reply. He sat back, feeling oddly lighthearted, and turned his attention to the feedback. The shapes froze, then after a dizzying moment without stimulus, fierce agony swept through him. It wasn't gradual this time; the new shapes brightened from blue through green and yellow to orange almost instantly. But he was not caught off guard. Though Peter took the lead in switching mind-patterns, Jesse followed deliberately, consciously visualizing the match.

It was a feeling beside which all past experience meant nothing. The pain ebbed to insignificance. And he was high, higher than he had ever conceived of being, and Peter was high too, and it seemed that nothing within imagination lay beyond reach. It seemed they joined somewhere in space, their contact closer than bodily touch. Kira and Greg too, who had been in the control booth, who were still there, perhaps, though their minds were linked with his, with Peter's, there was no distance between any of them. . . .

As the stimulus ceased, Jesse soared, mind now free from the effort of control; he was one with his body yet indifferent to its sensations. He was scarcely aware when they left the little room and went up, through the storerooms, into sunlit brilliance, into the warmth and laughter of friends' welcome, into a joy that would be his forever.

People grabbed his arms, embraced him, their exuberance reflecting and heightening his emotion. He was home now, one of them, never to be alone again anywhere. This was his Lodge, his world, his galaxy. Feeling an overwhelming surge of energy, Jesse seized Peter's hand, and Michelle's, as they ran with the others to the waterfront and dove headlong from the rock into the bay.

Part Three

19

THROUGHOUT THE EVENING, surfeited after the delayed feast and filled with happy anticipation of a reunion with Carla, Jesse sprawled beside the fireplace, thinking that never before had he felt so completely free. Free not merely of the fear just past, but of all the fears, worries, and doubts that went with ordinary living. Fears that he would always be alone ... that life would remain empty ... that there was nothing that really mattered to him.... He had been seeking something after all, he realized—and had found more.

Peter had gone back to the city with Anne, rather than in his own plane, since he'd not slept the previous night. "He wasn't fit to fly," Greg said. "I don't know what's come over Peter. I never knew him to recruit before without weeks of evaluation. I never knew him to call in sick so he could stay at the Lodge an extra day, either. And as for going on dual with a novice stressed out to the extent you were, when he himself was under that much stress—well, he wasn't behaving rationally. Kira and I just sat there, in shock, waiting to pull you out fast if he collapsed."

"I knew it couldn't be as easy as he made it look," Jesse said. "But was there real danger to him?"

"No, with hindsight we know there wasn't. But if he'd misjudged you, if you'd not been so strong, you'd have taken him down with you; he'd—" Greg broke off, shaking his head.

"An instructor makes himself vulnerable to more than the effects of the stimulus," Michelle said. "He had been through a lot even before he went on dual—during your first two sessions he felt your pain, literally in his own body, as he would if he were healing someone. He wasn't suffering physically then, but the emotional strain drained him. And then to hear bad news about Ian—"

Chagrined, Jesse said, "That's why you urged me to wait for breakthrough."

"Don't worry about it," Greg assured him. "He did not misjudge. He never does, actually. You'll be pushed hard and fast—Peter's even talking about trying to get you ready for the Ritual before Ian dies, which is another sign of how far gone he is from normal caution. But he will not endanger you. He's too good at the job for that."

"He seems young for the responsibilities he has," Jesse reflected. "But it looks as if the Group consists entirely of young people. Am I the only exception besides Kira?"

There was an awkward silence. Finally Michelle said, "I guess there's no reason we can't be frank now that you're one of us. How old do I think I am, Jesse?"

He hesitated, deciding on the most tactful answer. Like most of the others, she appeared to be in her early twenties, though perhaps a year or two beyond. "I'd say about twenty," he replied.

"I'm twice that," Michelle confessed, "and some of us that you've met are older."

"Oh, you mean in local years. I meant Earth years, the way ages are counted most places."

"I do mean Earth years," Michelle said.

"That's not possible!" None of them wore makeup, and on the beach they went topless; there was no way they could conceal normal aging. "I thought you people didn't go in for things like cosmetic surgery," he said.

"Of course we don't. We control our physical reactions to stress, that's all. It's ongoing stress that causes aging— within limits, of course."

"We won't live forever," Greg said. "Ian's a hundred and thirty, now, and he's about to go. But we have to hack the Net to adjust some of our birthdates, so they won't lead to questions. Needless to say, outsiders would hunt us down trying to find our secret."

Open-mouthed, Jesse ventured, "How old is Kira?"

"She is over a hundred," Michelle replied. "She's been in the Group since its early days, when it was just a small gathering of Ian's friends."

"And Peter?"

"About forty-five, I think. I haven't asked him."

Stunned, Jesse struggled to readjust. Peter, whose youth and vitality he had envied from the beginning—three years older than he himself was? Kira, who despite white hair was trim, energetic, who swam topless like the others—over a *hundred*?

How old was Carla? Perhaps after all, there wasn't a large gap between her age and his own.

"There are no guarantees," Greg said. "The Group hasn't existed long enough for us to know if we'll all have extended lifespans. But we can pretty much count on not disintegrating from age before we die."

Jesse stared into the fire, slowly absorbing this. He'd been told there would be personal gain. It had been implied that this would include good health. But a longer lifespan . . . freedom from aging . . . it was beyond anything he had envisioned, despite all he'd sensed about the specialness of these people he'd come to care about. I'm still high, he thought. I shouldn't take seriously what I hear while I'm high. In the morning I'll find out I've been delusional.

After awhile he said, "It's a paradox, isn't it? We aim toward lengthened lives, yet at the same time toward acceptance of death."

"It's outsiders who are confused," Greg said. "They deny death, cling to pseudo-life, because they never get all they should out of living."

"But what *is* natural death," Jesse questioned, "if not

the result of aging? What is Ian dying of, if all diseases are curable here and he's not disintegrating from age?"

"Ah, that's the big question. In the twenty-first century, many scientists hoped genetic engineering could eventually cure aging itself. Some believed humans could become literally immortal. The conservatives who thought physical immortality would be a bad thing wanted research that might lead to it banned. They didn't need to worry. Such research has never gotten anywhere. Life expectancy is longer than it used to be—most people are active well into their nineties—but no matter how thoroughly bodies are repaired, old age remains 100 percent fatal. That's never been adequately explained in terms of biology. Something within the human mind controls it—the deep, unconscious part of the mind that's often called spirit."

"Are you saying that underneath old people *want* to die?" Jesse protested.

"Underneath, they seek something more than can be attained in life, something beyond, without which the struggle of living would have no meaning. Not necessarily the sort of afterlife depicted by religious metaphors. A person doesn't have to believe consciously in any form of continued existence—I'm not even sure whether I do. But there's a built-in human longing for a state of being we can't put a name to, a yearning that extra years can't satisfy. Eventually, everyone comes to a point where there's nothing more to be gained from living, even if the awareness of that fact is buried deep inside."

"Once you have tended dying people you will see, Jesse," said Michelle. "It's not like premature death. And it's not an escape from pain, either—you know now that it need never be that among our own people or those we serve as caregivers. Ian was well until a few weeks ago; now his body is shutting down. People simply die when it's their time to pass on."

Kira, joining them, said, "In the words of a very ancient poem, to everything there is a season . . . a time to be born and a time to die. And that's why the Vaults are such a travesty of life. Why stasis is the one end we ourselves can't bear to contemplate."

Yes, Jesse thought. They feared nothing except that. Tonight, he too feared nothing. Had he not become one of them?

But the next morning the elation was gone. He felt unreal, disconnected from the world around him, and his nerves were on edge; when people greeted him warmly at breakfast it was hard to respond. His head ached. Well, this was only to be expected after getting high, he told himself. The fact that it hadn't been a chemical high apparently had nothing to do with the immediate aftereffects.

Life at the Lodge went on as usual. The current residents took pleasure in it, as had those of the week before, seemingly oblivious to the dangers Jesse now knew they faced. He was awed by them. Collectively and in some cases individually, they were in peril of arrest for almost every crime in the book. Hacking, smuggling, conspiracy, evasion of monetary laws, involvement in the paranormal, maybe even fraud . . . and of course, murder. So too was he, Jesse realized. But the edginess he felt wasn't due to that. The carefree joy that the others displayed, that he'd felt briefly himself the night before, he now sensed was hard-won. So far he had experienced only the beginning of what it might take to win it.

In the afternoon Kira took him down to the lab for what she said was the first of regular sessions on dual. No pain was involved; he was simply told to watch the feedback and match the mind-patterns she created. It was harder to do than it had been with the spur of pain. His mind did wander. Not knowing the significance of the patterns made it tougher, but Kira said that at this stage, explanations would only confuse him. And perhaps frighten him, Jesse guessed— they represented altered states of consciousness, didn't they? He didn't feel as if he were in an altered state, but then, he wasn't asked to match any specific pattern for very long.

"It's natural for you to be uneasy for a while," she told him. "Your mind's been shaken up more than you realize. What you went through yesterday set things in motion that you won't be consciously aware of for some time. But you're going to be fine. Peter tells me you show great promise."

The second day he rose feeling no better. He was still sleeping in the bunkroom, but most others were not. More people had arrived, and for the first time, he'd noticed couples leaving the fireside together, headed, presumably, for the cottages widely separated among trees far back from the shore. Meals continued to be served potluck-style in the Lodge. Nobody treated him as a stranger; it was simply taken for granted that he belonged. But he missed Carla. Without her, the place wasn't as much fun.

Personal questions were no longer taboo, and by this time he'd learned more about the Group's members. There were about three hundred, only a few of whom came to the Island—which was owned by Ian and labeled Maclairn Island on maps—during any given offshift. There were other gathering places more convenient for some, including a safe house in the city where leisure hours could be spent in the company of fellow-members. All were welcome at the Lodge, however, except when the red pennant was flying. That meant a guest was present and it was open only by invitation.

The Group included adults of all ages, but because it was growing, those in their twenties did predominate. "Don't any of you have families?" he asked during breakfast.

"A few of the older people do," said Dorcas, who sat next to him. "In several cases their grown children are members. But it's rare among those of us who joined young. That's the catch, of course. It's the one way in which our life's unsatisfying." In a low voice she added, "It would be nice if we could have kids."

Was the Group so demanding, then, that they must abandon every facet of normal living? For himself he did not care; he had given up hope of a family long ago. But the young people should care. "I don't see why you can't," he confessed. "Peter said we're not asked to renounce attachments."

"Oh, it's not that," Dorcas said. "Not the Group, though that's what woke most of us up. The trouble is, we're unwilling to be bound by this world's rules. In the first place, natural conception isn't allowed here. In vitro fertilization isn't just an option, as it is everywhere—on Undine it's mandatory. And embryos are screened for a lot more alleged defects than we're willing to discard."

"Not only major problems that would cause suffering or mental incapacity," her husband Erik added. "We have no objection in principle to the destruction of embryos that don't yet have brains, any more than we view brain-dead bodies as persons. But the Meds' selection criteria are warped. They won't accept a genetic predisposition for *any* disease, or even for characteristics that aren't 'defects' at all, like shortness or obesity. They stick to an arbitrary standard of physical perfection; if it weren't for the Colonial League ban on germline genetic engineering, they'd be altering genomes to fit their narrow concept of what's ideal. Or trying to, at any rate—God knows what havoc that would create with personality. Most abilities can't be predicted by genetic analysis, so no one knows precisely what's lost in the screening process. But something surely is."

Jesse had noticed that the population of Undine seemed lacking in natural diversity; though skin color varied, virtually everybody was tall, slim and athletic. The thought of the uniformity being planned was disturbing. He'd heard that no prejudice existed in the colony. Now he saw that no one against whom prejudice might arise was allowed to be born.

"What if a woman gets pregnant accidentally?" he inquired, thinking that forced abortion, common as it was on overpopulated Earth, would be inconsistent with the Meds' policy of keeping bodies on life support indefinitely.

"That can't happen. Though women's contraceptive implants have to be taken out prior to IVF for hormone balancing, men's IVDs aren't removed. We're all required to have our eggs or sperm stored cryogenically, so they're available to use."

"Good God. Why don't they just cut everyone's tubes while they're at it, then?"

"They would, if League law didn't prohibit sterilization on colony worlds." Sadly, Dorcas added, "The screening of embryos isn't the only reason we choose not to have children. If we had them, you see, we'd want them brought up according to our beliefs. We wouldn't want them conditioned by Med propaganda."

Conditioned? Puzzled, a bit frightened, Jesse asked, "What harm would the Meds do to a normal child?" It occurred to him that he might not yet have been informed of all the horrors.

"Nothing as sinister as you're imagining," she assured him. "Only what happens everywhere, even on Earth. Except that here, it's more stifling. Kids aren't allowed much fun—no sports that could lead to injury, no exercise that's not supervised in gyms. No time free to just hang out. Never anything to eat that doesn't meet nutritional standards. And medication for every minor problem, so that they come to believe drugs are the answer to stress. Besides, we wouldn't even see them except during offshifts—"

"Not see them? Why not?"

"Everyone works on Undine," Erik explained, "just as in most colonies. Here, the Meds provide us with free child care, and for efficiency, kids live and are schooled in crèches during the five days of their parents' workweek. They can be taken home only during the five offshift days, and not even then if the parents have other plans."

"Crèches run by the Meds, I suppose."

"They're part of the Hospital complex," Dorcas said. "Newborns are taken directly to them and stay full time until they're old enough for untrained mothers to be trusted with. The crèche counselors are kind and loving, you understand. We have fond memories of our caregivers, just as kids often did in societies on Earth where it was the custom for upper-class children to be turned over to nannies and boarding schools. But here, there's no option. Child-rearing is considered the business of professionals, a matter of ensuring children's health. And if we tried to instill different values while our kids were home or prevent their receiving medical treatment we think is damaging, we would lose custody. There's less heartbreak not having them at all."

"I'm surprised they don't force you to have them. Most colonies want population growth, and Undine is closed to immigration." It had been explained to Jesse that if it were not, hordes of the rich would come from Earth seeking eventual preservation of their bodies in stasis. He himself had escaped deportation only because Fleet personnel had the right to remain on any planet to which they traveled.

"Oh, we contribute DNA," said Erik. "That's the main reason our germ cells are stored—in the year we turn twenty our contraceptive implants are temporarily removed for it, first the men and then the women later so both sexes won't be fertile at the same time. Since all conception is by IVF anyway, it makes no difference to population growth whether a child's biological parents are also social parents. The government's happy when people relinquish parenting rights. It means their eggs and sperm are banked anonymously and the Meds can decide which genomes to combine. Surrogate mothers are employed by the Hospital; it's a respected career."

"You mean there are kids in the crèches without social parents, kids with no families?"

"Yes, lots of them," Dorcas told him. "Their surnames are assigned by the computer from a list of traditional Earth surnames that haven't been used here before—that's why not everyone on Undine has one of the surnames of the original colonists." At Jesse's frown she added hastily, "There's no stigma attached to it. Peter was a crèche child. I don't know how many other Group members were."

"I thought Peter inherited wealth," Jesse said, more bewildered than ever by the local culture's oddities.

"Just his share of the pool, so far, though all Ian's assets will pass to him. When citizens go into stasis without descendants or adopted heirs, their funds are pooled and the income is divided among the crèche children. Since the highest-paid people are the least apt to have devoted time to child rearing, pool shares tend to be worth more than the average direct inheritance."

Well, he hadn't been close to his own family, Jesse thought. He hadn't missed it after leaving Earth for Fleet. The weakening of family ties on Undine nevertheless struck him as unnatural. But not so unnatural that the public would object, he realized with dismay. People who wanted their own kids could rear them five days out of ten. If it were forbidden entirely in favor of the government-favored crèche system, the voters would rebel.

He was beginning to get the hang of how things worked in the colony and how hopeless it was to think that political action could bring about any change. "Have you—the Group, I mean—ever thought of emigrating?" he asked.

"There's no way for us to become a true subculture on any world," Erik said. "We've investigated. It seems that we ought to qualify under freedom of religion laws, in principle anyway, if we posed as a religious cult. But no, the high priesthood of the medical experts is well established throughout the galaxy. Even where they're not the only government, their pronouncements override all issues of conscience."

Jesse's frown deepened. He had never thought about it that way, but it was true enough that no one, anywhere, would be permitted to raise children in a way considered bad for health. There were indeed conflicts between religious groups and health care authorities, and the latter always won. You never questioned that. You assumed the authorities knew best, just as religious dogma had once been considered infallible.

The medical authorities here were so far from infallible that he'd agreed with enthusiasm to take criminal action in opposition to them. For the first time he wondered, are they any wiser elsewhere? Is the only difference here that they've got police power?

"There are uninhabited islands on the other side of this planet," he ventured. "Couldn't you establish a new colony there?"

"We've no way to get there, let alone transport supplies," Erik pointed out. "Small boats and planes haven't the range, even assuming a one-way trip for lack of a power source for recharging—and since there's no native land life, we couldn't survive on an island that hadn't been terraformed. What's more, it wouldn't be allowed. The present government holds the charter for Undine, and surveillance from weather satellites would detect any attempt at unauthorized settlement."

Yes, and Fleet would soon put an end to it, Jesse realized. He had momentarily forgotten that independent colonies on the same world were prohibited. The Colonial League was determined to ensure that never again could a situation exist that might, in the future, lead to a global war. Thus the government established by the first colonists to arrive had legal sovereignty over the entire planet. He had never doubted that policy; now he decided that he'd been fortunate to have been assigned to freighter duty rather than Fleet's enforcement patrol.

It had not previously occurred to him that sometimes the only way to create a better society might be to start a new one.

20

FOR CARLA THE workweek seemed endless before it had barely begun. She could scarcely focus on the hacking required to alter Group members' telemetry data, much less on the duller, if safer, routine of her official job.

She had taken an extra shift the first night so as to be at the Hospital when Peter returned, had been waiting in his office, in fact. Though when he came in she'd known instantly, telepathically, that all had gone well with Jesse, she'd needed to hear him put it into words.

"He's everything I hoped for, and more," Peter had said. "The ways of fortune are very strange, Carla. Despite all we know, all we believe beyond established science, we'll never understand the miracle of synchronicity. We could never have foreseen the fate that brought this man to us—"

Carla stared at him in bewilderment. "Synchronicity? Fate?" This was not at all what she had expected him to say. It made no sense.

Startled, Peter came back as if from trance. "Forget I said that," he told her. "I'm tired. I haven't slept since the night before last and I've got a night shift ahead of me."

"You haven't rested?" She'd assumed he'd have gotten back to the city by noon.

"I stayed at the Lodge longer than I planned." In reply to her unspoken question he explained, "Jesse has an ability rare among people who choose technical careers such as space work; he's highly intelligent but not so analytical that he feels he's got to calculate every move. He's willing to let things play out, even when he doesn't fully understand what's happening. That means he has natural aptitude for our training—so much, in fact, that this afternoon we went all the way to breakthrough."

"Breakthrough? Oh, Peter—you haven't pushed him too hard, have you? He's all right?" Peter, at times, was prone to demand more of people than was prudent.

"He's fine," Peter assured her. "He got high. He's having a great night at the Lodge. I got high too, and then flying back with Anne, I crashed—me, that is, not the plane. I'm running on empty, Carla. There's more I haven't yet told you; Ian is dying."

She went to him, embraced him, sensing his need for consolation. Ian had been like a father to Peter ever since his college days. A retired professor then already over a hundred, he had sought paranormally-gifted young people to train as future leaders. He'd helped both Ramón and Peter through medical school—Ramón specializing in geriatrics, Peter in psychiatry—and after Ramón died, his bond with Peter had grown even stronger; he had adopted him legally as his heir. Everyone in the Group would grieve for Ian, but for Peter it would be the hardest, especially as it hadn't been long since the death of his wife, Lesley. Yet while still mourning the double loss, he would have to take on the full burden of leadership. Ian's wishes had been made clear. The Council could not possibly choose anyone else to succeed him.

It was no wonder Peter didn't seem quite himself. Still, what could he have meant by saying that fate had brought Jesse? From Jesse's standpoint, his detention on Undine had turned out to be a stroke of good fortune. But was it that important for the Group to include an offworlder? Or did he have some special talent of which only Peter knew?

Proceeding to breakthrough on the same day as testing was unheard of. That, on top of the unprecedented speed with which Jesse had been recruited, meant Peter was hiding something. Which of course she knew in any case, from the way his mind was closed to her. Among telepaths there was normally free exchange between close friends.

Suddenly a thought occurred to her. "Peter—your hurry to accept Jesse hasn't anything to do with me, has it?" she ventured. "I know that for years you've been thinking I should stop mourning, that only in a sexual relationship can I recover—" She flushed; this was a topic she would never before have discussed openly with him. She'd had to guard her own feelings, those she'd long known that she might have developed for Peter, were it not that until recently he'd been married. What she now felt for Jesse had set her free.

With brotherly affection, he stroked her hair. "You can never stop mourning the manner of Ramón's death," he said, "nor can any of us, as far as that goes. But it's true that there's only one bond powerful enough to heal you. I felt joy when I saw it might form between you and Jesse. The sooner it becomes possible, the better, though that's not my main reason for fast action."

She was silent. After a moment he continued, "In due course you'll know what's at stake with Jesse. I can't tell you, or anyone, until it's time for *him* to know, to make a deep and irrevocable commitment to the Group that I've no right to ask for until he's better acquainted with us and has made the Ritual pledges."

Carla's heart lurched. "Peter! You wouldn't put him in danger—"

"Not in the way you're thinking. Not of dying as Ramón did, I promise you."

She relaxed, chagrined at having allowed herself to fight the sensation of fear. She knew how to handle it—that was what Group training focused on, after all. Coming to terms with fear was the key to controlling effects of stress on the body. You must inwardly consent to the worst possible outcome in order to live free of worry. But there was one thing she could *never* consent to, never again dare to love anyone to whom it might happen. Was that why she'd held back even after Lesley was gone?

"For now," Peter was saying, "Jesse's welfare does have a great deal to do with you. Am I right in assuming you want a long-term relationship?"

"Well, Peter, I don't know if it's what *he* wants."

"I have every reason to think it will be." Peter looked away. "This is awkward. I don't like intervening in people's private lives. But—well, you remember how it was with you and Ramón—"

At the beginning, he meant, before their marriage . . . the long-ago time of her own induction into the Group. Ramón had sponsored her in the Ritual. Earlier, he had taught her not only Group skills but the nature of physical love itself. She'd been a virgin until then, and had not known how different it was for outsiders. She was not sure she knew now, despite the explanations she'd been given.

"It can't be as it was Ramón," she acknowledged. "I'm the experienced one, now. That will be hard for Jesse, I suppose."

"You realize, don't you, that so far he has no comprehension at all of what an intimate relationship within the Group entails?"

"But you'll tell him, surely, now that he's through the test."

"He's not ready to understand quite this soon. It has to be absorbed gradually. If it comes up I'll tell him; but telling isn't the important part. He must be shown, Carla—if not by you, then by someone else. A lot depends on it."

Underneath she had known this was coming. She had blocked it out; she had not wanted to speculate about who would teach Jesse the things mere lab sessions could not. There were trained instructors, and she was not one of them. She was not qualified. . . .

"Carla, love's more important than training. It overrides, always! Not all newcomers fall in love, but when it happens, it's much better than the other way." Peter turned back to her. "But you must be willing. And I must know now, from the start, whether Jesse can count on your help."

"I'm scared of being swamped by memories, Peter. If that happened at the wrong moment, I could hurt him."

"Yes, emotionally, just as his own deep-seated fears may hurt you. Yet if the love is real, you'll get past that. Would he be better off with someone who cares less for him?"

There'd been only one way she could answer. Yet so much would hinge on her strength, not only their love, but Jesse's entire future! His whole outlook toward the powers of his mind . . . and perhaps, Peter had implied, some unique destiny beyond the commitment required of them all. . . .

"He won't see why we have to wait," she'd said sadly. Jesse had made love with women in the world outside; his expectations of sex would be different from hers. For that reason she must hold back from him. Any premature union between them would be disastrous.

"But when the time comes," Peter had reminded her, "he'll know it was worth waiting for."

The waiting, she now realized, was going to be hard.

21

JESSE'S LAB TRAINING session wasn't scheduled until evening—he learned that when not reserved by Peter, the lab was in constant use by others, not only for advanced training, but for games of some sort. The experienced people lined up to go on dual with each other; matching mind-patterns was a popular form of recreation. He didn't ask what sort of altered states they were playing with. He wasn't sure he wanted to know.

By noon he longed for action. Anything, even something risky like a rescue mission or retrieval of a body for burial in the bay. It would be easier than sitting around pretending to relax.

Greg, sensing his mood, suggested a scuba dive. "We'll go to a place you haven't seen," he said, "one we keep secret from outsiders."

In the boat, getting into his gear, Jesse found to his dismay that he was nervous. The old apprehension about deep water was returning—but that was nonsense! He'd done plenty of swimming by now and was gaining proficiency.

He was paired with Kira; the others had already submerged. "Jesse," she said as he went into the water, "diving may seem different from before, when Peter was supporting you."

Jesse held onto the gunwale with one hand, lifting his mask to reply. "He wasn't supporting me after the first few minutes."

"I mean he was supporting you telepathically, as he did

much of the time during your feedback sessions—for which the diving was a trial run."

He drew breath, trying to absorb this information. "The others know only that you're relatively inexperienced and they'll need to keep an eye on you," Kira went on. "I can help the way Peter did, but I won't unless it's necessary. We'll be making a long swim, then going into an underwater cave."

"I should never have needed that kind of help," Jesse said, embarrassed.

"Yes, you should. We deliberately put trainees in situations where they do need it, because only under the spur of emotion can new mind powers be learned. Including receptiveness to telepathic support, which is essential to the more advanced ones." She smiled encouragingly. "Your fear of water was a lucky break for us—confrontations with the phobias some newcomers have are harder to set up."

I can't believe I'm hearing this, Jesse thought. From a woman over a hundred years old, about to plunge underwater with her on a planet I never heard of till a few weeks ago? The sense of unreality that had plagued him these past two days was stronger than ever. What the hell, he decided. Just go with the flow.

He replaced the mask and dove, Kira after him. The water in previous dive areas had been clear, offering a full view of Undine's weird, primitive sea life. But here it was murky; Greg, ahead of him, carried a torch. Jesse focused on following it, trying not to be aware of anything else. Not to think of the mass of water over him, the bottom below, the bodies buried there—but no, not below him, for in the boat they had come far from the burial site. He breathed steadily, imagining the mask and air gauge as part of a spacesuit. Then all at once he recalled, *don't resist the fear. Let it come. It's supposed to come.* . . . After some time, the sensation of water around him became quite pleasant.

Kira guided him through the underwater cave entrance. To his surprise, they broke surface and swam into shallows.

Their torches shone on rocks sloping up out of the water, onto which they climbed. Further on, no torches were needed. Pulling off his mask, Jesse followed Greg and Michelle, wondering why the darkness wasn't total. As they rounded a boulder and came into the main room of the cavern, he saw a shaft of light from high above. It came from the sky, as, he realized, did air.

Jesse looked around him. Kira knelt at a low ledge of some kind, fumbling with a battery-powered lamp that was evidently kept here. All of a sudden it flared into bluish brilliance. The wall over it was illuminated, revealing a pyramid of painted words with letters too small for him to make out. A list of some kind? Names? Yes, certainly, Jesse thought. This was a memorial; it couldn't be anything else.

"You are now in the only cemetery on this world," said Greg. "Or the closest equivalent, anyway. Everyone ever buried in this colony is listed here, except for a few who were destroyed in accidents. They're in the bay, where it's deep, where we can't reach the bottom. It is a better place for them than the Vaults."

God, Jesse thought, everyone . . . yet the list was not very long. These were the only people who had escaped the stasis vaults, the only ones whose bodies were totally dead! He had been told, but it had not really penetrated until now.

"What if some intruder finds the vent and lowers a rope down here?" he asked.

"They won't. The Island is off-limits to trespassers, but just in case, the shaft's booby-trapped—it will collapse if it's ever disturbed."

Michelle was opening a sealed plastic sack she had carried. It contained not lunch, as he'd supposed, but greenery. She arranged it on the ledge next to the lamp, which was a sort of altar. Kira was still kneeling, deep in thought or perhaps prayer. Michelle stepped back and stood beside him, silently looking up at the names.

"We knew them all," she said finally. "At least some of

us knew each one, because they wouldn't be here except for us. They were the people in our hospices."

"Peter's wife Lesley is among them, too," Greg added. "She died last year when a sailboat they were in capsized in a freak storm. She was trapped beneath it and drowned before he could get her into the life raft, and then when he wasn't able to revive her, he had to sink the raft to keep the rescue squad from taking her body. They might have got it breathing even though her brain was dead. So he hung onto a life preserver in that storm for hours, until a search was launched—he'd ditched his phone to explain why he hadn't called for help before it was too late."

"Good God," Jesse murmured. "Are you saying that if they'd known there was a raft, he'd have been accused of murdering her?"

"Oh, yes. He'd have been convicted for sure—especially since the authorities frown on sailing in the first place. Hazardous sports aren't actually illegal for adults on outlying islands, at least not yet, but people who engage in them are viewed as irresponsible. He's given up sailing now to keep his job, and the fact that we scuba dive here isn't mentioned in the city."

Convicted . . . exactly what, Jesse wondered, might have happened? What was the penalty for murder on a world where all police power was vested in the medical establishment?

Kira rose and came to him, her eyes conveying more than grief. "Jesse," she said, reading this thought. "You know underneath what's done to murderers here. Don't pretend to yourself that you're uninformed."

He had known all along, of course. There was only one thing the Meds could do with murderers when crime was viewed as treatable illness. They would use drugs, ostensibly to cure, perhaps sincerely thought to cure—drugs that would damage the brain. It was done elsewhere, routinely, to anyone considered dangerously psychotic. Chemical lobotomy, it was sometimes called. . . .

Peter, a gifted telepath, more skilled in controlling his mind than Jesse himself could yet imagine—those talents depended on the brain. New mind-patterns, new states of consciousness, higher brain functions than orthodox science was even aware of . . . Damage to the brain would be worse for him—for anyone in the Group—than for its usual victims. They risked losing what they most valued . . . just to decently dispose of dead bodies?

"Not just for that," Kira assured him. "There was no chance of anyone suspecting him when he handled it as he did. Since he can control his body temperature, he wasn't even in danger of hypothermia. We take risks only for the living, though when they die in our care we're stuck with bodies to bury."

But caregiving was not their sole reason for defying the law, Jesse thought. Their primary goal was to use the power of mind. *In order to gain volitional control, you must be wholly, unreservedly willing to lose control—to let what comes, come,* Peter had said. That was true in a larger sense. . . .

He struggled with the idea, unable to fully grasp it. Kira said, "This is the choice the world forces on us. To become all we can be, we risk being totally destroyed. Yet we can't choose not to, Jesse. We're human beings, not mere bodies; we can't live as if we were less. This is what we're pledged to. This is who we are."

This is who we are . . . For the first time thinking of the Group as "we," not "they," Jesse let it sink in. He knew he would never go back to Fleet.

22

AFTER RETURNING TO the boat, they anchored near the shore and opened the lunch box. As he ate, Jesse stared at the bay and the expanse of pale blue above, dazed at the realization that for the first time in his adult life, he'd become a world-dweller. He'd spent his adolescence counting the time till he could get into space, and later, during leaves, he'd sensed nothing worldlike in his surroundings. He'd visited cities, not worlds; once away from their spaceports you couldn't see more than small patches of sky. To a spacer, worlds were something to observe from orbit. He had never before felt oriented to a planet's surface. He found that he liked it.

He turned to Kira, more than ever impressed by her incredible agelessness. "How did you get involved in the Group?" he asked.

"Many years ago, when I was a young doctor, I thought I knew how to preserve health," she told him. "But a time came when I saw that I was wrong."

"You're a doctor, Kira?" said Jesse, surprised.

"A cardiologist, yes," she told him, "though I no longer believe much of what I was taught in medical school. I've retired from the Hospital now, but I manage the Group's healing house and hospices."

A retired cardiologist capable of such work when over a hundred must know what she was doing, Jesse thought. She was certainly not like the wackos his sister used to hang out with, even if she did claim that mere mental training could affect health.

"I got disillusioned," Kira went on. "People have searched for the causes of illness century after century, and some specific ones have been found—although not as many as the Meds would have you believe. You'd think that after all this time there would be less illness, wouldn't you? That especially here, in a colony where genetic disorders have been eliminated by screening of embryos, where contagious disease has been wiped out and even cancer can be cured, that fewer people would get sick than on Earth? But that's not what has happened. There's just as much sickness as there ever was, if not more, the same as on Earth—though less of it's fatal than in the past. As soon as one condition becomes curable, another takes its place. And here, where continuous medical care is not only free but mandatory, there is more illness than in any other colony in the galaxy."

"Well, that's not surprising," Jesse said, "considering that people here are chased around by cops in ambulances aiming to convince them that they're sick."

"True, but it's more complicated than that," said Greg. "On one hand people are made to worry about their health, yet at the same time this place is too damned safe. Even potentially-risky sports are discouraged—and too little challenge is as stressful as too much. Human beings naturally crave it; on Earth they're apt to get into trouble by searching for excitement. Here, the craving is simply frustrated. Once our ancestors got past the challenge of pioneering on a new world, there was no legal outlet for it."

"Our health and safety laws are largely self-defeating," Kira agreed. "But stress isn't unique to Undine; it's the main cause of illness everywhere. Human nature doesn't change when specific diseases disappear. Science has known the biochemical mechanisms underlying stress responses since before the age of space colonies, and still the Meds don't know how to deal with them. They will never learn, because their premises are all wrong."

"On Earth, stress reduction's promoted in a big way."

"Yes," Michelle said, "but that's backwards. You can't reduce stress! Merely *living* involves stress; it always has. Long ago people died of other things before stress caught up with them. But physical response to stress is a normal process—as normal as breathing—and over time it causes damage. There's always some aspect of the body that's most vulnerable, no matter how much repairing of parts is undertaken. Fixing one just throws others off balance, which is the main reason our Hospital causes more illness than it cures."

"You can't just not fix things," Jesse protested. "Medical technology is what prevents those other ways of dying."

"Of course it is," Greg said. "We have no objection to

medical technology where it's appropriate. It's great for dealing with injuries and acute conditions. We use its techniques in our own healing house when necessary, and we go to the Hospital for major procedures like limb and organ replacement or eye surgery. But it can't compensate for the effects of normal stress."

Kira said, "Since way back in the twentieth century, people have been conditioned to believe that all their problems ought to be considered medical problems—even that they ought to seek medical attention when they aren't sick, just in case they might get sick later. And so-called preventative medicine *doesn't* prevent, except in the sense of shifting the odds of getting one disease instead of another."

"Rearranging the deck chairs on the *Titanic*," Michelle agreed.

"Huh?"

"Oh, that's an old saying about a ship—not a starship, an ocean liner on Earth—that was doomed to sink. I don't know if it was a real one or just a legend."

"Take cardiovascular disease, for example," Kira went on. "For several hundred years advocates of preventative medicine have been raising alarms over the fact that it's the leading cause of death—"

"I always wondered," said Jesse, "which other disease they thought should lead."

"My point exactly. Actually, despite all the propaganda, the percentage of deaths due to cardiovascular disease has risen steadily, for the simple reason that past scourges like cancer and Alzheimer's can now be cured. Nothing is going to change that, short of the appearance of some new infectious plague that wipes out a significant part of Earth's population. Exhorting people to spend their lives trying to avoid it merely brings illness on earlier by increasing their ongoing stress level."

"Are you saying stress-based illness can't be prevented, then?"

"Not by medical science. And not by any other physical

means, either, except indirectly. All sorts of alternative practices are legal on Earth, and their advocates say many of
the same things we do about mainstream medicine—but
the alternatives don't work, either. They're based on the
same underlying fallacy."

"When it comes to treatment, most of those practices
help some people, some of the time," Greg added. "But then,
so does standard medicine. All health care theories, except
for a few wholly spiritual ones, assume that the way to avoid
illness is to do something to the body. In the long run,
whether it's high-tech drugs or herbal remedies or nutrition
or physical manipulation doesn't make a whole lot of difference. Some things do less direct damage than others. The
end result doesn't change."

Jesse considered this. "Accepted treatments have been
proven better than placebos in controlled trials, haven't they?
Doesn't that mean they're effective?"

"For well-defined illnesses that are already established,
yes. But not in terms of overall health and longevity."

"What's more, in most trials the placebo works for about
a third of the subjects," Kira said. "Often the percentage is
much higher. All that's required for the treatment for to be
judged better is for it to work on more subjects than that,
not necessarily a lot more. So in reality the majority of patients treated with powerful drugs aren't really helped by
them, not to mention the people who weren't sick in the
first place. Decade after decade, century after century, this
fact has been carefully ignored—not only by pharmaceutical companies, who have an obvious motive for suppressing
it, but by well-meaning doctors who want to believe they
can help people and patients who want to believe medication will help them."

"But placebos wouldn't help if the patients stopped
thinking they were drugs."

"No. What the placebo effect does is to mobilize the
body's own healing ability—but not for long, not after a person starts to doubt."

"I don't think it's just a matter of believing," Jesse insisted. "Doctors, and sometimes even faith healers, cure people with no faith in the treatment."

Kira laughed. "Peter and I heal skeptics, too. Many of us in the Group do."

"You use some sort of telepathy, though," Jesse recalled uncomfortably.

"So do faith healers," she informed him. "So do alternative practitioners who are successful with skeptics. And so, in fact, do talented physicians. It's on an unconscious level, of course; they don't know they're doing it. But apart from strictly mechanical procedures like surgery, one can't be an effective healer without giving some form of telepathic help. That's been true since the beginning of time."

"Oh, Kira, I can't believe that!"

"You'd rather not, I know."

Jesse was silent, listening to the waves lap against the nearby shore. It was true that he didn't like the thought of widespread telepathy; for some reason it chilled him. "I'm getting more and more confused," he admitted finally. "You say stress is universal and stress-based illness can't be prevented, yet you all stay healthy, and supposedly I'm to be trained to do the same."

"We said it can't be prevented by *physical* techniques," Greg told him. "With the mind—that's another story. Telepathy acts on the unconscious mind, not on the body directly, just as the placebo effect does. And we ourselves learn to consciously control our bodies' reactions to stress, so that they aren't damaged by it."

"So Peter said. That seems pretty fantastic to me."

"He taught you to control pain, didn't he? The same principles apply."

"But that didn't affect my body—only my perceptions."

"Jesse," Kira reminded him, "he did explain that your brain, which is part of your body, is responsible for your perceptions—and that you were controlling what your brain did. It's more complicated, of course. The biochemical responses of the nervous system are involved. You don't need to know the scientific details, but you'll find that volitional control works."

"It's not as new a concept as you may think," Michelle said. "I've read up on its history. As long ago as the twentieth century, experiments showed that simply *being in control,* or believing that you're in control, has a big impact on biochemistry—not just in people, but in rats. Those early studies produced evidence that people who have control over their situation are healthier, and have fewer illnesses, than people who don't."

"Which, incidentally, was absolute proof of the objective value of freedom," Greg declared. "Needless to say, the Med government here has discounted it. But medical science never followed through even on Earth. People want to believe magic pills will ward off illness, and the drug companies don't want them to believe otherwise."

"Neither do the health care professionals, I suppose," Jesse reflected grimly. "Even where it's not a matter of political power, their prestige and their jobs depend on keeping patients dependent."

"Besides," Michelle said, "free choice in action isn't enough. It helps; for instance, that's why diet came to be considered an effective prevention strategy even though widely different diets all made the same claims—in most cases it's the *control* people exercise, not the food itself, that improves their health. To get really significant control of bodily responses, though, you need more than indirect effects. You need to use conscious volition."

"And that's what you'll learn to do in the neurofeedback lab," Kira said. "Nobody can learn it just by thinking about it, and even with our advanced lab technology it couldn't be learned quickly without the telepathic help we provide. But once you do learn, you'll be permanently protected. You'll feel emotional stress just as anyone does, but you'll be able to keep it from damaging your body."

"And from being detected in your compulsory health

checkups," Greg added. "It's a matter of self-defense if you don't want to be forcibly medicated."

Turning away, Jesse reached over the side of the boat and trailed his hand in the water. There was something disturbing in the thought of having to control his bodily processes, something he couldn't put a finger on. And earlier, it had been implied that the training would involve experiences more frightening than mere lab sessions. . . .

Kira, picking up his thought, said, "There are psychological barriers to learning these skills that you're not yet ready to understand. It takes a good deal of courage, Jesse. As you've probably noticed, we put a lot of emphasis on dealing with fear. The aim's not to turn you into some sort of hero, but—among other things—to help you stay healthy."

"I'm still not sure I see the connection."

"No, because you've been conditioned by Med propaganda," Greg said. "You've been taught to believe that your body is a machine to be controlled by physical intervention. We use drastic methods to break that conditioning, starting with what you went through during testing."

Michelle added, "Some of the things we do would seem impossibly hard if we described them to you now. You'll find you're able to do them—even, in most cases, to enjoy doing them. And that will enable you to handle ongoing everyday fears without letting stress wear you down."

Well, Jesse thought, life in the Group wasn't going to be boring. "If that kind of control takes aptitude and courage to learn," he protested, "then isn't it unrealistic to say that medicine ought to rely on it? Even if it weren't for the political situation here, I don't think the majority would go along with the idea. Surely they wouldn't give up all drugs."

"No, of course not," Kira said. "Outsiders often do need medication, especially after stress has done lasting damage. In any case, without the techniques we've developed comparatively few people can alter the mindset they've absorbed both from conditioning and from mass telepathic influence. There's no way around that in today's culture, nor would there have been in past centuries. Our discoveries can't help the majority at this stage of human history."

Greg said, "We see the worst of it here because of the compulsion. But on Earth things are just as bad as far as conditioning goes, and the problem is harder to recognize. It may never be surmountable there."

"I guess not, when learning to stay healthy by your methods seems to require paranormal ability on the part of the instructors. That couldn't become widespread anywhere, even in the future." Nor would he want it to, Jesse thought nervously, putting aside the remainder of his unfinished lunch. He was suddenly aware that he was no longer hungry.

"Well, of course control over our bodies isn't the only thing we learn—" Michelle began, but Kira frowned and shook her head. "As I'm sure Peter told you, we're not trying to transform society," she said. "We're simply experimenting with the kind of advance we believe will come in the future, trying to find out if the development of new mind powers is practical for different kinds of people over a long period of time."

"As a vanguard—yes, he said that. But even supposing we find it works with everybody who joins us, and enough telepaths can be found to instruct, how could humanity ever make the transition?"

Michelle hesitated. "There's just one possibility," she said finally. "If kids could be brought up from earliest childhood according to our principles, without any conflicting influence and in a supportive telepathic environment—"

"But that could never happen."

"Not as far as civilization as a whole is concerned. But there might someday be a new world, a colony established specifically for that purpose—and ultimately that world would be on the cutting edge of human evolution. Other colonies would emulate it."

Kira nodded. "One of the reasons colonization is vital to evolution is that only separate colonies can experiment with new ways that can't ever prevail within the established mass culture of Earth," she said. "Undine has tried one experiment, and it's a miserable failure. We trust that someday, others will try the opposite approach."

"A future like that is beyond our power to bring about, of course," Greg said, hauling in the boat's anchor. "But we're collecting data in the hope that we can pass it on. We consider ourselves stewards of that knowledge, and we take steps to ensure that even if we're wiped out by the authorities here, it won't be lost."

Jesse drew breath. He had not realized that the goal was so far-reaching. A world where illness was truly abolished—not by policing people, not by herding them into the care of professionals and manipulating their bodies, but by teaching them to use their own minds. . . . He would not, of course, want to be personally involved in the telepathic side of it. But after all, it would take centuries to come to fruition. Such a colony would start small, like all colonies, and would have to remain isolated. Those who established it would never see the culmination of their hopes.

Just as the Group here on Undine would never see even the beginning. And yet somehow, imagining such a goal *felt* right. He was thoughtful as they headed back across the bay toward the Lodge, and at first did not notice the sound of an approaching plane.

"That's not one of ours," Greg remarked. "Not unless somebody's put more money into extra power than shaving half an hour off the flight warrants."

Then, as the plane swooped low over them and touched down only a short way ahead, Kira rose up, reaching for the scuba masks and shoving them hastily under the seat. "Dear God," she said, "it's an air ambulance. The police."

23

"JESSE," KIRA WENT on urgently, "can you swim a little way without fins?"

"Yes, but—"

"Get into the water, now! Michelle, you too—he hasn't enough experience to swim alone, and anyway it wouldn't look natural. Angle over to the swimming cove and mix with the people there."

"But why?" Michelle protested, as Greg cut power and the boat slowed. "Jesse's not wanted by the Hospital anymore, is he?"

"No, I don't think so. But Peter left strict orders that his presence here must not be known to any outsider. I don't think the police will note who's at the Lodge; they never have before. Still, we mustn't take the chance."

Jesse went over the side and held onto the gunwale. "Do they come often?" he inquired in dismay.

"The health inspectors show up unannounced about twice a year, but it's nowhere near time for them. They were here only a few shifts back, and found no violations; we keep all the contraband food downstairs. I don't know what's up, but I'm in charge and I should get to the dock before they collar someone else. So go—and stay on the swimming beach until I send for you."

He obeyed and struck out toward the shore, Michelle beside him. Swimming in the open bay without fins took all his attention; his stroke still wasn't efficient and he soon tired. After what seemed a long time, they reached the rocks and climbed onto them. Half a dozen others were lounging there. "You've become a swimming addict, Jesse," Dorcas laughed, "if you can't even wait for the boat to dock to get here."

"It's no joking matter," Michelle told him. "The police are at the Lodge, and Kira said they mustn't see him."

Instantly the group sobered. "The police? Why?" demanded Erik.

"I wish I knew," Jesse declared. "I was legally discharged from the Hospital, or so I thought. I haven't had a chance to commit any crimes since." Unless, he thought grimly, being an accessory to murder counted—but they had no way of knowing he was involved in that, had they? He realized suddenly that no one else now at the Lodge had been; all those people were back in the city. Had someone been caught and forced to give names? Oh, God, could they have gotten *Carla's* name?

That was a much more frightening thought than the possibility that they knew his. If Carla were to be arrested, they might find out about her hacking activities. It was hard to believe that having merely witnessed a burial could be proven, much less severely punished. But hacking—a lot of hacking, over a long period of time . . . That was a serious crime on most worlds. He had been uneasy ever since he'd learned that Carla regularly engaged in it. She was, he'd been told, only one of several hackers in the Group; others did what needed to be done while she was away from the city, since the Lodge didn't have Net access and it would be too risky in any case to log on remotely. Nevertheless, she was the most active of them, and she knew many secrets that the Hospital would no doubt try to extract. . . .

Greg had said that if anyone but Peter examined her after an arrest, she'd be given truth serum. That might be true even if she was accused only as an accessory to murder. They would want to learn the source of the body. Was it certain that Peter would be permitted to deal with his employee, as long as she wasn't considered his friend? Or was that a mere hope, based on the fact that neither he nor Carla could be replaced?

Not for the first time, Jesse wondered how the Group dared to take such risks. Did they expect to operate indefinitely without a slip somewhere?

Perhaps the slip had already occurred. *Something* had happened. Kira had made plain that the arrival of the police was not normal. They were evidently conducting some sort of investigation. Though the dock was not visible from this beach, he would see the plane take off—and yet she'd said to remain here not just until it went, but until she sent word.

Time passed. Jesse, in turmoil, tried to talk casually with the others; but they were all on edge, all apparently as much in the dark as he. They were wet and, as the sun dropped lower, shivering. Finally Michelle said, "The rest of us weren't told to hide, and none of us here today except Kira are involved in anything that requires concealing our friendship with Peter. It would look strange to stay here so long after getting out of the water. We've got to go back to the cottages, if not the Lodge itself."

"Why didn't Kira keep out of sight?" Jesse asked. "If she manages the healing house and hospices in the city—"

"Kira has been in the Group since long before any hospice work or hacking was started," said Dorcas, "and her friendship with Ian is common knowledge. So of course it's known that Peter is her friend, too. That's one reason they put her in charge of the Lodge when they're away; she has no anonymity to lose. If she were ever caught and given truth serum, we'd all go down. But the Meds aren't likely to suspect someone over a hundred years old of being involved in crime."

One by one the others gathered their things and left the beach. Alone, Jesse felt himself getting more and more agitated, and his nerves weren't helped by the arrival of a second plane, identical to the first. He longed to *do* something, anything rather than simply wonder. The afternoon dragged on.

At last, when it was near sunset, Greg appeared. "Thank God," Jesse greeted him. "I was beginning to think they had you all in handcuffs."

"They paid no attention to us," Greg said. "But they did arrest Valerie."

"But why? What had she done?" Jesse wasn't well acquainted with Valerie, a young, mousy woman who seemed the least like a potential activist of anyone he'd met.

"I don't know," Greg said. "I'm not sure they even told Kira. The ambulance officers will be leaving in a minute, but they locked her in their plane while they inspected the whole Lodge again, and the cottages, too."

"Is there anything around for them to find?" Jesse asked. "I mean, even if they got downstairs, they wouldn't discover—"

"Oh, no, not the door to the lab. There's not a chance they'd see that; all the food in the freezer is legal and they'd merely glance at it. You'd be safe if you could get down there, but you'd be seen trying to reach the elevator. The workmen from the second plane are apparently going to stay a while; they brought in boxes of stuff."

"Stuff? What sort of stuff?"

"I have no idea. Kira couldn't talk to me privately," Greg went on, "but telepathically, she made me aware of what you're to do."

Telepathy again . . . even for specific instructions? No doubt, Jesse thought, he would have to get used to the idea, uncomfortable though it was. "So, am I going to be on this beach all night?"

"You may have to stay away longer—but not here. Did you climb the hill above the Lodge last week? Peter usually takes guests there."

"Yes, the place with the view," Jesse replied. "I guess I can find it again—the trail was well worn."

"Okay, you're to wait there until someone comes for you. That might not be until tomorrow. I've brought your clothes and something to eat." Greg produced a small duffle bag of the sort used to hold beach towels. "Don't open it until you're far out of sight. It's your Fleet uniform, which fortunately I found in the bunkroom you've been using when I went to get you something to wear. If they found *that*, they'd know for sure that you're staying here, and they'd remember."

"I take it they haven't asked for me by name."

"Not as far as I know." Greg gripped his hand, and smiled. "Cheer up, Jesse! None of us believe they're going to arrest you—Kira's just following her instructions to keep your presence here secret. Peter may be thinking that since he was the doctor who discharged you from the Hospital, for you to be seen among his friends might lead his colleagues to ask questions. He's not admired by them, you know, especially not by his boss, the head of the Psych department. The man's an ass, and he's always accusing Peter of being too quick to release the patients under his care."

That made sense. Peter's early discharge of a patient he knew socially might indeed look suspicious. For him to be seen here could put them both at risk. He might be picked up and sent back to the substance abuse unit . . . and worse, Peter's cover would be jeopardized. Jesse headed for the trail, chagrined that he had not figured this out sooner and determined to stay well hidden.

But there remained the question of what the police were doing here, why they'd arrested Valerie and what sort of "stuff" they were now foisting on the occupants of a peaceful private retreat. Surveillance equipment? This seemed the sort of world on which it would be employed if they had any reason for suspicion. He would have to leave the Lodge permanently if there was a camera. And, Jesse realized, he did not like that thought at all.

When he was well into the woods, jogging not only for speed but to work off the chill, he got out of his wet swim trunks and put on the clothes Greg had brought. The familiar Fleet uniform was welcome for its warmth and the protection it offered against the branches intruding on the narrow trail—and yet it no longer seemed his own. For twenty years he had worn it, or variations of it, and had considered it part of his identity. Now in less than ten days he had become a different person. The change frightened him a little, not the danger into which he'd fallen but the strangeness of the powers the Group seemed to think he might develop. Nevertheless, he *had* changed. It would do no good to worry, for he did not doubt that belonging to the Group was worth whatever might be asked of him.

At the top of the hill he sat and watched the sun sink into the sea. He could see the roof of the Lodge from here. Strange, he hadn't noticed that satellite dish when he'd come here before . . . no, not strange! It hadn't been there before. The Lodge had had neither Net nor phone service, which, people had assured him, wasn't missed when the whole idea of the place was to isolate themselves from the world outside. Why would Peter suddenly go to the expense of installing it?

He wouldn't. The authorities had evidently just done so. What was it Carla had said, there was no medical telemetry from outlying islands because they had no satellite uplinks? This one did now, and it was the answer to a lot of things. For some reason, the police had had a warrant for Valerie, and they had found her. In the process, they had discovered that there were too many people at the Lodge to be without health oversight. As soon as they'd radioed that information, the second plane had brought men to work overtime outfitting the place with retinal scanners and high-tech toilets.

The next morning, after a rough night sleeping on the ground with nothing to eat but the chocolate he found in the duffle bag, he saw the official plane take off, followed shortly by one of the Group members' smaller ones. Soon thereafter Erik and Dorcas appeared carrying breakfast, which they shared with him before all three hiked down the trail. Greg, they said, had gone back to the city early to inform Peter; personal phones now worked, but it wouldn't be safe to discuss yesterday's developments on the phone.

"I hate to tell you, Jesse," Erik said as they approached the Lodge, "but you can't use the bathrooms anymore, except for the one downstairs."

"I suppose not. My DNA is on record and Carla can't hack a steady stream of data from the Island, day and night. I guess when I'm not down where the lab is, I'll have to keep on visiting the woods."

24

KIRA CALLED THEM all together at lunch, speaking seriously and sternly. "Valerie meant no harm," she said, "but she behaved foolishly. She failed to answer the summons for her mandatory health checkup, even after the second notice. She's fairly new to the Group and perhaps she didn't realize that by inviting arrest and calling attention to herself, she might put us all in danger. But everybody needs to be clear about this: we do *not* openly disobey the health laws. We circumvent them when we can, when there's small chance of being caught, but we can't afford to do so merely out of defiance. Only to help the sick or dying do we put ourselves at risk."

"What will happen to Valerie?" Jesse asked.

"She'll be fined, and she'll get the exam, of course—probably an intensive one like yours, because they assume that anyone who evades a checkup must be hiding symptoms. We hope she'll be in the Hospital only a few days, but—" Kira frowned. "In her case there's a chance she may be kept longer because of her past history. I can't tell you more than that; it would violate medical confidentiality. But Peter may have to take action, which is another reason why her recklessness has hurt us."

Jesse scowled. By nature he wasn't hot-tempered and he had never been inclined to resist authority, but he'd never before been in a situation where there was much to rebel against. The more he saw of this world's government, the more he felt like telling it to go to hell . . . and yet it was clear why they couldn't do that.

"Another thing," Kira went on, "who left chocolate in the upstairs pantry? If I hadn't come across it and sent it to Jesse, it might have been discovered—and that would have been more than a health violation. It would have been proof of smuggling."

"I think it must have been Valerie," Michelle said.

"She's not used to the Lodge, and she was in charge of cleanup after dinner the night we brought it up for dessert."

Was importing chocolate the equivalent of drug smuggling here? Jesse wondered. Had he eaten a small fortune last night, munching whole bars of it out of hunger?

That afternoon Kira took him to the lab again. "I'll be teaching you a new mind-pattern today," she said once the sensors were in place and she was settled in her chair. "While you're watching the feedback, I'll talk. Just focus on what I'm saying and leave matching to your unconscious mind."

The visual patterns of the feedback, now that no dimension for intensity of stimulus was involved, were multicolored and of great complexity. They were hypnotic. Kira had told him that though actual hypnosis was one of the states into which he could be led, that particular mind-pattern would—for obvious reasons—not appear while they were working on dual. Nevertheless the huge wall-filling display drew him in, making him giddy and sometimes slightly nauseous.

Jesse was still uneasy at the thought of going into altered states of consciousness. It didn't seem to have happened to him yet, unless you counted the state of not minding pain, and he couldn't help wondering what it was going to feel like. Still, all the others, even Carla, had apparently experienced such states repeatedly—not to mention Kira herself, who despite old age seemed to consider it routine. He hoped she wasn't sensing his apprehension. Resolutely, he focused on the feedback pattern, determined not to shrink from whatever was about to happen to him.

"Oh dear," Kira said, all too aware of his nervousness. "I'd not stopped to think what you must have seen in spacers' hangouts during shore leaves. There are many kinds of altered states, Jesse. Those useful to us aren't as disruptive as the ones you're worrying about."

"Not like tripping out, then?"

"At this stage, no. Later, we'll teach you to deal with

that sort of thing as a protection, in case you experience it spontaneously, and in the future you might choose to seek mystical illumination. But basically, an altered state of consciousness is simply a state of mind in which your perceptions are altered. There's an infinite variety, counting the ways they overlap—our software filters them, so you see only the mind-patterns we're concerned with. There isn't anything deeply mysterious about such states, even undesirable ones. As I'm sure you know from past experience."

"Me? I never tried street drugs even as a kid," Jesse stated, not sure whether this was a situation in which you were supposed to say that, or one of those in which you'd hesitate to admit it.

"There's something you're not counting, isn't there, Jesse?"

It took a moment or two to grasp what she meant. Then, feeling stupid, he confessed, "Well, I did get drunk sometimes." Of course Peter would have told her; the reason for his detention on Undine was a matter of public record.

"On purpose. To alter your perception of reality."

"Yes. I don't think I'll ever want to again, Kira."

"Not with alcohol, not after we've shown you better ways. But the desire to alter perception is a universal human impulse, Jesse, and there's nothing wrong in it. There have been cultures that handled it relatively well. The modern culture of the Meds, which has dominated at least since the twentieth century, isn't one of them. It is schizophrenic— on one hand it promotes fulfillment of that impulse through a vast variety of potent medications prescribed for every conceivable instance of human dissatisfaction with life, and then it wonders why people turn to substances of their own choice in pursuit of the same goal."

"I never thought of it that way."

"Most people don't," Kira said. "Hypocritically, Med culture condemns people for the very error it has instilled in them from birth: the idea that controlling perception through chemistry is a good thing. And then it turns around and subjects them to still more drugging, which aims to correct that error while simultaneously reinforcing the same misconception."

"Well, but medical drugs are different—"

"From illegal ones? Good God, Jesse! You don't think legality has any real connection with the principle involved, do you? That's entirely a political matter, even on Earth. The public is led to make certain drugs a scapegoat while consuming many that are equally damaging—and even those can't be obtained by personal choice. The monopoly on drugs, including prescription drugs, is the means whereby the government-endorsed medical establishment maintains control over people where ostensibly, it lacks the direct police power it has obtained here."

Jesse frowned. "There's a line, though, isn't there, between mind-altering drugs and others?"

"All psychoactive medications produce altered states," Kira told him. "That's what they're for—antidepressants, for instance, alter the way people perceive the world. And many other medications affect the brain and thus produce unintended cognitive 'side' effects. Mind-altering drugs aren't limited to those that interfere with rationality."

"Is rationality what separate good states from the bad ones, then?"

"No. Some states that interfere with reasoning ability are aberrations—psychosis, for instance—but others, such as dreaming, are normal. And still others, if induced in the right way, have legitimate uses."

"Are you saying that even drastically altered states aren't harmful in themselves?" He should feel reassured by that, Jesse thought. He didn't. Moment by moment, his wish to avoid such states was growing. He longed to be away from the lab, out in the fresh air where he could think clearly, gain time....

"They can be. Some people's minds aren't stable enough to get out of such states; others are prone to violence. Peter takes care not to recruit anyone who's susceptible to the dangers."

No wonder the Group needed a professional psychiatrist—and Peter was good at the job, Jesse reminded himself. He could be trusted not to mess with people's minds in unsafe ways, couldn't he? "I don't see why entering such states this way isn't just as risky as doing it with drugs," he admitted.

"If you're thinking that neurofeedback technology like ours could cause harm in the hands of an incompetent instructor, or one with destructive aims, you're right," Kira agreed, "which is why we'd keep it hidden even if it weren't illegal. But as long as both participants have been proven qualified, it's not dangerous." As the shapes of her feedback swerved away from his, she went on, "The bad thing about drugs, apart from the damage they do to the body, is not the states of consciousness they produce but the fact that they force such states on people not equipped to handle them. And they deprive even capable users of volition until they wear off—that's where the hazards lie."

"And from what I've heard, bad trips can recur without taking more of the stuff," Jesse said, striving to keep part of his attention on the display.

"Yes—which goes to show that the mind itself is what produces states of consciousness; drugs merely open the door. So if you can control your mind, you can get in and out of various states by volition alone. Shamans have been doing it for millennia, but for us it's easier because of the feedback."

"I don't see how just making patterns with my brain can do that," Jesse declared.

"The visual patterns are only symbols, remember—just as the metaphors used in traditional spiritual practices are symbols. We associate them with the way our brains are operating. The actual instruction comes from the teacher's unconscious mind to the student's."

The two feedback patterns before him now matched,

Jesse saw. He felt strange, as if he were hearing Kira's voice from far away, but it wasn't an unpleasant feeling. He was very calm, breathing slowly and deeply, and the nameless terror he'd felt had abruptly vanished. "How soon will I get into a new state of consciousness?" he asked.

"You're in such a state right now," Kira told him. "I'll prove it to you—but keep watching your pattern, don't let it diverge from mine." She called out, "Michelle, put the heart monitor on-screen, please."

He had wondered why they continued to use the heart monitor when he wasn't being stressed by pain. Now, below the matched mind-patterns, its characteristic graph appeared. The rhythm of the beats was regular, the way he'd seen them in countless vid dramas. He tried not to think of the dramas in which heart rates flatlined.

"We don't use this particular technique with anyone who has heart problems," Kira said. "Peter has access to the Hospital's files. We know you're okay, since you've just had a very thorough physical exam."

Well, Jesse thought, at least something useful had come of it. And then he thought, did Peter subject me to that exam because he planned to recruit me? But how could he have known he wanted to before I'd spoken more than a few words to Carla?

"Your attention's wandering," Kira said. "Focus on your brain feedback; keep it steady."

Jesse complied. "Now," Kira went on, "speed your heart up. Imagine that you're running, racing perhaps, and your pulse rate's going up—"

Unbelievably, it worked. He could see the spikes of the rhythm contract.

"Now slow down," said Kira. "Stop running, rest. Relax and let your heart beat slowly, more slowly . . . but not too slow. Don't slow it any more."

"This is unreal," Jesse murmured. "People can't control their hearts just by thinking about it."

"Yes, they can. Yogis have controlled their hearts, and

more, for centuries. But it took them time and effort to learn. You do it instantly right now because, through matching mind-patterns, you're already in the appropriate state of consciousness."

"But surely I can't keep on doing it. Not without watching the feedback."

"Eventually you can, after you've had more practice." Kira frowned. "Normally we don't introduce heart rate control this soon in the training. Peter was very specific; he said you were to learn it immediately, that we were to focus on it before anything else and get it out of the way. He didn't tell me why. When I protested that it might be too stressful for a beginner, he assured me that you're up to it. But I think one reason he chose me as your instructor was my knowledge of cardiology—just in case anything were to go wrong."

Is this a game? Jesse thought, seeing his heart rate accelerate again as a chill spread through him. Is she trying to shake me up, or is she really worried?

"I'm sorry," Kira said quickly. "It's not a game; I spoke thoughtlessly. Still, sooner or later you have to face the fact that it's scary to have control over your own heart. Peter's decisions are usually wise and never unwarranted. If he chooses not to tell me what's back of this one, I'm sure he has due cause."

Deliberately, Jesse gave his attention to the visual patterns, reminding himself that it was okay to fear his control might slip, that instead of fighting that he must let it happen . . . and on the monitor, he watched his heart slow and then stabilize.

"You're getting the hang of it," Kira said reassuringly. "In time, you'll learn to control more kinds of stress responses, and you'll learn to get into states of consciousness without external assistance."

"And this will protect my health?" It seemed too simple to be true.

"Ultimately, yes, after it becomes unconscious. Of course

it won't work if you just do it once in awhile. You have to train yourself to react this way, instead of the instinctive way, automatically—when you're actually under stress. Not just major stress, but ordinary ongoing worries and frustrations. That's the hard part."

It would be, Jesse realized. But it was why they all seemed so carefree, despite all the real worries they faced. He was not sure he could ever reach that stage. On second thought, it was not at all simple. He didn't see how to even begin.

Wanting to change the subject, he said slowly, "If psychoactive drugs produce altered states, then the ones they use in the Hospital . . . on people who commit serious crimes, I mean . . . wouldn't our training enable us to overcome the effects?"

Kira shook her head. Soberly she told him, "It might, to start with, but that's one experiment the Group's not going to try, any more than we're going to kill ourselves to find out if there's an afterlife. Those drugs cause physical damage to the brain, just as electroshock and psychosurgery do. They've never been given to one of us, so we don't really know how long a trained mind would retain control—volition depends on the brain, after all, even though it's not physical in itself."

"Not *physical*?" Puzzled, Jesse questioned, "What is it, then?"

"You may as well ask what telepathy is," Kira told him, "and we don't have an answer; we only know what we can do with it. Though in some traditions, healing and other forms of psi have been attributed to energy vibrations of some sort, that's simply one of the metaphors—one we don't use, because we don't encourage the notion that anything physical is involved." She got out of her chair and detached the sensors from his body. "Enough training for today. Now go out and run, or something, to clear your head."

25

JESSE INDEED FELT a need to exercise after the training sessions. Running on the beach at low tide, as well as the swimming he'd begun to enjoy, was a welcome diversion from the things going on in his mind. He had also, belatedly, realized that the work of maintaining the Lodge was shared on an informal basis. No one had asked him to pitch in, but floors didn't sweep themselves, nor did fuel appear magically for the fireplace. So now, after a short run, he set to work replenishing the woodpile, finding it pleasantly exhausting to swing the axe.

That night he woke in the dark with a backache nearly killing him. Oh hell, Jesse thought, is this going to start again? He'd had it on shipboard a few times for no apparent reason. Fleet medics had examined him and found nothing wrong. It came on suddenly and then, over several days, gradually diminished. This time, he supposed, he'd thrown his back out chopping wood, though it was odd he hadn't felt it happen. The pain was worse than usual. He did not get back to sleep.

In the morning he dragged himself to breakfast, unable to stand erect but determined not to let the agony show. People looked at him, then carefully looked away. "What's wrong, Jesse?" Kira asked, showing less sympathy than he expected.

He told her, feeling somewhat sheepish. Everyone in the Group was healthy, after all—nobody ever displayed the slightest sign of disability. And knowing what he now knew, he could not even say it was because they were all so young!

"Rest today," Kira told him. "We don't have to go to the lab."

All morning he lay on the beach in the sun, wondering why his joy in the place had evaporated. It wasn't that he wanted to be elsewhere. He didn't even feel restless, as he had the three days before. But his uneasiness had grown.

His back continued to ache fiercely. He didn't bother to move when the others went up for lunch. Then clouds formed, the first he'd seen on the Island, and before long a drenching rain forced him indoors.

By evening, he could scarcely walk. He settled on the cushions near the fireplace and Dorcas brought him a plate. She didn't seem very concerned about him, nor did the others. It was unlike them, Jesse thought—there was usually so much empathy within the Group. Now they were withdrawn, seeming, almost, to be deliberately avoiding eye contact, though their conversation was friendly enough. Had his dark mood put them off, or did they simply scorn human frailty? His back hurt more than ever, but he'd be damned if he was going to mention it to anyone.

Finally, after several hours, Michelle spoke up. "For God's sake, Kira," she said. "Put Jesse out of his misery! If he hasn't caught on by now, he never will."

Everybody brightened, their warmth suddenly restored. He'd indeed never catch on, Jesse thought—not to the thinking of these people; the surprises in their reactions were unending. "What have I done wrong?" he asked humbly.

"It's what you haven't done," Greg told him. "Jesse, think! You have been going around all day in so much pain that we're worn out from sensing it. And we've been wondering why. We've been waiting to see how long it would take you to put two and two together."

"I don't see—" he began, and then it hit him. A backache was no different from induced pain. He had been resisting, hoping it would go away, despite the vivid lesson he been given in how to alter perception. *Let go!* he told himself. *Let it hurt! It doesn't matter. . . .*

The ache lessened, became bearable. After a while he found he could enjoy the music. When the evening was almost over Kira moved to his side. "How are you feeling?" she asked.

"Better, thanks. Much better. I think I'll be able to sleep."

"Better? Jesse, it's not supposed to be merely 'better.'"

You are not supposed to suffer from pain *at all,* ever again. Did you think what Peter taught you was just for the lab, with no practical use?"

"You mean what I did during the breakthrough, when I literally didn't mind it? Over a long period like all day?"

"Of course. Your brain can work the same whether you see feedback or not, after all." She smiled. "We know perfectly well that you aren't yet experienced enough to do it on your own. But you need to start trying to. That's why we didn't ease it for you as we would have for an outsider. Come downstairs now, and I'll help you."

In the lab, Kira went on dual with him again, sharing his natural pain—which she claimed to literally feel, telepathically—to form the feedback pattern. He found he could match with it quickly. He didn't get high, but the pain no longer bothered him. It was just there, in the way mild heat or cold might be there.

"The relief won't last," Kira warned. "You'll have to keep reminding yourself, visualizing the pattern, over and over. In time, you'll learn to do it without thinking. After that you'll have to rely on common sense to tell you when an injury needs treatment."

"Kira—why was I so blind? How could I go through a night and a day suffering pointlessly, after I'd once learned?"

"There are good reasons," she said. "Since the question's come up, I'll tell you, though you may not be ready to hear."

They went back upstairs and out across the porch of the Lodge onto the damp beach. The heavy clouds had blown past, but mist dimmed the stars.

Kira said, "Usually we don't have this conversation until a person's been with us longer. But Peter said to push you. Frankly, I don't know what's going on with Peter. He says he's moving fast with you because he wants to learn the reactions of an offworlder. That's nonsense. Human reactions are the same except where cultures differ radically, yet the culture of Fleet is much like Undine's, and you haven't been exposed to the telepathic undercurrents on

Earth for twenty years. So it's not a valid experiment. Even if it were, Peter would never exploit a trainee! It would be contrary to his basic ethic."

"I don't think I'm being exploited," Jesse said. "I agreed to accelerated training. I want to get on with it."

"Perhaps," Kira said. "But he closes his mind to me in a way that's not like him. He's seemed troubled for some time now, since the week before you arrived. Maybe it's just that he's preoccupied with grief for Ian, and with worry about what's to come when Ian is gone."

"I guess it will be hard on the Group to lose the leader," Jesse said.

"Hard for all of us, and not only because we love him. But especially for Peter, who will have to take his place."

Jesse had not realized this. But of course, it was obvious. There could be no doubt about Peter's qualifications to lead. "What exactly does the head of the Council do?" he asked. "Aside from presiding at ceremonies like the ritual Michelle mentioned?"

"Presiding at the Ritual is a bigger responsibility than you know," Kira said, "but that's not the problem. No new leader can be what Ian has been to us. Peter cannot fill his shoes. There will never be another like Ian; he is psychically gifted beyond any but the greatest spiritual leaders who ever lived on Earth. If he were not, there would be no Group, no hope of achieving our goal on even a small scale."

"And the goal depends on these—gifts? Not just the system he developed?" Jesse had been told that the neurofeedback lab had been established by Ian and that it employed technology so far unknown in the world outside.

"The training we give our people depends on telepathic aid to a much greater extent than you've seen so far," Kira explained. "And that's okay. We're here to provide it. But in the beginning there was no one but Ian. He developed the mind skills we rely on, personally on his own, and was able to pass them on only through paranormal talent that far exceeds what any of the rest of us can hope to attain. He is literally ahead of his time, perhaps by centuries."

Jesse tensed, shifting his weight and feeling his back start to ache again. The constant references to telepathy continued to make him uneasy.

Kira sighed. "Anyway, you asked why it didn't occur to you that you could get rid of your pain. To begin with, it's a matter of habit. When you feel pain, all your past experience tells you it's unpleasant. You don't question that. Your brain keeps on functioning the same way it has since you were born. But there are deeper reasons why you let yourself suffer, why you have a backache in the first place. It's not from chopping wood. Jesse, unconsciously you *want* to suffer—not for some perverted, unhealthy reason, but because that is a normal response to certain kinds of stress. It takes your mind off things you'd rather not be aware of."

"Oh, I don't think so, Kira—"

"Of course you don't. By definition, unconscious choices of this kind are not accessible to your thinking mind. But they are part of being human. Everyone is subject to them sometimes, at some point in life. You have been placed under extreme stress—and the stress is going to get worse, which you know underneath but would just as soon not contemplate."

Jesse was silent. This was, of course, true.

"As we were saying two days ago, most illness is caused by stress," Kira went on. "Not stress like what you went through during testing. You're okay with that. Humans are genetically equipped to deal with crises. But ongoing stress, stress that comes from what's going on in your mind, is another matter. Instinctively, you respond biochemically when you're stressed, and that affects your heart, your nervous system, your immune system—even your muscles—in ways that would enable you to act fast if you were in danger. It's often said that these responses damage the body because they last longer than nature intended, but there's more to it. The results of prolonging them are psychologically useful."

"That doesn't make sense! Are you saying people get sick on purpose?"

"Yes, though the purpose is unconscious, of course. When this was first understood, it was viewed by some as if it were a fault that victims of sickness should be blamed for, and because that was so wrongheaded, most refused to believe any purpose exists. But it's a constructive one buried deep in our biological inheritance. A tired, stressed-out caveman didn't fare too well fighting predators; if he got sick, not sick enough to kill him but enough to keep him home from the hunt, his genes were more likely to be passed on. That genetic programming still affects us, though today's stresses are different and they no longer have any impact on evolution."

Peter, too, had said something about evolution, Jesse recalled. He'd said it was time for humankind to grow up. . . .

"We're learning to overcome our programming. But— here's the hard part—unavoidably, the very process through which we teach you to handle stress creates *more* stress. In the first place many of the skills you need can't be learned except in crisis situations. And in the second place, those skills in themselves add another very severe stressor on top of what's required to awaken them—which you're now beginning to feel, and which your unconscious mind will resist."

"Catch-22, you mean."

"Not quite that bad. You'll get through this stage. But for now, you're lucky you don't have something worse than a backache."

That was hardly a comforting thought. Developing skills to protect his health seemed like a great idea, and yet somehow . . . he was not sure, Jesse realized, that he really wanted to become Superman.

"That's just it," Kira said seriously. "You *don't* want to be Superman. Nobody does! For starters, people don't want conscious control over their bodies—it's too much responsibility to carry. Just as kids want the safety of home and parents, no matter how much they may think they long to escape, adults want someone to rely on for care. In modern society, that means medical care. It's the reason people give control of their lives to the Meds. You've seen where that leads, but it's not easy to accept the alternative."

No. All your life, you assumed that your body would function, your heart would go on beating, without any conscious attention. That you didn't have to worry about managing such things because they were totally beyond your control. Knowing that you *could* control them would involve loss as well as gain. . . .

Kira reached out for his hand and squeezed it. "To rely on your own mind, even in defiance of built-in responses like pain that nature supplied to protect you—that's very, very scary, Jesse. The sooner you admit that to yourself, the better off you'll be."

Slowly, thoughtfully, Jesse said, "I didn't want to turn off natural pain. I didn't want so much power as that; I couldn't trust myself with it."

"That's why we had to use artificially-induced pain— severe pain—to teach it to you. Given a choice between using that power and suffering mildly, your unconscious mind would have backed off from it—as today, in fact, it did."

He did not intend to back off. He'd accepted a challenge, and he was going to see it through. Even though he felt shaky inside and wasn't at all sure, underneath, that he still wanted to. . . .

Now wasn't the time to think about that, Jesse decided. Tomorrow was the start of a new offshift, and Carla would be coming back to the Island.

26

TONIGHT I'LL BE with Carla, Jesse thought, waking free of back pain to a sky clear of clouds. All his friends except Kira had gone; by lunchtime new planes were coming in.

He was kept busy meeting yet another new set of people, hoping with each arrival to see her among them. Finally, from the Lodge porch, he saw Anne's red seaplane circle, and went down to the dock to watch it land.

Carla was the only passenger. He ran to her and she embraced him, her smile joyous. But to his dismay it was a sisterly embrace, the hug customary among all Group members. When he moved to kiss her she clung for a moment—then dropped her arms and stepped back. "No," she said gently. "It's too soon."

"Too soon, Carla? No, it's not. I love you, you know that! Don't you?"

"Yes!" she said. "I love you too, Jesse. If you hadn't joined the Group, I don't think I could have borne it. But for now—wait. Don't expect more than what we had last week. Please."

"But why?"

"Because I ask you to. Because it's best, and I can't give a reason."

They walked back along the dock in silence, their footsteps loud on the wooden planks. Carla gripped his hand, but would allow him to come no closer. Bewildered, he had no choice but to let it ride.

And that was the way it was for the entire five days of her offshift.

Carla was vibrant, fun—to be beside her remained a joy to him. They were apart only during his sessions with Kira, although never, he noticed, alone. With the others, they swam and hiked and lounged on the beach. They ate together; they sat together before the fire. There was warmth and affection and an emotional closeness even greater than he'd known with her before. And there were undercurrents of desire. But nothing more. Not even, as the days passed, the mere friendly kind of touching with which they'd begun.

God, Jesse thought, was there some obscure colonial custom no one had told him about? Was he supposed to ask her to marry him first? Marriage was rarely mentioned in the Group and, he'd assumed, not viewed as essential. If Carla wanted marriage, though, he'd be more than willing to go through the formalities. He had already decided he wasn't going back to Fleet.

But you couldn't propose marriage to a woman you'd never even kissed.

Peter, Jesse recalled, had foreseen that there might be a problem. But Peter didn't come to the Island; he was spending the offshift with Ian. So Jesse couldn't consult him. The last day ran out with nothing changed, and before he knew it, Carla was gone.

The next five days without her passed slowly. He continued training with Kira, gaining control not merely of his heart rate but his blood pressure and, she claimed, his biochemical responses to stress. "Yes, the mind can do that," she told him. "It's long been known that under hypnosis, people can have biochemical reactions unlike those of their normal state. That's true of multiple personalities, too— sometimes each personality has different medical disorders. So there's no doubt that the unconscious mind controls biochemistry, and what your mind can do, you can learn to do intentionally."

In addition to working with Kira he was required to spend time matching prerecorded mind-patterns, alone except for a computer operator in the control booth. This included sessions under mild stimulus; he must learn, Kira said, to manage pain without assistance. Surprisingly, it wasn't hard. He went quickly into the state where pain didn't bother him, and came close, in so doing, to getting high. It was a great feeling. He knew that once he could do it without feedback, he would be free of physical pain for the rest of his life.

And yet, quite apart from his worry over the way Carla had acted, inexplicable anxiety nagged at Jesse. The training troubled him more and more. Some sessions elated him, yet when the near-high wore off, he didn't feel good about them. He was, in fact, feeling less good than in the beginning about everything, despite his liking for an increasing number of friends. He supposed this was due to stress, produced not only by Carla's rejection of intimacy, but by the buried fears of which Kira had warned him. But there seemed to be something else, just below the surface . . . something that was not quite right.

He was glad when Peter arrived before Carla returned. Somehow, Jesse thought, he'd gotten off on the wrong foot with Carla. It had been made plain that a relationship between them would have the Group's approval. Her desire for it had been unmistakable. So what unspoken rule had he violated? He was ready to seek the advice Peter had offered.

Jesse approached him after dinner, finding that he needed no words to convey that he wanted to talk privately. They went out into the dusk and walked along the beach. "You're doing great, according to Kira," Peter said.

"With the training, yes, I guess so. It—bothers me sometimes."

"That's okay, Jess. New ways of using your mind are bound to throw you off balance, but you are making progress. I hear you can manage pain by yourself, now."

"I'm not quite comfortable getting elated by those sessions," Jesse confessed. "Isn't it akin to masochism?" He had not known he was going to say this, had not consciously thought about it, but realized as he spoke that it did concern him.

"No. Masochists get pleasure from suffering; you feel none till you are past it. You're elated by achieving full control with your mind."

"I'm—not sure there aren't sexual feelings attached to this."

Peter shook his head. "Not the unhealthy kind. Believe me, I know. I got as far as dual with a masochist once, through carelessness in checking him out beforehand. It was not an experience I'd care to repeat. Incidentally, he could not learn the new mind-pattern. He did not really want to."

"I'll take your word, but—damn it, Peter, there's something wrong."

Frowning, Peter asked, "You haven't been on dual with anyone but Kira, have you?"

"With Michelle, once. I was—in trouble, and she pulled me out."

"Oh, God. I should have warned her. She's not fully trained and she hasn't the background to predict misinterpretations."

"It wasn't her fault. I was overtired and she told me to quit, but I was stubborn. She came out of the control booth and went on dual, using the arm stimulators—"

"So then, I suppose, you got aroused without knowing why, which led to this line of speculation." Peter sighed. "It was a reasonable concern, but it happens to be off base. Given a choice, would you have played kinky games with Michelle or gone to bed?"

"I see your point." Jesse flushed with relieved embarrassment. He had indeed felt like taking Michelle to bed; if she'd been someone he'd met in a bar, before meeting Carla, he might have suggested it. And yet . . . it hadn't been like seeing a woman in a bar. There'd been something more, something disturbing, though at the time it had seemed as if it would be better than any encounter, ever.

Peter appraised him. "You're still troubled."

With a psychiatrist you couldn't hide anything. What the hell, with a psychiatrist of Peter's caliber, why should he try? "It's not just the masochism thing. I don't know what it is. My—reactions, maybe. To people I've only just met." He wet his lips.

"Yes," said Peter gravely. "Jess, you are going to have some confused feelings for a while. I can assure you they're nothing to worry about."

"I've never worried about things like this before."

"Don't start. Your reactions are normal. Among us relationships are not quite like those in the society you're used to, that's all. They're more—intense. And where no serious commitment is intended, things happen more quickly."

Jesse stared at him, grasping, as he often did, more than had been said. "God, Peter, you know! It's not only when I'm on dual. It's all the time. When I first came here I felt like I'd known you people for years; now I'm starting to feel some sort of a current between us. Don't get me wrong, but even with you—"

He broke off, horrified. He had felt this with Peter when they got the high. He still felt it. He had not admitted it to himself until now.

"It's not what you think," Peter said. "You're not changing your orientation or anything like that. We do get people who're bi and don't know it, but you're not one of them. I have your psych record, and in any case I can usually sense it." Seeing the look on Jesse's face he added, "I'm not, my-self—bi, I mean. You'll be able to sense it too, in time."

"I always heard there's no way for an observer to tell."

"There are a great many things we sense that outsiders don't. We have more senses."

Jesse frowned. "You're talking about ESP," he concluded. "You and Kira read thoughts and project feelings. Are you saying all the others—"

"Yes. And to you, at first, those feelings may seem like sexual feelings, because they involve a closeness between people that comes only through sex in the culture familiar to you."

"But Peter, *I* don't have ESP."

"Yes, you do. Most people do, and I certainly wouldn't bring in anyone I couldn't establish a two-way rapport with. I can pick up your thoughts and project concepts to you; you know that."

"It takes ESP on my part for you to do that?"

"Certainly. Logic tells you it does, but you haven't wanted to recognize it."

Jesse pondered this. "I would not have trusted any of you as I did, if I had not sensed more than I knew I was sensing."

"That's right. Even though you weren't consciously aware of it, you judged us by ESP and found us trustworthy; otherwise you wouldn't have agreed to join us in the first place."

"You say I haven't wanted to recognize this—though I could have, from what you told me the first day. Why, Peter?"

"Because it is paranormal in your eyes and therefore frightening. As you lose that fear, you'll learn to develop the ability consciously. Even before that, though, you'll feel currents, because you're interacting with those of us in whom it's already developed."

Jesse tried to piece things together. "Then when we were on dual, when you communicated the skill to me by telepathy, I felt something I'm misinterpreting."

"Yes, but there was more to it than the skill, and more than trust. You and I have forged a strong emotional link because of what we went through together. With us it will have no sexual component. But in the case of potential sex partners a shared high, especially following stress, often does lead to bed. Such a link plus sexual attraction is better than either one alone."

"That's why you wanted me to work only with Kira?"

"Kira comes across as grandmotherly. You have enough to worry about without going on dual with an attractive woman like Michelle at this stage—she should have used her common sense." As an afterthought, Peter added, "On the other hand, Michelle doesn't know how you feel about Carla, so she may have assumed an offworlder would be lonely. She's no tease; I wouldn't have her on the staff if I couldn't trust her intentions."

"You're saying whatever might have happened would have been okay."

"If you had wanted it, yes. If it weren't for your love for Carla, it would have had advantages."

Jesse frowned. "I've never been one to move too fast, not with a woman I respected. This seems a bit like, well—"

"Casual sex? It's the exact opposite. There can be nothing casual in telepathic sharing; what you'll lose your taste for is sex with women who can't offer that. Sharing bodies but not minds is what you object to in quick encounters anyway, isn't it?"

"Yes." Jesse laughed. "Did you know that on some worlds now it's in to buy sex with androids? The idea always turned me off, and till now I didn't know why."

"I'd laugh too," Peter said, "if that were not a symptom of the trends we're fighting here. Perhaps you're not aware that medical science now accepts androids as aides in sex clinics. In my outpatient work at the Hospital, I'm expected to employ them."

"God, Peter. Do you?"

"You don't want to hear about the things I do in that place."

Though this was said lightly, Jesse perceived that something far more troubling than the use of androids lay behind it. Sorry to have stirred it up, he said quickly, "I still don't understand. The first few days at the Lodge, before I was brought in, there was no sex between any of you. Now you've said there's even more of it here than in the world outside."

"We did hold off on your account," Peter said, "as we always do with outsiders. It is—different, with us. You would have known there was more to it than what you're used to, and we couldn't have explained."

"Different? Sex itself?" Jesse had thought he was past being surprised, but some things, after all, were basic. . . .

"Physically, it may or may not be, depending on whether you've previously experimented with so-called mystical practices that sometimes led to spontaneous telepathy even in ancient times. But that's not what I mean. The real difference is what happens in the mind, Jess. You feel undercurrents between us when we're not engaged in sex; those are nothing to what you'll feel when we are. And that in turn is nothing to what you will feel during personal experience."

Jesse thought about it. "Is this what Carla has been hiding from me? Why she won't let me close?"

"Yes. It would be impossible for her to hide it if she allowed herself to become aroused to even the slightest degree. Since we live in the world outside, we do have to learn self-control in that respect. And when we bring guests to the Lodge, we sleep in bunkrooms; it makes things easier."

"I'm not a guest anymore."

"Don't press her, Jess. Follow Carla's lead; she'll have good reasons if she holds back, and you're not ready to understand them. But you mustn't misunderstand, either. If you get mixed signals, bear with it, okay?"

An appalling thought struck Jesse. He burst out, "I didn't misread her, did I? It isn't just what you say has been going on with everyone?"

"No, Jess! With you and Carla it's real! But among us, more happens in a long-term relationship than sex. The bond it creates makes things possible that could not happen otherwise. It's not all pleasure at first, and needless to say, Carla's not an experienced teacher. Besides that . . . the past will haunt her. She's a widow, you know, though there's no such legal status here."

"I didn't," said Jesse, wondering why Carla had never mentioned a former husband.

"She came to us young," Peter went on, "and married a fine man, one of our leaders, with whom she was deeply in love. For many years they were happy together. Then, five years ago, he died in very terrible circumstances. It's not my place to tell you about it; maybe she will someday, but I wouldn't advise you to ask her, because it's a painful subject. She has shown great courage in carrying on as well as she has. But she's never considered a new relationship until now, and for both of you it will be extremely demanding. You will have to make allowances, Jess, and perhaps take a kind of responsibility you can't yet imagine."

"I'll do whatever's best for Carla," Jesse declared.

"I know you will," Peter agreed. "If you had not assured

me that your interest in her is serious, I wouldn't have allowed her to come here last offshift, perhaps not for several weeks."

"Meaning that if I'm serious, I can wait even for a simple kiss?"

"Exactly. Absorb what you've heard so far. Before I leave for the city again, I'll tell you more."

But Peter was already telling more, telepathically, Jesse guessed. Or was what he'd now grasped merely his own double take on what had been said?

These people had paranormal powers to a far greater degree than he did, if in fact he possessed them at all. Carla expected a partner to have them. She would not be satisfied by ordinary sex; she would want mind-to-mind contact he did not offer. Would it be, for her, like making love with an android? Not quite that bad, yet there was a gulf between them after all, and he did not see how he could ever bridge it.

Michelle, evidently, had been willing to accept an amateur, had perhaps thought even to extend her instructor's role! Was that how most of them did it? It was not his way; he could not imagine himself doing that . . . yet he sure as hell was not going to practice at Carla's expense. And besides, it was all too true that he feared such powers. Fear and love were not a good mixture, not in bed, certainly. . . .

He wondered why Peter seemed so sure that in time, things would work out.

27

WHEN HE MET Carla at the dock the next morning, Jesse found himself shy and awkward. He looked at her with longing, torn between an impulse to abandon all restraint and kiss her, and a foreboding that the relationship he'd expected was never going to be possible. Throughout the day, as they took part in the usual relaxed routine of the Lodge, he reached out with his mind, hoping that by some miracle he'd be able to sense her thought as she had so often sensed his. He felt nothing. Even the easy companionship they'd had was gone.

Carla was obviously keeping herself under rigid control. He did not doubt that she wanted him as much as he wanted her. After awhile it occurred to him that she too was painfully frustrated, that he was failing her, hurting her, by not being what she must have hoped he'd become. Then too, she still suffered from a tragedy in her past, Peter had said. He wanted desperately to take her into his arms and comfort her, yet knew he could not. It was true enough that they couldn't embrace like mere friends anymore. It would have to be all or nothing now, and for the foreseeable future it was apparently going to be nothing.

Ironically, he no longer felt any conscious fear of the paranormal. If an ability to sense minds had made him trust the Group from the beginning, then it must be a good thing. If all of them possessed ESP, then how could he not want it for himself? Yet despite Peter's assurance that he had such abilities, he could find no trace of them within—not even enough to sense the currents he'd been feeling the past few weeks. The closeness he'd felt to new friends seemed to have lessened.

To Kira, as they came up from the lab one evening, he finally confessed this. "Is there any way I can learn to be . . . telepathic, like the rest of you?" he asked, without much hope. If there were a mind-pattern for that skill, it would surely have been offered before now.

"The first step is wanting to," Kira replied. "You have to really want it, Jesse—want to go further than receiving unconscious projections, as you do in lab training."

"Damn it, Kira, I do want it! I'll do anything you think will help," he declared. He found himself less embarrassed to admit worries to her than to Peter, and he'd come to rely on her wisdom in such matters.

Kira hesitated. "Your older sister was interested in the

paranormal, I've been told. Why didn't you share that interest? Why did you never investigate what was known about psi on Earth?"

"Because I thought all that stuff was nonsense," Jesse declared.

"No. Because you were afraid it was not nonsense."

He considered this. "Please don't take offense, but you're off base there. Before I met you people, I did not entertain the slightest suspicion that there could be anything in claims for the paranormal."

"Consciously, perhaps not. In a scientifically-oriented person like you, the suspicions are repressed far below the surface. There's nothing unhealthy in that; it's a valid form of self-protection. What's more, in terms of evolution it has been an adaptive response for the species. Our forebears could not have progressed to the stage of offworld colonization if people had been busy exploring their inner powers instead of the galaxy. But we are ready to move on, now."

"Things like that have been said for a long time," Jesse maintained. "I did hear enough from my sister to know that line's not new. It shows up in Earth's literature; you see it particularly in speculation of the late twentieth century. Humankind must turn to inner space, people argued. It didn't happen."

"We're lucky it didn't; if it had, we would not be here. There would be no colonized worlds and Earth itself would be a wasteland."

"You're saying it's a matter of evolution, then, not just chance." He had heard enough from her, and from others in the Group, to know they believed all trends in human civilization were part of a natural sequence, the only alternative to which was extinction.

"We hope and believe that we are forerunners," Kira declared. "Human civilization has gone as far as it's possible to go along the road that leads to the stasis vaults—which, if you'll pardon the pun, are a dead end. So we must strike out in a new direction, not only for preserving our health but for empowering our minds. And the two are re-lated. As we've told you before, our methods of training and of healing depend on telepathic communication."

"But if it's possible, if it leads to the good I've seen here, why aren't people everywhere doing it?" Jesse protested. "Sure, the Meds object for political reasons, even where. they're not as strong as they are in this colony. That can't account for the widespread disbelief among the public."

"No," Kira agreed. "The paranormal is not easily ac-cepted, Jesse." After a pause she went on, "I can tell you why, but you'll understand better if I show you. We've held back with you until now because unlike trainees with previ-ous interest in psi powers, you share your culture's attitude toward them. Are you willing to experience a form of com-munication more intense than what you've received uncon-sciously?"

He nodded, feeling cold, knowing that something over-whelming was about to happen to him, here in a Lodge that he loved, with people he cared about—people who cared for him, yet would not let him hide from fear. They went out onto the dark porch and sat on the steps. The breeze from the bay smelled faintly of salt, he noticed, though that was unusual; Undine's sea was far less salty than Earth's. He found himself picturing Earth more clearly than he had for years.

Kira's hand closed on his, then tightened. "Our ances-tors drew back from awareness of the paranormal," she said quietly, "but not because they foresaw that our species' sur-vival would depend on space colonization. They reacted just as you do, and for the same reason. Over and over, scien-tific evidence was presented for the existence of telepathy and other psi powers. By most people, especially other sci-entists, it was ignored, blocked out of consciousness—often angrily denied. Because if it exists, then everything famil-iar to you about your mind, your world, stands open to chal-lenge. There's nothing firm left to cling to. And if you have paranormal powers, who knows what you might do to disrupt the world, unwittingly, perhaps even unwillingly? Might you not lose control? Might your mind even disintegrate, perhaps? No sane person wants to confront that—"

"God, Kira, what are you doing to me?" It was plain what she was doing. She was giving him the concept telepathically as she spoke; she was not letting him off with mere words.

"If I gave you only words, you wouldn't take them seriously, any more than most people who've heard or read them in the past have taken them seriously. Any more than you took what was happening to you here seriously before Peter spelled it out for you. You still don't want to believe that it was *your mind* doing something so far removed from everyday reality."

That was true. He didn't want to! He wanted to be back in Fleet, back even on Earth, on the seacoast of his childhood—back home, where there wasn't any question about what minds might do.... I should never have gotten into this, Jesse thought despairingly. I can't do this. I'll lose control. . . .

Kira squeezed his hand tighter, but her voice was gentle. "Weren't you taught something early on about the fear of losing control?" she asked.

Jesse pulled himself back to firm ground. *It's not an arbitrary test,* Peter had said. *In order to gain true volitional control, you must be wholly, unreservedly willing to lose control—to let what comes, come, with full consent to the consequences.* He had passed the test. He'd been warned that the circumstances under which he had passed it were only a prelude to something that couldn't be taught in a lab setting. And he was damn well not going to let the consequences throw him.

"The first step is wanting paranormal abilities, but the second step is acknowledging your fear of them," Kira told him. "You started to acknowledge it a few days ago—but then you retreated, told yourself that you didn't need to be afraid because you don't have them after all. That's why you stopped sensing even the currents of thought between friends."

"But how could my fear be stronger than my love for Carla?" Jesse protested.

"I suspect Carla is closing her mind to you," Kira said, "just as Peter has closed his to me since he's been hiding something. She doesn't have to let you sense what's she's thinking unless she wants to, you know. Right now you're not ready to share her thoughts, yet she knows your sensitivity has been growing. So she can't feel as free with you as before."

"How can I move ahead, then?"

"We'll help you," Kira promised. "We have ways of doing that, well-established ways. But you must fully accept your fear in order to get beyond it."

It was all tied together, Jesse realized. Fear of altered states, of responsibility for controlling his body, of the paranormal . . . that was much more troubling than the fear of getting caught by the law. The Group's illegal activities seemed almost incidental to these inner issues. . . .

"Of course they are," said Kira, offering confirmation that he was indeed able to project thoughts. "Our healing and hospice work is a sideline. We fell into it because we couldn't stand by without helping those we had power to help. But it's not what we exist for. Our real work is here, among ourselves."

"Just learning to use our minds?"

"Proving that what we do is possible. That we're healthier and happier than people bound to the premises of Med culture—though health too is a side issue, since it's not at the top of our scale of values. The goal is to prove that the mind has more power than has previously been recognized. This is the key to the future, Jesse. The proving, not the work we do in the world outside."

"How can we hope to influence the world?" Jesse demanded. "Can what a few hundred of us do here really lead to the establishment of some future colony where everyone possesses advanced mind powers?"

Kira's face clouded. "Not in any way we can yet see," she admitted. "But they couldn't spread if nobody made a start."

28

PETER, WHO WAS spending his first offshift at the Lodge since the installation of the satellite uplink, seemed even more troubled by it than anyone had expected him to be. It was not so much that he was outraged by the invasion of Ian's private island—although he was, and said that Ian was, too—but that it appeared to worry him. Carla reported that he'd been preoccupied even at work. "I don't quite see why," she told Jesse. "It's a nuisance not to be able to use the upstairs bathrooms, but as long as those of us who can't reveal our friendship with Peter don't use them, we're safe. It's not as if they could learn any of our secrets just because medical telemetry can now be transmitted."

Jesse's blood turned icy as he recalled his initial speculation. "Carla—maybe he's afraid they planted bugs in the Lodge, too. Maybe they *did*. Have we done a sweep?"

"Oh, Jesse, things like that don't happen here. The government has no need for non-medical surveillance. It wouldn't occur to the Meds that there could be opposition apart from individual cases of people ignoring the health laws. They'd have to bug every house in the city if they wanted to find out who complains, and mere talk isn't illegal."

"Except what *we* talk about—smuggling, hospices, burying bodies—"

"If they had any suspicion about those things, they'd have arrested us by now. It wouldn't be hard to find evidence if they were looking for it."

True enough. That, Jesse thought, was what had bothered him all along. He was not sure whether the Group was foolhardy or naive, but he suspected the latter. Lacking experience with what happened on more heavily-populated worlds, its members viewed spy dramas as they viewed fantasy. Of course they hadn't done a bug sweep; they wouldn't know how. The equipment for sweeping probably didn't exist on Undine, and if it did, the process of acquiring it might create suspicion where none had existed.

Carla hesitated, then pointed out, "We wouldn't need electronic equipment to find a bug if there was one, you know. There are plenty among us who could locate it clairvoyantly. Peter certainly could."

"So then what's he worrying about?" Jesse questioned, trying to cover the dismay this new piece of information stirred in him.

The uplink itself bothered Peter more than the bathroom modifications, despite the fact that it provided phone and Net access that might be useful in emergencies. "I've been expecting it," he had admitted. "But I hoped it wouldn't happen quite so soon. All the outlying islands will be linked in before long, and I suppose we were put high on the list when the police noticed a lot of guests at the Lodge. That they authorized overtime work, though, and left a crew here all night—"

"That did seem strange," Kira had agreed. "Establishing medical telemetry for offshifters after years of letting it go is hardly a high-priority job."

"No. Which means they've pushed up the deadline for universal coverage. And once they have it—" Peter broke off, and would say no more on the subject.

He had earlier confirmed that hiding his friendship with former patients was a concern. Jesse was not the only person for whom he'd arranged release from the Hospital, though out of respect for their privacy he did not name the others. Valerie was evidently one of these people. Carla, who kept Peter's records, surely knew the whole story; but she wouldn't talk about it. She did, however, reveal what had happened after Valerie's arrest.

"We got her admitted to the surgical ward," she told Jesse. "If she'd been sent to the psych ward, Peter wouldn't have been allowed to handle her case, not when it was known she'd been staying at the Lodge. So it was important to make sure she was put under the care of some other doctor who's in the Group."

"How could she be sent to the surgical ward if she didn't need surgery?"

"I hacked the radiology report," Carla explained, "to make it look as if she had a uterine tumor."

"Didn't anyone look at the actual MRI scan?"

"Only Susan Gerrold, our gynecologist. They're stored in the database—no one else would have occasion to call up that file."

"But surgery—how could she fake that? There'd be a whole team present."

"She didn't fake it. The idea was to keep Valerie hospitalized long enough for the people on duty to forget that she hadn't reported for a checkup voluntarily."

"You mean she really cut her open?" protested Jesse, appalled.

"Yes, she performed a hysterectomy, since Valerie didn't want children anyway. Susan's a healer as well as a surgeon; Valerie wasn't in any danger, and of course, she knew how to manage postoperative pain. The recovery time was what they faked—Susan healed her internally the first time she examined her in private. But the incision was left to heal naturally, since it had to be seen by the nurses."

"I thought we were opposed on principle to unnecessary medical procedures."

"Sometimes we have to compromise," Carla said, "when it's a matter of preventing something worse."

Puzzled, Jesse persisted, "Would a psych evaluation have been worse than surgery for someone who'd done nothing illegal beyond trying to escape a medical checkup?"

"For Valerie, yes. She has reason to fear it, which is why she refused to respond to the Hospital summons in the first place."

Carla wasn't telling him all she knew. Moreover, the

whole thing sounded too much like a scheme that might yet be uncovered. "Carla . . . why should you and the surgeon endanger yourselves for Valerie? She got into trouble through her own poor judgment. Was protecting her from its consequences worth the risk?"

"In the Ritual we pledge to support fellow-members, Jesse," Carla replied. "So we'd have helped her avoid psych detention even if there'd been no other reason. But in this case, there was. Valerie knows the Group's secrets. We can't afford to have members examined in the psych ward by anyone except Peter—other doctors might use truth serum, you see, for psychiatric reasons even if they didn't suspect any wrongdoing."

God, Jesse thought. That was all too obvious; he wondered why it had not occurred to him before. "What if the delaying tactics didn't work?" he persisted. "What if they call her back for a psych check anyway, since her having resisted medical examination seems to call for one?"

"I don't know," Carla confessed. "Peter will think of something."

"Peter is too softhearted," said Kira, coming in on the conversation. "He should never have recruited Valerie; she is not stable enough, and he knew it. But she's alone in the world and he felt responsible for her, though he couldn't bear to subject her to the kind of therapy the Hospital would have forced him to provide. I don't know what will become of him if someday one of us faces a major criminal charge."

"Has that ever happened?" Jesse asked.

Carla dropped her eyes, "Once," she said shortly. "Peter wasn't allowed to take the case."

"From what I've seen of Peter, I imagine he could handle it. 'Soft' isn't how I'd describe him."

"Of course not, not in the sense of weakness," Kira agreed. "Peter is very strong indeed. But he empathizes. That's a good thing in most situations, and yet if he were forced to give harmful treatment to someone over a long period, it would wear him down. It would destroy him, I think."

"Let's not talk about it," Carla said, keeping her voice steady. Jesse could see that she was disturbed by this topic, and cursed himself for bringing it up. Group members survived awareness of danger by accepting it and then setting it aside. He must not question the risks they took. That served no purpose, since they were in too deep to back off. All the same, his knowledge of Carla's peril frightened him.

From now on, Peter decreed, all patients who'd been hospitalized under the care of any Group doctor, as well as members who were involved in illegal activities in the city, must avoid medical telemetry from the Lodge. Since the one bathroom they could use was downstairs and was reachable only through the locked lab, he enlisted volunteers to build a permanent latrine in the woods, far enough back from the cottages to be considered a camping convenience if it was ever noticed. Jesse took on coordination of the job, while Liz, who was a history buff, downloaded pictures from the Net of the interior and exterior of a small hut called an "outhouse." This was typical, she explained, of structures common on Earth before the invention of indoor plumbing. It was a bit hard to believe that for generations families had relied on such crude facilities, but on the other hand, what else could they have done? The advent of the flush toilet had indeed been progress. Too bad the progress hadn't stopped there, before the addition of electronic sensors.

"Why can't the police still find people the same way they found Valerie before there was any telemetry at all from here?" Jesse protested.

"They can if they're hunting for someone," Carla told him, "which is a good reason for not openly defying the law. But actually, now that we've got to enter false data for everyone whose presence here must be hidden, it won't occur to them to search outlying islands. The telemetry doesn't show specific source locations within the city—it's only because of the separate uplink that it would show where we are." Seeing his expression, she added, "Stop worrying! I'm no more likely to be caught hacking telemetry data for a lot of people than for a few."

"Won't they notice if what you enter doesn't match previous days?"

"Don't worry," she assured him, "Peter and Kira have taught me enough about medical data to put in variations that won't be flagged by the system, even in cases like yours where it's all been faked, or where I have to modify actual sensor readings to conceal conditions our people don't want reported. If anyone ever questioned the figures they'd blame equipment failure; the Meds couldn't imagine there being a motive for hacking health data. It's not as if these were financial records."

Carla's offshift on the Island passed too quickly; soon she was gone again, with nothing more than conversation having passed between them. Jesse tried to forget that at any moment in the city, her hacking career might be brought to an abrupt and disastrous end. His own problems, though less alarming, were more than enough to occupy his full attention.

Learning skills in the lab was one thing, but making practical use of them was another. He was mortified to think that suppressed fear of psi might still rule his unconscious reactions—despite Kira's assurance that this was normal, it was a blow to his self-confidence. A starship captain, afraid of capabilities possessed by hundreds of colonials? Not that he'd had much experience in confronting fear while ferrying freighters in Fleet . . . had his whole life been built on illusion? he wondered. Had he clung inwardly to a boyish image of what spacers were like, despite all-too-clear knowledge of the reality, simply because he'd possessed the title and uniform he had coveted during his youth on Earth?

At times these doubts troubled him. Then, at other times, he thought of space crews he'd shipped with, and was jolted by the thought of what they would say if they knew what he was worrying about. Difficulty in controlling his own biochemistry? An inability to become telepathic? They wouldn't call him fearful; they'd call him crazy! They would scorn such ideas, and laugh. He himself would have laughed only a few weeks ago. He wished he still could; it would be more comfortable. He longed to be back among people who never stretched the bounds of normality. . . .

But of course he didn't, really. He longed to be with Carla—with her in a more intimate way than she now seemed likely to permit.

He dreamed of Earth sometimes. He'd hated it while he was there and had vowed never to go back. Now, he knew, he never could. That illumined it in his memory—the proverbial greener pasture. Actually very little of Earth was green anymore, and hadn't been since long before his birth. Undine, on the other hand, had green islands along with a sparkling blue sea and clear sky that during his waking hours inspired him with its beauty. But in his dreams Earth, and the home he'd left behind, were a refuge. Jesse was not unperceptive. He knew perfectly well, when awake, that it was the stirrings of his own mind he sought refuge from. Kira, when he confessed this, told him that having nostalgic dreams was a sign of strength; she said that to many people, the terrors of the mind appeared as monstrous forms in nightmares. He supposed he should feel fortunate not to have seen any.

As the days passed, he was in limbo, not knowing what was to become of him. It was like being in hyperspace, Jesse thought—you'd set an irrevocable course and left normal space, relying only on what you'd been taught to tell you that you would get back to it. There were no mileposts along the way. You couldn't see the stars. You saw nothing, in fact, beyond the interior of your ship. And if you were exploring new regions, you couldn't be sure there would be anything at all where you emerged.

He had no idea what his future would hold if he managed to achieve what the Group expected of him. He couldn't live at the Lodge forever, and besides, Carla worked in the city, where there would be nothing for him to do. Though he'd mentioned to her that he wasn't qualified for onworld employment, she had told him not to worry. "Peter has connections," she'd said. "He's got some important job in mind for you, I think, something he's not willing to talk about yet." In a troubled voice she'd added, "I hope it's nothing dangerous. He seems to believe you'll play a special role in the Group, one he's got to make sure you're ready to take on."

Special role? This seemed unlikely, considering that he was the least-skilled among three hundred members and had no natural bent toward psi whatsoever. Still, Peter seemed not to doubt he would get through the training. He maintained that his aptitude was high . . . and looking back, Jesse could see he'd been taught the rudiments of volitional control on the first day. Yet he couldn't seem to apply them to daily living. That tolerance of failure had been among the lessons did not occur to him for some time.

The prospect of personal danger was less disturbing. If he could just get on with it, accomplish something worthwhile . . . but life in the Group wasn't like that. Carla had been hacking for years and she would keep on doing it. If she ever did marry him, would he have to be afraid for her, day after day, for the rest of their lives? Sooner or later she would be caught! The Group's hope of lasting forever was built on illusion. And yet, Jesse thought, there was no way out of the situation that required it to exist.

29

THREE DAYS INTO Carla's next visit to the Island, Peter himself took Jesse downstairs to the lab. Jesse performed well, as he usually did during training sessions; only the carryover into real life seemed beyond him. Silently, he despaired of ever altering his inner biochemistry enough to influence his health. "You're trying too hard," Peter told him, "which defeats your purpose. Remember, you can't do it by force of will. Volitional control means letting go—forming an intention and letting your unconscious mind take over. You have proven ability to do that in a crisis, so we know you're capable of it. But it takes years to become automatic, Jess."

"Years?"

"Of course. You didn't think we became what we are overnight, did you? You're learning basic skills quickly—much more quickly than most people do, since you're here every day. As far as preserving your health goes, though, it depends on continuous sensing of how the rest of us do it, plus an ongoing commitment to practice those skills and use them when you feel your body reacting to emotions. No one expects more of you than that."

"I'm expected to turn into a telepath," Jesse said, rather bitterly, "and that's something that can't be taught."

"It can and will be," Peter said seriously, "when you're ready. When you can overcome the fear of your own power. That's going to happen, Jess. If necessary I'll give you some kind of push—but I may not need to. You're in the process of making a very difficult adjustment. Don't be too impatient with yourself." Then, brightening, he added, "Forget problems for now. We're going to have some fun tonight."

Peter's idea of fun, Jesse knew, was unlikely to be relaxing. Well, that was okay. Any break from inner uncertainty would be welcome.

When they got upstairs Jesse saw from the Lodge windows that several large bonfires had been built on the beach, below the high tide mark. To make coals for a barbeque, maybe; it wouldn't be dark for hours and the day was too warm to sit near them. They were being tended by a mere handful of people.

"Are you free, Jesse?" asked Bernie, coming in from the porch. "We could use some more wood."

Jesse followed him to the woodpile, which to his surprise he saw was almost depleted although he had replenished it only the day before. Kwame and several others were chopping up more logs; he joined them, then helped to haul loads down to the beach. If a barbeque was planned, a large crowd must be expected—and indeed, he noticed that the red pennant was flying from the dock. That meant guests were coming. He hadn't thought the Group ever brought multiple guests to the Island.

As dusk came on, the fires had been raked down to coals. Several more plane loads of people had arrived, and Carla warned Jesse not to mention the Group's secrets, or even its existence, to anybody he didn't know. "The guests are from our front group," she said. "Tonight's event is one of the ways we attract potential members."

"With some sort of cookout?" He was astonished.

"No," Carla said. "We're going to eat now, early, in fact."

The buffet tables had been moved onto the Lodge porch, since the guests weren't invited inside, and the food offered was lighter fare than usual. Jesse and Carla helped themselves to sandwiches and sat on the beach, some distance from the others, to eat. He could tell that she wanted to talk privately.

"I've never understood what the front group does," he admitted.

"It's just a gathering of people interested in the paranormal. They think it's all speculation, of course. We offer lectures, discussion groups, and so forth—plus some colorful ceremonies that provide an outlet for those attracted to the magical and mysterious. And about twice a year, this, which requires just a few hours of training, yet is very impressive."

"What is it, then, if not just a feast?"

Carla hesitated. "A firewalk," she said. "Walking barefoot on the coals."

"Barefoot . . . on hot coals? You're kidding."

"Haven't you ever heard of it? It's common on Earth, and not only in cultures where it has religious significance," she informed him. "Starting in the late twentieth century, it was done by thousands of Americans who actually *paid* to attend firewalking workshops. Ian studied what was written about it. It's illegal here, which is why we do it only on the Island."

"But Carla, such a thing's not possible! Those coals out there would burn human feet to a crisp—I could barely get close enough to rake them."

Carla smiled. "Hardly anyone gets burned. You'll find that you don't."

"*Me?*" He had known they would confront him with more trials—"drastic" had been the term used, he recalled—but this . . .

"Not you alone, of course; we all take part. It would have been nice if we could have done it your first week here—then our powers wouldn't have been such a shock to you after you were recruited. Also it's a better confidence-booster when a novice has to overcome real fear, which you won't, now."

"I'm glad to hear that," Jesse said dryly.

"You've nothing to be afraid of," she declared. "You know how not to suffer from pain, so even if you are burned, it won't matter. We can heal you quickly, after all, whereas with guests we'd have to go through the charade of using medical burn treatments."

"That's true, I guess," he agreed dubiously, "though I can't say it makes me exactly eager for the experience—"

Carla, watching his face, broke in, "I'm teasing, Jesse! Of course it will be challenging—that's the fun in it. But you won't be burned. Very few people get worse burns than small blisters even in untrained groups on Earth, and with us, no guest ever has. Peter can judge telepathically, you see, whether a person is in enough of an altered state to try it."

"Altered state? I haven't been taught a mind-pattern for that one."

"Remember, firewalking was done on Earth long before neurofeedback was invented." She frowned. "Not having real-world experience with useful altered states prior to lab training may have handicapped you, Jesse. Better late than never."

"But in the world outside, getting into altered states requires drugs, except maybe for gifted individuals."

"No, not at all!" she said, surprised. "There's the traditional way, the time-honored way, that's produced them in gatherings throughout history."

"The traditional way?"

"Mob psychology, the uninformed call it. Or mass hypnosis, though it's rarely true hypnosis. It's telepathy, group telepathy, triggered by a charismatic leader. What do you think inspires heroic deeds in wartime? Or religious ecstasy? Or riots and violent demonstrations, as far as that goes—it has been used for evil as well as good. Fanatics like Hitler and Osama bin Laden were all too good at putting their followers into altered states. But on the whole, it's a positive force."

"And you're saying Peter can—trigger it?"

"Oh, yes. He could even if the rest of us weren't trained telepaths, and since we are, it's even simpler. All he has to do is rouse concerted enthusiasm and we'll carry the novices along."

"You mean the guests—people without any mind training at all—will *do* this, not just watch?"

"Most of them will. People with no special skills have been doing it for centuries on Earth. Skeptics try to pass it off as some strange physical phenomenon; they say the coals aren't really hot or don't conduct heat, or something. They can't bring themselves to admit that the mind has such power; it would shatter their belief system. That's exactly what it's for, of course. Underneath, the scoffers know that, which is why they deny vehemently that it's real."

"So why didn't we do it earlier, while I was a guest, if that would have been better?" he asked curiously.

"Because we don't have enough wood to build big fires often."

Jesse had wondered about the extravagant use of wood while hauling it. The trees on the Island, genetically engineered on Earth for terraforming colony worlds, were fast growers; new ones were planted frequently. But it would not take many fires such as had been built today to deplete them faster than they could be replaced.

"This is a bit ahead of schedule, actually," Carla went on, "but Peter thinks it's important not to wait any longer. Maybe he wants to recruit others before Ian dies. He took a chance subjecting you to the test without your having firewalked first—I'm still not sure what the hurry was. Most people who join us have motives different from yours, you know. They're seeking something you don't yet quite want to believe in."

She was troubled, Jesse realized. No doubt she sensed his deep doubts of his paranormal potential. Could she, through the unconsummated love they shared, see into him more clearly than Peter, the expert? Or had Peter had second thoughts? Would he be tested again tonight, and found lacking?

She looked at him, pleading with her eyes for him to share her confidence. "He asked you to talk me into this," he realized.

"To explain it to you, yes," Carla admitted, "and to make sure you get into the spirit of it. Come on, Peter's about to start."

People were clustering around the Lodge porch, sitting on the steps and on benches; the buffet tables had been pushed back. Peter, wearing his blue shirt, stood in their midst; he looked younger and less preoccupied than he had since the first week Jesse had known him. He suddenly became aware of how the man had changed recently. The looming responsibility of full leadership evidently had been weighing on him, or perhaps merely grief in anticipation of Ian's passing. The ability to forget cares and enjoy life, so central to the Group, had in his case seemed to fade. But tonight, at least, he did seem to be having fun.

Next to Peter stood a slim, brown-skinned man Jesse hadn't met. "That's Hari," Carla said, "one of Ian's protégés. He's a Council member and the teacher for the front group.

He also gives training in some of the more esoteric psi powers to those in the Group who want to experiment with them. Between those two things and his official job teaching anthropology at the university, he rarely has time to come to the Island."

"How large is the Council?" Jesse asked.

"Just five—Ian, Peter, Kira, Hari, and Reiko. I guess you haven't met Reiko yet, either. She's a university professor, too. She teaches history and sociology, but her real work in those fields isn't revealed to outsiders. It's coordination of our research on how unconscious telepathy shaped human progress in the past."

The group hushed and Peter began to speak, welcoming the guests to what they believed was simply his private island retreat. There was an air of excitement; Jesse realized they'd looked forward to this occasion and had high expectations of being transformed by it. Hari would have prepared them for believing in the power of mind to protect them from burning. Firewalking wasn't meant to be an ordeal, he realized. Probably those who did it successfully would get high.

Unconvinced though he was that he would be among them, he had no choice about making the attempt. He sure as hell wasn't going to balk at anything Carla asked of him, even apart from not wanting look like a coward. Don't think about it, he told himself. Just do it. Just hope to be put into enough of an altered state to pass muster if Peter checks up before letting people try.

Peter went on talking, instructing the listeners to acknowledge and face their fear. "Don't try to hide it," he said. "It's normal, and it's good! The whole point of walking on fire is to discover that fear needn't hold you back from anything you want to do. If we weren't consciously afraid, we'd never learn that. . . ."

Which was, of course, the same advice he'd been hearing all along, Jesse realized. What was the matter with him, that he apparently still had fears he couldn't identify, much

less face? Was he suppressing them even now? It was true
that he had no reason to fear burns. He knew pain wouldn't
bother him—yet minute by minute his dread of them was
growing, not fading. It was mortifying. These others, the
guests, would suffer agony if they failed; how could he be
more frightened than they were?

Carla took his hand, tightened her fingers on his. It was
the first physical touch she had allowed for weeks, and his
heart began to pound. "It's okay," she whispered. "You're
supposed to be scared your first time, Jesse! Admit it!"

He couldn't admit it, not to her. He focused on what
Peter was saying. "You must be willing to be burned . . .
paradoxically, the only way to control your mind is to let go,
and let whatever comes, come. . . ." As Peter continued, elaborating on the principles of volitional control, it all came together for Jesse. There was no difference in method between
dealing with pain, or controlling his blood pressure, or even
preventing his skin from burning. He had managed to do it
during the test. Could he possibly, in this new crisis . . . ?

"It's up to you to choose whether to walk or not," Peter
said, "and if you don't feel ready for it, you mustn't try. I
will judge you individually, but that's not a substitute for
feeling that you'll succeed. People who don't feel they're protected can get severely burned—it happens sometimes,
though it has never happened here. People who aren't focusing their attention can also get burned. I have walked
on coals many times, but even I would be burned if I let my
mind wander."

The sky was dark now, and the coals glowed red on the
beach behind them. Peter took off his shoes and rolled up
his pant legs, telling the others to do the same. As he came
down from the porch, everyone rose and turned to face the
fire. Up-tempo music emerged from speakers that had been
moved outside; Peter used a wireless mike to be heard over
it.

"I'll go first," he said, "and then the people who've had
experience. After that we'll come around and check each

one of you. When you enter the bed of coals, move quickly—but don't run. Keep walking, and whatever you do, don't stop before you're across. Once you have taken the first step, you'll find it's easy to go on. You'll notice heat, but not on the soles of your feet. The coals may even feel cool. . . ."

I can't believe I'm doing this, Jesse thought, moving into the single-file line now snaking toward the fire. The people ahead of him he recognized as Group members; Carla held back so that he was directly behind her, the first of the novices. The volume of the music swelled. So too did the excitement and confidence of the participants. He had gained enough sensitivity during his weeks at the Lodge to be aware that this was indeed enhanced by unconscious telepathy. It occurred to him that under its influence he might finally make contact with Carla—but no, he must focus now on what he was about to attempt.

The line circled the fire rather than heading directly to it, so that Peter was visible to everyone as he stepped onto the red-hot coals. He was calm, smiling; firelight reflected onto a face already illumined by an inner glory. This was beyond mere fun, Jesse saw. And in that moment he wanted more than ever before to become like Peter, to experience whatever it was that made him—made all the Group members—what they were. He had thought he'd achieved it, that first day, the day he'd freed himself from pain . . . why had he never felt that freedom again? Why was he terrified at the thought that the fire might give it to him?

One by one, the experienced firewalkers followed Peter, sharing Peter's exultation. Almost before he knew it, Carla stood at the edge of the coals. She did not hesitate. Her arms held out for balance, she moved forward, and in four steps, she was across. Jesse knew he must not hesitate either. What the hell, what would it matter what became of him if he could not match Carla's courage?

Peter had come around to judge the waiting novices; he smiled at Jesse and nodded. "Go for it," he said.

Then to his own surprise, Jesse became suddenly, inwardly, sure that he was in some way protected—not by Peter's reassurance, but by the state of his own mind. The nameless terror he felt was not of burning. He hardly knew when he took the first step. The coals were not very hot under his feet; they felt like beach pebbles warmed by the sun. More intense heat rose around him, enveloped him, and he strode quickly ahead to get away from it. Two steps ... three ... four ... and the fire was behind him. Incredibly, his feet weren't even blistered—the feeling in them was normal.

Carla, then other friends, hugged him exuberantly. They were high, he realized. This was the kind of triumph that produced natural highs, that had done so even in him on several previous occasions. It hadn't done so on this one. Her excitement fading, Carla stepped back, and he watched disappointment, even sadness, overtake her. "Oh, Jesse," she murmured, "I'd hoped—"

To share a high with him? He recalled the high he'd shared with Peter—he'd have given *anything* to experience that with Carla! And perhaps to share more; had she been hoping that tonight it would become possible? Peter's words echoed in his mind: *In the case of potential sex partners a shared high, especially following stress, often does lead to bed....*

But Jesse was not high. He felt none of the inner joy that had transformed the others, including, by now, most of the guests. Knowing he could walk on coals unharmed was not a comfort to him. In fact, the sense of foreboding that had plagued him the past few weeks seemed stronger than ever.

30

BY MID-MORNING THE guests, who'd camped in the woods, were gone, and the bed of ashes had been washed away by high tide. The memory of the firewalk seemed unreal to

Jesse. He saw no concrete evidence that it had happened, certainly not on his feet, which were unmarked when he examined them. And though his mind assured him it *had* happened, what, after all, did that signify? He'd been told firewalking wasn't limited to Group members and had even been common on Earth among ordinary people in the past. Incredible as not being burned might seem, it was not really a sign that he was progressing.

The day was hot; after lunch he and Carla hiked along the shore, wearing only light shirts over their swimwear. Not having been particularly eager, he was soon ready to turn back. But Carla, as always, was full of life. He had been, too, his first week on the Island, Jesse recalled wistfully. He was vaguely aware that his loss of that vitality signaled conflict in his unconscious mind. It held him back from enjoyment and also, no doubt, from the immunity to aging he was supposed to acquire. Yet he couldn't shake the worries that weighed him down.

For Carla's sake, he went through the motions of having fun. "Come on," she said. "I'll race you to the point." She was off, leaping from rock to rock where the rising tide lapped between them. Jesse followed, pretending that he felt young and carefree.

And then, with a shriek, Carla disappeared.

"Carla!" Jesse shouted. His heart pounding, he rushed to the place from which he'd seen her fall. There wasn't a big drop; she was lying on the pebbly shore not far below him. As he scrambled down to her, she turned onto her back. "I'm okay," she said. "A rock gave way under my foot. I didn't break anything—I just need to stay still a few minutes." But she was not okay. There was blood on the stones beside her, and more blood gushing from a long gash on her leg.

"Oh, God, Carla." He tore off his shirt, wondering whether a bandage was going to be enough. A wound bleeding that profusely might need a tourniquet. She might go into shock. They were too far from the Lodge to call for help; he would have to carry her. . . .

He knelt beside her, wiping her leg with a corner of his shirt to examine it. The laceration was longer than his hand, and deep; she'd evidently fallen onto a sharp rock. It must be incredibly painful, he thought in dismay—and then he remembered that Carla, like everyone in the Group, was immune to physical suffering. For the first time the full significance of Kira's warning struck him, the warning that once he stopped minding pain, he'd need common sense to judge when an injury needed treatment. His common sense now told him that whatever Carla might think, she did need it.

"I'm okay, really," she insisted. "Look, the bleeding's already stopping."

Incredibly, it seemed to be. Where he had wiped the blood away, little more appeared. But it wasn't possible that it could stop! He had not even put pressure on it.

"Jesse," she said, smiling. "I know you haven't been taught yet. From your face, I guess nobody has even told you. We control bleeding just as we do other physical responses. If I were in the City, where outsiders could see, I wouldn't dare do it this fast; I'd have to let them treat me. Here, I'm free to heal myself."

"You—you're stopping it with your *mind*?"

"Of course. The way you can control your pulse rate and your blood pressure, when you remember to do it."

Startled, he brought the frantic racing of his heart under control. But to halt bleeding was hardly the same—it was a higher order of capability altogether, surely. And in any case, a wound that wasn't bleeding was still an open wound. He had to get her to the infirmary downstairs in the Lodge.

"No," Carla told him. "I don't need the infirmary for a flesh wound. If I'd broken a bone, it would have to be set. But I can heal this easily. Just let me rest here a little while."

"I'm taking you back," Jesse declared grimly.

"No! I need to be still." She sat up, bending over and gripping her leg with both hands so that the edges of the wound were pressed together. "If you want to help, hold it for me, so I don't have to stay in this awkward position."

Mutely he grasped her leg between his hands, and she lay back on the sun-warmed pebbles. What good this would do, he could not imagine. A wound as deep as hers would take days to heal even if it didn't get infected. She was apparently shocked past reason; he could only trust that before much more time passed she would come to her senses and let him carry her.

There was no sound but the small waves lapping against the shore. Carla's eyes were closed and soon she was half-asleep, yet her color was normal and she was breathing evenly. Despite his fear for her, Jesse could see no grounds for believing she was in immediate danger, certainly none strong enough to justify forcing her to move against her will. Kira could clean and stitch the wound later.

Time seemed to crawl, but looking at his watch, he saw that less than half an hour had passed when Carla sat up. "You can take your hands away now," she said.

He did so—and stared in amazement at the dark red line of a newly-healed scar.

"Oh, Carla," he whispered, unable to express—or even form—a coherent response. He should feel nothing but joy . . . nothing but his relief that she was all right. He cared more for Carla's well-being than for anything in the strange new life into which he had been plunged—more by far than for the hope he'd had of a union between them. Yet all the confusion, all the doubts of the past weeks crystallized in this, and he knew it for the end of that hope. He would never be Carla's equal, never the equal of any of them, whatever they might try to teach him. Despite Peter's denial, they were not human, but superhuman. They could not turn him into one of them. Perhaps they'd never really believed they could; had they not admitted they were experimenting with an offworlder?

No wonder he couldn't learn to sense her thoughts. Carla knew he could not; that was why she would not let him get close, although with the part of her that was merely human, she too had hoped. It was, he reflected, like the ancient myths of men who fell in love with goddesses—even when attraction was mutual, there was a gulf that could never be bridged.

He could not stay with the Group, he thought in despair. It would be torment for her, as well as for him, if he tried to. There was nothing else for him on Undine. Peter, somewhat mysteriously, had insisted that he leave his funds offworld; so though no liners came here, he might be able to bribe a freighter captain to grant him passage. Had Peter known it might come to that? Known that he would have too much pride to remain as a misfit if he failed to become truly one of them?

They walked slowly back to the Lodge, saying little. Carla, too, seemed subdued, troubled; Jesse wondered if she had read his mind. What he'd been thinking must have hurt her, yet how he felt wasn't subject to choice. Guiltily, he realized he was relieved by the possibility that he might not have to put it into words.

All through dinner they sat apart, talking with others, going through the familiar routine of camaraderie at meals and around the evening fire. Now that Carla was fully dressed her leg was hidden, but the glimpse he'd had of it on their return had showed him that the scar was already fading. Its impact on his emotions, he knew, would never fade.

At the fireside Peter spoke quietly to him. "It's still bothering you," he observed. Carla had evidently—perhaps telepathically?—made him aware of what had happened.

"No, I—" Jesse broke off, knowing that he would not be allowed to get away with less than frankness. "Yes," he said in a low voice. "It's awesome, too awesome to be true. I can't quite believe that it's entirely human. That someone I care about is more, physically, than flesh and blood. That we could ever be—normal together, when I'm not on her level. There's too wide a gap . . . as if she were alien."

"All right," Peter declared. "This has to be cleared up, here and now." He turned to Anne, beside him, and spoke louder. "Do me a favor, Anne. Go down to the infirmary and bring back a sterile knife."

Carla, across the circle, burst out, "Please don't, Peter! Not for my sake!"

"We can't let it ride," Peter said. "The problem's dragged on too long."

"Maybe that's true," she admitted through tears. "Maybe we have to accept that not everyone can adapt to our ways. Not even everyone's who's strong! We knew from the start that Jesse's background is different, that he would never have sought us out of his own accord. I love him for what he is, not for being like us! I'd rather see him go than try to make him change."

"It's not for your sake, Carla—it's for his. We need Jesse, and he wouldn't be happy now as an outsider. He's seen too much."

Jesse nodded. "I have," he agreed miserably. "It's true that I won't be happy. But I'd only hurt Carla by staying, Peter. Another demonstration won't help. I don't doubt that you can cut yourself and heal instantly. Probably a lot of you can; I know you heal other people. But that just makes it worse. I'm . . . out of my element here. I'm doing my best to learn what you're teaching me, but I'm never going to have paranormal powers myself, in spite of what you've said—even in spite of having walked on hot coals. I can consciously control normal functions that used to be unconscious, and that's as far as I'll be able to go."

"Self-healing *is* a normal function," Peter pointed out. "You had cuts and scrapes as a kid, didn't you, and they healed?"

"Sure, minor things. It didn't happen overnight."

"So we simply speed up the process. The real miracle is that the human body has this capability—a capability people take so much for granted that they don't notice how truly incredible it would seem if they had never heard of it before."

"Well, it's not just speed, Peter. A really serious, deep wound—profuse bleeding, like what Carla had—wouldn't heal naturally."

"No? What about surgery? How do you think people heal from that?"

"They have medical care—" Jesse bit his lip. He could hardly fall back on the Meds without denying the Group's most fundamental convictions. What did medics actually *do*, to heal a surgical wound?

"They stitch it up," said Kira, "because in nature healing does take time and during that time, the edges of the wound must be held together. They stop the bleeding faster than would happen naturally, so that too much blood won't be lost. They make sure the wound doesn't get infected. None of these things in themselves bring about healing. Only the body can do so, under the control of unconscious processes."

"You're saying these can be made conscious, like the others I've been learning? Surely there's more to it than that."

"Nothing more," Peter said. "Bleeding can be consciously controlled; that's an ancient skill that will be taught to you in the lab, in due course. The knitting of flesh can also be controlled when there's need. Even by you."

"I don't believe so, Peter."

"No, because you're thinking someone who heals rapidly is 'more than flesh and blood,' as you say. Fundamentally different from yourself."

Jesse didn't reply, and for some time no one spoke. He sat listening to the music, the thrilling synthesized music that normally elated him, knowing he could no longer feel comfortable in the Group even if Peter urged him to stay. It had been so good. He had learned so much. He'd had friends he cared about, a woman he'd hoped to marry, everything he'd always wanted and more. And yet he could never really fit in. There would always be the knowledge that there was power in the others—in Carla—beyond anything a normal man could aspire to.

Anne returned; she handed a surgical scalpel silently to Peter, who said, "You've got to get past that feeling, Jess. We can show you there's nothing weird about healing."

"Watching again can't change anything," Jesse protested, and then wished he had kept quiet. Though he knew Peter wouldn't suffer pain or be permanently harmed, the prospect of observing a deliberately-inflicted injury wasn't appealing. But that was why he would be required to watch. In the Group, all the things you shrank from were to be faced unflinchingly.

Peter rose, holding the scalpel. Kira came from the kitchen with an armload of towels, which she piled on top of a cushion placed front of him. The others moved in close, forming a tight circle. Carla, on the far side of the fireplace, was white-faced; Jesse wondered why she was so upset. She could hardly be expecting him to faint at the sight of more blood, even if she'd come to realize he could never adapt.

"Okay," said Peter, turning to Jesse, on his right. "Hold your left arm over the towels there, and grip the wrist with your right hand."

Jesse froze. Peter could not mean . . . But of course he did. His projected thought was clear, probably had been clear all along. How, thought Jesse, could I have been so afraid as to close my mind to him?

"It won't hurt, you know," said Kira gently, "unless you let it."

Something Peter had said at the time of the first breakthrough echoed in Jesse's mind: *Pain usually can't be isolated from harm. Injury, torture, almost always involve the fear of bodily damage. Only in rare circumstances can an untrained person deal with both fears at once. Here, we take them in sequence.* He had not stopped to think, then, what "sequence" implied.

"We don't expect you to initiate healing by volition at this stage," Peter said. "We will guide you telepathically, all of us, as we would an outsider unaware of what was happening. You will be aware, and you'll feel, in your own body, that it's possible—that you are not different from Carla after all." He smiled encouragingly.

Jesse got to his feet. Oh, what the hell, he thought, trying to maintain that attitude as he thrust his arm out and held it steady. This was like everything else he'd been led to do, most recently at last night's firewalk. He must be willing to accept whatever happened, that was the only way to stave off panic ... panic would interfere with telepathic reception. At the same time, he must turn off pain ... but he must be willing to accept pain, too, if it came, because to resist would mean losing control ... except that he mustn't resist loss of control either.... He couldn't remember it all in words, but the lessons had been burned into his mind. Stressed again, he felt the unconscious memory surge up in him. You didn't have to reason it out! You just *knew*. Just as you knew how to fly a fast ship without thinking through every touch of the controls.

Peter's knife slashed through flesh, a long cut from forearm to elbow, almost as deep as the bone. The arm, too, remembered; with a detached part of his mind Jesse realized that pain there, having been repeatedly dealt with, was easier to manage than it would have been in some other part of his body. He felt the slash, but it didn't bother him. Blood spurted and then flowed freely, dripping on the towels. For a moment he was gripped by instinctive terror. But then other feelings overrode it. Superimposed on the memories and on the instinct was the knowledge that he was already healing, of how it felt to heal. He was drawing the power to activate healing from the focused minds of his friends.

As if from a distance he heard Peter's voice saying, "Move your right hand from your wrist and press the wound together—it can't heal while it's gaping open." He did so, finding it easy; his hand was not even shaking. Within moments the bleeding stopped, just as it had with Carla. The flesh began to knit. It didn't hurt, but he wasn't disengaged from the process. He was aware that he was *doing* something, with guidance from outside, but nevertheless something that demanded his full attention. It was an indescribable feeling, just as the control over pain was indescribable—a feeling that, once experienced, would never again be beyond reach.

In a little while he glanced down at the arm and saw only an angry red scar.

"It will fade," Kira told him, wiping dried blood from his skin with a damp towel. "Perhaps not as fast as Carla's, but by tomorrow you won't know by looking that it was ever there."

"But I'll know in my mind."

"I hope it will be reassuring knowledge, Jess," said Peter.

"I—I don't think I can say right now." He was shaking with released tension, with the aftermath of fear, and he knew that the knife hadn't been what frightened him.

He'd been lying to himself before. He had not been depressed because he was different from the others. On the contrary, he'd been afraid that he was *not* different. That he was truly . . . paranormal, as they were. That the transformation set in motion was a matter not just of learning skills, but of freeing something in his mind—something that would separate him forever from all he'd known of himself in the past.

Peter took his hand, gripped it. "Did you think I would let you start on a course you weren't fit to finish?" he asked with warmth. "If you trust us, Jesse, it's time you began trusting yourself."

Slowly, Jesse nodded. And suddenly there was a shift within his mind, as if from black and white to color in a film, or perhaps the adding of a new dimension. He became aware of depths previously filtered from consciousness. Now that the break with his past self had come, he felt no regret. He had turned his back on Fleet; why had he feared to surpass the burned-out Captain he once had been? Why had he not known that metamorphosis would heal him? It had done so almost instantly, as the wound had been healed. In fact, he was getting high. There was no longer any barrier between him and Carla. . . .

She had sensed the change in him and, now radiant, threw her arms around his neck. As her joy blazed clear in his mind, Jesse knew he had never before guessed what conscious telepathy would be like. He looked down at her, seeing nothing but her desirability. The feelings he'd tried so long to suppress overwhelmed him; he was aroused past possibility of control. He seized her, not roughly but not gently either, not in any sense tentatively. Carla didn't resist; her response was eager. They stood motionless by the fireplace, locked together in the kiss, as oblivious to outer concerns as if they had been alone.

I will not wait any longer, Carla, he thought. This is not a time to be held back by fear—not even the fear that I haven't enough to offer you.

And Carla whispered, "Of course not. You're free now. This is what we were waiting for."

Part Four

31

INCREDULOUS, JESSE GAZED at Carla, seeing only her, as if Peter and the others did not exist—and in fact, they all seemed to have disappeared. Yet if this was some kind of dream, it didn't seem like dreaming. It seemed more real than anything else had lately, as if he were at last awake. What had happened to his promise to do only what was best for her? he thought with chagrin. Despite his new confidence in what he'd become, he still wasn't a true telepath. . . .

Carla smiled. "So far you've been mixed up about telepathy," she informed him. "We don't gain conscious control of it and then use it to enhance sex; it's the other way around."

"You mean it was meant all along for me to gain it . . . from you?"

"Yes! Sexual arousal is an altered state, you see—when are you least distracted by rational thinking, if not during sex? It releases latent psi power in a way nothing else can. Among us telepathic control's always learned from a partner."

Then why have we been wasting time? he wondered, kissing her again.

We didn't waste time. It couldn't happen until you got over the fear of being paranormal, she told him. *You'd have found that . . . inhibiting, perhaps even physically—as you guessed earlier tonight.* They were down on the floor cushions before Jesse realized that his tongue was touching hers, that there was no way she could have spoken this aloud.

Where shall we go? he asked silently. He still hadn't been into the private cottages and did not know if any were empty. Yet he wasn't quite so uncontrolled as not to realize that though the common room seemed deserted, they were still beside the fireplace, presumably in full view of everyone else in the Lodge.

They won't come back here tonight, Carla told him, unbuttoning her shirt. *Why do you think the circle dissolved so quickly? Committed couples lie by the Lodge fire their first time together on the Island—it's tradition. The others have their own memories. No one will intrude on us.*

He was not in a mood to doubt it, or even to question how such a strange piece of information had been imparted to him. He pulled off his clothes, fumbling with them in haste, with eyes only for Carla's now-bare body. Her breasts were firm, tanned from the sun, perfectly formed. He had seen them when she swam, but had been careful not to notice. He noticed now. He fondled them; her flesh was cool, touching his, as he drew her closer. Yet he knew it was cool only by comparison, for he himself was burning. It was as if the fire enveloped them both, and the light in their minds merged with it. . . .

I love you, Carla, he told her, exploring her body further. *I've never loved anyone before. Not like this, not feeling minds merge like this.* He knew, without words, that she loved him, would always love him, in a far deeper way than he had ever experienced. It was indeed more than physical union, and more than the ordinary union of intimates. Their minds were merged. He felt hands touch his thighs, but they were not her hands, for hers were on his back; somehow he felt *his* hands touching *her.*

That the physical sensations would be shared had not occurred to him. God, would they feel each other's climax, too? It was possible. Nothing, no matter how strange, was impossible tonight. . . .

He did not have to ask himself whether she was ready for him, or be concerned with any of the usual things one looked for in a woman's reactions. He knew. He knew from her mind alone that she too could bear no delay. As he entered her, he was sure; he did not even need to see her face. He knew, also, that it was his mind that had aroused her. No slow preliminaries had been required precisely because his own arousal had been projected into Carla's mind.

Arousal did not really depend on physical stimulation, he perceived. How could it ever have, when fantasies could arouse? To depend on the purely physical was a mechanical way, a deficient way. The androids used in clinics could do that as well as a man. It would degrade Carla when she expected the arousal only a man could offer her. No wonder she'd wanted to wait until his mind was free enough to project it, sensitive enough to feel her body's response.

Simultaneously, they climaxed. He had never experienced anything like it, never imagined such a feeling. It was all the best of sex as he'd known it previously, along with what *she* felt too . . . and it was more than physical sensation. Their minds were one, and not merely for sensing pleasure. They saw images through each other's eyes: the fire from double perspective, faces, a starry sky. She saw space as he had seen it, and he in turn saw her world. . . .

And then, in an instant, the joy was shattered.

Abruptly Carla cried out—with anguish, not passion— as an image more vivid than the rest loomed in their joined minds. The Vaults . . . Jesse recoiled in shock. The stasis vaults . . . metallic walls, bodies in steel boxes shaped like coffins, bodies still breathing, and through the lid of one box, a man's face. . . . *Oh God, no, not now, this wasn't supposed to happen now! Jesse, I've failed you. . . .*

He rolled onto his side, still holding Carla in his arms. *Don't let it matter,* he begged. *I'm sorry, I don't know what made me think of it....* The image faded, leaving him breath-less, drained.

"I've failed you," she said aloud.

No, you haven't! He knew that he must not let the sexual release break their telepathic link, as it very well might if he were not still high. He evidently still felt subconscious fear of his new power, else why this most horrifying of im-ages? Though he had never seen Undine's vaults, he knew the look of stasis units from his Fleet training. Here, they'd become a metaphor for death—the death of his former self, perhaps, though he had believed himself already reborn....

It's my fault, Carla insisted. "That came from my mind, not yours. I ... couldn't help it ... I'd thought I could shut it out...."

"No, how could it have been from you?" *Are you as afraid of the Vaults as that, when you're younger than I am?* Per-haps only a few years younger, he realized; he still did not know her age. But she was a long way from the prospect of dying.

"It wasn't fear that set it off," she whispered. "It was memory ... memory and grief. I couldn't help remembering the first time I made love beside this fire."

He pulled her closer to him, trying to suppress his dis-may. "The man is ... in the Vaults? It was his face we saw?" He had been told that she was a widow, but had not stopped to think what that must mean on this world.

She was crying. "He was young ... his body is in the Vaults, still young, forever!"

Jesse knew he mustn't shrink from the idea. He had seen just the overflow, the part that she, her ESP enhanced by physical arousal, had not been able to hold back. She had unconsciously projected it because she needed his com-fort—she'd turned to him with love and trust. Could he be strong enough to help her confront a fact that repelled him?

He had to be. If emotion enhanced psi power, then his love for her would make him strong. "You haven't failed me," he insisted, feeling her tears wet against his skin. "Let's share it all—all the things you have not told anybody in words. Let me help now, while I'm high enough to do it."

His strength must outlast the high. Telepathy, he now saw, involved far more than mere projection and sensing of specific thoughts. It meant sharing feelings, not only during sex, but as an ongoing link between intimates whose potential for it had been fully awakened—painful feelings as well as good ones. It was this he had unconsciously feared, this the Group required of its members. The physical skills were trivial beside the need to deal not only with one's own deep emotions, but those of lovers and friends.

Carla had perceived his most private feelings from the beginning, he realized. An hour ago he'd have been mortified by that thought. Now, he was no more shy about sharing his inner self with her than about the nakedness of his body. Yet he had never before truly loved another person, never been really close to anyone during the empty years in Fleet . . . he was not sure he knew how to respond to *her* pain. He hoped that at least he could manage not to make it worse.

32

THE FIRE BURNED low, now. They lay in the dark, uncovered both physically and emotionally, aware only of their concern for each other's distress.

"You couldn't understand just from thoughts," Carla said with sorrow. "There are things you still don't know about this world."

Jesse pressed closer to her, feeling her heart beat in rhythm with his own. Peter had warned that her husband had died tragically, that he must not ask her how—but did that apply, now that she had revealed what haunted her? It would be better for her to talk about it than to keep it bottled up inside.

"I've got to tell you someday," she agreed. "We can't keep

secrets from each other anymore. Besides, you need to be aware of what can happen."

He waited, cold despite the warmth of her body next to his. He had begun to sense some horror too terrible for comfort.

Carla turned her face toward him, white, stained with tears. "Ramón was—executed," she said. "For aggravated murder."

"Executed!" Jesse could not conceal his astonishment. He'd been on enough worlds where execution hadn't been outlawed not to be bothered by the thought of its existence, and in fact Fleet had been known to execute mutineers. But here, where death was not even recognized . . .

"Of course they didn't call it execution," Carla said. "Killing someone would be beyond the pale as far as our law's concerned. But that's what it was."

"But if they didn't kill him—"

"The world outside doesn't look at entry to the stasis vaults as death," she said bitterly. "It's maintenance. It's immortality. It is not capital punishment to send someone to the Vaults prematurely; it's simply a matter of not wasting treatment on those beyond benefit."

"Oh, my God," said Jesse. "Healthy people?"

"Only those who commit the worst crimes—aggravated murder, or some major financial crime resulting not from sickness but from greed. It's thought to be a deterrent, so the victims . . . aren't even sedated . . . though they die right away, of course. . . ."

"You mean he was put in there *conscious?*" Jesse whispered, sickened. To bury condemned men alive was beyond any atrocity he had imagined could occur on a civilized world.

"Peter says consciousness is lost almost immediately when the stasis maintenance AI takes over," Carla said. "Only we don't really know how long some sort of altered state lasts in stasis."

"But Carla," Jesse said, trying to absorb this, "people unconscious in stasis aren't dead! On the old starships they used to travel for years in stasis—this colony was founded that way. The stasis units from the founding ship were transferred to the Hospital, and more like them were added. Surely he—your husband—could be wakened someday, if we could find a way to rescue him—" What had Peter been thinking of, not to tell her this? he wondered. Or did he himself know only because of the history he'd learned in Fleet?

"No," she told him. "The AI isn't programmed the same as it used to be on starships. Bodies normally put into stasis are already brain-dead, after all, and can't breathe without ventilator tubes. The mix used doesn't supply enough oxygen to the brain for it to live. People who have been executed are just as dead as the others."

"Oh, Carla." How, Jesse wondered, had she managed to retain her vitality, her usual joyous spirit, when burdened by this unspeakable memory? Her husband surely had been innocent. Peter had called him a fine man; he could not have been a real murderer. Burying a body would be called murder, but the consequence of that was treatment—not execution. . . .

She lay silent in his embrace for a while, then pulled away, propping herself up on one elbow while she told him the details. "Ramón was a doctor who specialized in treating old people," she said. "He hated what his job required of him—when his patients neared death he had to put them on life support, and eventually authorize sending them to the Vaults. He kept on because it gave him a chance to get some of them into our hospices, and to help others telepathically before they died. Just as Peter's job enables him to help the criminals he has to drug—"

Jesse cringed. He hadn't known Peter was forced to do that.

Carla continued, "Ramón made a point of getting to know his patients, and when he found someone who didn't want to die on life support, he steered that person to a hospice before it was too late. If the person was already in the Hospital, he faked the chart so he could arrange a discharge. We still do it that way—we have other insiders—and of course it's dangerous. Without telepathy, we'd never know which patients can be trusted not to reveal that the hospices exist. They have to abandon their families, after all. When they disappear, we have to say they're in the Vaults."

Cruel, but necessary, Jesse realized. They would die soon anyway, and actually would be in the Vaults if there were no deception.

"There was an old couple, very devoted to each other, that Ramón had known a long time," Carla went on. "Usually he didn't tell anyone but the patient about the hospice; it was too risky. The wife's condition deteriorated suddenly, however. She couldn't walk out of the Hospital on her own and she'd always hated the thought of life support—he couldn't bear not to act, so he let her husband help him take her to a safe house. But the husband, who wasn't even sick, couldn't disappear. He had to go home, and he wasn't able to deceive their daughter for long. She got the truth out of him—she wanted her mother's body preserved indefinitely by all means possible. She reported Ramón to the authorities and sent an ambulance to the hospice. When it got there, the woman had just died and was shrouded for burial; the body was cold. And there were others there, dying, who'd been Ramón's patients."

"But if only one dead body was involved, why was this worse than what we all do when we dispose of bodies? Why was it called aggravated murder?"

"He confessed to letting her die, Jesse. It was a worse crime than others partly because he was a doctor, and had falsified charts; the Hospital's authority depends on the public placing absolute trust in doctors. Still, he might have got off with treatment for insanity. But he couldn't allow that to happen. Peter was barred from the case because everyone knew he and Ramón had been friends since their medical school years—and if he'd been drugged by anyone else, they'd have gotten our secrets from him."

Yes, Jesse thought, that had always been the biggest danger. He had not let himself recognize the one way in which it might be circumvented.

"We're more careful now," Carla told him. "We don't keep more than one patient in a single safe house, and other precautions are taken. But in Ramón's case they suspected conspiracy. They would have found out I was the one who hacked into the files that showed those people in the Vaults, and they'd have learned the names of the hospice caregivers who hid when they heard the ambulance coming. Peter and Kira would have been compromised, too—perhaps even Ian. Ramón had to make them think he was solely responsible. So he convinced them that he did it for money, that he was holding the patients hostage until their families paid off."

"That's fantastic," Jesse protested. "There were no ransom demands, and besides, if they questioned the husband—"

"He was judged mentally incompetent, which he may have been; he went into shock when he found out about Ramón's arrest and was sent to a residential care unit."

"Even so—"

"People believe what they want to believe," Carla said, "and the authorities here don't want to believe anybody could object to stasis. Financial motives are easier for them to understand. Besides, Ramón passed a brain scan and polygraph test—he controlled his physical reactions. And on top of that, he was projecting telepathically."

"I thought telepathy couldn't be used to lie."

"It can project genuine feelings, and he genuinely wanted them to believe him. I had to use it too," she added. "I had to go to the hearing and pretend to be shocked by his crime, not to save myself—I didn't care what happened to me at that point—but for the Group. All I could do for him was help him protect us."

At the cost of his life, Jesse thought, awed. His own worries seemed trivial beside recognition of what commitment to the Group might really mean.

"I never want to talk about this again," Carla said, blinking back tears. "I can't bear it . . . just the thought of him, of anyone, being shut in that thing, the lid coming down, aware even for a few moments of what was happening . . . it terrifies me. I know it can't ever happen to *me*, but I couldn't *stand* it. . . ."

He held her tight. There didn't seem to be any solace he could offer, beyond loving her. Could he possibly live up to the standard of a man like Ramón?

"Oh, yes, Jesse," Carla whispered. "I can't forget Ramón . . . God help me, I can't stop seeing his face. I so wanted tonight to be perfect for you, and I've spoiled it. But I love you! That's all that matters now."

She nestled against him again. They lay there, sharing silently, while the fire slowly died. Not until she slept did Jesse rise to unfold a blanket that lay folded by the hearth. She woke as it touched her, welcoming him, the old grief now thrust from consciousness.

"I want to marry you, Carla," Jesse said.

Carla smiled at him. "You already have, according to Group custom."

"Just by our coming together?" He was surprised; this didn't seem to match what Peter had told him about relationships.

"By coming together, sharing our minds, with that intention," Carla said. "We're not like outsiders—we don't need words. I *knew*. You knew too, didn't you, that we both were committed?"

"Yes, but aren't there formalities?"

"To make it legal we'll have to register in the city, but that's just signing documents. The formality as far as the Group's concerned is making love by the Lodge fire. I wouldn't have done it here if I hadn't already been sure you wanted to marry me. Fire is a symbol, Jesse—especially this fire. After the Ritual you'll understand why."

Jesse put more logs on, recalling that he had always sensed something at gatherings around this fire, some special bond between people that was less evident anywhere else. Why else, considering the wood shortage, would they light it every night regardless of the weather?

"Of course the Group will give us a wedding feast," Carla went on, her eyes sparkling. "But our marriage took place here. Since you didn't know, we could do it again to make sure."

He took her in his arms and they made love again. This time, when their minds merged, no dark memories intruded. He knew that they were forever bonded, not merely one flesh, but one soul.

33

THE WEDDING FEAST would follow the Ritual, Jesse was told. Carla had gone back to work in the city the night after their marriage. He had wanted to go with her, could not imagine another five-day wait apart from her. But Peter had persuaded him to stay and finish his training. "I'd like to hold the Ritual the end of next week," he said, "assuming you feel ready to make a commitment." Jesse had agreed with enthusiasm. No doubt remained in his mind about committing himself to the Group in whatever way the mysterious Ritual demanded.

The marriage was not to be legally registered after all. Peter had insisted that Jesse's offworld funds must stay offworld, and that he must therefore not be officially viewed as a permanent resident of the colony. "We may need access to those funds suddenly," he'd explained. "You can borrow all the money you want from us, to be paid from your accounts if and when we use them. But Undine's tax authorities mustn't find out that they exist."

Furthermore, a legal marriage would document Jesse's connection to Peter through Carla. Though her association with Peter away from work was carefully concealed, in time someone might notice if his assistant married a patient he'd discharged under questionable circumstances. They might even start wondering about her own relationship with her boss. That would not happen merely from Jesse and Carla living together, since medical telemetry did not pinpoint people's location within the city.

It was just as well anyway not to register the marriage, Jesse thought. Since learning of Ramón's execution he had worried more than ever about the risks Carla ran. She had explained that besides the Group's other hackers, many people had access to the Hospital's database—she'd have been suspected only because she was Ramón's wife. Now she was *his* wife, and it would be best if the authorities didn't know that, in case he was ever accused of murder.

He would be told little about the Ritual beforehand, Kira said, except that it was a happy occasion, always followed by celebration with which wedding festivities would combine well. "I must say, though, Jesse," she went on, "that I think Peter is rushing it. It was heartless of him not to let you go with Carla—you should be together the first week of your marriage. And you will need more experience in deep telepathy, which only she can give you. She'll be here several days ahead of time, which he says will be enough. All the same, he's thinking more of himself than he is of you, which isn't like him."

"Himself? What difference does the date make to him?"

"He still wants Ian here," Kira said grimly, "and he claims Ian wants to come. He says Ian's dying wish is to initiate you, though he's never met you! Personally, I doubt that Ian can even get here, let alone survive the Ritual in his weakened state. It's true that it's something he'll find hard to let go. But if he should try it and fail—"

"Is it dangerous?" Jesse asked, surprised.

"Oh yes," Kira admitted. "You will be warned. But you are in better condition for it now than Ian is. Peter should know that, but he doesn't want the final responsibility of judging you at the moment in which you are placed at risk. Ian has always had that responsibility. Peter's hoping against hope that he'll be spared it one more time."

Troubled, Jesse said, "I trust Peter's judgment."

"So do we all. I don't mean to frighten you, Jesse. Peter is more than competent to handle the Ritual. But he has a tendency to expect a trifle too much of people in lesser matters, and knowing that, he doesn't yet quite trust himself." She shook her head. "As to the lesser matters, he is asking more of you than he should by hurrying this last week of lab training when you've just been married and should enjoy yourself! Some of the things we have to do won't be pleasant."

This proved to be an understatement. During the five days of Carla's absence Jesse spent long hours in the lab. To begin with, he was required to get into the states he'd been taught one by one, without feedback, blindfolded so that only Kira could see the patterns. Then other stressors were added—loud noise, blinding light, and finally sporadic pain. Combinations of states were demanded; he had to control various physiological responses simultaneously. Sometimes he worked with Greg instead of Kira, deprived of her familiar presence. He and Greg were good friends, but Jesse could make no telepathic contact with him and soon understood that his role in this exercise was to intentionally shake him up.

Kira taught him to control bleeding, first on dual but eventually without help. The cuts were superficial and quickly healed. "You're ahead on this," she said. "Peter jumped the gun last week, and in that, I think he was wise. There was a larger issue than your ability to self-heal. But usually we don't deal with deep wounds until later."

"The training goes on after the Ritual?" said Jesse, with dismay born of exhaustion.

"It's a lifelong process, Jesse," Kira told him. "But it won't be as intensive. You've a lot left to learn before you're fully protected against stress-based illness. Besides that, there are states of consciousness not everyone cares to experience, and paranormal powers only a few people have begun to investigate—plus some common ones, such as re-mote viewing, that for some reason Peter feels you shouldn't get involved in yet. How far you'll eventually choose to go is up to you."

The fifth day started normally, on dual, with Kira show-ing him a mind-pattern he'd never seen before. He matched it easily enough, wondering what new state of conscious-ness it represented. And then, suddenly, he drew back, stuck by a terror so intense, and so astonishing, that he scarcely recognized it as fear. He wanted only to withdraw, hide, not just from the dizzying visuals but from everything. . . .

"God, Kira," he gasped, his face white. "What's happen-ing to me?"

"Look at your feedback now," she said calmly.

It showed panic—the same as the worst of the panic he'd experienced his first night in the lab. Jesse struggled with it, but couldn't seem to pull out. Unbelievably, he froze, though reason told him there was nothing whatsoever to be frightened of. Trapped, helpless, he was caught in a loop: groundless panic produced more panic engendered by his helplessness.

"I don't understand," he protested weakly. "What brought it on? There's nothing—no pain, nothing wrong—how can this be happening to me without any cause?"

"It's hard when you can't see a cause," Kira agreed. "But actually, Jesse, this is an encouraging reaction right now. I led you into an altered state that you're not yet equipped to handle. If that had been tried before you had any training, nothing would have happened—you'd simply not have been able to follow. The fact that you reacted consciously shows that you've developed a great deal of strength."

It didn't feel like strength. It felt like hell. "Why do I feel terrified? What's wrong with me?"

"Nothing. I know it feels as if there is, but all that's happening is that your unconscious mind is on the alert. It interpreted an unfamiliar state as threatening—so you feel fear."

"But there's nothing to be afraid of."

"No. And so there is conflict. The human mind strives to maintain a status quo. It does so with respect to your body as well as your psyche. So, when there's conflict, it fights, and if it can't win, the adrenalin keeps flowing. People's sensitivity to that varies. You are not as sensitive as some; that's why nothing like this has ever happened to you before."

"You mean it's *normal*? Other people feel this way?"

"Oh, yes, due to all sorts of conflicts—often for weeks at a time. But Med science doesn't recognize it. It looks for deep-seated psychiatric causes or arbitrary chemical imbalances, neither of which is a valid approach to the situation."

"I've always felt that way about headshrinking. I take it Peter's not the kind of psychiatrist who goes in for it."

"Not usually. There are cases where it applies, but they're exceptions. Much harm has been done by generalizing from them to the average sufferer. On the other hand, depth psychology does at least acknowledge the mind's primacy. Belief in physical causation is worse."

"Aren't there ever physical causes?"

"The proximate causes are physical. Neurotransmitters produce physical effects. And these can be relieved chemically. In the Hospital or even in Fleet, you'd have been treated that way at the first sign of symptoms like those you're now having. Are you sorry not to be offered such relief?"

"Kira, that's a loaded question. The way you ask it tells me there's some reason why I shouldn't be sorry. Some reason besides being willing to pay a price for all I've learned here, I mean."

"The price of mind power is never arbitrary," Kira said. "To live in peace with it, you must learn to deal with groundless anxiety. There may be . . . recurrent episodes. You may wake in the night, in terror, without knowing why. The episodes will be brief—I'll teach you how to recover. But you will know, deep down, that the panic may recur."

"You're making it sound like a literal bad trip."

"That's exactly what it is. The only difference is that it won't harm you, whereas if it came from a state forced on you by drugs, it could."

Still sick with fear, shivering, Jesse asked, "Are you trying to warn me to expect evil as well as good from paranormal powers?" It occurred to him that such powers could be turned to what tradition on Earth called black magic, Satanism, or the dark side of the Force.

"What you feel is not evil," Kira declared. "The evil use of such powers is an all-too-real possibility, but you won't come up against it within the Group because both Ian and Peter have been very careful not to recruit anybody who's susceptible. They've occasionally had to deal with outsiders—but that's another story. You have enough to worry about right now without hearing *that*."

"What's the aim of putting me through this, then?"

"Think of it as an inoculation," Kira said. "You are about to move to the city, where neither Peter nor I will be on hand to cope with emergencies, and though Carla can help you, she's not a trained instructor. There won't be lab equipment available in any case. Through the use of this equipment, we have opened your mind to the alteration of consciousness. We've done it rapidly, intensively, in a mere fraction of the time this process would haven taken if traditional non-drug methods had been used. There are more potential altered states than you've imagined, Jesse, and you're now vulnerable to experiencing some of them spontaneously. If that happens it can be terrifying, and as you are learning now, terror feeds on terror. You need to know how to handle it. You don't want to end up in the psych ward at a time when Peter doesn't happen to be there."

Horrified, Jesse burst out, "Could that happen?"

"It happens frequently—but not to our trained people. We make sure they have experience to protect them."

"So you're going to teach me to . . . turn this off?"

"Yes. But not right away, Jesse." Kira looked at him

with compassion. "There's another kind of protection I have to give you first. The process involves some suffering, but what you'll gain is worth that. Okay?'

He wondered what would happen if he said it was not okay. But he did trust Kira's wisdom, and he'd gone along with too much to balk now, so he nodded.

She took him from the lab into the infirmary, where she opened a cabinet and produced a hypodermic. "I'm going to give you something that will make you sick," she said. "I know you still feel frightened without cause, and that will make this particularly hard to bear. There is no physical antidote. It will not simply wear off. I can of course heal you if necessary, but you need to learn that your own mind is capable of doing so."

Jesse drew breath. Well, they had done it to him many times in the Hospital and he had survived—but either they *had* used an antidote or it *had* worn off.... "What sort of symptoms will I have?" he asked."

"Nausea and cramps—similar to what you had in the Hospital, but more severe."

Jesse lay down on the cot. Kira gave him the injection, then left the room. What followed were among the worst hours of his life.

He broke out into a cold sweat when the nausea hit; it was indeed more severe and persistent than it had been in the Hospital. The cramps proved almost unendurable. He found himself unable to stop the pain as he had learned to do—internal pain was somehow harder to manage. Dimly, he perceived that the baseless terror with which he'd begun might have something to do with this. The fact that he was constantly dragging himself to and from the bathroom also interfered with control of his feelings. His terror progressed from being groundless to a specific fear that Kira would leave him alone until he somehow made his mind cure him—which meant she might never come back.

By the time she did return he was so weak he could

hardly speak. "Kira . . . I feel like I'm . . . dying. I don't want to ask for help, but—"

She put a cool hand on his forehead, and he felt her sympathy rush into him, reviving him. "This is a harsh lesson," she said gently.

"And I've failed."

"No. It will serve its purpose." She helped him back into the lab, went on dual, showed him a new mind-pattern. He matched it quite quickly, and the sickness faded. "Remember it," she cautioned. "This isn't something we'd want to repeat for practice."

Definitely not, thought Jesse. "Kira—if I'd had this training before I was in the Hospital, could I have thrown off what they gave me?"

"Yes, though you'd have been wise not to reveal that you could."

"Then . . . I'm in danger of being picked up again. That's what you're trying to protect me from."

"Possibly, though the risk is small. You might also get sick naturally from something like food poisoning. But that's not the main point of the lesson." Kira paused, then continued, "Jesse, I didn't drug you—we don't believe in drugs, after all. What I injected was distilled water."

He was not sure he'd heard right. "What made me sick, if not the injection?"

"Your mind made you sick. On ancient Earth, witch doctors killed their enemies with curses. Prisoners told they'd been poisoned sometimes died with the symptoms of poisoning. And people today often get sick merely because the Meds say they're sick. If informed by a trusted authority that sickness is imminent, then the mind will produce sickness—even yours did."

"The placebo effect in reverse?"

"Yes. The technical term is 'nocebo.'"

"And I fell for it," he said ruefully. "In spite of all you've been saying these past weeks."

"That very fact proves that it's the mind, not the body,

that determines your well-being, doesn't it? All the training has been aimed toward making you understand this. Just an intellectual understanding's not enough, though. It needs to be a deep, gut-level understanding."

"Well," Jesse said dryly, "gut-level knowledge is what I got, certainly."

"As we warned you in the beginning, we use drastic methods to break the conditioning people acquire by living in a Med-dominated culture. Have they worked for you? Have you become unconditionally sure that the mind can determine physical responses?"

"Yes," Jesse declared. "I believe it, Kira."

"Good. You'll need to, during the Ritual. Remember it, when the moment comes in which you must defy your deepest instinctive fear."

He was too tired, and still too shaken by unwarranted fright, to ponder this. It took another hour of work on dual before he managed to absorb the fact that groundless anxiety, like any other fear, would not go away until he was willing for it *not* to go away. Once he'd mastered the knack of not letting it bother him, however, the anxiety lifted. It seemed incredible that he could ever have panicked over nothing. He knew that if it did happen again, he could ride it out.

"Congratulations," Kira told him, as his spirits began to rise. "You've come a long way. Whatever Peter's motive was for pushing you so fast, his experiment succeeded. I wish you joy with Carla, Jesse. You've earned it."

34

THE DAYS AFTER Carla returned were idyllic. Jesse had never known so much happiness; every hour with her was joy, but the private ones were beyond description. They moved into one of the cottages—only temporarily theirs, of course, since different people came to the Lodge during different weeks— and spent a good share of their time there. That time brought him more than sensual pleasure. That sex could lead to altered consciousness had been known to many cultures, she told him, and though the goals and symbols of the traditions that had used it that way on Earth weren't the same as the Group's, some of the same techniques applied. He wondered, once he'd been shown those techniques, why he'd ever thought mere minutes long enough for lovemaking.

Carla helped him to achieve stronger telepathic rapport than he'd thought possible. It wasn't only that the two of them became one during physical arousal—that, she said, sometimes happened even to people without paranormal skills. It would have proved the existence of telepathy centuries ago if not for the widespread fear of recognizing such powers. Now free of that fear, Jesse let her teach him to sustain their link, to reach with his mind and receive knowledge from hers. She assured him that once gained, this skill would be lasting and could be used apart from sex, not only with her but with others. "For working as a healer," she explained, "which you may do later on. But especially for the Ritual, when you'll draw on power from us all."

He was not worried about the coming Ritual, despite Kira's admission that it involved danger. Carla would be with him. She seemed to be looking forward to it. Having found that the Group's methods always turned out well, he saw no reason to be afraid.

On the morning of the appointed day, Peter took him to the lab for one last check of the abilities in which he'd been trained. It was a grueling session, and although he performed flawlessly, Jesse found himself getting more and more nervous as it progressed. Finally it dawned on him that Peter was causing this, deliberately stirring fears he'd thought were behind him—even to the extent of leading him into the mind-pattern for groundless anxiety.

"Damn it, Peter," he burst out, "you're trying to scare me! You can't do that, you know."

"I thought not," Peter agreed, "not this way, anyway. But I had to make sure." He sat up, pushing back his headpiece, and the dual feedback patterns on the wallscreen blinked off. "If you did not have enough confidence by now to be absolutely unshakable in the use of your skills, I could not let you go through with the Ritual tonight. Yet you must have the impetus of fear to gain the mind power it will demand. So you need to feel some apprehension."

"And with clever games, you're setting me up to do so," Jesse observed.

"I suppose it seems that way. But the danger of failure is real." Peter reached over and gripped Jesse's hand. "Jess, from here on things get serious. There will be no more games, and you can be badly hurt if you take this warning too casually."

"Not telling me what to expect is a game in itself, though, isn't it?"

"No," Peter said. "If I described what we'll do in advance, you would be so afraid that you wouldn't be able to do it."

"So you simply . . . test me. The way we began."

"Not 'simply,' but yes, tests are inherent in it, not only of your courage but of your trust in us. You could not do what we'll ask of you without our telepathic aid—our rapport with each other is the foundation of the Group, and to become one of us you must be willing to rely on it. Furthermore, if your belief in what you pledge is less than unconditional, if you merely pretend to yourself that you believe, both you and others will suffer. But that's not going to happen." He smiled reassuringly. "You have been thoroughly prepared to attain the necessary state of consciousness. And it's an awesome experience, Jess. We'll all renew our commitment as you make yours, and we'll get high; but you will start out high and get higher than ever before."

"Exactly what am I committing myself to?" Jesse asked, realizing that no one had ever been specific about it.

"Nothing you've not already decided to do. You'll pledge to live by the principles we've taught you and to support fellow-members, just as they will support you."

"Is that all?" He had hoped he'd be asked to take on some significant task. He was impatient, now, to see action.

Peter, sensing this thought, hesitated. "That's all as far as the Ritual is concerned. Before long, Jess, I may ask you for a further commitment. I can't talk about that yet. If Ian should say anything that implies special plans for you, keep it to yourself, okay?"

"Ian's coming, then?"

"Yes, thank God. It will be his last Ritual, his last visit to the Lodge—so this is a bittersweet time for us. I hope you'll forgive us if our joy in your celebration and wedding feast is mixed with sadness."

That afternoon more people began to arrive on the Island; boats and seaplanes were moored in the bay since there wasn't room for them all at the dock. Jesse and Carla slipped away and walked along the shore to a secluded cove far from the swimming area. The weather was glorious, the sky a more vivid blue than was usual on Undine, the sun warm. They spread a blanket on the flat rocks, stripped, and made love. "I'm supposed to get you high," Carla told him. "You have to start out high the first time you go through the Ritual."

"I thought I was expected to be apprehensive," he said, "though I don't think I can be if we do this, Carla." He was already in high spirits, and she was skilled, he knew, in arousing even better feelings. No thought of danger could touch him; the future seemed cloudless as the sky. Whatever happens next, he thought, there will never be a day to surpass this one.

Later, they stood on a rock by the water, watching the sun drop into the bay and mists begin to rise. Carla was more beautiful than ever in the fading light, he thought, her dark hair tumbling over her shoulders, her slender body silhouetted against the backdrop of silvered waves. It was a picture he would carry with him forever. They kissed one last time, then headed back to change clothes for the evening's celebration.

He was still high when they entered the Lodge, and not at all frightened. "You'll get telepathic help from everyone," Carla had told him. "And especially from Ian, because he's *good*. He won't let you come to harm."

"Better than Peter, even?"

"Ian trained Peter. He originated most of our techniques." She gave him a radiant smile. "Just follow his lead and don't lose focus. You're going to be fine."

The tables in the common room had been pushed against the west windows to make space for a large assembly. Adorned with greenery, they were set buffet-style in preparation for the wedding feast. The floor cushions near the central fireplace had been taken up; the people were all standing. They were animated, even exhilarated, by the rousing music that filled the room—synthesized music, tracks Jesse hadn't heard before. There was a beat to it that stirred his soul and made him want to soar.

Peter and Kira, in a corner away from the others, beckoned to Jesse; he and Carla joined them. "Reiko just phoned," Kira said. "Ian was dressed and ready to come when she went to get him, but his legs were weak and he collapsed. He may live a few weeks longer, but he won't leave his bed again."

"I'm sorry," Jesse said. "Look, we don't have to have a feast tonight. Nobody will be in a mood for it."

"We're going ahead with the wedding feast," Peter said. "There's a crowd here that would be disappointed to have come for nothing—not to mention all the food that's been prepared. We don't look on approaching death from old age as cause for mourning, Jess, however deeply we grieve personally."

"What do you mean, come for nothing?" Carla said. "The Ritual—"

"Can't be held tonight without Ian," Peter stated.

"We've been over this," Kira declared. "He will never come again, Peter. He'll be bedridden until he dies. You know what has to be done. Will you stand here and tell Jesse when he's ready for commitment, worked up to it, that you lack the strength to fulfill your own responsibilities?"

Peter's face was white. "I'm not prepared. No official appointment has been made, and since Reiko's not here the Council can't vote—"

"That's a formality, and you know it. You have been Ian's backup in every Ritual for the past five years; everyone's aware of his wishes. You are his heir in every sense, not just the legal one. You've been carrying most of the leadership load anyway lately. There's not a remote chance that the Council will choose anyone else."

Jesse stared at him, puzzled. To shrink from a hard task was so unlike Peter that he wondered what he was misinterpreting.

"I can't risk it," Peter said stubbornly. "Not tonight, not with Jesse—"

"When, then, and with whom?" Carla demanded. "Jesse and I are married, Peter! Is he to come to the city, vulnerable to risk but uncommitted, without the pledged support of the Group and the empowerment you, and you alone, are fit to give him? Or are he and I to live apart while you work up courage to do what Ian has relied on you for?" She spoke angrily; Jesse had never seen her so upset.

Peter met her eyes, though his own were agonized. "No," he conceded. "I must take this on now for Jesse's sake—and for the Group's, so that it won't disintegrate when Ian dies. If you of all people can trust Jess to me—"

"I trust you as I've trusted Ian," Carla declared. She turned to Jesse. "It's pointless to ask whether you trust Peter," she said, "because you wouldn't be here without that. But in the Ritual, a deeper kind of trust is needed. You must believe not just in his sincerity but in his judgment and paranormal skill, and if either of you falters, you will—come to harm. Peter himself won't be in danger. He is afraid only for you."

"It's up to me, then," Jesse said. "We seem to be at a point where the future of the Group depends on whether we go ahead with this thing. I don't know much about what it involves, but I understand command decisions. I am expendable, Peter. You are not. That's all there is to it; we don't really have a choice."

"If I fail with you, we all lose—lose more than anyone but Ian yet suspects."

"Then that's the chance we both take. But if you withdraw we all lose, too, and it's not a chance but a sure thing."

"You're right, of course," Peter admitted. "We have to do it. Yet I'm endangering you by my fear—"

"Are you? From what you've told me, fear should facilitate whatever psi powers you have to use."

"God," Peter murmured. "You're right there, too. Has it been so many years since I was truly afraid that I'd forgotten?"

"If so, Peter, you need this more than I do," Jesse said. "Perhaps we're talking about more than one empowerment here."

Peter nodded slowly. "We'll proceed as planned. Kira, you're Jesse's sponsor—"

Carla broke in, "I want to sponsor Jesse."

"I'm not sure that's wise," Peter told her, frowning. "It's been a long time for you, and considering what's happened in the interim—"

"Jesse is my husband; it's my right. And I want to renew my own commitment fully, not just with a candle." To Jesse she added, "The last time I took an active part was when Ramón sponsored me. Peter is afraid I will be . . . distracted. But if my love for you isn't stronger than old memories, how can I live up to the pledge?"

After a pause, Peter said with reluctance, "Okay. Risk increases power; love increases it still more. I'm not myself tonight—I spoke from my own self-doubt again."

"It's heavy responsibility, taking on two of unknown strength your first time presiding," Kira agreed. "But you are up to it, Peter."

"Will you be my backup, Kira?"

"Of course, if you wish, though Hari is better qualified."

"You know Jesse better than Hari does; you're already bonded with him. Hari's set to be torchbearer."

"All right, then; let's get started." She raised her voice, calling on people to assemble.

35

EVERYONE GATHERED AROUND the fireplace, not in a ring as usual, but in a semicircle several rows deep. On the open side of it, across the fire from the others, a smaller semicircle was formed: Peter at one end, Kira next to him, then Carla and finally Jesse, spaced so that he was facing Peter. Their crisp white shirts gleamed against the dark backdrop of the wall behind them. It was the first time Jesse had seen anyone wear white at the Lodge. When he and Carla had dressed in the fresh clothes she'd produced, he had assumed she'd chosen white to symbolize their wedding. But Peter's and Kira's shirts, open-collared and short-sleeved, were identical to his own.

Candles, as yet unlighted, were distributed to the people, who were now hushed and expectant. Someone turned the lights and the music down to background level, so that the fire became the room's focus and spoken words were clearly audible.

"Ian's deepest wish was to be here," Peter began, "but that has proved impossible. And so from this day forward we must carry on without him." A murmur of sorrow spread through the listeners, then gave way to silence.

"We're gathered tonight as witnesses to Jesse's commitment to the Group," Peter continued. "In the Ritual of his pledging we will renew our own commitment, remembering the time when we too faced the fire and for the first time felt its power to inspire our lives."

Carla had told him the Lodge fire was symbolic, Jesse recalled. To him, it now meant their marriage, and she'd said others had similar memories. But people gathered around it every evening, laughing and joking, eating, singing bawdy songs as well as ballads. It was a symbol of fellowship, surely—of happiness and home—but he found it rather strange that the same symbol had been chosen for something as solemn as he'd understood the Ritual to be. It seemed more comforting than inspirational.

Peter spoke on, summarizing the precepts of the Group and its goal of proving that it was possible to live by them. To trust in the primacy of mind over body. To develop skills outsiders would call paranormal. To enjoy life without succumbing to worry or fear. To reject maintenance of brain-dead bodies in stasis as a travesty of life and to accept death in old age as natural, whether or not survival of the spirit might follow. . . .

Jesse had rarely heard this last idea mentioned in the Group. It was apparent, from the way Peter phrased his remarks, that members differed in their feelings on the issue, as was the case with all religious matters; and yet he sensed that majority felt existence continued in some way after death. Was that why it meant so much to them to keep the dead out of stasis? he wondered suddenly. Did they believe their spirits were entrapped as long as their bodies were maintained? Such a notion was oxymoronic, surely— spirit, if it existed, would by definition depart once life was gone. Still, glancing at Carla beside him, he shuddered at the thought of what her awareness of Ramón's preserved body must be doing to her. It wasn't a matter of logic. Her image of him could hardly be divided.

There was a short pause; then Peter concluded, "In silence, let's commend ourselves to whatever Power we hold highest, each of us in our own way." This did seem to be a time when you'd want to pray if you were so inclined, Jesse thought, suddenly apprehensive. For him, it was not quite prayer; he had never adhered to any formal religion. But he knew that he was about to be tested in some unimaginable way, a paranormal way, evidently, since no physical peril could arise in this setting. He'd been told he would be at risk, and that could mean only that they would do something to his mind—something so overwhelming that Peter feared he might come to harm. He appealed to whatever force might prevail in the universe to make him strong enough to withstand it.

After several minutes had passed, Hari—also wearing white—stepped forward on the opposite side of the fireplace, carrying a tall unlit torch. He plunged its head into the fire and then raised it, blazing. Turning, he extended it outward, and one by one the assembled people approached it to light their candles. Then he came around to the participants' side and stood behind them, holding it aloft.

To Carla, Peter said, "Do you wish to sponsor Jesse in his commitment to the Group, sharing the peril of his pledging, and do you believe him qualified to undertake this commitment safely?"

In a clear voice Carla answered, "Yes, I do."

Peter then addressed Jesse directly. "Do you accept Carla Francesco as your sponsor, knowing that her participation may increase your danger?"

"I'm happy to accept her." But not happy to have her share the mysterious peril, he thought. Why would anything done to his mind affect her?

"So be it," Peter continued. "Jesse Sanders, do you confirm the pledge you have made to keep everything you know, or may learn, of the Group and its activities secret from outsiders, now and forever, at whatever cost to yourself?"

"I do," Jesse replied.

"Do you by your own free choice commit yourself to live by the precepts of the Group, as I have stated them?"

"Yes, I do."

"Will you support fellow-members of the Group in all ways, even at the risk of your personal safety?"

"I will." This meant more than he would have assumed before his introduction to telepathic sharing, he knew. He was pledging to support them not only by his actions, but, when occasion arose, through ESP.

"Do you believe that your mind has power over the well-being of your body, and that it can protect or heal you from sickness, injury and pain?"

"I do."

"Jesse, are you willing to confirm your commitment by proving your trust in that power?"

"Yes, I am." Had he not already proven it on several occasions? To ask for formal consent after the fact seemed rather anticlimactic. And yet he knew the climax of the Ritual was still to come.

There was another moment of silence in which Jesse sensed that Peter was probing him telepathically, far more deeply than in the past. It was not unpleasant. He was high; Carla was beside him and she was high too; and he felt at ease within this gathering of good friends. He was committed to them and to the promises he had made. The strong connection among them ... the soft yet exalting music ... the flicker of nearly two hundred candles beyond the fire ... there was no past, no future, but only this moment, frozen in time forever. . . .

Hari lowered the torch he carried, thrusting its pole horizontally between Kira and Carla so that the flame, at waist level, was poised over the fire's edge. Tension mounted among the watchers. Using words sanctified, Jesse guessed, by long tradition, Peter said:

"Unfaced fear is the destroyer. We will acknowledge fear and accept it, we will go past it and live free.

"We will trust the power of the mind over all restrictions, whether imposed from within or by the world outside.

"We will act always through volition, allowing neither internal nor external pressures to enslave us.

"We will support one another unfailingly in fulfilling this pledge.

"We believe that we are stewards of a flame that will illuminate future generations.

"And we now seal our commitment with the symbol of the mind's power, which is fire."

Across the semicircle, his face lit by the torchlight, Peter smiled encouragingly. His normal ebullience had returned. Jesse returned the smile, trusting him, unafraid now of whatever mental shock might be coming. He sensed that their telepathic link had become nearly as strong as his bond with Carla.

The torch blazed between them, so close Jesse could feel its heat. Then suddenly, incredibly, Peter stretched out his right hand and thrust it into the flame. He held it there, undamaged.

"Place your hand on mine, Jesse," he said in a low, commanding voice.

For a second Jesse did not grasp what was meant. But Kira spoke quickly, also as a command. "Do it, Jesse. Now."

Jesse knew that if he stopped to think, he could not do it, and that if he did not, that would mean leaving Carla, his friends, the Lodge—everything that now mattered to him. It would be a total repudiation of the Group he had come to believe in, the pledge he had just made. And even more, it would be a rejection of his own power, the thing in himself that during these last weeks had begun to fill the emptiness of too many years. Having tasted what it was to move beyond the merely human, he could not drop back. The free choice essential to that power had become no choice at all, for he knew that he would rather be physically burned than give up all that he truly valued.

This knowledge came to him instantly, without rational deliberation, as a whole. He was less aware of it consciously than of what he was receiving from the Group, from Carla, from Kira—and of course from Peter. They were giving him a sense of *how* to do it, so that though he was willing to be burned, and knew he must be willing, at the same time he knew that he need not suffer any more harm than Peter himself had. That knowledge, too, came instantly. No more than a few seconds had passed.

Without hesitation Jesse thrust his hand forward to touch Peter's, letting it be bathed by the flames.

He had thought he'd been high before, thought he knew what it meant to be high—but all that was nothing, compared to this. He was hovering somewhere in space beyond the planet. There was no space, no time, nothing left of the physical or mundane. There was only fire, a flame of light that enveloped and warmed him, but did not burn. All the universe was light. He was one with it, and with the others, yet was also himself; he trusted himself as he never had while worldbound.

At the edge of his perception, he knew Carla's hand, too, was in the flame, and so was Kira's. In the opposite semicircle, beyond the fireplace, the others' fingers touched the flames of their candles, thus magnifying the collective power of the minds merged with his. He felt no pain, nor were his hand and arm damaged. They were impervious to flame. It was surreal . . . except that it seemed that nothing in his life had ever been real until now.

Peter was drawing his hand back out of the flame; only with psychic prompting did Jesse notice. He withdrew his own, realizing that though he had been conscious only of eternity, mere moments had elapsed. There was no end to the power of the human mind, he thought, awestricken, staring incredulously at his unburned fingers. It could do *any-thing*! At the moment, this fact did not scare him, though he guessed that once the high wore off, he would be unnerved by it. It was too late to ask whether he really wanted the degree of power he had assumed.

"It's what we live by," said Carla. "This is who we are, and we can't deny it. We can't betray our foretaste of what humans may become."

He turned to her and they embraced. The others came to him and one by one embraced him, Peter first, then Kira, then all the rest, first laying their candles on the fire as Hari had now laid the torch. Greg, Michelle, Bernie, Anne, Kwame, Ingrid, Nathan, Liz, Erik, Dorcas . . . the friends he'd come to know as family, others meeting him for the first time, all pledged to him now as he to them, for as long as he lived. . . .

"What was that part about you sharing—even increasing—my danger?" Jesse said to Carla when the others had moved away. "You weren't a novice."

"Peter's less experienced than Ian in sustaining grouped minds. Immunity to flame can't be attained by any person alone, Jesse, not even after long practice. It requires the support of everyone who participates. If either you or I had panicked or lost focus when we were in such close rapport, all four of us would have been burned."

Jesse tightened his arm around her. None of them had handled fire before without Ian present, he realized with awe. If he himself had faltered, he'd have brought Peter down, too. No doubt burns could have been healed, but shaken faith in the leader would have been irreparable.

He and Carla stood staring into the fireplace for a few more minutes. Then, as the mood of solemnity faded and the volume of the music swelled, they went joyfully to the tables spread with the wedding feast.

36

WHEN CARLA WENT back to the city for her next workweek, Jesse went with her. Though he still didn't know how he'd occupy his days while she was working, neither of them wanted to spend more nights apart. They planned to return to the Island almost every offshift, as she had even before his arrival. Once used to the company of telepaths, Group members spent as much free time together as possible, and friends tended to congregate; hers favored the Lodge over the other safe gathering places.

Carla had neither friends outside the Group nor any contact with relatives. "My parents didn't take me out of the crèche often," she told him, "and I left home for good right after I finished school." Having left home himself in youth, Jesse considered this both natural and fortunate—keeping Group membership secret must be awkward and painful for people close to their families. How, he wondered, did anyone hide a transformation as overwhelming as that of the Ritual? He supposed the impact of that miracle would wear off, eventually. But each time he looked down at his unburned hand, he was struck anew by awe at what had happened to him.

Before he left the Lodge, there were formalities. Jesse found that there were, in fact, passwords to learn—he had not met all the members, and in the city might need to identify them. Also, to his surprise, Peter asked for his consent to hypnosis.

"Since Ramón's death I've given hypnotic protection to those at high risk," Peter explained, "hospice caregivers, for example. It doesn't interfere with the conscious mind, but does reduce the risk of Group secrets emerging spontaneously from a drugged mind. An expert investigator could extract them, but at least it would keep them from slipping out during casual talk with nurses or other patients."

"And you think I should have this—protection."

"Yes, as a precaution, before you live in the city with Carla. But we're not going to put you at risk of getting caught with bodies, Jesse. Not except as a witness to burials here on the Island."

"Why not? I'm as willing to take that risk as the rest of you."

"I know you are, but there are reasons why it wouldn't be wise."

"I thought I was supposed to learn to care for the dying," Jesse protested.

"Yes, eventually, but not in the city with anyone likely to die while you're present. Originally I assumed that Ian would die at the Lodge, as he has always wished."

The discussion closed there; Peter would say no more. The hypnosis was done in the lab, and Jesse remembered nothing of it afterward. He was glad of it, however. The idea that he might involuntarily endanger Carla haunted him.

She'd told him few details of her hacking activities. But as they waited on the city dock for a water taxi after mooring Peter's plane, she said sadly, "If Ian is in a hospice, I suppose I should inactivate his file."

"No," Peter told her. "Ian said specifically that we are not to list him as in stasis before he dies. He has no family, after all, to inquire about him. I am his only legal heir."

"But Peter, it's dangerous to leave his file active. Someone in geriatrics may remember him, and what if he's called for a mandatory health check?"

"He had one a few weeks before he got too weak to pass it. He asked for it, in fact, because he knew what would soon happen."

"Ian *asked* for a health check? Voluntarily?"

"It surprised me," Peter admitted. "He said he must do it to prevent being caught later, when they wouldn't release him." At Carla's frown he added, "Yes, I know—it's contrary to the policy he himself established. We reject so-called preventative care except the minimum required by law. But something made him believe it would be important for him to remain free without our having to hide the fact that he's still alive. Did I ever tell you that he has precognitive dreams?"

"No," said Carla. "Literally, you mean? Paranormal dreams?"

Peter nodded. "His abilities are far greater than ours, and precognition is, after all, a known psi talent, particularly among people experienced in remote viewing, as he is."

Jesse, surprised, said, "Are you saying some people really foresee the future?"

"In dreams it's fairly common, though I've never had such a dream myself. Ian rarely discusses his dreams, but he's told me about some of them. The most recent made him feel he has something left to do in life, something that will require his action to be publicly acknowledged."

"He's kept out of the public eye for decades," Carla protested. "What sort of action could be required of him?"

"He doesn't know. He can't even be sure that the dream was a true premonition; he never is, before events provide proof. But he asked me to tell you, Carla, so you'll be sure not to inactivate his file."

Ian also, Peter said, had expressed a strong desire to meet Jesse. They had been settled in the city only two days when Peter came by Carla's apartment after work and accompanied them to the safe house where Ian was now living under Kira's care. "I'll feel honored to meet him," Jesse said. "But why would he ask to see me, a stranger, when he's dying?"

Peter was silent. Carla said, "He presided at the Ritual for all the rest of us. It's hard for him, I suppose, to think of members coming in that he doesn't know."

Kira met them at the door. "He tires very quickly now," she warned. "Don't stay too long."

Having been told that Ian was a hundred and thirty years old, Jesse had not known quite what to expect—but certainly not the vital, magnetic man he found. Ian, propped up on a couch in a room that looked nothing like a sickroom, did not even appear to be ill, let alone dying. He was thin; his hair was white and sparse; his skin was pale, almost translucent. But his eyes were alive with power as well as wisdom, and his voice was clear.

"So this is Jesse," he said. "Sit beside me, Jesse, and let me get to know you."

At a loss for what to say, Jesse approached the couch. Hastily Peter pulled a chair next to it for him to sit on and for that, Jesse was thankful; in another moment, he thought, he might have found himself kneeling.

There was silence. He longed to pour out his feelings to this man who was, he sensed, far more than he had guessed, despite all he'd heard of him these past weeks. And then he became aware that he didn't need to. The telepathic link between them surpassed any he had experienced, even his link with Peter during the Ritual. If Ian wanted to know him, he had only to draw on that link. Words would be awkward and superfluous.

In the same moment, he knew why they all loved Ian, and knew that he, too, loved him and would weep at his death. But he would grieve for his own loss and the Group's, not for Ian's sake. Ian would die because it was time. He would not, Jesse felt, be extinguished. He knew this was an irrational feeling, against all his own past convictions, but he could not shake it.

"I wanted to be at your Ritual," Ian told him. "but I found my legs would not support me. And then that night, I learned why they would not, and never will again. I dreamed again—Peter, hear this—and knew I dared not go to the Lodge. If I had gone, I might not have had strength enough to leave it again."

Peter said, "It's been your hope to eventually die at the Lodge ever since you built it, nearly a century ago. Why should you have to leave it?"

"Because there is something I must do that I can't do there. I have no knowledge of what it could be. But in the dreams, I know I'm needed, just as I knew—" He broke off, turned back to Jesse. "Will you take my hand?" he asked.

Jesse gripped the firm hand offered him. "I wish it could have been in fire," Ian told him, and he knew this for high praise.

"I will do it in fire here and now, if you ask me to," he said sincerely, ignoring Kira's frown. He was sure beyond question that with Ian he *could* do it.

"No matter," said Ian. "I can probe you without that; your mind is strong." Then for a moment it was as it had been with the Ritual torch, and he was free of time and space again, high again. . . .

Ian looked into his eyes and said, "I trust you, Jesse."

Then his fingers loosened and he lay back against the couch pillows, exhausted but apparently at peace.

Kira pulled the coverlet up over his shoulders, motioning them to go. Wordlessly they left the room. All the way home in the cab Jesse was silent, wondering what it was that Ian trusted him to achieve.

37

PETER TOOK JESSE aside as they prepared to leave the Lodge for his second week in the city. "I didn't want to intrude on your honeymoon," he said, "but if you've got some free time, I have a suggestion to make. Would you be willing to take on a job this workweek?"

"That would be great," Jesse said with enthusiasm. He'd dreaded having nothing to do in the daytime but more sightseeing.

"You won't enjoy it. It's low-paid work nobody wants, so we offer our services through the regular channels for Hospital volunteers. We ask most recruits to try it, during offshifts if they're currently employed, because it promotes comprehension of our goals."

"That's okay by me. What's the job?"

"Stasis vault attendant."

"Good God. I suppose it's a matter of 'acknowledge and accept our fears'?" Such a demand fit the Group's uncompromising policy of facing reality, certainly.

"For some, it is," Peter agreed. "But you'd be surprised, Jess—many of our recruits haven't the sense to be horrified by the idea. People who grow up in this colony have an idealized picture of happy eternal sleep. Pictures of the Vaults are never published, you see. Only those who've been into them know the reality. Your route to us was not typical, after all. We do most of our recruiting among people attracted to the paranormal, and we steer them into vault work before commitment, often even before approaching them. The shock is sometimes what starts them questioning Med policy."

"Well, it won't be a shock to me," Jesse said. "I saw the stasis deck on an old starship at the Fleet academy. Of course that's not the same—stasis for space travel was once necessary for colonization. The people placed in those units expected to wake, and nearly all of them did. But it doesn't take much imagination for me to picture vaults full of dead bodies."

"I realize you don't need the experience for the same reason most of our people do," Peter said. "For you, though, simply working in the Hospital—"

"Yes," Jesse said, chilled. "There's that." Peter was too good at his profession not to be aware that he hadn't been planning to go anywhere near the place.

"The only problem," Peter said, "is whether you can keep it from Carla. You realize, don't you, how she feels about stasis? We're all repelled by the thought; when we pledge to live past other fears, we project our normal human fear of death onto it. But she has a true phobia."

"She has good cause," Jesse declared. "I certainly won't mention it to her."

"Can you keep it out of your mind when you're telepathically joined?"

"If she can, I can," Jesse declared, "and she has, after our first night. The image she projected was quite accurate, incidentally. Does that mean she was put through this— ordeal?"

"Yes, when she joined us, before she was married to Ramón. At the time of his execution, I was sorry. But no one could have anticipated that happening to someone she loved." He sighed. "If she came to me for professional help, I could cure her of the phobia even now; I've helped recruits conquer worse ones. But she is not a trainee, so it's not my place to stir it up when she hasn't asked me to."

"Best to let it ride," Jesse agreed. "It's not as if she would ever have to see stasis vaults personally again."

"You're no longer a trainee either, Jess. You don't have to do this. But Carla said you were looking for some sort of challenge, and it's all I can offer right now."

"I think I do have to do it," Jesse said. In the Group you didn't turn away from things you found distasteful. "And yet—I wonder, Peter, whether it's right for us to take part in something we're so opposed to. As a matter of principle, shouldn't we refuse to work in the Vaults? Maybe even sabotage them?"

"We couldn't help matters that way," Peter said. "Public opinion wouldn't be changed by our refusal. As for sabotage, tempting as it sounds, it couldn't be done short of blowing up the entire building, killing all the patients and staff in that part of the Hospital. We don't take risks, let alone lives, for the sake of the dead."

Jesse couldn't argue with that. "I guess what bothers me," he confessed, "is that I don't see how we hope for even a moral victory. I'm not looking for martyrdom, but if we never protest publicly—"

"We can't win by your criteria," Peter said. "You're a man of action; you see winning as having an impact on the system here in this colony. That's not how human evolution works. There is a cumulative telepathic influence on culture, Jess. It has sometimes been called the collective unconscious, sometimes described as a sort of psi field, but never understood as the very significant factor that we in the Group know it to be. We have studied history in this light—Reiko's a professional historian and she can tell you the details. And so we believe that, as the Ritual puts it, we're 'stewards of a flame that will illuminate future generations.'"

"You mean that literally, Peter? That individuals influence the future in some way apart from what they pass on through public actions or words?"

"Yes, in the long run, if enough people are involved. And in any case, the individuals benefit. We win simply by being who we are. By living up to what we've pledged, by helping others when we can, by looking ahead to an era when there will be more of us. Not by futile attempts at forcing society to change."

Yet there had been hints that Peter had something active in mind for him, Jesse thought—even that Ian did. . . .

The next morning he waited until Carla had gone, then followed her to the Hospital and reported for work in the Vaults. Merely entering the building, donning orderly's garb and walking through miles of antiseptic corridors fraught with memory of his imprisonment, was daunting; before he even got to the stasis section he was unnerved. His discharge had been legally signed, still he wasn't listed as "cured." And in any case, there would eventually be mandatory check-ups, a prospect he'd tried to put out of his mind.

He knew he could stand anything the Meds might do to him, short of mind tampering. He was not physically afraid. After a while, he perceived that the idea of being forcibly controlled was what frightened him—the thought of finding himself helpless in the hands of alleged authority. That concept was what the Med establishment stood for. It was what the Group resisted. Seeing this, he understood as never before what his Ritual pledges meant, understood how the Group could win without changing the world outside. He understood, too, why Peter had sent him here. But that did not relieve his nerves.

The Vaults occupied many floors, a bewildering maze of chambers lined with row upon row of metal stasis units stacked ceiling-high, separated by narrow aisles. Only their ends were visible; they slid out like drawers in a morgue. Jesse had seen this on the old starship, though on a lesser scale—but those units had been empty. There was a wholly different feel to it in the presence of death masquerading as life. Dead bodies forcibly made to breathe, hearts kept beating by force . . . the control of well-meant authority extended past life into death, forever. . . . Throughout human history there had been tyranny, but always before there had at least been escape in death.

The work of a vault attendant was to check the indicator panel for each unit to make sure there were no malfunctions. He was given a phone with which to summon a technician in case any were found. This seemed to Jesse an unnecessary task, since the whole system was AI-controlled and malfunctions presumably would be detected by the central computer. It took him a while to realize that it was psychologically important to the Hospital staff, and the public, to believe that not-quite-dead loved ones were, in fact, cared for by human beings. Manually checking the panels served the same purpose that checking the control board did on a starship—a starship was AI-controlled, but you nevertheless kept a full-time watch on the bridge. You didn't leave it unattended until the computer triggered an alarm.

The Meds weren't defrauding the public. They truly believed in their mandate to preserve life as they defined it. That was the true horror—the travesty. The belief that personhood resided in literally mindless flesh. His function here was to maintain the fiction by treating the bodies as he would treat sleeping passengers.

He had expected the panels would show no names, but only numbers. He was wrong. That made it worse, somehow. It wasn't the same as names on tombstones . . . was it? Perhaps, Jesse thought, traditional interment had also been a charade. There were, after all, old tales of the dead rising from cemeteries, ancient superstitions that once had inspired true fear. Abhorrent though it seemed to him, he knew some Earth cultures had gone on preserving dead bodies, burying them in silk-lined caskets encased by concrete so they could not cleanly decompose, until the space for such burial had literally run out. Peter was right, he thought despairingly. Most people wouldn't stop equating persons with bodies, and if stasis technology became affordable elsewhere, the maintenance of the brain-dead would spread from world to world. The reality would continue to be repressed, as it always had been.

He did not read the names. He carefully looked past them, in terror lest he come across Ramón's. Everyone he knew must have relatives in here, he realized—even the crèche children who didn't know their identity. But death before old age was extremely rare on Undine. The vision brought to mind of old people was not quite so horrific as that of those sealed in prematurely.

At least he told himself it was not. On the fourth day of his circuit of the Vaults, Jesse learned otherwise. The lights on a panel before him indicated trouble. For a moment he thought, what the hell? Why call a technician to restore breath to a body long dead? But then he pictured what decomposition inside the sealed unit would mean . . . it would not be clean, certainly. That was an old fear of space travelers placed in stasis on the long trips, trips where no one stayed awake to deal with malfunctions. It had happened infrequently, but the result had been all too gruesome. Since this body couldn't be removed from the unit, he decided, it had best be maintained.

The technician came; the automatic racking mechanism was activated and the unit slid out from the wall, then lowered. The translucent cover opened. Within lay the body of an old woman. It was not breathing; the face was blue despite the ventilator tube protruding from the mouth. The veined hands, lying at its sides, were also blue. Oh God, Jesse thought. Can't they let it go? Is it not past restoration? Do they never dispose of them decently? He had never asked what would happen in such a case.

Nor did he find out. "It's not too late to save her," the technician said happily. "All we need to do is move her to a different unit." Metabolism being far lower than normal in stasis, going a short time without breathing was okay—lack of oxygen to the brain could not damage a corpse already brain-dead. Following instructions, Jesse unracked an empty unit—some were left in each chamber for use as spares—and suppressing his repugnance with difficulty, he helped transfer the flaccid body into it.

After the technician had gone, he retired to the nearest lavatory and was sick.

38

JESSE THOUGHT, AFTER actually seeing a maintained body, that keeping the image from his mind when with Carla would prove impossible. He walked home the long way, head down, staring into the canals, while he got his emotions under control. But it proved easier than he expected to deceive her. Their telepathic contact was not constant; she had already begun to teach him the knack of closing his mind, a skill as necessary for living among telepaths as the ability to open it. If she sensed that he was troubled, she did not mention it. Not until much later did it occur to him that Carla knew perfectly well what newcomers were required to do and had carefully refrained, during his week of vault work, from asking how he spent his days.

As for their hours of lovemaking, no thoughts of mundane life ever arose. Jesse was long past the stage of thinking during sex; it was a timeless altered state in which he knew only the sensations of the moment and the unity of his mind with Carla's. That this was not a state exclusive to the Group astonished him. Carla assured him it had been practiced by the ancients as well as any number of occult groups throughout Earth's history, described in many old texts though sometimes couched in symbolic terms. In the Group it was merely extended to the stage of full conscious telepathic communion.

"I don't get it," he protested. "I understand how knowledge of paranormal stuff got suppressed, but *sex*—well, there were eras when talking about it was taboo, I guess, but from the mid-twentieth century on—"

"Well, you see," Carla said, "It does lead to the so-called paranormal to do it this way. That's why rites involving sex were often condemned as the work of the Devil. And it's why most people gave information about them a wide berth long after the taboo on sexual frankness disappeared. You'd think the books on what some called mystical sex would have been popular—yet they were widely ignored, just as the serious books about ESP were. It was the same unconscious fear, Jesse. Instinctively, people knew where prolonged sex could take them, and they didn't want to go there."

The same fear he himself had felt . . . the fear that had kept him apart from Carla until he learned to trust his own powers. People gave up sensual pleasure to shut out awareness of telepathy, just as they preferred sickness and treatment to the belief that their minds' power could heal them. It seemed crazy, viewed that way, yet he had lived for years in the world outside without guessing that he was doing it. Would the majority ever change? Not without the support of their culture, he realized. But the Group wasn't a culture, not even a subculture, and it couldn't become one without children. . . .

He had long ago stopped minding not having kids. Now, with Carla, he found himself wishing they could make a baby. He'd had no such thoughts during previous sexual encounters. Was there some genetic imperative, he wondered, that was activated by a committed relationship? Carla felt it, too. "I guess it's my biological clock ticking," she said, "because I never cared when I was with Ramón. Of course we'd both been brought up to view natural conception as primitive, even uncivilized. With you, I sense how on other worlds it's seen as the fruit of love."

They were free to have a child by IVF if they chose to— legal marriage wasn't a requirement—and in some ways the idea was tempting. But there was a reason why Group couples didn't, in addition to those Dorcas had explained to him. No one really knew what part inheritance played in paranormal abilities, but genes surely had some influence, just as musical talent ran in families. Most Group members had been selected for telepathic potential. If two were to mate, their kids might display paranormal gifts in child-hood, before knowing enough to conceal them, and would be in danger of being viewed as mentally unbalanced by the Meds. They'd be given drugs to suppress those abilities. Worse, the Meds might learn what genes were responsible, and discard all future embryos that carried them. Those risks were too great to ignore.

Besides, Jesse thought, it wouldn't be fair to the kids. Taught one thing in the crèche, another by part-time par-ents, they would grow up conflicted. If the Group's ways were to spread, they should be absorbed from childhood on, and that could never happen in this colony. It troubled him. Perhaps, Jesse thought, it was because he, unlike all the rest, was an outsider and not yet resigned to the policies in place on Undine.

That was not the only problem he faced. A larger one was the question of what to do with the rest of his life.

He had tried not to think about it while at the Lodge. The training, the new friendships, his love for Carla . . . he'd been fully absorbed by these, not wanting to look ahead. The only decision he'd made beyond commitment to them was that he would never go back to Fleet.

"Do you miss space at all?" Peter had asked him once. Jesse knew that Peter, like most Group members, was fas-cinated by space though without hope of leaving Undine. The colony's monetary restrictions were an unbreachable barrier against offworld travel, unless a person was fortu-nate enough to have both passage and living expenses paid for by someone, or some institution, on Earth.

"I miss what I once expected from space," he told Peter. "But not what it turned out to be. Not ferrying freighters, never seeing anything beyond spaceports that all look alike."

"But the command—you liked that, I think."

"I did, but freighter crews aren't large, you know. There's not a lot to do in space, even for the Captain; it's all auto-mated except for departures and arrivals in orbit. You can do only so many of those before it gets to be routine. For a long time I hoped for promotion to a liner; when I was young I dreamed of someday commanding a colonizer. That, I'd have liked! But the time came when I knew it wasn't going to happen."

Peter seemed about to say more; Jesse could sense that he had thoughts on the subject—but abruptly, they were cut off. His mind was closed to probing. Perhaps, Jesse thought, he was hiding private pain. Peter, too, might have had dreams when he was young. He hated his job at the Hospital, though his work there was vital to the Group.

Apart from a few exceptions like Peter, members had fulfilling careers unrelated to their Group activities, an aspect of their lives not evident from their relaxed lifestyle at the Lodge. In the city, Jesse became all too aware of what he'd realized his first night in the colony—he would not be able to get a job. He had no documentation, no resumé. Being AWOL from Fleet, he could mention neither his education nor his experience, and in any case, as a former starship captain he would be considered overqualified for the jobs available. The only work not demanding credentials would be farm or mine labor on outlying islands.

He was fit only for retirement. It wasn't a happy prospect.

Money would not be a problem. He had ample offworld funds against which he could borrow—not directly from Peter, who dared not maintain connections to Group members that would be traceable by the authorities in case of trouble, but from a wealthy member named Xiang Li whom he had met only once. So it wouldn't be as if Carla were supporting him. Still, he could hardly sit alone in their apartment all day, and working out at the gym, which was compulsory for all city residents and which he hated, filled no more than an hour. At the Lodge, during offshifts, there at least was maintenance work to be done and a chance to run and swim, opportunities the canal-laced city lacked. But that wouldn't be enough. He could not stay idle for a lifetime.

After the first week he'd tired of exploring the city. There were few streets, and therefore no land vehicles except cabs, trucks, and of course ambulances. Narrow walkways paralleled the canals, which could also be navigated by water taxis, but these were not scenic walks. The buildings were drab and functional, in contrast to the beauty of the Lodge, which had spoiled him for the efficient architecture typical of colonies. Then too, no trees had been planted in the city. It had grown from a mining camp on a barren island of a nearly-lifeless world into a crowded metropolis in which every available piece of ground was fully utilized. The public beaches were crowded and their accessible areas confined to the shallows, cordoned off by ropes from the deep water considered too dangerous for people to swim in. Recreational boating, like all other sports that might lead to injury, was prohibited. Having few other pastimes, many citizens turned to the city's numerous gambling parlors, which were legal and heavily taxed. Jesse was no more attracted by them than by the bars that no longer drew him.

Nor had he much contact with friends. The Group members he knew were those who favored spending their free days at the Lodge or on other islands. Although he was welcomed at the safe house where others gathered, to go there without Carla, when most of the others went as couples, was awkward. Moreover he soon found that it was frequented mainly by people connected with the university—both faculty, such as Hari and Reiko, and students. Having never attended college himself, he had few interests in common with them and felt out of place. He supposed he could enroll in classes; he'd be given advanced standing for his Fleet experience and a degree would qualify him to teach math or engineering. But that wasn't a career that appealed to him.

He met Kira for lunch several times. She was staying nights with Ian, but was relieved by other caregivers during the day and thus was free the same hours he was. Jesse found himself letting off steam to her about the Group's inability to take action. "It's all very well to tell ourselves we'll have a long-range effect on human evolution even without personal descendants," he declared. "But what if something happens to us? To most of us, I mean, if we're ever caught?"

This had begun to worry him during the daytime hours, when he had too much time to think. As an offworlder he could see what the Group, inured to risk, seemed blind to—its very existence was at best precarious. Sooner or later, some member would be caught and forced to expose others; it was admitted that the hypnotic protection provided could not withstand psychiatric probing, much less investigation of suspected conspiracy. "If they ever searched the Lodge thoroughly and found the lab—"

"That won't happen," said Kira. "Someone's always there who knows where the hot switch is."

"The hot switch?"

"To destroy the lab and infirmary. Did you think we leave them unprotected?"

Jesse winced. The precaution was wise, of course. But the Lodge was a sacred place, a sanctuary, and it pained him to think that it too was in danger. An explosion large enough to take out the lab would bring the whole building down. And after that, how could they go on training new recruits?

"If we die out," he insisted, "we can't have any mysterious telepathic influence on the future."

"We do keep written records," Kira told him, "not only here in the lab, but with a contact on Earth to whom they're transmitted in code. If we fail, our effort won't be totally lost. Someday, somewhere, others will benefit from it."

"Peter mentioned offworld contacts. I don't see how the Group enlists them when no one can leave the planet."

"Ian studied on Earth when he was young," Kira explained. "He won a scholarship that paid his passage and living expenses, which was how he got around the restriction against spending his own money offworld. That was long before he founded the Group, of course. But he made friends there that he's kept up with. Several of them are deeply committed to our cause and are entrusted with our secrets. Only the Council knows their identity."

Jesse tried picturing Ian as a college student on Earth, and found the image incongruous. "What field did he study?" he asked, curious. Scholarships covering the cost of interstellar passage were not lightly awarded.

"Neuroscience. He became a research neurologist, not a practicing physician, and was considered brilliant; he could have had his pick of positions on Earth. But after taking some time off to investigate spiritual healing traditions, he chose to come back here and teach at Undine's medical school. That gave him time to privately pursue his own unorthodox insights into the relationship between the brain and the mind, and ultimately to establish our neurofeedback lab."

That accounted for the difference between the Group's view of mind power and the more common vague, metaphysical view, Jesse reflected. It was based on accurate knowledge of the brain. Yet even so, mainstream science wouldn't accept it, despite Ian's recognized brilliance. And there was nothing he or anyone could do to change that. . . .

"It's time you started seeing the positive side," Kira said. "The healing. Though it's on a small scale, we do help people."

With enthusiasm, he agreed to accompany her to the Group's city healing house the next morning as an observer. But before morning came, Valerie was arrested again, and he could give thought to little else.

39

CARLA WAS WORKING at the Psych Department's front desk that afternoon when Valerie was brought in. Sometimes she substituted when the admissions clerk went on break; it was pure luck that she was doing so now. The ambulance officer had Valerie in handcuffs. The girl was pale, her eyes despairing, with uncombed hair obscuring part of her face. She seemed really not to recognize Carla—if she had merely been concealing the connection between them, she'd have made telepathic contact.

Valerie? Carla gasped in dismay, knowing she mustn't speak to her aloud. No one here was aware that she knew this woman. For more than one reason, it must remain that way. "What's the charge?" she asked the officer crisply. If it were a purely medical arrest they would not have used cuffs.

"Attempted escape. We had a warrant for completion of her last checkup—there was some kind of foul-up and she was released too soon, before Psych signed off on her chart. But when we picked her up, she tried to run."

"Okay. You can take the cuffs off; I'll confine her," Carla said, in as level a voice as she could manage. Inwardly she tried again to reach Valerie, who was enough of a trained telepath to have gotten through the Ritual last year. *Valerie, respond to me! You can't go to pieces now! We have to plan. . . .*

It was no use; all she sensed was a dark cloud of apathy pushing down terror. Valerie was evidently in her depressive phase. She was bipolar, and would have been diagnosed as mentally ill even on Earth. Peter had brought her out of it; he had doctored her chart to make it appear that she'd completely recovered—which she would have done in time under his guidance, if only she hadn't panicked when summoned for a routine health check. She had been okay during her lab training, which Peter had found often enabled unbalanced people to function. For the Ritual she had been high, in her manic phase, so none of the other members had guessed that she'd been one of his true patients. That was confidential information, of course; Carla had not told Jesse, who had never been informed that he frequently recruited them.

In Peter's view, so-called mental illness was not really

illness at all unless the patient was violent. Especially in the case of schizophrenics, it was often merely a matter of spontaneously falling into altered states of consciousness, which could indeed be helped by training in volitional control over such states. Moreover, schizophrenics were often psi-gifted. Sometimes indiscretion in the use of psi was the only thing that had labeled them psychotic. Bipolar disorder, however, was another matter. Peter could cure that, too, given time—but he was rarely given time. Unless he happened to be the first doctor assigned to a case, a bipolar patient was usually halfway destroyed by drugs or electroshock before he could take action.

That was what had happened to Valerie. That was why she was so afraid of the Hospital that she'd made futile attempts to evade capture, why she'd agreed to undergo unnecessary surgery in order to escape psych examination. She would never be wholly normal, no matter how good the therapy Peter gave, because her brain had been damaged by electroshock. Underneath she knew that, and was terrified by the prospect of more.

"It's a ruinous, barbaric practice that should have been outlawed centuries ago," Peter had declared. "Attempts were made to outlaw it on Earth. They didn't succeed because ostensibly, the process was improved—opponents had objected to the pain it involved, the horrifying seizures, and when those problems were eliminated, they were lulled into thinking it isn't harmful. That as long as anesthetics and muscle paralyzers are used, shock treatment is a legitimate medical procedure. But of course brain damage never does anyone any good; it simply makes its victims too confused to be depressed."

Among the effects of electroshock, Carla knew, were permanent memory loss, reduced intelligence, and sometimes suicide. Not to mention disorientation. Sick with dread, she realized that if Valerie was subjected to it again, she might be too disoriented afterward to keep the Group's secrets. What, for instance, if she called out to Peter for help? What if she begged for his help beforehand, in the hope of rescue?

They would not let him treat her now that it was on record that she'd been staying at the Lodge. Her case would be assigned to another doctor, and if Peter tried to release her she would simply be brought back. Worse, his discharges of other inpatients might be reevaluated—even Jesse's. That might happen anyway if the discrepancies in her chart were noticed. Damn it, why had Peter gambled by recruiting her?

Carla knew why—he'd thought Valerie would be safer within the Group than free in the city without lab training or the support of friends. Peter would do *anything* to save someone from electroshock. He would risk his own life . . . as perhaps he had, if she should let slip any remark about the hospices. The memory of Ramón's execution welled into Carla's thoughts, momentarily overwhelming her. It would not matter that Peter had not been caught in possession of a body. If they found out about the hospices and traced deaths to them, he would be held responsible—he would make sure that he was, to protect Kira and other caregivers. Whether or not anyone else was implicated, he would be condemned.

Forcing herself to seem casual, she rose and took Valerie's arm. "You'll be okay," she lied. "We just need you to check with the nurse."

Valerie, trembling, followed her mutely into an exam room, where Carla pulled up her chart on the monitor. Was there any way to fix it so that her history would be over-looked? She didn't usually hack from exam-room consoles, but it was technically possible; the only extra danger was that a staff member would come in before she could clear the screen. There was nothing she could alter that would help, however. She had already hacked this chart exten-sively in arranging for the surgery, but had not dared to remove the original diagnosis. Its absence would be ques-tioned, especially since Valerie was all too obviously depres-sive right now.

Sitting down on the edge of the chair to which Carla had guided her, Valerie mumbled, "Peter said I wouldn't have to come here again."

"Valerie! You mustn't speak of Peter by his first name—he's Dr. Kelstrom here, remember. You can't talk about having seen him anywhere else."

"Oh, that's right," Valerie agreed. But now her underlying thought came through: *Does it really matter? I don't think anything matters much anymore. . . .*

Carla knew enough about psychiatry to realize that this was a classic symptom of major depression. Valerie had not really forgotten her Ritual pledges; she was simply incapable, in her present state, of seeing significance in them or in anything else. Somehow, she had to be jolted out of it. That was precisely what electroshock was alleged to do, albeit at far too high a cost to be justifiable. If only it were possible to consult Peter . . . but he had left early today and wouldn't be back until morning. By morning, it might be too late.

Carla's mind whirled. The hysterectomy . . . what if Valerie talked about *that*? Her surgical scar would still be evident; though Peter or Kira could have erased it after her release, it had to be visible during future checkups. If Valerie, disoriented, mentioned that she hadn't really had a uterine tumor, someone might look at the MRI scan. Then there would be hell to pay. What possible conclusion could the authorities draw other than that hacking had been done?

They would see no motive for it. But they would try to find one. They would investigate everyone who had access to the database, herself included. And they would press Valerie for information. The hypnotic protection Peter had given her wouldn't hold up against direct questioning. If she was drugged with truth serum, she would talk, and there would be no hope for the Group to remain hidden; but even if she wasn't, she might say enough to doom those directly involved.

Like Susan Gerrold, the surgeon who had operated. They

would call her in. And she would be trapped—there was just no explanation she could give for having operated on a woman whose MRI showed no abnormalities. To get to the bottom of it, they might use truth serum on *her*.

That risk could not be allowed to remain, Carla realized. Better a mysteriously-lost MRI than conclusive evidence against Susan. Her mouse poised over the exit icon, she prepared to log off her own ID and log back on again with the backdoor password she used for hacking.

The door opened and the intake nurse appeared. "You can go back to the front desk now, Carla," she said. "I'll take over."

At the front desk there were too many people around; she could not hack there, nor would she have an excuse for looking at Valerie's chart—the points from which it had been accessed under legal IDs could be traced. Hastily Carla brought up a file directory window, located the MRI image, and hit Delete.

"What are you doing there?" demanded the nurse. "This patient's no longer one of Dr. Kelstrom's, so you're not authorized to add notes."

"Just entering the time of readmission," Carla replied evenly, doing so. There hadn't been time to switch IDs. Which meant that the deletion of the MRI would be recorded under her own ID until such time as she could get back on in private and repair the log entry.

In all years she'd been hacking, she had never before done anything illegal under her own ID.

And she had accomplished nothing beyond protecting Susan. There was still the much larger danger of what Valerie might reveal. There had to be a way to make her grasp what could happen to the Group if she wasn't careful! She was devoted to Peter and would never bring harm to him while she had free choice. . . .

Telepathy might do it, if she could get through to her. Even if Valerie wasn't responsive, she had been taught to unconsciously absorb the telepathic projections of her instructors. That was a large part of Peter's success with patients. Carla didn't have the gift he and Kira did, nor had she received instructor's training. But her emotion now might be strong enough to override Valerie's withdrawal.

They would have to be in the same room, and she must be sure no doctor would walk in on them. Carla called up the staff schedule. God, they'd assigned her to Dr. Warick, the department head! Peter despised Warick, who not only favored aggressive treatment methods, but was heavily involved in Hospital politics. For Valerie to be examined personally by him was the worst thing that could happen. Warick would be on the defensive, angry because a bipolar patient had slipped out of Psych's clutches and had been allowed to relapse. He would want to know why. And he would want to gain credit in the eyes of the Administration for restoring her to health, which by his definition, meant replacing any vestige of disturbance in her mind with the compliant, unthinking serenity of a zombie.

However, it was late in the day and Warick would not see Valerie until tomorrow. She would be locked in a room alone, terrifyingly alone, for the night. Possibly Peter could find some way for her to escape before morning, despite the fact that escape from the psych ward had always been deemed physically impossible. In any case, Carla saw with relief, she would be able to visit Valerie uninterrupted. Like other staff personnel, she knew the keypad code for the rooms in the main ward, although it wouldn't get her past the security of the locked ward where violent criminals were kept.

She waited until the end of her workday, knowing that in the confusion of the shift change nobody was likely to notice who belonged where in the maze of corridors. Then she moved fast. There was a master chart showing patients' room numbers; Valerie's was at the far end of a hall. Closing the door quickly behind her, she found the woman huddled on the bed, with her knees drawn up and her face buried in her hands. *Valerie?* Carla probed. *It's just me, Carla. I'm Peter's friend, you know. . . .*

"Is Peter coming?" Valerie whispered, raising her head.

"He won't be able to come. Peter is in danger, Valerie. You have to help him."

"Me? I can't—I'm no good at anything. He'd be better off if he'd never tried to cure me."

The element of truth in this made it all the more tragic. Low self-esteem was another symptom of depression; Carla knew better than to argue. But she saw that she had struck the right note. Peter's welfare was the one thing Valerie still cared about, the one concern that could rouse her out of her apathy. *Valerie, you have to remember!* she insisted, throwing all the force of her own turmoil, her own fear, into the projection. *Remember the Ritual, your hand touching Peter's and not being burned, remember what you promised then. . . .* Though Ian had presided at Valerie's Ritual, Peter had been her sponsor. It was likely that she was attracted to him—many of the young, unattached members were, although he tried to discourage that.

What can I do to help when I'm locked in here? Valerie ventured.

Remember your pledge to keep the Group secret! If you let anyone find out about that secret, Peter will be arrested . . . he might even die.

I don't want him to die!

No, of course you don't. So you must keep his secret, the secret of all of us who are his friends. Most of the other doctors aren't his friends. Promise me, Valerie, that you won't tell the other doctors anything about Peter.

I promise. . . .

And you won't even tell them his name. No matter what happens, you won't mention Peter's name.

Valerie nodded. *I won't say his name.* Carla hoped she would hold to that.

40

AS JESSE WAITED for Carla to get home from work, appre-hension rose in him. She was late. She had never been late before without calling. He could not help remembering what the long-term Group members seemed not to mind: they were in danger, all of them, always. And especially Carla, because of the hacking she did.

When she came in, one look at her face told him his fears weren't groundless.

He took her in his arms, sharing thought without words. They no longer needed sex for their minds to be open to each other when in the grip of strong emotion. Carla didn't attempt to hide anything from him. He knew, with despair, that the event he had dreaded—that they had all dreaded without letting themselves believe it could happen—had fi-nally caught up with them. They were on the verge of expo-sure. By tomorrow, the Group's existence might be known to the authorities.

And if not tomorrow, then some day in the not-too-dis-tant future. Whether Valerie was given truth serum or merely subjected to repeated electroshock, no promise she had made would have any bearing on the outcome.

After a few minutes Carla broke away. "I have to warn Peter," she said.

She used the Group's emergency password, alerting Peter to circumstances worse than she could reveal on the phone. After talking to him she was more scared than ever. Peter, she said, had understood the message, but hadn't implied that he would take action beyond informing the other Council members. That meant he didn't know of any action he could take. If he'd had a backup plan, he would have said something reassuring.

They waited. As a staff doctor, Peter could call up Valerie's chart remotely; he would know if anything hap-pened during the night. It wouldn't, of course. Nothing would happen until morning, when he was on site, and then it might happen all too quickly. Jesse realized, somewhat to his surprise, that Carla loved Peter—as a brother, to be sure, but nevertheless as deeply as she had loved Ramón. He, too, cared about Peter. He could not bear the thought of his being arrested. But that thought was obscured by his overwhelming fear for Carla.

She had hacked Valerie's chart using her own ID. If there was an investigation of the discrepancies, that would be detected. It would be unsafe, she said, to repair the log remotely. She had never hacked the database from her apartment because a record of unauthorized outside transmissions would be a sure tip-off that hacking was going on. She couldn't go to Peter's apartment, which he had left to consult Ian; nor could she go back to the Hospital without arousing suspicion. There might be opportunity tomorrow. Then again, by tomorrow it might not matter.

Abruptly she turned pale and ran to the bathroom. Jesse heard her being sick, heard the toilet flush repeatedly. He had never seen her like this; after all, Carla knew from her Group training how to deal with the physical effects of fear. Normally she was imperturbable. Was there something she had not told him? he wondered. His own dread grew; he was dizzy with it, sensing her agony even through the closed door. Finally, when he believed he could endure it no longer, she came back to him, wordlessly communicating the horror that had suddenly struck her. *What if Valerie does keep the secret, yet they arrest me for hacking and I'm examined by Warick because of the connection with her case . . . what if I'm given truth serum and Peter is found out through me?*

Jesse held her close, soothing her as best he could. There really wasn't any answer to that. The risk had always existed; every one them must have known underneath that they might someday involuntarily betray each other. Peter certainly had known it, and yet in the effort to forestall trouble he had rashly created a situation with more potential for betrayal than usual.

"Why did Peter ever think the surgery scheme would work?" he burst out . "I mean, it must have been obvious there was a risk of Valerie being picked up again."

"Yes, but if she'd been normal at the time—not in a depressive phase—they'd only have questioned her. And Peter . . . he just didn't want to believe she wasn't yet cured. He'd promised her that she wouldn't receive more shock treatment."

"Yet the ruse was based on the fear that she might be treated."

"That was Valerie's fear, not Peter's, except for his outrage at the whole idea of electroshock. He can't judge objectively when that's involved, and in any case he knew she couldn't handle the thought of being taken back to Psych."

"Aren't all of us pledged to face our fears?"

"Well, but she was his patient, Jesse, not someone who joined us from strength."

Kira had been right, Jesse thought—Peter expected much from his followers, but if they weren't able to live up to those expectations, his empathy was so strong that it overrode all other considerations. He was torn between his commitment to advance humankind and the compassion that had led him to become a doctor. How could he survive in a world like this, where his attempts to help people only put him in danger?

Perhaps he couldn't.

They didn't talk much more. There was nothing left to say. Eventually they went to bed and attempted to sleep. So far Jesse hadn't given thought to his own possible fate. Beside Carla's and Peter's, it hadn't seemed to matter. He himself had not done anything illegal yet. Unless they rounded up the whole Group, the worst that could happen to him was that he'd be retreated for alcoholism. But how could he stand it if Carla was drugged and punished? How could *she* endure if Peter, like her husband, was put into stasis?

In the morning she got up and mechanically pulled on

her clothes. She had to go to work, of course, to cover her hacking tracks if for no other reason. They lingered over their kiss before she left, agonizingly aware that it might be a long while before they kissed again.

After calling Kira to break his appointment for visiting the healing house, he settled on the couch, prepared for a long day with nothing to do but wait and worry.

Barely an hour later, Carla returned. "Jesse," she said quickly, "It's okay. Peter's safe, and so am I. He told me to take a sick day." But she wasn't smiling.

Slowly Jesse asked, "How much longer will you be safe?"

"From now on, unless something else happens. I fixed the data entry log, and the missing MRI scan will never be noticed. Valerie's file is—closed. Closed for good."

Seeing that it was hard for her to speak, Jesse held back his questions. Finally Carla added wearily, "Valerie killed herself last night. She slit her wrists."

"Oh, my God. Was she *that* depressed, or was it from fear?"

"Both, partly, Peter thinks. But it was more than that. She left a note. It said 'They're going to shock me again, and I don't want him to die.'"

41

BECAUSE EVEN IN desperation Valerie had remembered her promise not to name Peter, her suicide note was dismissed by the authorities as an irrational outburst of a sick mind. No one bothered to wonder what she had meant by it. Peter, however, was called to account by the department head, Warick, who as her current doctor was blamed for not having put her on suicide watch. Why, Warick demanded, had there been nothing on her chart about suicidal tendencies? This Peter could answer with complete honesty: Valerie had not been suicidal at the time he was treating her. Depressed though she'd been, she had never given any indication that she might take her own life. Since nothing could be proved to the contrary, and since Peter declared that the threat of more electroshock was enough to trigger suicide in anyone whose brain was already damaged by it, Warick was forced to let the matter drop. But the never-cordial relationship between the two had deteriorated into enmity.

There was no hope of the Group retrieving the body for burial, of course; it was still warm when found and had been sent immediately to the Vaults. Suicide was a felony in the eyes of the Meds, and the supercilious remarks made by news commentators on the Administration's mercy in keeping perpetrators "alive" made Jesse want to vomit.

Carla was deeply shaken by Valerie's death. At the Lodge, after a simple candlelight memorial service, she was finally able to talk about it. "I drove her to it," she said miserably. "She was weakened by depression, and telepathically I convinced her that she would harm Peter if she was questioned."

"Which she probably would have," said Kira. "Tragic as it was, her death was what saved him, and at least some of the rest of us."

"In the end, she wasn't weak," Peter said. "Make no mistake, I don't condone suicide. It's wrong, as the Group has always maintained. But it can be excused when the aim is to save others."

"Even though she didn't plan it rationally?" Carla protested. "It was an impulse that came from her fear of electroshock combined with the worse fear I implanted in her! She wasn't in shape to know what she was doing."

"She knew," Peter replied gently. "Carla, I spared you the graphic details earlier, but it's best that you know them now. People don't die from slitting their wrists as easily as the public thinks—it's often a mere gesture, a cry for help. Even if they're not found quickly, the blood tends to clot before they bleed out. Valerie lost a lot of blood, fast, despite the fact that she had no sharp knife and needed effort, plus her pain management skill, to cut herself up with eating utensils. And that means she bled out deliberately."

"Deliberately?" Jesse questioned.

"Our control over bleeding works both ways," Kira told him. "Valerie evidently hadn't forgotten her mind training."

"It's true that the aftereffects of electroshock predisposed her to suicide," Peter admitted, "so that when faced with more such treatments, she welcomed the thought of dying. And I'd be the last to say that's not a terrible thing. But we do her injustice if we assume she didn't have free will."

"That's what you've always said about mental patients," Carla recalled. "That their free will shouldn't be denied by well-meaning caretakers."

"Yes. Mental imbalance does not make people less than human. Warick, like the rest of the Meds, thinks anyone likely to commit suicide should be locked up for his or her own protection. He knows I disagree, so he's convinced that I purposely failed to note it on Valerie's chart. Ironically, I didn't, though I did alter other things when I put through her discharge. She wasn't in any sense suicidal until they arrested her the second time. But it's true enough that I wouldn't have recorded it if she had been, because nothing except danger to others can justify depriving patients of their human right to freedom."

Carla frowned. "I don't like the way Warick's been bugging you."

"There's not much to like about Warick," Peter agreed. "Unfortunately, he's my boss, so I have to put up with him."

"But he's going to get suspicious someday—"

"Of what? He has no reason to guess I've done anything illegal; the worst he can do is fire me, and he hasn't the power even for that without proof of misconduct."

"I suppose that's true," Carla conceded. But later, to Jesse, she said, "Warick makes me nervous. I get a bad feeling whenever he and Peter have an argument."

The next week, with the crisis past, Jesse began visiting the Group's city healing house with Kira. It had long ago been determined that he lacked the natural talent to be trained as a healer. Self-healing of relatively minor conditions was as far as he would be able to go. He wanted to learn all he could by observing, however.

The healing house was merely a safe house to which Group members came with illness or injury not amenable to self-healing and to which members of the front group were occasionally directed. The latter could not, of course, be given spectacular treatment like the rapid healing of wounds, nor did they need it, since injured people didn't hesitate to seek official care. Outsiders sought help only with problems the Hospital had been unable to cure. Back pain, undiagnosed stomach pain, headaches—these and other conditions brought on by stress were often severe and recurrent. Kira and others skilled in healing dealt with such problems telepathically, using mystical hocus-pocus as a facade.

"But can you trust the patients not to mention it to their doctors?" Jesse asked.

"Oh, yes—they're afraid their mental health would be questioned if they let it be known they were involved in any kind of mysticism. And even if they did report us, what we do with outsiders isn't illegal. We don't call it treatment. If a safe house were compromised we'd simply close it and go elsewhere."

The treatment Group members received *was* illegal. Though serious illness was rare among them, it did occasionally occur. Jesse was surprised to learn that even major surgery was done within the Group. But, he realized, it was not dangerous when no anesthetic was needed; surgical patients could remain awake, help to control their own bleeding, and afterward heal their own wounds. The Group included several skilled surgeons besides Susan Gerrold, the gynecologist who had operated on Valerie. Medical equipment was kept hidden in the city healing house for emergencies, though when possible members were taken to the Lodge.

With Carla, Jesse gradually developed his telepathic skill to the point where she pronounced him ready to learn how to relieve pain in others. He had seen it done by Kira in the healing house; people arrived in extreme pain and left free of it, for a time, when the healer, ostensibly, had done no more than touch them lightly. "It would be easier if we used a placebo or spoke of some mysterious form of energy," Carla said, "just as healers have traditionally done on Earth. But as a matter of principle, we don't want to encourage the notion that the cure is physical. Calling it prayer would also work, but we don't want to encroach on anyone's religion, or lack of religion. So we tell them the literal truth, that under our guidance their inner minds can free them of pain."

Her explanation of how to guide was a bit frightening at first. You had to sense telepathically what the patient was experiencing and deliberately *not* turn off suffering until you felt it fully in your own body—a technique that had been practiced in ancient times by shamans. Then, and only then, could you go into the state where you didn't mind pain, projecting into the patient's mind the way in which you did so, carrying her along. Jesse perceived that this was what Peter had done in teaching him, and was uncertain of his own ability to manage it.

"It won't be as hard as instructing," Carla said, "because the patient doesn't have to learn to do it herself. You suffer for only a brief time." During that time, you would have to be absolutely calm and steady, he knew. Any fear or doubt in your mind would be passed to the patient, who would then be left in worse pain than before.

During their next offshift at the Lodge she took him to the lab to try it, with Ingrid as a volunteer victim under stimulus. He found it easier than he expected to wait before banishing pain. When he knew he *could* banish it, the pain he shared with Ingrid didn't seem bad. And of course, that was what Peter had told him in the first place: the fear of losing control was much worse than pain itself. He could sense that the relief, when it came, had been initiated by

him—that Ingrid hadn't cheated by using her own skill—
and he found it a deeply moving experience.

Nevertheless, Carla was there to help and Ingrid had
past experience with the state of not suffering. Jesse knew
his own projection into her mind wouldn't have worked if
she'd been a frightened novice. He was not telepathically
gifted, despite his new-found ability to communicate with
other trained telepaths. A healer had to be able to project to
untrained people.

And so he was back to the same dilemma: he was happy
in the Group despite his ongoing fear for Carla, yet bored
and restless with nothing to fill his days. "Don't worry about
it," she said. "I'm sure Peter has something important
planned for you—otherwise he wouldn't have declared that
he doesn't want you distracted by advanced training."

This had come up during one of their first visits to the
Island; to Jesse's inner relief, Peter had overruled Greg's
suggestion that he should be progressing beyond mere re-
fresher sessions in the lab. The question "distracted from
what?" had not been answered. Jesse had supposed he was
being given time to assimilate what he'd learned and apply
it to daily living, an effort that since his Ritual transformation had become easier. That it might refer to an upcoming
task had not occurred to him—but if it did, what was Peter
waiting for?

"Right now," Carla continued, "he's too absorbed with
Ian, and what Ian's teaching him about taking over the leadership, to think about anything else. He doesn't often seem
to have his mind on his work at the Hospital."

That must be it. Even at the Lodge, Peter was no longer
the vibrant, carefree young man Jesse had first known there.
Learning his true age had altered Jesse's view of him, to be
sure; still there was a real difference, which Carla too had
noticed long before Valerie's arrest and had mentioned more
than once. Having met Ian, he could now see its source.
Taking Ian's place would demand all the strength and wisdom that Peter could muster.

Beside this, his own problem was insignificant, Jesse decided. In any case, there was nothing he could do but let it ride.

42

THE CITY WAS built on the largest of Undine's islands, which was long and narrow, with the spaceport and power plant occupying one end. The Hospital complex, containing the largest and tallest buildings in the colony, took up the high ground in the middle. The island's other end, crisscrossed by canals, was tightly packed with businesses, apartments, and a few private houses. If the population grew any larger, it would have to expand to the neighboring islands now devoted to mines and farms.

The West Shore waterfront was where the private boats and seaplanes were moored. Peter kept his plane in the area closest to the Hospital, but moorings extended a long way toward the tip of the island, separated from a row of upscale homes by a wide esplanade. On a bright afternoon Jesse walked aimlessly along it, farther than he'd gone before, and to his surprise found himself in front of the house where he had been taken to meet Ian. It had been dark then, so he hadn't noticed that it faced the water, but he was sure it was the same house. And, he recalled, he'd been told that the Group's hospices were always located on the waterfront for the simple reason that bodies had to be surreptitiously moved from them into planes. Cost was not a factor; the Group had plenty of local money available to spend on real estate, the ownership of which was registered in the names of members who kept a low profile.

He did not, of course, go to the door; he knew that Ian needed rest and received few visitors. Though either Kira or some other caregiver would be there, his daytime loneliness was hardly an excuse for intruding. But he stopped and sat on the low concrete wall at the water's edge, looking out at the brightly colored seaplanes and thinking that this was the only view Ian would ever see now. Ian must long to be aboard one of those planes, heading out over the sea toward his beloved Island . . . Jesse certainly did. He, even more than Carla, lived for the offshifts when they would be free to go there. Besides, the weekly flight itself was something he looked forward to, mere passenger though he now was. He did miss flying, though he'd never had opportunity to do as much as he'd have liked in shuttling between starships and spaceports.

There was a pier opposite the house with boats tied up, and a few shacks on it—the recharging station, water taxi office, and so forth. Idly, Jesse read the signs, noticing one that read "Seaplane for Charter." On second glance he saw that beside the sign was a large "For Sale" notice.

Suddenly, Jesse knew what he was going to do with his time on Undine.

There was no reason he couldn't run an air charter service. Now that the idea had come to him, he couldn't imagine why he had not thought of it before. Surely he could learn to fly a seaplane easily, considering his experience piloting shuttles. He would enjoy it. He could set his own hours. And it would be of use to the Group; there were always more people wanting to go to the Island than planes available to take them. Peter's willingness to arrange loans against his offworld accounts had so far appeared to be unlimited. He could buy the plane and charter business outright without making much of a dent in his retirement funds.

Eager to get started, Jesse proceeded along the pier to the shack with the sign. Not until he'd pushed the door open did he remember that he knew nothing about financial transactions in the colony beyond the fact that they were strictly regulated. Probably he should have asked Peter's advice, lest government red tape jeopardize the secrecy of his funds' true source. But what the hell, it would do no harm to inquire about the price.

At the desk within the shack, with his chair rotated toward the window and sea view, was a grizzled, bearded old man wearing an antiquated plaid shirt. He swung around as he heard Jesse enter. "Sorry, I'm not taking charters anymore," he said. "I'm closing down."

"I saw that you're selling," Jesse said. "What's your price?"

"Depends on the terms. You want just the plane, or everything?"

"The whole business—all the equipment you've got, records, moorage lease. I'll pay cash."

The man stared at him in astonishment. "Thought I knew all the pilots around here. Taught most of the older ones to fly myself. I sure hadn't heard there was anyone in the market for a charter business."

"I'm new here," Jesse admitted. "From offworld. So I'm looking for a good opportunity."

"Ever do any flying?"

"Not in seaplanes," Jesse hedged, "though I've been up in them with friends."

"It's not much different from flying land-based planes, or so I've been told. As you probably know they're all seaplanes here; the island's not big enough for an airport. But it shouldn't take you long to make the transition."

"Well," said Jesse, "I've only flown larger ships, under conditions not much like this world's. So I'll need a bit of instruction. Is there a flight school around here?"

"There is, but the guy who runs it will charge you as much as he charges the green kids he caters to, and not give you half the training you're paying for," declared the man with evident bitterness. "My instructor's ticket is still good. If you buy the plane, I'll throw in lessons."

"So let's see it. Have you got time to take me up now?"

For just a moment the old man hesitated, and Jesse sensed doubt in him. But then he said, "Sure. I'm Zeb Hennesy, by the way."

He led the way to a blue and white seaplane, moored directly at the pier. "The lease on this space is worth plenty," he said. "If you bought a new plane you'd be stuck way out, and water taxi bills run up fast."

Jesse had observed enough during his flights with Peter and others to be familiar with the routine of inspecting the floats and making sure that the plane had a full power charge. It was a beautiful machine that had obviously been carefully maintained. As he climbed into the copilot's seat and they taxied out for takeoff, his spirits soared. This was what he was meant to do. With this, his new life on Undine would be complete.

They accelerated, nose up out of the spray, and he could feel the decrease in drag when the floats began to lift. In a moment they were off the water. The plane climbed, and Jesse gazed down at the canal-threaded city. It was clearly dominated by the massive, glaring white Hospital cluster, which seemed even from the air to dwarf the featureless residential areas. He was glad to be away from there.

"Take over," Zeb said to him as they leveled off. "Let's see if you've got a feel for it."

Jesse took the yoke, his confidence rising with the passing minutes. The plane handled very differently from a starship's VTOL shuttle, of course, and was so much slower that he kept wanting to put on power. But after his trips in Peter's similar plane, he knew that it wouldn't take him long to get used to it. The only tricky part would be setting it down horizontally, on water.

"You're a natural," Zeb said, seeming rather relieved. "Mostly I'll just sit back and let you log the hours on dual you need for a license."

"It may take me a few days to raise the cash," Jesse said after they'd landed. The price mentioned had meant nothing to him, unfamiliar as he was with colonial money, but he could tell that Zeb wasn't a man who would cheat him. "Is it a deal?"

"Best deal I ever made," Zeb said. "Don't care about the money. I just—well, I wanted her in the hands of somebody who'd treat her right. Not one of those damn fool kids looking for joyrides these days. There's hardly anybody else in the market for used planes."

Most people in the colony who needed planes already owned them, Jesse realized, and they rarely had reason to give them up. Zeb was evidently reluctant to let this one go. With his developing access to people's feelings, he sensed the pain in him, and wondered why the old man was selling. He was past the age to retire, certainly, but if he didn't need the money, why not keep the plane for personal use?

They shook hands on the agreement, and Jesse, seeing that it was late, took a water taxi through the canals back to the apartment. Carla would be home before him, for once. He could hardly wait to tell her his news.

"That's wonderful!" Carla said, hugging him. He was elated all evening, and the next morning commenced flying lessons with Zeb. But Peter, when at Carla's request he met them in a safe house that night, was surprisingly unenthusiastic.

"I'm not sure it's a good idea, Jess," he said, frowning.

"Oh, Peter," Carla said. "Jesse loves it, and he needs to do something here."

"I know. But a long-term commitment like this—"

"I'm sorry if I misunderstood," Jesse said, somewhat stunned. "I had the impression that the Group wouldn't mind lending me as much as my funds will cover."

"It's not the money," Peter assured him. "We can't give it to you in cash; a transaction that large would have to go through a bank, and would be reported. But it would be perfectly legal for Xiang Li to invest in an air charter service, if you wouldn't mind signing paperwork to make it look as if the plane's securing the loan."

"Of course I wouldn't."

"So that part's okay. I just wonder if maybe you're being a bit hasty. You've only looked at one plane, after all."

"It's in great shape, and I like Zeb Hennesy. We hit it off right away."

"But you're not even licensed yet—it will be a while before you can carry passengers, and even longer before you have enough hours to carry them for hire."

"Surely you don't think I'll have trouble learning to fly a seaplane, Peter."

"No, no—certainly not. You'll make a great pilot. I've got an instructor's rating myself; we could log some dual hours for you going to and from the Island."

"Then what's the problem?"

"For one thing, you'd need to acquire permanent, legally-recognized resident status to operate a business here."

"Peter," Jesse said, "I can't live the rest of my life in this colony without the authorities noticing that I've become a permanent resident."

Peter sighed. "I suppose not," he admitted. "I guess we could hack credit bureau files to prevent your offworld accounts from being discovered, since you'll have some earned income to satisfy any tax investigations."

"Hack financial records? I won't have Carla risk that," Jesse stated firmly. Much as he wanted to fly, he wouldn't pursue it on those terms.

"No, of course not. All the financial hacking is done by our contacts on Earth."

"Well then, as you say, it will be awhile before I can get a commercial license. So we can take care of the red tape later, can't we?"

"Sure, go ahead and have fun flying—you deserve that," Peter told him. "I'll talk to Xiang Li tomorrow." But he did not look happy.

Puzzled, Jesse worried about it during the night, and finally an answer came to him. He had mentioned to Peter that the plane was moored in front of the house where Ian was living. In fact, Carla had said the one next door, which was owned by Xiang Li, was used as a hospice, too—that made it easy for caregivers to keep watch over two patients, when there were two, without exposing either of them to the danger of the other being found. Sooner or later, perhaps often, bodies would have to be moved out of those houses. And who would be better situated to transport them than a pilot with a plane at the pier across the street?

Peter had previously declared that he wouldn't be allowed to risk being caught with bodies. Why, Jesse didn't know. He was as fit to assume that risk as the others in the Group. There had never been any indication that he was not trusted. But for some reason, Peter did not want him to be endangered—just as, he now knew, Peter's reluctance to preside at the Ritual had stemmed from unwillingness to expose him to possible harm. Was it for Carla's sake, he wondered? Was it because her first husband had been caught, and for her to go through such an ordeal a second time might destroy her? Worse, might the authorities suspect her if a second partner—even if not her legal husband—was accused of murder? He too felt horror at that possibility . . . and yet he could not live on Undine without taking chances. The most fundamental rule of the Group was that fear must not be allowed to interfere with living.

He was not obliged to respect Peter's wishes. The Ritual pledges said nothing about obedience to the Group's leader; on the contrary, his commitment required him to support fellow-members. If they asked him to transport a body, as well they might if his plane was close at hand, he would do it. Knowing this, Peter had hoped he wouldn't get into such a position. He had backed down because he knew he was wrong to be ruled by anxiety. But excess caution was so unlike Peter that Jesse wondered if there was something more going on, some danger to the Group of which he himself was unaware.

That week was the happiest he'd known since coming to the city. The first day he did little more than acquire the ability to land the plane, practicing over and over without going far offshore. It was odd how nervous Zeb appeared to be about it, considering the many years of instructing he'd said that he had. Surely his young, inexperienced students had been slower learners. But once Jesse demonstrated that he could touch down safely, regardless of wind and weather,

Zeb relaxed. From then on, they flew all over the part of Undine within range. Once they even went to Verge Island, the farthest out in the cluster that had been settled, which of course covered only a fraction of the planet's surface. A few more of the larger islands also had recharging stations; Zeb took him to them, familiarizing him with the common routes and introducing him to the people he would meet during his required solo flights and later, when he began charter flying.

By the time the first offshift arrived, he'd had four days of instruction, three or four hours a day. On the last afternoon, he had soloed, with Zeb standing on the pier cheering him on despite, Jesse guessed, considerable pain at the sight of the plane he loved taking off without him. It marked the true transfer of ownership. Worse, Jesse knew, was the fact that for the next five days he would be taking it where Zeb could not go. With Peter as the official instructor aboard, he and Carla were going to Maclairn Island, which on maps was marked as off limits to landing. "I'm sorry," he told Zeb, "but my partner has a job, you see, and when she's free, we fly to a place her friends own. It's one of the reasons I wanted to have my own plane."

As he went through preflight inspection the next morning, Jesse was overcome with fullness of joy in the realization that the plane *was* his own. He had literally never owned anything before. He'd gone to the Fleet academy straight from school and in Fleet, with your life spent in space, you didn't have a chance to buy a house or a car or anything else people normally acquired. You didn't have a personal computer or video gear, since on starships those things were standard equipment. Even the locally-programmed phones used on shore leave were rented. He'd possessed nothing but his pocket datakeeper and the few clothes he wore when not in uniform.

Now he had everything, intangible and now tangible as well. Carla, friends, use of the Lodge he loved, the prospect of health and long life . . . powers of mind beyond his former imagining . . . a commitment to something important . . . and not merely a way to occupy his time, but a plane that belonged to him and a long-term occupation he would enjoy. If he were superstitious, Jesse thought, he would not dare to acknowledge so much good fortune. It drove his knowledge of the Group's ongoing danger into the background, so that he was scarcely aware that the trouble-free time could not last.

Peter, seeing his happiness, seemed reconciled to the situation. They took off in high spirits, looking forward to another relaxing offshift. Nevertheless, Jesse continued to sense that he was hiding something, something more than his concern for Ian. Had he told Ian? Jesse wondered. Did Ian watch from his window, aware that they were in this particular plane headed where he must wish he, too, could go?

Evenings on the Island, Peter went up with Jesse to teach him the fundamentals of night flying. The moon, so much larger and brighter than Earth's moon, made this easy; seaplanes were not limited to daylight as they were on most worlds. Circling the Island, looking down at it, Jesse had an overwhelming sense of attachment. He knew that never again would he want to be a worldless rover—and yet he couldn't quite forget that there was no refuge from the peril in which he and Carla lived on this particular world.

43

AT THE LODGE, despite the fact that the Net was now accessible, few people watched the news and phones were set to receive only emergency calls. Group members had little desire to be reminded of the world outside. So on their arrival back in the city for Carla's next workweek, Jesse was startled to find current newscasts heavily focused on a sensational crime. Several houses on the waterfront had been set afire during the past few days, and investigators had sought the arsonist in vain. Much speculation was being devoted to what sort of dreadful mental illness such a person must suffer from.

"Is arson that unusual?" Jesse asked. "Of course, I suppose that here the real firebugs, the pyromaniacs, are diagnosed young and drugged into passivity. And if it were insurance fraud, multiple houses wouldn't have been hit."

"There's more than just that to wonder about," Carla said. "It's not easy to set a house on fire; we have no accelerants—none of the petroleum products that exist on Earth. We don't have gunpowder either, since guns are prohibited here and none have ever been imported. To burn a building, an arsonist would have to either short-circuit its electrical system or use explosives from mining operations. Both those methods require time and skill."

That night another unoccupied house burned, and the furor grew. Peter, Carla reported, was upset about the city's mood. "I suppose he dreads what he'll have to do to the guy when he's caught," she mused. "Treating criminals is hard on him—he doesn't believe in turning them into zombies, but with this one in the public eye, there won't be a chance of going easy on the drugs, as he sometimes tries to."

"Maybe they'll be given during a shift when he's not working," Jesse said.

"The maintenance dosing, yes; an arsonist will be locked up for life. But Peter will have to order the medication and administer it initially. He got himself put in charge of crime treatment so as to help as much as possible in case of—trouble."

She shuddered, and Jesse understood why. No member of the Group except Ramón had ever been caught committing a felony, but they all knew it could happen. And people presumed guilty of violent crimes, such as murder or arson, faced consequences much worse than those of hacking. Peter would do what he could to lessen the mind damage inflicted on such a person. A member would be better off under his care than in the hands of an orthodox psychiatrist, as in fact any patient was. But he did not have the power to save a convicted criminal from being treated. He lived under constant threat of what the responsibility he bore might force him to do.

Jesse was too absorbed in flying to pay much attention to the arson news. In addition to solo hours, he continued to fly with Zeb. He became used to navigating by sight on the clear blue days, and by instruments when it was stormy. Their time in the air was counted only for his logbook; Zeb seemed even more eager than he to be airborne, and was "throwing in" far more lesson time than any paying student would expect. It seemed odd until, after a while, he saw that Zeb was saying goodbye to all that mattered in his life.

They had come to know each other well. Jesse had revealed his experience with spacecraft; his Fleet background was not secret, as the circumstances of his stranding on Undine were a matter of public record. He did not have to skirt unconventional views in discussing them, for Zeb, too, disliked the Hospital. "I'm due for a mandatory health check next week," he finally confessed, "and after that, I won't be allowed to fly. They'll take my license."

Too bad, thought Jesse sadly. Even on Earth, aging pilots eventually lost their licenses. Yet Zeb didn't appear to be incompetent. He was a skilled pilot and his reactions were sharp. "Why don't you think you can pass?" he asked.

"They'll test my heart," Zeb admitted, "and they'll find out about the pain I sometimes have. I don't fly charters anymore, Jesse. I'd have been scared to take you up if I hadn't seen you could handle yourself in the air."

So that was what was behind the early push on landings. Zeb went on, "I'm not afraid for myself, you understand. Sometimes I've wished . . . that it would happen when I was alone. I'd rather go down in the sea than go where they'll send me. I thought I might even take her down on purpose."

"Oh, God, Zeb."

"Don't worry. She's yours, now. But if you hadn't come along when you did—"

"Zeb, you've got a lot of good years ahead of you, even if you can't fly anymore. They can treat heart problems, after all. They can even give you a new heart."

"Sure they can," Zeb said bitterly. "They'll keep it beating even if being hooked up to machines during the surgery causes damage to my brain, which it sometimes does. Besides, you're new here. Maybe you don't know what they do with old folks who need treatment."

"Life support, yes—I've heard about it. But you're a long way from that. You're fine except for pain once in a while, and that can be fixed. I know you haven't wanted to get it checked when it meant losing your license, but once you do, you'll be okay."

"Once I do," Zeb said, "I'll be locked up."

"Locked up?" Jesse stared at him, perplexed. "You haven't done anything wrong, even according to the health laws."

"You don't think they let old people in danger of heart trouble out of their sight, do you? There'd be a chance of it happening too fast for an ambulance to get to them."

"You could have an implanted monitor."

"Sure, but I'm ninety-four, Jesse, so relying on that would be called risky. I might be out walking somewhere, or in somebody else's plane, nowhere near any resuscitation gear. So I'll be sent to a residential care unit where there's supervision. And sooner or later, I'll end up in on a treatment floor with no way out short of the Vaults."

"But you may live for years in shape to be active!" protested Jesse, knowing as he spoke that he shouldn't be surprised. Replacement organs, even cloned ones, did not work reliably in people over ninety; Kira had told him that this was because bodies are not mere collections of parts. And of course the Meds would not let old people risk dying for the sake of enjoying the time that remained to them. It wouldn't fit the policy of forced treatment.

He bit his lip, realizing for the first time what his pledge of secrecy was going cost him, what it must cost all Group members with elderly relatives and friends. He longed to assure Zeb that he didn't have to end up on life support, that when the time came he could die naturally, that his body would be flown to a place where he would indeed be buried in the sea. His was surely the sort of case for which Group hospices existed. Yet not only was Jesse unauthorized to reveal this, but no one else would be able to say anything, either. Potential hospice patients were never informed in advance; it would be far too dangerous.

And it wasn't as if Zeb's death were imminent. First would come incarceration in a "residential care unit" that would hardly be a pleasant place to live. . . .

"They're inland, on Hospital grounds," Zeb told him. "They've got plenty of windows, I'm told, but you can't see much of the sky, let alone the sea. The rooms have video and Net hookup; that's all most folks care about, I guess. But they're no bigger than cubicles. And the food's terrible— the Meds don't let you eat anything they think is bad for you, which makes no sense if all you're there for is to mark time till you die."

Jesse's heart ached for Zeb. Surely the Group could do something for him. What, he couldn't imagine. He hadn't been informed as to how people were smuggled into hospices when they were dying, either; it was considered unsafe to spread that information among members without a specific need to know. But he resolved to consult Peter or Kira the next time he saw one of them. He had to get Zeb's name on whatever list they kept of those to whom assistance would be offered.

At home that night, he told Carla. "Can't you alter his records, give him more time?" he asked hopefully.

She frowned. "We'd like to do that for everybody slated for a residential care unit," she said, "because once in, they can never get out again."

"Never?"

"Jesse, those places are secure. People are allowed out only for the day with relatives or friends, who have to show ID and sign custody papers—and what's more, the patients have implanted microchips that transmit heart data and track where they go. It's worse than the treatment floors of the Hospital, where we do have insiders to forge discharges. Nobody's ever discharged from a residential care unit."

"Carla, that's *prison*. For people not even sick."

"Of course. Do you think the Group isn't aware of that? It's all part of the tyranny we're fighting against."

"We're not fighting," Jesse protested. "We're just saving ourselves."

"And a few others, when we can."

"But not Zeb? Isn't there some way we can hide him?"

"Oh, Jesse. Even if we could get rid of the microchip, we can't conceal people forever! A lot of members have parents or grandparents they'd hide if it were possible."

He had not stopped to think of that. Carla's own parents were only in their sixties, and healthy; furthermore, they were strong supporters of the Med regime. On the one occasion when she'd taken him to meet them—introducing him merely as a friend, not as her husband—she had warned him not to criticize it. But other Group members must have loved ones facing the ills of aging. . . .

"This is a hell of a world," he declared, close to forgetting the joy he'd taken in it the past two weeks.

Carla didn't answer at first. Finally she said, "If I hack Zeb's record so that he won't be called for a mandatory check right away, can he be trusted not to mention the delay to anybody? You won't be able to tell him why he hasn't gotten a notice to report, you know."

"He'll keep quiet," Jesse assured her. "He values his freedom."

To Peter, two days later on the Island, Jesse expressed his misery about Zeb's fate. It overshadowed even the uplift he'd previously felt about flying.

Peter's own feeling, he sensed, went too deep for words.

He had no solution to offer. "Jesse, I'd hoped that as an offworlder you wouldn't have to face this," he admitted. "We've armored ourselves against it, here. It's a fact of life we've known since childhood. We hope, of course, to control our own health successfully enough to avoid residential care, but our loved ones—"

"At least he won't end up on life support, or in the Vaults."

Peter looked away, staring out across the bay to the horizon. "Carla told you, didn't she, that the people in residential care units have implanted microchips that send out heart monitor data and a location signal? Don't you realize what that means?"

"I know we couldn't hide him even if we could help him escape. How will we arrange hospice care, then, when the time comes?"

"We can't, Jess," Peter said sadly. "Not for anyone in a residential care unit. Our hospice patients are people who've been living independently. Even if it were possible to hide escapees from care units, we couldn't bury their bodies. The microchips would go on transmitting unless destroyed, and if we destroyed them, the authorities would know when and where it had happened."

"Oh, God." It was obvious, of course, but he'd resisted thinking it through. "Damn it, Peter, I don't see how you tolerate what we're up against here."

"We've had no choice—and things are going to get worse." He hesitated, measuring Jesse. "I'm going to tell you something I haven't told the others yet. It will be on the news in a few weeks, and I'd rather put off discussion until then. So can I rely on you not to mention it even to Carla?"

At Jesse's nod, Peter went on, "I know through my Hospital position that the government is planning to implant such chips in everyone on Undine—that was why they were in such a hurry to install our satellite uplink. Universal tracking has been the Administration's aim for a long time, and now, when the public's worked up about an arsonist on the loose, is deemed a favorable time for calling an election. There's little doubt that the measure will pass. The voters will see it as a reasonable safety measure, both for protecting their health through ongoing heart monitoring and for preventing crime." Bitterly he added, "The original colonists had too much independence to go to such lengths for the sake of preventing the few heart attacks not predictable through regular checkups. But in our enlightened era, all traces of respect for privacy have died out."

Jesse stared at him, horrified. "That will mean we can't hide *anyone* in a hospice, or bury any bodies at all."

"Yes. Our hospice work will come to an end. What's more, in our own old age we won't be able to die naturally ourselves. The implications are even greater than that. The authorities may start keeping records of people's movements, who goes to the Island and how often, for instance. Once information like that gets into a computer, it generally stays there, and of course it will defeat the purpose of hiding who my friends are. Whether or not our conspiracy is suspected, we'll be vulnerable."

"God, Peter. We're vulnerable already—we've been living on borrowed time. If we can't even hope to be examined by you if we're caught, the risk will be just too great. Besides, it's going to be almost impossible to train recruits. The heart rate variations in our lab work alone might attract notice."

"Unfortunately, yes. I've known about this since the week before you arrived. It's one reason I rushed you through your training."

"So what's to become of us?" No wonder Peter had seemed troubled. As leader, he might be unable to do more than preside over the Group's demise.

Peter didn't answer immediately. Then, seriously, he asked, "Jess, do you believe our goals are too important to abandon?"

"Of course. I've always thought we should be politically

active, and now we're going to have to be. There'll be no alternative if we can't stay underground."

"But since we can't win through politics—and there's no hope that we ever can—how far should we go to preserve our own way of life? Would you be for giving up many of the good things we enjoy to gamble on a better future, and more freedom, for ourselves and those who come after us?"

"I would, but I don't see what you're driving at," Jesse said.

"No, and I can't explain yet," Peter said slowly. "Ian and I have a contingency plan, but we've agreed not to reveal it until we're sure it can be attempted. Even the other Council members haven't been told. All I'm looking for right now is an idea of whether you'll back it when the time comes."

"You can count on me," Jesse assured him. He felt a pang of regret—just as he'd found a lifestyle with which he was happy, it looked as though he wouldn't have it long. But that would be true regardless of what Peter might propose. He would not stand for being perpetually tracked by an implanted heart monitor without taking action—if necessary, dangerous and possibly futile action. Nor could he sit quietly back and resign himself and his friends to an eventual end like the one Zeb Hennesy was facing.

44

WHEN JESSE GOT back from the Island, he found Zeb in a state of agitation. "My notice to report for a checkup was due while you were gone," he said "It hasn't come yet. I don't know what to do."

"Be grateful for whatever glitch in the system's holding it up," Jesse suggested.

"They're never late. The damn government computer's got a clock more reliable than sunrise. And my Net connection's working fine—my bills arrive on schedule."

"Well, I wouldn't worry about it if I were you," said Jesse.

"Enjoy as many days of freedom as you're allowed. It's the Hospital's error, after all."

"But will they admit that, or will they arrest me for ignoring a summons? I'm wondering if I ought to check it out—"

"God, Zeb, don't do that!" It hadn't occurred to him that Zeb would fear being blamed for failure to show up. If he inquired about the delay, Carla's tampering might be discovered, though she'd assured him she'd covered her tracks well. "As long as you don't tell anybody besides me that you knew it was due, you're safe."

"I guess you're right," Zeb conceded. "Who am I to question a gift of fate? Let's fly."

They were airborne most of that day and the next, hopping from island to island. Zeb was tense, anticipating that each day of flying might be his last. Jesse perceived with dismay that he'd become reckless, that if it were not for his own presence, he might be tempted anew to lose himself and the plane at sea. That might have been best, considering the alternative, he thought in anguish. The Group held that nothing but the aim of saving others could justify suicide. The line between self-destruction and natural death was firmly drawn. In principle, Jesse agreed, but when he thought of Zeb, strong, vital, locked for the rest of his life within the confines of a stifling institution where the only concern for him was to keep his heart beating. . . . And in the end, the Vaults after all. There would not even be the eventual sea burial he'd expected to give him.

It was near dusk when they reached the city on the second day. Jesse had enough dual hours for licensing by now and had given Zeb a chance to take the pilot's seat for what he believed was likely to be his final flight. Though privately, Jesse knew that no notice to report for a health checkup would come soon, Zeb still expected one to arrive the next morning. Perhaps it had been a mistake to draw it out when he couldn't say anything to alter that expectation. The suspense might be worse than the reality to which the man had repeatedly resigned himself.

As they descended toward the water on their final approach, Zeb let out a moan of pain. "Oh God," he mumbled, "Heart . . . knew it would quit—"

He gripped the controls, his knuckles white, struggling to hold on long enough to land. That proved impossible. With a sharp cry he fell forward, clutching his chest, and lay slumped against the yoke in front of him, prevented only by his shoulder strap from pushing the plane into a dive.

Jesse reacted fast. He hauled back hard on the copilot's yoke, at the same time putting on power. The plane shuddered, almost stalled, as it grazed the water. Then it lifted and began to climb. He could not turn from the controls to see, but he knew Zeb hadn't lost consciousness. Pain filled him, radiated from his mind with the magnified force of emotion. It didn't matter that Zeb wasn't a trained telepath; in a situation such as this, Jesse's own sensitivity more than compensated. The man was in agony. But there was no underlying fear. In spite of the pain, Zeb was feeling almost relieved at the thought that he was about to die in the air after all.

Reducing throttle, Jesse trimmed the nose of the plane lower, focusing on flying until he got enough altitude to level off. When he was sure the area was clear of traffic, he switched on the autopilot and leaned over, reaching between Zeb's legs for the handle to push back the seat. After managing to get his feet off the pedals, he felt for a pulse; it was faint, irregular. Zeb's eyes were closed and he was breathing erratically. There was nothing he could do for him as long as they were strapped in. He was not sure that there was anything he *should* do. Certainly Zeb would not want to go to the Hospital, not when he'd never again be allowed to leave it. Maybe, Jesse thought, it would be best to keep flying for awhile. . . .

But the moon wasn't up yet. In a few more minutes it would be too dark to land. He had no choice but to do so, hoping no one would be near enough on the pier to see Zeb's condition. Somehow he'd have to get him to a hospice.

The landing was rough; Jesse was too preoccupied to concentrate on touching down smoothly. The jolt as they hit the water revived Zeb to point of speech. "Jesse," he gasped as they taxied in. "Don't . . . call the ambulance. Please don't."

"Are you sure?" Jesse asked, knowing the answer but feeling obliged to verify it. "You might die if you're not treated quickly, Zeb."

"I . . . know. Maybe it's . . . just as well. Never be locked up, not before going to the Vaults, anyhow."

You're never going to the Vaults! Jesse wanted to say. Now he could prevent that, at least. It was unlikely that Zeb would recover without immediate treatment. But it was his choice to refuse it, and to make that choice was a basic human right.

For a moment he considered taking off again and going directly to the Island; there would be moonlight by the time they reached it. The Group would surely accept a body, even without prearrangement. But he could not be sure that Zeb would die before they got there, and he could not take him to the Lodge while alive. In theory, he was not even authorized to take him to a hospice, but to hell with that. He couldn't stay all night in the plane with a dying man, certainly. He would have to get him into one of the safe houses across the street.

Not the one Ian was in, of course. No outsider must know of Ian's involvement, and in any case, there was a policy of not keeping more than one hospice patient in the same place. He hoped the house next door was empty at present; if it wasn't, Zeb would have to be moved later. For now, there was no alternative. But he did not see how he was going to get him there. Zeb was in too much pain to walk. . . .

Yet, Jesse thought, he was supposed to be able to relieve others' pain! Could he possibly do that? He had practiced it only in the lab, with Group members. Healers could do it for outsiders, but it had been acknowledged that he had no talent for healing. All the same, he had to try. Even without the need for walking, he'd have had to—he cared too much for Zeb to let him suffer.

Gripping Zeb's hand, he reached out as he would to a fellow telepath, making an effort to share what the man was feeling. All at once, the pain came. It nearly swamped him. Instinctively he recoiled, almost slipped into the mind-pattern for pain control—but then, pressing his free hand against his own chest, he let himself experience it. *Zeb, oh Zeb, it doesn't have to hurt so much . . . I can ease it if you let your mind merge with mine. . . .* He knew his skill wouldn't be sufficient to guide someone who was terrified, but Zeb had no fear of death. Only the physical sensations had to be handled.

His left arm was on fire, the hand clutching Zeb's . . . the arm through which he'd learned to deal with pain . . . but no, it was Zeb's arm, wasn't it? The pain of a heart attack was often felt in the left arm; that must be where it was coming from. *Zeb, just let the arm float, it doesn't matter, the chest pain doesn't matter either, we won't suffer anymore. . . .* For an instant they were in full contact. Jesse was in control; he felt the pain abate as he shifted into the state where it did not bother him. And he knew that Zeb was following.

After a few minutes of deep breathing he unfastened his seat straps, then Zeb's. "Zeb," he said softly, continuing to project the mind-pattern, gradually allowing it to become automatic enough for him to talk. "It's not so bad, now, is it?"

"Seems to have let up," Zeb agreed. "I still feel it but I'm—used to it, I guess. I don't think it's going away."

"No. But could you walk a little way?"

"I'm shaky as hell, Jesse. Sick to my stomach, too. I can't get home. Have to wait till I feel better—or else, till it's over. Here in the plane's as good a place for that as any."

"I know a better place. Some friends just across the street."

"They'll call an ambulance."

"No, they won't."

"It's the law, Jesse. They have to."

"Trust me, Zeb!" The pain was really bad; he still felt it, although he himself was no longer suffering from it and for Zeb it was partially attenuated. "Come on, lean on me," he said. "We've got to go *now*."

He managed to get Zeb out of the plane and, holding most of his weight, started slowly along the lighted pier. God, if anyone should see—this wasn't a world where pretending Zeb was drunk would be helpful. If he was found with a man so obviously sick when he hadn't phoned for help, he would indeed be in violation of the law. It was near dark on a moonless evening, however. There would be no air traffic now, and it was late for strollers along the esplanade.

All at once, the silence was broken by the sound of sirens.

"God! They're coming for me," Zeb burst out.

"They couldn't be," Jesse assured him. "I didn't call, and nobody else knows you're sick. No planes have come over; we couldn't have been spotted."

"But if they drive by here, they'll see."

This was all too true. Desperately Jesse looked around for something they could sit on, as if they'd been merely enjoying the view of the stars, perhaps. There was nothing. The sirens were coming closer. As they approached, he did the only thing he could think of—he grabbed Zeb and threw both arms around him, turning him face to face in what he hoped would look like a lovers' embrace.

The ambulance drove on past.

But there were more sirens coming, more vehicles. At first terrified, close to losing his focus on the pain he had to control, Jesse let out a breath of relief. They were fire trucks! Looking to his left, in the direction they were headed, he saw that a house half a block down was on fire. The serial arsonist, apparently, was still active.

"It's our lucky day," he said. "Nobody's going to notice us; anyone around will be watching the fire. So come on, while we've got a good chance."

Supporting Zeb, who was gasping for breath but able,

with effort, to walk, they crossed the esplanade and street, then stumbled around the safe house onto its back porch. There were no lights in the windows and Jesse dared not knock. He could not be sure there were never outsiders there. The only thing he could do was leave Zeb concealed and go to the back door of the adjacent house, where, he hoped, Kira would have arrived to stay with Ian. If she wasn't there, it would be some other Group member, perhaps one he didn't know. He did have a password, and if worst came to worst, Ian could identify him—but Peter would not be happy if he disturbed Ian. Peter wasn't going to be happy anyway when he heard about the risk he had taken.

To his relief, it was Kira who answered his knock. "Jesse!" she said in surprise.

"I've got Zeb Hennesy out in back next door," he said. "He had a heart attack in the plane, and he doesn't want the ambulance."

"What have you told him?" she asked brusquely.

"Nothing! Nothing except that the people here won't call the Meds. God, Kira, surely you'll take him in—he's dying."

She frowned. "It's a terrible thing to say, but I hope you're right. The rules aren't meant to keep out dying people—the problem is what we'll do with him if he recovers. That's why we don't reveal our safe houses to anyone who hasn't been examined."

"I'm sorry, Kira, but there wasn't anywhere else I could take him. We barely made it this far. He's in a lot of pain. I—I relieved it some, but now—"

"You were able to do that for an outsider?" She seemed surprised.

"Well, he's a pretty close friend. Maybe that makes a difference."

"It does. An emotional tie makes a big difference." Kira sighed. "I suppose you had no choice about bringing him here. Do you vouch for him, Jesse?"

"Yes. He hates the Meds; even if he does recover, he'll never betray us."

"All right. Go back and do the best you can with his pain while I get the key."

Jesse went back to Zeb, who had collapsed on the steps, obviously in intense pain again. He put an arm around him and repeated the process of sensing it, letting himself feel it fully, and then trying to project the shift in consciousness toward not minding. It was harder this time; he perceived that the pressure of crisis had helped before. Kira would do it much better than he could. "Hold on, Zeb," he said. "A friend is coming. She's a retired doctor. She'll make you feel better, even if she can't cure you."

Kira came with the house key and together they got Zeb indoors and into a clean bed. He was slipping in and out of consciousness. "Have you got what you need to examine him here?" Jesse asked.

"I'm doing it with my mind," Kira said. "Telepathy, plus my healer's senses combined with my background in cardiology. You were right; his heart is damaged past repair. He hasn't long to live."

"There's no way you can—heal him?"

"No, no more than I can heal Ian. All a healer does is enhance a person's deep self-healing power. Zeb no longer has that power; he feels it's his time to go."

"Can he hear us?"

"Not at the moment. I'll bring him around in a little while; I need his consent to keep him here."

"It's damned ironic," Jesse said, "for it to happen now. He's worried about his heart for some time, and feared the summons from the Hospital that's due—but Carla just fixed it so that it's not going to come."

"You didn't *tell* him that!"

"Of course not. He still thinks it's coming any day. That they'll send him to a residential care unit when it does."

"Then it's not coincidence, Jesse. The unconscious mind controls these things. I can tell that he'd rather not recover—now I know why."

Jesse protested, "As I've heard it, the residential care

units are full of people waiting to die. Certainly the nursing homes on Earth are; it's often talked about. So the unconscious mind is hardly a reliable control on how long anyone lives."

"It is when the body's not interfered with." Kira told him. "It's nature's provision for dying when the time comes. But the drugs the Meds use override its influence on biochemistry, which is one of the worst tragedies of their system as far as old people are concerned."

"I'd say the worst tragedy is that Zeb can't live out his old age in freedom."

"Yes, certainly. But since he can't, it's understandable that he doesn't want to live it out in prison, not when he's been an active man with no interest in vids or reading."

"Kira," Jesse said reproachfully, "that sounds as if you're condoning suicide. I thought the Group believes it's wrong."

"We do. But why is it wrong, Jesse?"

He pondered it. Neither he nor the Group had religious objections. Peter had endorsed Jesse's own assertion that it seemed like cheating, that suffering was no excuse. He could not say why he felt this so strongly.

Kira said, "You don't believe refusing medical treatment is the same as suicide, though that's what the Meds would claim. You didn't try to talk Zeb into going to the Hospital, yet you wouldn't have let him ditch his plane on purpose." Whether she'd absorbed this thought from his mind or Zeb's, Jesse was not sure. "So underneath," she continued, "you do understand that there's a time to die. And it's the unconscious mind that makes that decision, Jesse. Suicide is wrong because to accomplish it, one must defy one's own unconscious mind, one's inner integrity. Someone who *really* wants to die doesn't need to take action. It happens naturally, as it is happening now with Zeb."

"It didn't happen that way with Valerie."

"And what she did would have violated her true self if it hadn't been for her wish to save Peter."

"You mean that as long as a person's alive, he or she unconsciously wants to be—whatever that person may think consciously."

"Exactly. If ongoing medical treatment isn't messing up the process, that is. But of course," she added, "the reverse isn't true. People can die without wanting to, and those who seek treatment voluntarily are apt to need it. That's why we have healers."

Zeb stirred, and Kira turned her attention to him. "Been dreaming I was home in bed," he murmured.

"You are in bed," Jesse said, taking his hand. "I'm here, Zeb."

"You didn't call the ambulance?"

"No. We won't ever call it. This is my friend Kira, and she'll find somebody to stay here with you."

"The pain's almost gone. But I'm—weak. Don't think I can get up."

"You don't have to get up," said Kira, "and you won't suffer from pain anymore. But Zeb, you might die. In the Hospital they could give you a new heart. Would you rather die here than go where they'd put you afterward?"

"Sure I would! But they won't let you keep me here, wherever this is."

"They won't know. No one will know—we can't even tell your family, if you have one. Do you?"

"I've got a sister. If she can't get me on the phone after a few days, she might call the Hospital. Then they'd search."

"If your sister calls the Hospital, Zeb, she'll be told you're in the Vaults. You won't have a chance to say goodbye to her. Is that okay with you?"

"Yes. Has to be. But what if I'm not dead by then?"

"The Hospital will think you are," said Jesse. "But when you do die, you won't be sent to the Vaults. I'll take your body in the plane and bury it in the sea."

Zeb struggled to raise his head. "Can't let you risk that, Jesse," he said, "but that you'd offer—" Tears welled into his eyes.

Kira said, "We don't approve of the Vaults. We don't send anyone's body there."

"Who *are* you people?"

"We can't tell you that. And you must promise never to tell where you've been or what we've said, even if you recover."

"Sure . . . I promise. You'd be in a hell of a lot of trouble if anybody found out."

"We would," Jesse agreed, "so I'm trusting you, Zeb."

"Jesse—you've been more than just an offworlder all along, haven't you? I could tell there was something about you . . . something you weren't saying—"

God, had he been as transparent as that? Zeb was the only outsider he'd known well since joining the Group, and though he had tried to keep his thoughts to himself, shielding them hadn't been easy. He had wondered how the others managed it for a lifetime, working side by side with outsiders.

"It's all right, Jesse," Kira said. "Zeb wouldn't have been conscious of questions if you hadn't helped with his pain. That sensitized him to your mind."

"I won't ask questions," Zeb said. "I'll just say thanks . . . while I can. I can't thank you enough for any of it, Jesse. For taking the plane, or for—this."

"Just sleep," Jesse said. "I'll stay here for now. Kira has to leave, but tomorrow someone else will come. You won't be alone."

In the next room, he pulled out his phone and called Carla. He could not tell her where he was—Group secrets were never mentioned on the phone—but he made clear that she shouldn't worry about his absence.

As Kira opened the door to leave, the smell of smoke blew in. "I forgot to tell you," he said. "A house down the street's burning; the arsonist has struck again."

"I don't like it," Kira said. "There have been too many in this neighborhood, for no reason, and who can say where he'll hit next?"

"Well, tonight, at least, I'm glad it was close," Jesse said, "because it was the diversion we needed to get here from the pier. Is it true, I wonder, that fate watches out for us?"

Seriously, Kira replied, "So far it seems to have been. Peter talks a lot about fate; I think he really believes in it. But we can't rely on it for protection, Jesse. You took a risk tonight—you had to. Just don't ever do it without real need."

45

IT WAS TAKEN for granted that Jesse would be the one to fly Zeb's body to the Island for sea burial. That would be his normal role as a friend even if he had not promised Zeb to do it personally. Neither Carla nor Peter was happy about it, but they knew better than to argue. Carla's fear for him was understandable. Peter's continued to perplex him. Why should Peter be more concerned about his safety than that of anyone else in the Group?

Zeb lingered for a while, and in the daytime Jesse stayed with him. Other caregivers took his place at night. Sometimes Zeb felt pain, and again Jesse eased it, finding that with practice his skill was increasing. "Kira," he asked when she came to check on Zeb's condition, "is it just because I know him well? Or could I someday—develop talent?"

Kira smiled. "It's a matter of empathy. You feel it for Zeb because he's your friend. A person born with the gift of healing starts out feeling it for everyone."

"Oh," he said, disappointed. "Then I guess I'm unqualified."

"Not at all. You were a loner all your youth, and Fleet reinforced that tendency. Now telepathy has opened your mind to feelings you'd never so much as imagined. You have a long life ahead of you, Jesse. You will grow."

Tending the dying, unpleasant as it was in some ways, did give Jesse insight, as he'd earlier been told that it would. Dying naturally in old age was not terrible. It was indeed unlike premature death. Zeb, though free of pain, was ready to go and unafraid. He'd had a good life and it was over; there was nothing left for him to cling to. Whether he envisioned anything ahead—anything that might be symbolized by flight into the wide skies he had loved—Jesse was not sure. They didn't talk about that, but he saw Zeb's eyes light up at times, as if he were looking forward and not back.

And whatever else might be said of such a death, it was better than the horror of the tubes and machines, the eventual entombment in the stasis vaults, from which Zeb's own unconscious mind had arranged escape. Jesse tried not to think about what Peter had warned was coming—the closing of that option even for aged Group members. They couldn't *all* end up in the Vaults, not after years of believing they could prevent it. . . .

During one afternoon Kira relieved Jesse while he took, and passed, the examination for his pilot's license. Whereas the transport of Zeb's body was expected to be a solo flight, he could not get a body from the safe house to the plane alone, and there was a chance that whoever helped him would need to come along if he was observed and had to leave in a hurry. Not that he wouldn't be charged with something far more serious than carrying passengers without a license if they were caught; still he felt it was wise to get the exam out of the way. He was not too sure of his ability to close his mind to unconscious telepathic sensing. Facing an official examiner later, with a guilty conscience about the illicit cargo he'd carried, would be harder.

The flight was likely to be that night. Because it was not expected that Zeb would live until morning, Carla had made an excuse to trade shifts with another technician so she would be free to go to the Island a day early if necessary. She could not bear the idea of not getting there soon after Jesse arrived. Thus she went back to work soon after dinner, and Jesse decided to sleep at the safe house instead of waiting for the summons that was almost sure to come. That would avoid the problem of transportation—to take a water taxi now would be okay, but they did not run past midnight, and to call a cab in the pre-dawn hours would look suspicious. Besides, he would like to be on hand during Zeb's last moments anyway, he thought. If Zeb was conscious he would want him there.

It was dark when he got to the dock and took a close look at his plane to avoid the need for preflight checking later. He was surprised at how nervous he felt. It was just a flight! The moon would be up, and he had made solo night flights before. No one could possibly know he had a body aboard, and anyway, there would be no other planes near him after he was in the air. The only danger lay in getting the body into the plane. Peter, who was next door visiting Ian, had agreed to help him. As was usual in the Group, they would carry the shrouded body across the esplanade concealed in a cargo container from which it would be removed within the plane, to lie straight across the back seats, prior to takeoff. This last was the tricky part; when anyone was around to observe, the helper had to come along and do it in the air before rigor mortis set in. But tonight the dock was deserted. There was no reason to expect trouble.

Jesse took deep breaths, calming himself, using the skills he'd been taught to lower his blood pressure and slow his pulse. Then he walked slowly back along the dock toward the house across from it.

And froze, sick with fear, his heart racing again. The house was burning.

Smoke rose from the roof of the kitchen, the room furthest from Zeb's. Through the window he saw a faint glow, not open flame, but a sure sign that fire raged beyond.

His first thought was that Zeb was probably still alive, and that to burn to death, helpless in bed, would be a horror past contemplation. Then too, tonight's caregiver— Ingrid, he thought—might be asleep if Zeb hadn't awakened and rung for her. Or worse, she might have been overcome by smoke. He ran toward the back door, which in anticipation of his late-night arrival had been left unlocked, conscious only of the need to rescue them.

But as he ran, another thought came to him. Ian, too, lay helpless in bed. He was in the house next door, the one on the side away from the fire. If this house was allowed to burn, that one might also catch—and even if it didn't, the firefighters would evacuate it. Kira and Peter were there. It would do no good to warn them; they would not leave Ian and they couldn't carry him out unseen. A cab wouldn't arrive soon enough for them to leave before the fire was noticed. So no matter what they did, all three of them would be arrested. Ian would be taken to the Hospital and soon, to the Vaults. Kira and Peter, having called no ambulance for him, would be convicted of attempted murder. They might even be charged with murder if they were suspected of having known Zeb was next door on his deathbed, especially since Peter was a staff doctor. In any case, for both to be involved would prove conspiracy. And if even one of them was given truth serum, the entire Group would be exposed.

The fire must be put out before it spread. If like the other arsons, it was an electrical fire, it couldn't be fought at its source with water. Jesse knew he could not extinguish it alone, or even with Peter's help. He had only one option. His hands shaking, he pulled out his phone and pressed the emergency key to summon the fire department.

They would come quickly—he heard sirens in the distance before he even reached the door. He hoped Zeb was already dead, or at least wouldn't live long enough to know that there would now be no sea burial. There was a chance he could save Ingrid. He ran to her room first and found her barely conscious; carrying her out the back door into the fresh air, he shook her alert. "Go next door!" he yelled. "Tell Peter to hide Ian and stay inside." He could not wait to see if she was able to.

He rushed back into the house, choking on smoke himself. Mercifully, Zeb's heart had stopped beating. There was nothing to be done for him. But, Jesse realized suddenly,

Kira's fingerprints and those of other caregivers must be all over the place. The arson investigators would discover them; with the city nervous about the serial arsonist, they would be very thorough. There would be questions about how a body happened to be in what was ostensibly an unoccupied house. And medical examiners would discover that Zeb had not died from smoke inhalation.

There wasn't time to wipe everything clean of prints. Yet if Kira was arrested Peter would not be the one to handle her case; her friendship with him was known. She'd be drugged by other doctors, and would reveal everything. Jesse froze. At all costs he must draw suspicion away from her. The blame for the death must fall on him alone. That meant there could be no escape for him even if it were physically possible. Which it wasn't—an ambulance was already out front; finding the door locked, the crew would be at the back before he could get away. The fire trucks were close behind them. If he tried to leave by the front door, he'd be seen.

In desperation he stared at Zeb's body. It was still warm; could they revive it, put it in stasis? Quite possibly they could. Cremation would be the next best thing to burial at sea—and besides, he had to make sure there would be no cause to question anyone but him. He made no conscious choice; he simply acted. Pulling the body off the bed, he grabbed it under the arms and started dragging it toward the burning kitchen.

Then, in dismay, Jesse remembered the most essential precaution of all. Letting go of the body, he pulled out his phone again and dialed Carla's number. Oh God, please let her answer! Please let her not be occupied with work that would prevent the use of her phone! He threw himself down on the floor below smoke level, trying not to cough. When he heard her voice he spoke quickly, starting with the Group password reserved for emergencies—he could not tell her anything in plain language, of course. "I need you to check the database," he said. "My friend Zeb Hennesy's wondering when he should report for a health checkup. The notice should have come some time last week. He's afraid it may have gotten lost." Ignoring her startled gasp, he whispered, "I love you, Carla," and hung up, willing her to understand what she must do. If only telepathy worked over a phone connection . . . was it possible, perhaps, that silent communication did work at a distance when the need for it was urgent?

The smoke was thick by this time; to drag the body he had to stoop low. As he neared the kitchen, the intense heat of the fire enveloped him. He remembered the firewalk, of how red-hot coals had seemed cool . . . but he'd been in an altered state then, and had drawn on telepathic support. He was not now immune to heat, much less to the open flame he'd handled during the Ritual. Now, he would be burned. Yet he must get Zeb's body into the fire, and the ambulance officers must see him do it.

Grimly, he dropped to the floor and crawled forward, pushing the body ahead of him. The heat became scorching, searing, and he could scarcely get breath enough to keep moving. Smoke cut off all sight but the blaze of the inferno ahead. Its crackle and roar overpowered all other sound, so that he did not hear the firefighters approach.

They broke the front door down and crashed through just as Jesse staggered to his feet and, with abnormal strength born of crisis, lifted the body. Heedless of flame, he heaved it past the burning remains of the kitchen doorway. At the same time, the ambulance crew rushed in from the back. Strong hands grasped him, not bothering to avoid a grip on his blistering forearms. He was too stunned by smoke to deal with the pain.

That Zeb couldn't be revived was obvious. "Got a psych case here," an officer said. "He's murdered a man and set the house on fire to cover up."

"Not likely we've got more than one arsonist on the loose," his partner commented. "I'll bet this guy set the other fires, too. Anyway, there's a lot of people who'll be glad to hear there's somebody in custody."

By this time the roof was ablaze. As they carried him to the ambulance, Jesse could see the firefighters pumping water from the bay, their hoses stretched across the esplanade. A crowd had gathered on the dock to watch and lights had been turned on. In the background, above the reflections on the water, he glimpsed the blue floats of his plane. He was dimly aware that he might never fly it again.

Part Five

46

WHEN CARLA GOT Jesse's phone call, she was at first bewildered by what she was hearing. Zeb was wondering when to report for a health checkup? But Zeb was dying! She had inactivated his file days ago, listing him officially as in stasis.

Yet Jesse had used the Group's emergency password.

With growing apprehension, she realized that the cryptic message could mean only one thing. Zeb, or his body, had been found. They would be checking his identity. She must reactivate the file before anyone discovered that it had been tampered with—and she must undo what she'd done to delay his health check summons, too, backdate it to the day it should have been sent out. Otherwise, it would be apparent that someone had been hacking the files.

She hurried to her own desk and with shaking hands, logged onto the Net with the backdoor password she alone knew, praying that no one would approach close enough to observe the file displayed on her monitor. Usually she hacked only when sure that others in the area were well occupied, or from Peter's office, which she must not be seen entering during a shift when he wasn't present. It was hard to focus, hard to proceed with the necessary speed without fumbling at the keyboard. If Zeb had been found, did that mean Jesse had been caught moving his body?

Oh God, it mustn't mean that ... yet no ambulance crew would have gone to the safe house. No one had been into that safe house but Group members, other than patients who were now dead.

It didn't add up. If Jesse had been caught, he wouldn't have had a chance to use his phone. He hadn't sounded right; his voice had been muffled—still, to call her, he must have been free. Had Zeb not died after all? Could he have recovered miraculously, left the safe house and gone somewhere he might be seen?

The files repaired, Carla forced herself back to the work she had been doing, wondering how she could last through the rest of the shift. If she said she was sick, she could leave now, find Jesse ... but no, he would expect her to be here. He might need to call again, want something else done that required computer access. At least he would let her know he was all right.

She waited, pulling out her phone repeatedly to stare at it. No call came in. She *knew* something was wrong. Telepathy? It sometimes gave warning of distant trouble—not verbally, but through visions or simply knowledge.... She was afraid of that knowledge. She tried to shut it out, at the same time aware that she could not bear not to know. Finally, she logged onto the Net again and ran a search, first for Zeb's name—he was now listed as "murdered, body unrecoverable"—and then, in terror, for Jesse's.

Jesse had been involuntarily admitted to the Hospital two hours ago. He was charged with murder and arson. The only reason he hadn't yet been brought to the psych department was that he was presently being treated for smoke inhalation and burns.

Carla felt faint, might actually have fainted had her training in stress control not taken over. It wasn't hard to guess what had occurred. Arson? The safe house was in the area where the arsonist had been active. It was a likely target, being apparently unoccupied, as all the other burned houses had been. No medical telemetry was transmitted from the bathrooms of safe houses—that was another detail she routinely arranged through hacking—and heavy drapes prevented lights being noticed from the street. So evidently it had been set afire . . . and Jesse had taken the blame to prevent anyone from finding out that it was a hospice. To prevent an investigation that might expose other caregivers who'd been there, perhaps even reveal that there was another safe house next door. He had spent time phoning to save her, when he might have escaped. . . .

No. He couldn't have escaped without setting off a hunt for everyone who had left fingerprints. He could say nothing in his own defense, and she could not defend him. If conspiracy were to be suspected, the inquiry wouldn't end with those who'd cared for Zeb. Even Xiang Li, who owned the house, would be investigated, and Xiang was involved in many of the Group's financial affairs. One thing would lead to another . . . how could the Group have been so blind as not to have foreseen that? But of course, no one could have anticipated a safe house catching fire. Serial arson was an unprecedented crime in the colony. That was why its citizens were so aroused. . . .

Chilled, she realized that they were perhaps sufficiently aroused to demand a scapegoat. And it was all too obvious who the scapegoat was likely to be.

She had never believed such a thing would happen. Not twice! And if it couldn't happen to her twice—to two husbands—did that not protect Jesse? She'd told herself it would. But that had been foolish. It was hardly a coincidence that both the men she'd chosen to marry had been outstanding people, strong and committed to risking themselves to save others. After Ramón, she wouldn't have been attracted to anyone who was less. Underneath, she must have known Jesse would be in danger precisely because of his courage.

Her mind whirled. She must go to him! But she dared not do so until she was sure he was alone. Even then she might not be able to see him; he was in custody and would be in a locked ward. No one outside the Group knew she was his wife. It wasn't even known that they lived together, and only Zeb had been aware that she flew with him. This, like their friendship with Peter, must be kept from the Hospital authorities—otherwise she'd be watched too closely to help him later.

Later . . . later, would he be drugged senseless, his mind destroyed? As a presumed murderer, he'd be given something much worse than mere truth serum. She had never seen the victims in the criminal ward; Peter had not allowed her to work in that place. He did not talk about what went on there. She knew it was a source of deep pain to him. How could Peter possibly endure the ordeal of inflicting its horrors on Jesse? Yet if he evaded it, Jesse would be turned over to some psychiatrist who would treat him more harshly. Peter's personal involvement was the only hope Jesse had.

She knew there would be no release for him. He would be held responsible for Zeb's death, not merely for disposing of the body, and for burning the house he'd been found in even if not for torching others. He would be declared mentally ill and permanently incarcerated. The Group could no more devise an escape from a secure ward than it could free dead bodies from stasis.

Unable to hold back tears, Carla dropped her head into her arms, folded on the desk before her. The world blurred. She could not bear awareness of what he'd be forced to endure. Nor could she bear the years ahead, trapped here with one husband brain-dead in the vaults above the ceiling, the other brain-damaged behind a solid wall. She would crack up; she'd be a psych case herself before long. . . .

Time passed; she became aware that the shift was ending. By supreme effort she steadied herself and shut down her computer, preparing to leave. She'd been trained to control her body and mind, had she not? Jesse needed her. The Group needed her. She could not crack up, now or ever.

Where to go, until she could find a way to reach Jesse?

Her normal shift was now starting, but she had traded and would not be expected to stay here. Yet she must talk to Peter. He'd gone to Ian's house last night, would have seen the fire. Had he found out about Jesse's arrest? Even if he had, he could not come to the Hospital until his regular arrival time. If his off-work acquaintance with Jesse became known, the case would be taken away from him; thank God they'd hidden Jesse's presence on the Island. She could wait for him in his private office now; people on this shift were used to her going there.

Peter was late. He must be checking with the Hospital's legal department, Carla realized. Would they really accuse Jesse of serial arson? The more she thought, the more she wondered how a fire could have been started in the safe house when there'd been a caregiver present. If Jesse had been there, he surely would have heard the arsonist break in. It must have started before he arrived. He must have seen the house burning, gone in deliberately. Even so, it was strange that Ingrid would have slept through a break-in—she'd have been alert, in case Zeb rang the bell given him to call her. If he'd already died, she'd have stayed awake to tell Jesse.

There was a couch in Peter's office. Carla collapsed onto it, attempting to reach a state of consciousness in which she could bring her body's stress reactions under control. She had thought that she knew how. In the years since Ramón's death she'd had plenty of practice. But for the time being, her skill seemed to have deserted her....

When she opened her eyes Peter was standing over her, his face lined with pain. They needed no words at first; even their telepathic exchange was wordless. What they felt was instinctively shared, and was too overwhelming for verbal expression.

After awhile Peter spoke. "You know, don't you, that I've got to be very hard on him? In public, or anywhere I can be overheard, I can't show the slightest sign that I believe him to be anything but a sick and violent criminal. If I don't treat him aggressively enough I will be taken off his case—and that would be disastrous not only for him, but for us all. The hypnotic conditioning I gave him won't withstand psychiatric probing, not after his mind is weakened. And I'll be forced to . . . weaken it."

"I know. And I know what it will cost you, Peter." Peter would suffer as much as Jesse did, if not more. Jesse, once his brain was damaged, would stop caring.

"I never really thought I could be brought to such a pass," Peter admitted. "Oh, God, Carla! How are we going to get through it?"

She rose and put her arms around him, not sure whether she was giving comfort or seeking it. They clung to each other.

"I'll be in telepathic contact with Jesse, of course," Peter reflected, "though I don't know how long that will last. Some psychiatric drugs suppress paranormal functioning, and I'm required to use them on people with hallucinations. What we give to murderers just makes them lethargic." His tone was bitter.

"I need contact with him, too," Carla said. "You've got to give me duties in the secured area."

"It would be hell for you."

"It would be worse never to see him," she insisted, "besides being worse for *him*."

"In the beginning, maybe. I'll make some excuse to send you in there. There's a rec room for the patients; you won't be able to say much aloud, but since you're so close telepathically—"

"How much time will we have after the start of . . . treatment?" She knew he wouldn't retain mental clarity long, though she could not believe that even brain damage would extinguish the love they shared.

"No permanent damage will be done for ten days, at least. He'll fight it. He won't give in as long as he's physically capable of resisting."

That would just make it harder for him, knowing the

fight was futile, Carla thought. Had he known from the time he entered the burning house?

In agony Peter burst out, "Of course he knew! He sacrificed himself for us—and I had to stand there, aware that he was doing it. I had to watch while they carried him to the ambulance. And the most terrible thing is that it might have been better for the Group if he'd taken his chance to escape."

"I don't understand!"

"He called the fire department to save the house we were in. If he hadn't, if he'd gotten out after rescuing Ingrid—"

"Then you'd have been arrested! Ian would have been sent to the Hospital and soon to the Vaults. You and Kira would have been implicated, and through you, all the rest of us." She saw more clearly, now, why Jesse had allowed himself to be caught; before, she'd assumed only the safe house had been involved.

"I suppose so," Peter conceded. "But oh, Carla, Jesse was the only hope the Group had. I'd give my own life, if that could free him."

Carla stared at him in shock. She sensed that he meant this literally. "I would, too," she whispered. "I love him. But you, Peter—the Group couldn't exist without you."

"It's unlikely that it can continue to exist without Jesse. He is less expendable than I am, Carla. A very hard time is coming to us—to everyone, not just those of us who care about him. There was a possibility that Jesse could have . . . made a difference. The difference between failure and our future survival."

"But *how*?" She had always known he considered Jesse special, but this . . .

Peter answered, "I shouldn't have said that. You have enough to bear without hearing it, and you mustn't tell anyone else yet—but since it slipped out, I guess I've got to say more. Before long everyone in this colony will be implanted with heart monitors containing tracking chips. It means the end of neurofeedback training, and certainly of our hospice work, including our own eventual burials—" At Carla's gasp he went on, "Ian and I have known this for some time. But we had a plan. Ian had a dream, an earlier precognitive dream than the one I've already mentioned to you—and in that dream, Jesse played a key role. That's why I moved so fast to recruit him."

"Ian dreamed of Jesse? Before he'd even met him?"

"Before he knew of his existence. From information I later shared with him, he made the connection. Perhaps I should have told Jesse. Yet it would have been unfair to lay it on him before the Ritual, and afterward, I feared he hadn't yet developed enough telepathic control to keep the secret. If only I'd confided in him, he might have seen how important it was not to risk himself. I failed to realize that in preparing him for a job demanding strength, I would make him too strong to sit back and wait to be given one."

"He was strong underneath to begin with, Peter. He'd never have avoided risk."

"I know that, really. Yet now I can't help wondering if I could have done something differently, somehow avoided this end to all we've been striving for."

"Did the dream show specifically what Jesse accomplished?" Carla asked.

"Yes. But it's best forgotten now that it can never come true."

"Peter," she said with excitement, "if it was a precognitive dream . . . doesn't that mean that whatever Jesse did in it is going to happen? That there's some way we can free him we don't yet know about?"

"Precognition isn't predestination, Carla. The future shown by a dream can always be changed. And we don't even know that it was real precognition. The content made us believe that it was. But there is never any proof beforehand."

She bowed her head. For a moment her despair had lifted; and now, to know Jesse had lost not only everything he'd had, but some mysterious destiny. . . .

"I've always had faith in providence," Peter said slowly. "Jesse's detention in this colony seemed more than coincidental—"

"Synchronicity, you once said to me."

"Yes, and this doesn't change that; the dream occurred the very night he arrived on Undine. Statistically, the odds against that are incalculable. If fate didn't send him to us for a purpose, what's left to believe in?"

"We believe what we say in the Ritual, Peter."

"That we are 'stewards of a flame that will illuminate future generations'? Those are hollow words if the Group can't continue."

"That we trust in the power of the mind," Carla said, hoping she still trusted it. "Our own minds, as long as we're alive—even if Jesse must lose his."

"You put me to shame," Peter murmured. "For it to be me whose faith is faltering, when you've faced Ramón's destruction and now Jesse's—"

"The burden you bear is greater than mine. Not only because of what you'll be forced to do to Jesse, but because you've got to lead the Group."

"I'll be no good as a leader if I lose faith in our future."

"What does Ian say?" she asked, grasping for something to hold to. Ian always had answers; he was not one to let Peter give up in despair.

"I haven't told Ian about Jesse's arrest," Peter said, "and I don't intend to. Why inform him on his deathbed that what he's worked for all his life is going to be wiped out, that even the paranormal dream he believed in was mere illusion? It would be cruel. We mustn't let him find out, Carla. I think it would kill him."

47

JESSE LAY IN a room much like the one in which he'd awakened many weeks ago, when his life on Undine had begun.

But the window of this one was barred. This time, there would be no escape from the Hospital. Though he'd offered no resistance to arrest —had even invited it—he'd acted fast, conscious only of need to protect the others. He had not, until now, let himself think of what it was going to mean.

At first, the reality of what had happened to him had not sunk in. It was simply not believable that within the space of a few minutes he could have lost all that he had gained on this world . . . friends, the Lodge, flight in the plane he had possessed so short a time . . . and Carla. The rest faded to nothing when he thought of losing Carla. Never again to lie in her arms, or in anyone's, for that matter . . . never to be fully a man again. . . .

Never even to be master of his own mind. If any doctor but Peter got control of his treatment, he might lose not merely the new control of mind and body in which he'd acquired confidence, but the mental capacity he'd taken for granted as a starship captain and indeed, as a normal human being. The psychiatric drugs used on criminals would reduce him to a childlike parody of a thinking adult.

He was terrified.

So far, the pain of his burned hands and forearms had not bothered him much; since recovering from smoke inhalation he had been able to control his perception of it. But his ability to do so was slipping as the panic in him grew. *Be willing to lose control, to accept the worst that can happen* . . . volitional management of pain, as of other brain functions, depended on that outlook. But he could not accept the prospect of brain damage! It would deprive him of volition, and the fear of this had begun to make it happen. Pain was beginning to overwhelm him. He was almost glad; unavoidable focus on his body drew his attention from the anguish of thinking.

There was no question of his healing the burns, though he knew that in principle his mind was capable of it. With Carla's help or Kira's, they could be healed quickly—but not here in the Hospital, where the nurses would observe abnormally fast growth of new skin. Probably even Peter wouldn't dare to let that occur. He would be obliged to go through medical burn treatment, which, though much improved over the long process it had involved in earlier centuries, was nevertheless said to be painful. Jesse resigned himself to it. It would be a welcome respite; he did not think they would send him to the psych ward until he was physically recovered.

In this he was mistaken. Soon after sunrise a nurse came to change the bandages. "Your hearing will be held this afternoon," she announced calmly, and then, her eyes meeting his, she whispered, "You can trust me—I am a steward of the flame."

Startled, Jesse nodded. It was the Group recognition password. Peter must have sent her. Could they have worked out some means of escape, despite past warnings that for criminals it was impossible?

"Speak softly," the nurse cautioned, "and take as much as you can from my mind in silence. Nod if you understand." He did so. The pain receded; she was relieving it for him telepathically as she dressed the lesions. And perhaps doing more—if she was to be the only one to dress them, rapid healing under the bandages would not matter.

"My name is Olivia," she said, "and I work in the residential ward where you'll be taken." *I will pass messages to you at times when Peter can't speak to you openly....*

Her thought was clear. Jesse nodded, and she went on, "Dr. Kelstrom will be in charge of your case—" *... and it's absolutely vital that he remain in charge. You must not appear to recognize him....*

He nodded again. Although Peter had supervised his case when he was held for alcoholism, he had not shown himself at that time. Officially, they had never met face to face, and any hint that they'd done so outside the Hospital would be disastrous.

"There will be other psychiatrists at the hearing," Olivia

said, "including Dr. Warick, who's the head of the psych department. They will question you. Be prepared to answer." *They won't show much sympathy for you—in their eyes you're a violent criminal. But they're not intentionally cruel. They merely believe that you're sick.*

Warick—the man Peter despised, the one Carla feared might be getting suspicious of Peter. "Will there be anyone appointed to defend me?" he asked. Surely, even on this world, some sort of judicial system must exist.

"It will be a medical hearing, not a judicial one," she replied. "And for what you have done, there can be no defense." He sensed that she was implying more than that he'd been caught red-handed. There could be no defense because only by convincing them that he was guilty could he ensure that the Group would not be implicated.

Are they likely to sentence me to . . . electroshock?

No! That's used on depressive patients, not criminals. She did not add what he already knew, that brain damage produced by drugs could, in the long run, be just as bad.

Olivia laid her hand on his forehead. *We're all pulling for you. We will support you in any way possible. From now on, forever, you will be in our thoughts and prayers.*

Forever? Had they no hope, then, after all? He knew, of course, that they had not; there hadn't even been hope of getting Valerie out. If they couldn't have rescued Zeb from a residential care unit, they certainly couldn't rescue anyone from incarceration in a ward for the criminally insane. Even so, it was chilling to sense her certainty of it. He was glad to know they were behind him—and, he recalled, they were pledged to support fellow members telepathically as well as through action—but telepathy worked only at close range. . . .

Late that afternoon Jesse was taken under guard to the front desk of the psych department, where he'd unrealistically hoped to see Carla, and on through a secured door into the hearing room. Because of his bandaged forearms he was not handcuffed, but was instead strapped to a chair confronting the table behind which Peter and three other psychiatrists were sitting. Peter's face was expressionless. He was projecting, *We must not communicate even silently. I'll come to you later, alone.*

The formidable Dr. Warick, who was presiding, called in the ambulance officers as witnesses to the circumstances under which Jesse had been apprehended. They testified that Zeb had evidently been bedridden in the house and that his body might have been revived sufficiently for preservation in stasis if Jesse had not shoved it into the burning kitchen. After they were dismissed, Warick spoke.

"Jesse Sanders, you are guilty of the murder of Zeb Hennesy and of arson. Do you deny this?"

"No," Jesse said steadily. "I was responsible, though I wouldn't call it murder."

"We're aware that your mind is sick and you may not realize the import of what you've done," Warick informed him. "But for the record, if it did not seem like murder, what do you think it was?"

Jesse had decided to tell the literal truth about Zeb's death. As long as he could present it as a personal opinion not shared with confederates, it wouldn't endanger the Group—and it would give him some satisfaction to inform these self-righteous medics that on other worlds, at least, views unlike theirs did exist. "As you must know, I'm new to Undine," he said. "Where I came from, natural death is the choice of many people. Zeb Hennesy was my friend. He was ninety-four, and he knew his heart would soon fail. He didn't want to be locked up in a residential care unit."

"So you helped him to die. Assisted suicide may be an accepted practice in uncivilized societies—"

"This was not suicide. Zeb had a heart attack while we were flying. All I did was take him to a place where he could die naturally in peace."

"Death is not natural. It happens only when medical care is denied. Do you mean to say you thought it peaceful for your friend to suffer the aftermath of a heart attack without even pain medication?"

"He was not in pain," Jesse stated, realizing that this wouldn't seem credible.

"Deficient in empathy," observed one of the other psychiatrists. "Typical—psychotics have no awareness of the feelings of others."

Nodding, Warick said, "You took him to an unoccupied house instead of calling the ambulance. A normal person would have known that he needed care."

"I cared for him myself. For several days." This was self-damning evidence, Jesse knew, but if the time of the plane's last flight was checked, they would realize that some caregiver must have stayed in the house. Providentially, his choice of hiding place could be legitimately explained. "The house we were in belongs to a man from whom I've borrowed money," he added. "I had previously agreed to rent it from him, though he wasn't aware that I'd moved in." Xiang Li, he knew, would back this story if he was questioned; Peter would see that he was warned.

"The fact remains," Warick admonished, "that you expected Zeb Hennesy to die and either persuaded him to adopt your warped view of death, or ignored his pleas to receive medical help. Whether you knew it or not, that was murder. And it's apparent that you did know it, because you set the house on fire to conceal your crime. You were so obsessed with the thought of covering it up that you attempted to burn the body, thereby depriving him of his last chance to live on indefinitely."

"We may be jumping to conclusions about this man's motive for arson," said the third psychiatrist, a hard-faced woman. "Anyone who pushes a revivable body into flames instead of pulling it out, burning his own arms in the process, is deranged, possibly a pyromaniac. After all, the other recent fires were in the same neighborhood, and Jesse Sanders' whereabouts at the time they occurred are unknown."

Jesse stared at her in horror. The other fires? That he

would actually be blamed for them had not occurred to him, despite the casual remark of the ambulance officer during his arrest. Yet he was vulnerable. No one knew where he had been. He could not reveal that he'd been living with Carla, much less that he'd ever gone to the Island.

Peter spoke for the first time. "There is no evidence that this man set the other fires," he said. "If he were the arsonist, why would he rent a house he planned to burn?"

The woman turned to him. "He's unstable," she said. "You know that better than anyone, Kelstrom—wasn't he under your care when he was brought in weeks ago after resisting treatment for alcoholism? He's an AWOL Fleet officer, abandoned on this world and probably desperate. And his experience in Fleet would have given him the technical skill to sabotage power circuits. They were all electrical fires; what are the odds that someone else started them?"

"He's an intelligent man, and as you say, he does have technical skills. Obviously it was a copycat crime that he hoped would be blamed on the serial arsonist—a mere ruse to dispose of the body."

"Perhaps," said the second psychiatrist. "Perhaps, in that case, he knows the arsonist; how else could he have copied the method when no details of it have been made public? We can't be sure without a full examination under drugs. I suggest that we perform it here and now."

"He's my patient," said Peter. "I have the right to proceed with him as I see fit. The fact that he committed murder and burned one house is not in question; whether he set more fires or not will make no difference to his treatment. I prefer to hold off on truth serum until I've had a chance to evaluate him."

"It seems to me that you were insufficiently cautious when he was under your care before," said the woman. "His record shows that you overrode the recommendation of the substance abuse department when you discharged him from the Hospital. You perhaps underestimated the danger he posed to society."

Oh, God, Jesse thought. If they turned him over to any-one but Peter . . .

"He posed no danger to society at that time," Peter de-clared. "He had done nothing worse than get drunk."

"Which shows a weakness of mind that was evidently exacerbated by the loss of his captaincy in Fleet. He was left without an occupation, at loose ends, on a world where he has no ties. I should think you might have foreseen the result and called him in for weekly checkups. If you had, Zeb Hennesy might be alive and we might have been spared a disastrous series of arsons."

"The public is suffering from mass anxiety," added the second doctor, "that won't abate until we announce that the arsonist is in custody—"

Peter, in desperation, broke in, "Let's not forget that if it weren't for that anxiety, the government wouldn't be call-ing an election to approve universal microchipping."

Warick eyed him, frowning. "I thought you were against the extended use of monitor chips, Kelstrom."

"I am. But I lost that fight long ago, and I don't want to see my patient made into a scapegoat now that stirring up the public over the issue of crime control has served its purpose."

"Are you suggesting that any of us deliberately—"

"I saw the inflammatory press release. I know the Ad-ministration hasn't pursued the hunt for the arsonist with as much vigor as the public assumes."

There was dead silence. Warick glared at Peter as if he too were considered dangerous, and Jesse sensed that Pe-ter, despite his long-standing dislike of the man, was startled by this reaction. An odd tension between them had devel-oped instantaneously.

"No doubt it would now be convenient to let people go on assuming that crime is rampant," Peter continued, seem-ing to convey more than he was saying in words. "But by God, Jesse Sanders isn't going to be delivered up to the media as an example. Not while I'm in charge of treating the criminally insane—which is a job I don't recall any of the rest of you wanting to take off my hands."

Peter must be damn sure they wouldn't do so, to risk such a gamble, Jesse thought. What if it failed? He was dizzy with fear, sick to his stomach. If he was given truth serum by anyone else, he would helplessly betray both Peter himself and Carla. That must not happen. He'd give his life to protect them, as Ramón and even poor Valerie had done, if that were possible . . . he'd prefer death in any case to slow destruction of his brain. . . .

"All right, Kelstrom," said Warick, ignoring frowns from his colleagues. "We'll adjourn for now. But keep in mind that your handling of this case will be observed and your records will be open to inspection. You have an unfortunate tendency to use less aggressive treatment than a diagnosis warrants. Remember that we aim to provide therapy, not merely give custodial care to patients who retain delusions."

Jesse shuddered. To him the psychiatrist said, with genuine sincerity, "I'm truly sorry that science has as yet no way to cure your mind fully. It's possible that you'll never be able to understand that you're sick. But we can at least relieve you of the thoughts we know are troubling you. In some societies you would be punished for your crimes. Here, we know them to be merely the result of illness. I promise that you'll receive the best care this Hospital has to offer."

48

THE DOCTORS ROSE and left the room. Orderlies unstrapped Jesse and took him through a different door. As it clanged firmly shut behind him, he glanced back, seeing that the only exit through it involved not merely a keypad but a retinal scanner. He did not believe he would be given occasion to exit.

The small white room to which he was taken was, he supposed, his permanent cell, although no doubt some euphemism would be used for it. Its window, like the one in last night's room, had bars. The view through it showed merely the blank wall of the next unit in the far-reaching Hospital complex. So much for any hope he might ever see the sky, Jesse thought. There was a narrow bed, a chair, a low cabinet for staff convenience, and plumbing facilities— nothing else. He wondered if he'd be given any clothing other than pajamas and a robe such as he'd worn to the hearing.

He was very frightened. It had been obvious that Peter would be forced to order him drugged, even if not in a permanently damaging way. And it seemed all too possible that other psychiatrists, perhaps Warick himself, might get control of his case at some future time if not now. If they did, he would be unable to avoid exposing everyone . . . how could the Group have believed the precautions were adequate? But of course nothing like an arson investigation had been foreseen.

The hall door opened and Peter came in. His face was grey, drawn. It was the first time Jesse had seen him look his true age. "We can talk quietly for a few moments," he said. "Only a few. Then . . . I'll have to start you on medication. When it's had time to take effect I'll add truth serum and examine you in private—but don't worry, I won't ask the wrong questions. If necessary I'll edit the recording before anyone else hears it."

"Thank God it's you, Peter. For a while I was afraid I might be facing the real thing."

Peter dropped his eyes, then with evident effort raised them. "Jesse—did you think I'd have some way of faking the long-term treatment?"

"Why yes, unless Warick interferes."

Steadily Peter said, "I can't save you, Jesse."

In shock, Jesse whispered, "Not at all? You mean not even from . . . brain damage?"

"The pharmacy nurse will be present and the medication is computer-dispensed. If I tried to fake a dose even once, I'd be taken off the case, and it would be worse for you if administered by someone else."

"You—you're going to give me a damaging drug *yourself?*"

"I wouldn't be on hand to provide telepathic help if I ordered a nurse to inject you while I hid in my office."

Jesse swallowed, and did not reply.

"There's no way out, Jess," Peter went on painfully. "If I let another doctor take over, he would probe after you're . . . defenseless. The hypnotic protection I gave you will hold only as long as no one suspects it."

"Oh, God, Peter." This was unreal. Peter had subjected him to ordeals so many times—it was impossible not to feel that this, like the others, would turn out okay . . . he had plunged his hand into flame on Peter's command, and had not been burned. . . .

"Yes. The hellish part of it is that you've trusted me not to harm you. Believe me, if I could spare you this I'd do anything, pay any price—"

"Not if it meant harming the others. I wouldn't want you to. What I trust you for now is to see that I don't implicate Carla."

Peter nodded. "Yes, of course. The next hundred days or so will be crucial. Later on, though, it won't matter what you say; it will be dismissed as mere loss of touch with reality."

"Does the drug do *that*? Cause dementia, confusion of imaginings with real life?" Appalled, Jesse felt his knees weaken; he sat gingerly on the edge of the bed.

"No," Peter assured him, "but the Meds believe you're sick to begin with, so after you've been here awhile, they'll view you like any other mental patient whose memory is unreliable. Anything you say against me or Carla will be called paranoia." He too sat down, pulling the chair close. "We haven't much time left," he warned. "The nurse will show up any minute, and then I'll have to proceed. She mustn't notice anything out of the ordinary."

"You've done this before?"

"To violent patients, yes. I abhor it. This particular treatment isn't justified for anyone. But actual killers do need to be treated; many of them really are ill. And schizophrenics who are violent haven't stable minds to destroy, at least I tell myself that. I try not to think of what they might become if I were given a chance to heal them."

"Peter . . . it doesn't work—instantly, does it? Will I be able to think straight for a little while?"

"It acts fast, but at least ten days will pass before any permanent harm is done. That used to take much longer before they 'improved' the stuff—on Earth, drugs like this have been forced on mental patients for centuries, but in many cases the damage was reversible." He spoke bitterly. "It's not meant as punishment, you know. In theory, you will be relieved of all anxiety, and will live out your life in happy unconcern, like an innocent child."

"But in reality?"

"I won't lie to you. It's extremely unpleasant at first. I won't describe the effects because that might become a self-fulfilling prophecy. Your training will help you cope for a while, but you mustn't let anyone see that the drug's slow to affect you—if you do, I'll be compelled to increase the dosage. Later . . . I can't even imagine what it will be like for someone with a mind such as yours—"

"Peter, I haven't the courage for this," Jesse confessed, realizing with horror that after all the ordeals, all the past triumphs that had made him trust himself, he now wanted only to die.

"Nor have I," Peter said. "But losing it wouldn't help either of us. All we can do is make the telepathy last as long as we can."

He leaned forward and took Jesse's bandaged hands between his, pressing gently; the remaining pain in them intensified briefly, but after several minutes it ceased. "I've healed your burns," he said, "though we can't let that be seen yet. Olivia will unbandage them when it's time. And you'll have other visitors from the Group. Someone will come every day—always."

For the rest of my life? Jesse thought in despair. It could

be *years,* years when he might not even recall that there was a Group. . . . There was only one thing in Peter's power to give him, and that, he could not ask for, knowing that it would be denied. The Group's rejection of assisted suicide was unconditional. He wondered if the volitional control he'd learned might extend to the stopping of his own heart.

To Jesse's shame, Peter sensed the thought and reacted. "There's something I've never told you," he said slowly. "When you first came to this world, Ian had a dream in which you were involved. And so he and I have believed that you—well, that you had a destiny in the Group, a role on which our future might depend."

"You mean one of his paranormal dreams? Precognition?"

"He thought so, yes. He's never sure until after the fact, but this was especially vivid, and parts of it have already been borne out."

"That's why he said he trusted me," Jesse said, recalling how uncannily sure Ian had seemed, despite having met him only briefly.

"Yes. To tell you the details now would only give you pain. But if you suffer brain damage, the dream cannot have meant what we felt it meant. And so I must say either that it did not—that the faith I've placed in beneficent fate has been false—or that there's hope, Jesse. I see no possible way of escape for you. I don't dare tell Ian what's happened because he might not survive the blow. Yet . . . his dreams often do come true."

"I'll try to . . . hope," Jesse said. "Forgive me, Peter, for what I was thinking."

"You're going to be all right," Peter told him. "No matter what happens. There's so much we don't know about the mind—we can't say the brain is everything. We know it *isn't!* We know ESP isn't physical. We receive knowledge in altered states that can't come from the brain. You may lose no more than the ability to communicate with us—"

A nurse—not Olivia, but an older woman—appeared at the door. Soundlessly Peter continued, *What if . . . you don't*

lose even that? I never did this to a trained telepath before. . . .
He rose and took a syringe from the tray offered by the nurse, prepared it. Jesse took control of his body, breathing deeply, calming his racing heart. For as long as he could, he would use the skills he had been taught; he would stick to the   commitment   he   had   made.

Now God help us both, Peter said silently, and plunged the needle into Jesse's arm.

49

THE WORST THING in the hours after Jesse's first injection was that he could not stay still. Sitting, walking, lying down—it made no difference; he felt compelled to move, yet movement offered no relief. He paced back and forth, back and forth, in the tiny room, longing to stop but finding that his legs moved of their own accord. Many times he threw himself across the bed hoping to rest, only to find himself rising within moments, unable to relax for even a short time. His skin crawled. He felt like screaming. And a nameless terror, different from his dread of mental destruction, grew and grew until he was sure that he was already insane.

Peter came to him several times before his shift ended, telepathically projecting what healing he could. That helped for a while, but did not last. *This is a common side effect,* Peter assured him. *Don't blame yourself if you can't overcome it alone.*

After a long time, when dawn brightened the window, he calmed his mind enough to recognize the emotional part, at least, as the sort of groundless panic Kira had taught him to cope with. He visualized the mind-pattern he had learned from her, holding it in consciousness so vividly that it shut out all else, and finally, for a while, he slept. But in the morning the physical sensations were as strong as ever, and he resumed pacing, helpless to control the restlessness of his body. When Peter appeared with the pharmacy nurse for his second injection, he almost fought back in anger; only the thought that violence might bring other psychiatrists kept him from it.

This phase won't last, Peter told him. *I can give you something to lessen the torment, but it will accelerate mental dullness and apathy....*

Jesse pulled himself together. *No. I'll take this over being a zombie, as long as there's a choice.*

I thought so. You're not one to accept defeat. You can never be defeated by involuntary reactions, Jess. All that matters is your inner choices. Even after you lose awareness of them, that will remain true.

He was still very much aware—far *too* aware of what was happening to him. But he was buoyed by the knowledge that he'd chosen to be.

Later in the day, Carla came.

"Olivia's home sick today," she said aloud. "I'm here to change your bandages." That, he realized, had been planned; Olivia, a Group member, could not really be sick. Peter had simply arranged an excuse to send Carla to his room.

They dared not embrace; there was always the chance that a nurse might walk in. But they joined wordlessly in their minds, striving for courage to spare each other pain. They were not very successful at it, since the looming horror of their future left no other thoughts to share. Jesse was not sure that separation would have been worse. Still he couldn't have endured not seeing her, and he knew she felt the same way. Was this the last time? Or, over the years to come, could other excuses be found?

Carla's hands were steady as she wrapped new bandages, concealing the fact that his burns were already healed. "There's a rec room," she said, "where you'll be allowed to go after they're sure you're thoroughly enough medicated not to be violent. I'll have duties that take me there sometimes."

Peter had told him about the rec room. A place for watching television, playing simple video games, and socializing with fellow patients, most of whom actually did have sick minds. It was not an inviting prospect. It was worse than what Zeb, at the age of ninety-four, had believed he could not face. He himself was more than fifty years younger. God, how many of those years would it take before his unconscious mind provided the escape that Zeb's had?

Carla, sensing this thought, broke into tears. Against his will, Jesse too began to weep. The drug had begun to weaken him. He could not trust his self-control anymore. "Go, Carla," he told her. "I don't want you to see me this way."

"You need me!" she protested. But she, too, was afraid of breaking down completely; they both knew that. *Oh, God, Jesse! I love you—I love you so much . . . and yet the only chance we have of staying sane is to keep a grip on ourselves. . . .*

I love you, Carla. I'll always love you, even if I stop being able to show it. Let's remember . . . the good times.

He went over those times in memory after she had gone—his first week on the Island, when he'd loved her before knowing their lives would be shared . . . the night they'd lain by the Lodge fire . . . the Ritual and the wedding feast. . . . His tears would not stop, and the most terrible part was that he was no longer trying to stop them.

The next morning Peter took him to his office and, in private, subjected him to questioning under truth serum—a process he said he could put off no longer without interference from Warick. As before, Jesse's mind was foggy during the examination and he did not know afterward what he had said. But unlike the first time, he did not fully recover. He formed thoughts only slowly, through a haze. It was like being trapped in the deep water that had frightened him as a child, unable to rise, unable to swim—yet except for brief periods when he roused and struggled in panic against the murkiness, he was not particularly frightened. He was past caring what went on around him.

Time passed: another night, another injection, another stuporous day. Jesse let Olivia help him wash and change clothes, which he could not do alone as long as his hands were bandaged. He barely grasped her assurance that Kira and other friends would visit him as soon as he was permitted to go to the rec room. It didn't seem to be important. He stared blankly at the window. He ate when he was told to, mildly irritated by the interruption of the apathy into which he'd slipped.

Peter continued to appear as often as he could find a chance. Only at these moments did Jesse's mind come alive. His telepathic ability, so far, was undiminished. In fact, perhaps because of the dimming of his normal faculties, it seemed stronger than ever. He was aware of Peter's empathy, and it strengthened him, staving off total despair. At the same time, he felt Peter's own pain; but even that was better than having no feeling at all.

Late on the fourth evening, as he was trying unsuccessfully to sleep, the door opened, sending a flare of brilliant light into the darkened room. Jesse turned over, shading his eyes, wondering what further indignities the night nurse might subject him to at this hour. But it was not the nurse who entered. It was Peter again.

I've just come from Ian, Jess, he began silently. *He insisted I must speak to you right away.*

Abruptly, inexplicably, Jesse's mind cleared and an image of Ian filled it. Ian wasn't supposed to know that he was here. *I thought you weren't going to tell him I was arrested,* he protested.

It was on the news several days ago—they showed your picture. In a low voice Peter continued aloud, "Neither Kira nor I ever imagined he would see it; he's so weak now that he doesn't watch the news. But tonight he got an impulse to look at the Net archives. I suppose that came from telepathic leakage of aggregate emotion—everyone's grieving for you, and he is sensitive to projected feelings that normally wouldn't be perceived consciously. He was angry with me for not informing him when it happened."

Yes, thought Jesse, Ian would hate being shielded from

bad news. In his own one brief encounter with him, it had been plain that the man's capacity for dealing with trouble was unlimited. . . .

"Ian needs no protection from anything," Peter went on. "I should have known that. Perhaps because I could barely cope with my own feelings, I didn't want to give the impression that I was burdening him with them on his deathbed."

Jesse found himself sufficiently roused to manage conversation. "I take it he wasn't as upset as you feared he'd be by finding out that his dream about me wasn't precognition."

"He didn't react the way I expected. By the time I arrived he'd had a few minutes to get hold of himself, of course; Kira said he was stunned at first. But then, he was somehow . . . revitalized. As if he felt that in the face of a blow to the Group, it was his responsibility to take command again. He made us tell him every detail of what happened during the fire, much more than Kira had said before, when she didn't mention your presence. He wanted the details of the case against you, too."

"I don't suppose he might have found a . . . loophole?"

"There's no loophole to find, Jess. If he'd seen one I haven't, he would surely have told me. What he did tell me was stranger." Peter sat down on the edge of the bed and laid his hand on Jesse's shoulder. Jesse began to feel healing calm spread through him and knew that once again it was being given to him wordlessly, as Peter talked.

"Ian sent Kira out on an errand," Peter continued. "Now that he's physically helpless she never leaves him alone in the house, but I told her I'd stay until she got back. I assumed he wanted to discuss the dream with me privately, as he has many times in the past. But he didn't mention that, and he wouldn't let me bring it up either. Instead, he ordered me to take you a message. He said, "'Tell Jesse that I trust him *in all ways*. And tell him not to lose courage.'"

"I suppose he meant he trusts me not to betray the

Group, no matter what's done to me here in the future."

"That's all it could mean now," Peter agreed. "What puzzles me is why he considered it urgent that you be given such a message tonight. We all trust you; none of us have ever suggested that we might not. Yet Ian would not even let me wait for Kira to return. He said he'd be perfectly safe alone for a few minutes and that I must come to you now, without delay. That I must make sure you don't give in to fear and despair."

"I don't plan to," Jesse said grimly, "but the stuff may deprive me of choice."

Peter looked at him with compassion. "Has it been bad today, Jess?"

"Nothing I can't tolerate. As I'm sure you know, though, when I'm fully awake my nerves are raw. I feel I'm . . . slipping, on the verge of losing control."

"That's partly anticipation. When you do lose higher brain functions, you won't care as much—which is a terrible thing to contemplate, but which will be mercifully dulled later on."

Jesse bowed his head and did not answer. That had already happened, for a while, and the time would come when he couldn't shake himself back as he had just now.

Thoughtfully, Peter went on, "Jess, Ian's wisdom has always been reliable. And what he said wasn't just for me to pass on to you. He intended it for both of us. He looked me in the eye and declared that whatever happens, we mustn't lose faith in our own destiny. It was almost as if . . . as if he'd had some inner experience, some revelation, that assured him things will turn out all right."

"Like a near-death experience, you mean?"

"It's conceivable. He can't live much longer, and his second dream—the one he's felt requires him to hold on until he's performed some mysterious final action—must seem less impelling now that we know the first one can't come true. NDEs aren't confined to people whose hearts stop, especially in the case of those accustomed, as he is, to experimenting with altered states. Perhaps his optimism is mere illusion, an old man's wishful thinking. But after so many years of being guided by him, I can't write it off as just that."

"It would be nice not to. But hasn't the Group always maintained that we mustn't shrink from harsh reality?"

"Yes. That's what's so strange, Jess. Ian would never abandon that principle, not even when all he's worked for goes up in smoke just as he's about to die."

"Well, my loss is hardly as significant an event as that."

"Yes, it is," Peter said unhappily. "You have never been told how significant you are to the Group, and it's just as well now that no one will ever know. But Ian knew. He can't have failed to admit to himself how much has been lost. I only hope he doesn't have a delayed reaction and die tonight in his sleep—his advice to me, his whole manner, was all too much like a farewell."

50

AFTER PETER LEFT, Jesse felt himself falling toward sleep, and knew that Peter had done something hypnotic to make that happen—as, long ago, he had given him sleep after pain on the first night of his testing. Because he'd slept little since his arrest, he was out for many hours. Then, toward morning, he began to dream.

He dreamed of Ian. At first only Ian's face, his wise eyes, loomed in his mind. Then they were in the Lodge that Ian had built, where they had never met in reality, and the flame of the torch was between them, and Jesse stretched out his hand to meet Ian's, bathed in flame, as he had done with Peter. And Ian asked, *Do you trust in the power of your mind, Jesse?* And he replied, *I do, but it's being destroyed.*

And Ian said, *No. There's something in the mind that nothing can touch, short of death. When we affirm the power of the mind, we're affirming that! We have said it all along by committing ourselves to the idea that the mind has primacy over the body.*

Yet we don't shrink from truth, Jesse thought, *and the truth is that the mind depends on the brain. Peter said so. My brain is going to be damaged....*

Peter doesn't know everything. And yet even he is aware that telepathy isn't physical. If it were, how could we be communicating now?

We're not, Jesse reminded himself. *I'm dreaming.*

The inner mind, the being that is you, does not depend on the part of the brain that drugs can weaken. When reason is lost, even when memory is lost, that essence remains. Once it is gone, life too is gone—the body that remains is braindead. You're not going to die, nor will you lose consciousness....

In the way of dreams, the fire faded. Ian still held his hand and they walked somewhere together, along the shore of the Island, then out across the sea into the air; and he looked down as if from his plane, with the Island a green oval against the vivid blue of the bay. Ian was tall and strong, as he must have been in youth, not as he'd seen him in life as an old man, dying. *Oh, Jesse,* he said, *I don't mind dying—I'm ready to die—yet I wish I could go where you are going....*

They rose higher until the air turned black, and they were in space, space as Jesse had seen it for years before ever coming to Undine. The familiar stars were around them. And Ian said, *I trust you, Jesse, and I think I envy you....* And then they looked down on a world again, not Undine, not Earth, but a different world that he had never seen. It was a golden world studded with sapphire seas, a wild world with no sign of habitation. Jesse looked around and the stars were gone—he was in a starship, on the bridge of a starship, and Ian was no longer in sight. But he knew that somehow Ian still depended on him, the Group depend-ed on him, if he lost courage the Group could not survive....

Carla could not survive. He could not let go of his mind's

core, could not give in to pressure or fear or despair, because if he did, Carla would die.

Go to her, Ian commanded. *What's happening to you in the Hospital does not matter. It can't weaken love. When all else is lost your bond with Carla will still be strong. Go to her, and see that telepathy isn't dependent on your body. She doesn't need to be physically present, any more than I do. Go when morning comes. . . .*

Jesse awoke, startled, the vividness of the dream still overwhelming any other awareness. He saw that it was daylight. He looked down at his right hand, astonished to find it still bandaged after feeling it healthy and whole in Ian's hand, and before that, unburned while touching Ian's in flame. His eyes were wet. He felt stunned, bereft, at having awakened just as he was about to see Carla. *Go to her,* Ian had said, yet he could never go to her again. . . .

His mind, except for memory of the dream, was groggy. He felt detached from the world of the Hospital. He was not really sure what was going on around him, and he didn't especially care. A nurse came and gave him another injection; Peter didn't appear, and he did not bother to wonder why. He used the plumbing when reminded to do so. He ate what was put before him. None of it seemed to matter. Had not Ian said it didn't matter?

Only what had happened in the dream mattered now. And what would have happened if he'd gone on dreaming. *Go to Carla,* Ian had insisted. . . .

Carla? Alone in the room again, Jesse probed the distance, trying to find her. Ian had said she didn't have to be physically present. He closed his eyes, and his surroundings receded. *Carla, are you there?*

Jesse? Are you . . . speaking to me, really? But you can't be, we can't exchange thoughts by telepathy when you're not even in the room . . . yet I thought I heard your voice.

It makes no difference where I am. Or where you are. All that matters is our loving each other.

Oh, if only that were true!

It is true. Ian said so.

When? I never heard him say that. He's always told us that only fleeting images come telepathically over distance.

In the night. In my dream.

But now we're awake, at least I am. I'm at my desk.

I know. It's a white desk, clean, with just your keyboard and monitor on it. I can see the page you're looking at, yellow background, blue characters in three columns.

Jesse! You've never seen my desk! You can't possibly know the format of the file I'm working on. . . .

I can see it as if I were there. And you . . . You're wearing a sweater over your uniform . . . I've never seen that dark green sweater before.

It's old, I was chilly this morning, so I pulled it out of the bottom drawer. Jesse, this isn't happening. I'm imagining it. I already know what I'm wearing, after all—this must be coming from my own mind. . . .

Yes, it's coming from your mind to mine, just as we see through each others' eyes when we make love. But it's real, Carla.

I want to believe it is. If we could keep on talking this way . . .

We can. Maybe not in words, but the other way, the wordless way—that will go on forever. I won't lose the deep things . . . just the surface. Just a way of life that I'll grieve for. It will always hurt, not being able to touch you. But I'm not afraid anymore. I'm not going to be destroyed, even if it looks that way from the outside.

But Peter says—

Peter doesn't know everything. Not yet, though perhaps in time I can tell him. Or maybe Ian will.

Jesse, give me some proof that I'm not just hoping! Something I can check on that I couldn't guess.

Okay—when Olivia comes to change my bandages, I'll tell her that I dreamed of being in space. Of Ian walking out into space with me. I'll ask her to tell you that.

In space? What a strange dream—taking Ian into your

own memories . . . do you long to be back in space, Jesse? Oh, God, I wish you were there, that you were free!

Don't, Carla! he urged, aware that for the first time on Undine, the knowledge that he'd never again be in space stirred sorrow. *That's all over for me now, and anyway, I wouldn't want to be away from you. It's best forgotten. Let's just share . . . without words. Let's imagine ourselves back at the Lodge. . . .*

All right. I'll go into Peter's office, so nobody will interrupt. He's not here today. It's not like him not to show up without leaving a message.

Jesse followed her, in his mind, to Peter's private office. She closed the door and lay down on the couch. She did not undress, but that made no difference; he saw her body as clearly as if it had been bare. He felt the sensations he would have felt, had he been kissing her. They went beyond kissing, and their bodies reacted normally. As always, they felt each other's climax.

Afterward, they remained in wordless contact for a long time. The love between them was not lessened by his fading brain power. Nor did his sense of self diminish. He was still Jesse. He would always be Jesse. He reached out to Carla, giving her comfort, letting her know she need no longer be afraid for him.

51

CARLA SAT ON the couch in Peter's office, deeply shaken by what she had just experienced. Had it truly been real? There was nothing paranormal about reaching sexual climax alone, aroused by fantasy. But still, in the morning, at work, when she had done nothing to precipitate it—and to have such a strong conviction that the same thing had simultaneously happened to Jesse . . . surely the stimulus couldn't have been *just* fantasy, or mere memory. . . .

She had never heard of telepathy over distance being so

specific, or so prolonged. And yet, there was one thing she couldn't possibly have imagined. It would never have occurred to her that he would lose all fear of the fate awaiting him. That he would try to comfort her, sure that medication could not destroy his soul.

There was a knock at the door and Olivia came in. "Jesse said you were working in here," she said. "I can't imagine how he knew—though I suppose as Peter's assistant you sometimes do. Anyway, he gave me an odd message for you, Carla. He said to tell you that in his dream last night the eras of his past were mixed, that he was in space again, yet Ian was with him. Not in a starship, they were just floating among the stars."

At least some of it was real, then! Carla hesitated. If it was all real, if she had not been merely fantasizing, Olivia could provide more verification—she was a medical nurse, after all, and would not be embarrassed by the evidence she might have observed. Jesse, with his hands heavily bandaged, could neither bathe nor change clothes without her help. She flushed, wondering how to raise the subject.

Olivia, being telepathic, answered the unspoken question. *Jesse's okay that way,* she assured her silently. *Most of the patients aren't, you know; the medication tends to make them impotent. That's not the case with your husband.*

"Thanks, Olivia."

"The drug's been slow to affect his mind, too. In fact he seemed better this morning than yesterday. Don't worry, I won't tell anyone else—Peter warned me that outsiders mustn't get the idea that the dosage is too low."

It was not a matter of dosage, Carla knew. Jesse had discovered something. He'd learned that there were compensations. Not that the trade of normal life and rationality for enhanced telepathic ability was one he'd willingly choose—but the drug had to be responsible for the unprecedented distance over which they'd communicated.

With reluctance, she pulled herself together and went back to work, wondering moment by moment when Jesse would contact her again. Could that happen even after she left the building? If not, how could she ever go home? What would she do during offshifts? And how could she work and communicate with him at the same time? It was pure luck that no one had come by her desk while they were conversing; to an observer she'd have appeared to be spaced out. . . .

At the end of the workday, she was afraid to leave. She could not bear to think that he might try to reach her and fail; his time sense, his connection with the real world, might be so impaired that he couldn't keep track of her schedule. In desperation, not knowing what to do, she returned to Peter's office.

It was dim; the drapes had been pulled. Carla switched on the light and to her astonishment, saw Peter slumped over his desk. Slowly, he raised his head. His face was white, frozen, and his mind was shut tight against her probing. She had never seen him look so shaken, not even when they'd first faced awareness of Jesse's condemnation.

There was only one thing she could think of that would affect him so profoundly. "Has Ian died?" she asked gently, assuming that he must have. Was it coincidence that Jesse had dreamed of him, or had he somehow sensed his passing? Ian floating in space could have been a dream symbol of death.

"No. Not yet." The emotion she perceived in Peter was something between elation and anguish. "Carla," he went on quickly, "Jesse's going to be released."

"Released?" She wasn't sure she was hearing it. This second shock seemed so unreal that she wondered if she was hallucinating—in an altered state, perhaps, through which what she'd needed for sanity was being supplied. Perhaps the whole day, even the conversation with Olivia, had been some sort of waking dream.

"Yes," Peter confirmed. "Tomorrow he will be free to go. He'll recover in a few days."

But if this were true, Peter should be smiling. "*How?*" she asked.

"I can't speak of it now. I—I need time to adjust." He started to rise, but sat down again as if his legs would no longer support his weight.

Bewildered, Carla burst out, "Aren't you glad about it?"

"Glad? That's too mild a word. The joy I feel for Jesse, for you, is unlimited—and for the hope we now have of saving the Group, it's more like awe. But it has come at a terrible price."

"What price?"

"You don't want to know now, Carla. Believe me, you don't. Go to Jesse tomorrow, and be happy. Don't ask for more pain; it will come to you soon enough."

"Peter . . . you haven't sacrificed *yourself* in some way—?" It was apparent that he'd suffered a blow, that it was a struggle for him to keep his composure.

"No. No act of mine could have accomplished this; it was taken out of my hands. And now . . . I have a responsibility. We have to carry on, all of us—it's more important than ever before. Something's happened that . . . obligates us."

"To keep the Group going? Of course."

"To fulfill Ian's dream."

"That means Jesse . . . tell me, Peter! What will Jesse have to do?" He'd just been given back his life through some miracle. She did not want him handed new obligations.

"I can't tell you, or anyone, before I tell him—in principle, he has a right to refuse, though I don't think he'll want to. And he won't be in shape to make that choice for several days yet."

"Will what you're planning put him danger?" she asked fearfully.

"We will all be in danger," Peter said frankly. "It will be no worse for him than for the rest of us."

"Of course it will be worse! You *can't* let him risk being subjected to psychiatric drugs a second time!"

"No. It won't be that sort of danger."

She turned white. "Not . . . like Ramón!"

"Oh, no, Carla—not that. Not stasis! God willing, in the future none of us will ever risk that again." He shuddered, as if Ramón's death loomed even more vividly in his memory than in her own.

"Well, it can't be anything as bad as either of those," she concluded with relief.

"Jesse will welcome the plan," Peter told her. "One reason I didn't tell him about it sooner was that I didn't want to raise his hopes before I was sure it could be tried. But there will be very great difficulties." He sighed. "I'm not up to dealing with them now, I'm not thinking straight. But we've got to make a start. There's a lot I need to explain to you, a lot you too will have to accomplish—"

"Me? Anything, Peter, just so it doesn't keep me from Jesse."

"His safety, and the Group's, will depend on you, Carla. On your hacking ability, especially during the next few days."

She drew breath. "More data to be faked?"

With evident effort, Peter pulled himself together. "Though Jesse has been cleared of the worst charges, he'll remain on probation for destroying Zeb's body. After his release from the Hospital, he will be required to report to me weekly as an outpatient. That's okay as long as I don't lose control of his case. It will even help us, because he'll have a legitimate reason to see me regularly in private. The problem is that he'll be microchipped—"

"Dear God."

"We're all supposed to be microchipped eventually; to Jesse it will simply happen sooner. What it means, though, is that outside the Hospital he can't ever go anywhere I'm known to go. Including the Island—it's no longer possible for him to hide there."

"Oh, Peter. He loves it so." And so do I, Carla thought, yet I won't go without him. . . .

"In the long run it won't matter," Peter said cryptically. "But right now, we have a dilemma. Jesse *must* go to the

Lodge once, later this week. A meeting of the Group will be held, and it's essential to the plan for him to be present. So you've got to hack the system to keep his location from being detected."

"But Peter, it can't be done! That's why we can't get people out of residential care units."

"I know you can't defeat the tracking system permanently. If you could, universal microchipping wouldn't threaten the Group's survival. All the same, just this once you have to make it look as if he were somewhere else—on Verge Island, maybe, so you won't have to tamper with transmission from most of the flight. And if at all possible you should set it up in advance so that you can go with him."

"What if I fail?" she whispered. Location tracking was a real-time operation; planting time-activated code to alter incoming data would be far harder than merely hacking into files and changing values manually, as she'd done in the past. It was well within her programming capability, but still . . .

"They're likely to watch his movements for at least a week after his release. If they tie them to mine, I'll be taken off his case and placed under suspicion. You know what that could lead to." Peter sighed. "I may be asking the impossible. Yet I can't believe that after all that's happened—all the sacrifices that have been made—we can be defeated by this one small obstacle. Not when the Group's future is at stake, which it is."

"I'd better get started tonight. I don't dare log on remotely; we've never risked using an identifiable Net address. Yet I'll need to stay home with Jesse while he recovers."

"That's another thing," Peter said. "Since you're my assistant, it can't become known that he lives with you—he can't ever go back to your apartment. I'll arrange for him to have his own, in one of Xiang Li's buildings, since their association is already accepted. Kira will take him there tomorrow; the Hospital knows she sometimes works as a pri-

vate nurse and it's reasonable for me, as his doctor, to engage one. You'll have to sneak in after dark and make sure
you're not observed."

"Always?" If they could never go to the Island and never
be seen together in the city, how were they going to manage
year after year?

Don't worry about that now, Peter advised, exhaustion
once again overtaking him. Aloud he said, "I've ordered sedation for Jesse tonight. Go tell him that when he wakes
he'll be freed from this place—I'm not up to seeing him.
Then get some rest while you can. Tomorrow will be time
enough for the hacking."

"Peter, I can't leave you like this," Carla said, longing
to rush to Jesse, yet aware that for the first time within
memory, Peter's strength might not hold. Jesse would be
all right now. Peter was obviously near collapse.

"I have to be alone for a while," Peter declared. "You
can't help me. Stay with Jesse until he's back to normal,
and wait for a summons to the Lodge. When I get there, I'll
be fit to take on the role I've inherited."

52

WHEN JESSE CAME fully awake, he was in a strange bed, a
wide bed he vaguely recalled having shared with Carla. She
was standing near him, silhouetted against a sunlit window. Disoriented at first, he assumed for a moment he must
be dreaming again. "What happened?" he asked. "How did I
escape?"

"You were released," Carla told him. "I don't know why;
Peter wouldn't tell me. It's official, though. You were cleared
of the most serious charges."

"But they saw me burn Zeb's body—"

"Yes, so you're still on probation. You can't be seen with
me except when you visit Peter's office as an outpatient.
And—you are microchipped, Jesse. The authorities will keep

track of where you are; that's why you're here in your own apartment instead of in mine."

"Microchipped?" he echoed in dismay. "Permanently?"

"Yes, but it's going to happen to us all, soon, Peter says. He's got some long-range plan for dealing with it."

"He told me that once, too. I guess I can't complain about being the guinea pig, after what I've been saved from." He flexed his hands, savoring their release from the heavy bandaging that had been necessary to conceal their healing. "I don't see why the Meds let me go. Did they find evidence against the real arsonist after all?"

"I just don't know, Jesse. Peter said there was a—a terrible price for your freedom. I don't think he meant money. If the authorities could be bought, he'd have gotten you out sooner. He said that we're all now—obligated. And he was more upset than I've ever seen him, despite being happy for you."

"Oh, God. What have I done to the Group by letting myself get caught?"

"You mustn't think that way!" Carla declared. "You saved Kira, probably Peter and Ian, too—maybe even the rest of us. Everyone admires you for what you did."

"Am I—normal, Carla? Was I given enough of the drug to damage my brain?"

"You're fine now. You've been recovering for nearly four days—Peter said you should sleep it off, so Kira sedated you hypnotically. That's why you have no memory of her bringing you here."

"The last thing I remember clearly was our minds joining when we were separated. When I was locked up alone and you were somewhere else, but it didn't matter, we came together anyway . . . was that real?"

"Yes. Kira said that by lessening your capacity for normal awareness, the drug must have put you into a state that enhanced your telepathic power. It was awesome, Jesse, though hardly a method we'd have chosen."

"There's a better way to enhance telepathy," Jesse

agreed, reaching out to her. Carla took off her clothes and got into bed with him. They made love in relief and gladness, sharing their bodies and minds fully. Afterward they both slept, free of the past week's anguish.

Late in the afternoon Carla's phone woke them. While she was talking Jesse rose and showered, feeling not merely normal but great. When he came out of the bathroom he saw right away that the respite from stress had been brief. "Are you well enough to fly?" she asked. "We're wanted at the Lodge—now. Ian died this morning. Kira said that Peter wants everyone to come."

Jesse felt a surge of grief. His dream of Ian was still clear in his memory; it was as if the contact with him had been as real as his telepathic contact with Carla. Knowing that he was gone hurt, just as it must hurt those who'd been privileged to be among his longtime friends.

They dressed quickly and grabbed sandwiches to eat in the plane. It had been moved from the dock near the burned house, where it might be watched; Xiang Li, as the lien holder, had arranged for it to be moored in a basin closer to the apartment. Carla could not go in the water taxi with Jesse, she explained, and she disguised her face with heavy makeup when she set out to walk, hiding her hair under a tightly-wrapped scarf. By the time she got there, he had completed the preflight check and was having the power cells recharged.

Taxiing away from the recharging station, Jesse could scarcely believe that the bad time had happened. He was totally himself in the air. It didn't seem possible that he had, for a few days, been less than himself. Now all his senses, all his perceptions of life, were suddenly illumined, and he knew that he would never again take its wonders for granted. Despite the happiness he'd found on Undine, the old emptiness and futility had not, until now, been completely behind him. It had taken the near-loss of his mind— and the discovery of its imperishable essence—to show him that Peter was right in insisting, *we win simply by being who we are.*

Carla spoke over the hum of the engine. "There's something you have to know, Jesse. I didn't want to spoil your joy sooner than I had to—but this is our last trip to the Island. The microchip reveals where you go, and so avoiding medical telemetry's no longer enough to conceal your presence there. More than ever the Island's not safe, if Ian has died. Peter owns it, now."

He stared at her, for a moment crushed. Never to go to the Lodge again? Never to walk on the shore or swim in the places they had swum together, never to sit side by side before the fireplace where they'd first made love? It would be hard. And yet, it was a small deprivation beside the one he'd just escaped; the pain of mere exile could not touch him.

"My joy's not spoiled," he told her. "I have my mind back—and I have you. There are other islands, Carla—dozens of them! I saw a lot of nice ones when I was flying with Zeb. We could build a cabin of our own—"

"You're forgetting that I can't be known to associate with you," she said sadly. In the plane she'd removed the grotesque makeup, but it would have to be reapplied.

"I've been thinking about that," he said. "Since I'm not under suspicion anymore, knowing me won't endanger you. If the only reason you can't be seen with me is that you're Peter's assistant, maybe you should quit your job—marry me legally and pretend to hate him for what he did to me while I was hospitalized. I have plenty of assets to borrow on; you don't need to work. We could live full time away from the city, just go in once a week when I have to report to him as an outpatient."

"I never thought of that!" Carla exclaimed. "Oh, Jesse, we could—except I have to be on hand for the hacking, you know. Speaking of which, the only reason we can go to the meeting tonight is that I hacked the tracking system. I coded the patch to activate when we reach Maclairn's coordinates. It will show you're on Verge Island; that's close enough for our flight path to seem right. But I put a timer on it, because it's not safe to leave a routine like that running too long. It will self-destruct, so we have to leave for Verge at sunrise."

"Carla, it doesn't sound safe for you to have done it at all! Much as I want to see the Lodge once more, and to take part in Ian's burial—"

"Peter said it was important. He wants you for more than the burial; this Group meeting was set up even before Ian died. I think . . . he's going to reveal the secret he's been keeping from you all this time."

"You mean Ian's dream?"

"You already know about that?"

"Not what happened in it. But in the Hospital, when I . . . wanted to die, he told me Ian had dreamed about me. That if my brain were to be damaged it couldn't have meant what they thought, and yet Ian believed it did. That I shouldn't lose hope of a miracle." Awestricken by abrupt recognition of what this signified, he added, "Carla, Ian was right! There *was* a miracle, so his dream must have showed the future!"

"But what about the other one, the recurrent dream that was keeping him alive because he thought he had something important left to do in life? That didn't come true—he's gone now." She frowned. "After all the weeks he lingered, I wish he hadn't died today, of all days. I'm worried about Peter, Jesse. He was already suffering from some burden too terrible even to tell me about, on top of the ordeal he went through with you. Mourning for Ian at the same time may be more than even he can bear up under."

"Never doubt Peter's strength," Jesse told her. "The worse things got in the Hospital, the more I drew on his courage—and he was always there for me, telepathically, in spite of what he was forced to do to me. I knew it was agony for him, but he wouldn't back away. I could feel the steadiness in him, and knew I could rely unconditionally on it. He's not going to fold, no matter what happens."

The sun had set by the time they reached the Island.

There were more planes moored than he'd ever seen there; he had to find a spot far out in the bay. A small boat approached; Bernie was shuttling arrivals to the dock. Well over two hundred people were gathered on the beach in the moonlight—just sitting, subdued and silent. "What's everyone waiting for?" Jesse asked.

"The body, I guess," Bernie said. "Peter must be sure we won't be caught with it, because there's going to be a formal funeral. I was told to watch for you and Carla and send you into the Lodge. Kira said to hurry."

Hurrying proved difficult; people pressed around Jesse when they caught sight of him, surprised and excited to see him back among them. Evidently they'd all been grieving for him—he had not realized how many friends he had. He found himself moved nearly to tears by the welcome.

As quickly as possible, he and Carla made their way across the beach and up the steps into the Lodge. As they entered, Peter came to Jesse and embraced him warmly. Immediately Jesse sensed something new, an emotion different from Peter's deep concern for him in the Hospital and earlier. He was no longer seeing him from the standpoint of instructor and therapist. Nor was it merely the embrace of an equal. It was almost as if Peter were looking to him for support.

There were nearly twenty people seated around the central fireplace: Kira, Hari and Reiko, plus Ian's closest friends, some of whom he hadn't met before. Peter turned to them and said, "Now all your questions can be answered. This is Jesse Sanders, onetime Captain of the starship *Eureka,* who sacrificed himself to protect us—and for whom Ian has now given his life."

53

THERE WAS A stunned silence. Incredulous, Jesse and Carla stood motionless, joining the circle only when Kira motioned them to sit. "Peter has just been formally installed as head of the Council," she said. "But he would tell us nothing about Ian's death until you arrived."

Peter remained standing. "I can speak of this only once," he began, "so I've waited until you were all here. After this meeting we will go out to the others, to the ceremony of mourning for Ian, and I will be forced to speak again. But there I will say something briefer. They'll hear the rest—though not the whole story—on tomorrow's news. As Ian's adopted heir, I managed to get a media hold for the purpose of notifying those standing in lieu of kin. It would be unthinkable for you to hear it from anyone but me, but bear with me, please, if I—" his voice broke "—if I find it hard to tell."

The crackling of the fire was loud in the silence. Painfully Peter went on, "The burial ceremony tonight will be symbolic. As some of you may have guessed, we cannot retrieve Ian's body. It has already gone to the Vaults."

Carla let out a cry and Peter placed his hand on her shoulder. "Carla, this will be hard for you to hear," he said. "I wish I could spare you, but even if it weren't to be reported by the media, it's essential for you to know."

Jesse moved closer to her and put his arm around her, resolving to support her through what promised to be a difficult hour. Ian had given his life . . . for *him*? To secure his release? How could that be? They would all have mixed feelings if it was true, but especially Peter, who had loved Ian so deeply. Yet in Peter's embrace there had been no trace of ambivalence. There was sorrow in him, but no regret.

"Five nights ago," Peter announced, "Ian sent Kira and me away on contrived errands. While he was alone he called for an ambulance." At the gasps of disbelief he paused briefly, then went on, "He was taken to the Hospital. When he arrived there, he confessed to the murder of Zeb Hennesy."

"But that's crazy!" Jesse burst out. "He wasn't in the same house as Zeb's body."

"No," Peter said, "but that's not the way he told it to the authorities. Furthermore, he convinced them that he set the fire himself, expecting it would be blamed on the arsonist who set the others."

"He lied to save me? *Why?* He didn't know me—he met me only once." But, Jesse recalled, in that one brief meeting Ian had *seemed* to know him. He had declared that he trusted him, and earlier he'd seen him in a dream. . . .

"That's not the strangest part," said Reiko, the first of the others to recover her voice. "I don't question Ian's wisdom. If he chose to go to such lengths to save you, Jesse, he had good reason. But why did it work? We are all accountable when people die in our care; we have always known we'd face murder charges if we were caught. The authorities wouldn't have believed you were innocent merely because Ian claimed to have been in on it. Why didn't they hold both of you?"

"Ian didn't confess simply to letting Zeb die," Peter said. "He stated that he killed him intentionally, out of mercy, because he'd talked to him earlier in the yard between the two houses and learned that he hoped for death. He said he smothered him with a pillow and started the fire to cover up the crime."

"A mercy killing?" Kira protested. "But Zeb wasn't suffering, and in any case Ian couldn't leave his own bed. Besides, euthanasia's against everything we believe, everything he taught us. He would never have said that."

"The authorities know nothing of our beliefs," Peter pointed out, "nor did they know Ian was bedridden before he called them."

"I admitted responsibility for Zeb's death," Jesse protested, "so even at best I'd be considered an accomplice. And that implies conspiracy—"

"Ian was careful not to imply it. He testified that he'd never met you and that Zeb had said you expected him to recover. He claimed to be overcome by guilt at having let an innocent man be blamed for more than destruction of the body. The supposition now is that you didn't know what Ian had done, that when you entered the burning house and found Zeb dead, you assumed his death was your fault and burned the body in the hope of not being caught. And since the only evidence that you set the other fires was the belief that you'd set this one, you've been cleared of serial arson."

"That's great, but what made Ian think the authorities would swallow such a story? The doctors who questioned me weren't easy to fool. Why didn't they give him truth serum?"

"Because he turned himself in and seemed remorseful. He was given merely a brain scan and polygraph test, which he passed easily by controlling his physiological reactions. Dr. Warick examined him personally and pronounced him sane, as of course he was." Peter's voice dropped; barely audibly, he added, "You were diagnosed as mentally ill because you didn't grasp any need to prevent Zeb from dying naturally. To kill someone in cold blood, on purpose, is a much more serious crime."

"Intentional killing while sane is *aggravated* murder," someone said. "The penalty for that—"

"Yes," Peter said, fighting back tears. "Ian agreed that conditional on Jesse's release, he wouldn't dispute the charge. Did you think he died just from the stress of confessing?"

Carla had been getting paler and paler; Jesse, sensing her mind, held her tighter. "Oh God," she pleaded, "Not like Ramón! Please, not like Ramón—"

"Nothing less could have saved Jesse," Peter told her gently. "He did what he had to do. He believed it was the action his dream foretold—as perhaps it may have been."

Kira, usually so composed, was weeping. "Had they no mercy?" she murmured. "They couldn't release him, of course, but he was a hundred and thirty years old and he was already dying. Couldn't they have waited for death to take him?"

"It's surprising that they didn't," Peter agreed. "For them

to have sent such an old man alive into stasis will hardly win political support for the Administration, criminal though they believed him to be. A lawyer might have got him an exemption despite the agreement he'd made, but he refused to let me call one. I suppose he thought delay might jeopardize the deception."

Carla whispered, "You *knew*, Peter? The night before Jesse was released, you knew this was going to happen?"

"He was brought to the Hospital the previous night, yes. I knew by morning, and I could do nothing. He ordered me to make no effort to stop it."

For long moments they all were silent as the horror welled into their minds and was telepathically shared. How, Jesse wondered, could he live with this? Ian had been the head of the Group since its inception, its focal point. It would have survived his natural death and burial, but to know that Ian had gone conscious to the Vaults, that his body still functioned there, while he himself was free . . . he couldn't possibly prove worthy in his own eyes, let alone those of the other members.

And yet . . . Ian must have been in the Hospital the night of the dream . . . the dream where they'd walked hand in hand. Ian had known then he, Jesse, would be released, had known his own death was imminent. Was it possible that it *had* been telepathy? Had Ian come to him while he slept, as he himself had later gone to Carla? Had there been a real message in that dream, not just mixed-up images from his memories—some clue to what Ian had expected of him?

Finally Peter spoke again. "I was there this morning," he said slowly. "Ian's last request was for me to be with him at the end. He wasn't afraid, any more than he'd feared the natural death that would have come soon anyway. And his last words were very strange. 'You never really understood,' he said to me, 'and for the Group's sake I couldn't tell you. I still can't. But know that this won't matter in the end.'"

"Never understood what?" asked someone.

"I can't say," Peter confessed. "What could he possibly refrain from telling me for the Group's sake, when he knew that I'd have to lead?"

"The part about his execution not mattering is clear, at least," Reiko said. "It can only have meant he believed that the Group will not be weakened by the manner of his death—that we will go on."

"Of course," said Hari. "We will carry on as always. Ian *was* sane, and he must have had stronger cause for what he did than a desire to save one man from destruction. He had some hidden purpose, even if we don't know what it was."

"One man?" Kira burst out. "Are you a fool, Hari? Don't you see that Ian did what he did not only for Jesse but for Peter, whom he loved? It was agony for Peter to drug Jesse, and to keep on destroying him gradually, day by day—after that, to see him every workday for the rest of his life, long after Jesse himself had been reduced to the point of not caring—it would have broken Peter! He would never have abandoned Jesse, yet his self-esteem would have been eaten away. Ian knew that, and knew, too, what it would do to the Group for such a weight to fall on its leader. We need look for no hidden purpose beyond that."

God, Jesse thought. He'd known how painful it was for Peter, but had not grasped what that would mean in the long run. And to Peter, it could happen again, if some other member were caught and condemned; there would be no second escape for him. How could the Group go on as usual, knowing this? How had they ever imagined that it could? To be sure, Peter didn't expect it to, not after they were all microchipped. . . .

"I know Ian did do it partly for my sake," Peter agreed, "or at least he would have, if he'd had no other purpose. One of the reasons I didn't want to tell him of Jesse's arrest was that I knew he'd feel pain at the thought of what I would suffer in the years ahead."

"So I assumed at the time," Kira said, "which was why I too tried to keep it from him."

"But in fact," Peter went on, "there *was* a hidden purpose. There is a secret Ian and I shared. It wasn't meant to be revealed in this shocking way, but there's no longer any time to spare—the situation now demands that we act quickly. Ian gave his life to save the Group, not just two of us. And we must dedicate ourselves to fulfilling his hope for our future."

54

EXPECTANTLY, THE PEOPLE in the circle fixed their eyes on Peter, who stood tall in the firelight, his weariness and sorrow overcome by the need to inspire his listeners. "Tonight the Group must make a decision that will change our lives forever," he said. "Ordinarily I'd bring it to the Council privately first, but Ian's close friends have a right to hear more than I intend to say at the funeral."

Under the circumstances, Jesse decided, that included him. He made no move to leave. Carla, nestled against him, was crying softly; his heart ached for her—and for Peter. He wondered if they could ever again live as if they were carefree.

"As you all know," Peter began, "in his last weeks Ian had a recurring dream that convinced him he mustn't die before performing some action he could not specifically foresee. Ultimately he believed that freeing Jesse was the action required of him—not only for Jesse's sake and mine, but because he'd had an earlier dream, one he confided only to me."

"Was that what he referred to in the note he left?" Kira asked. To the others she added, "When I got back to the house and found Ian gone, there was a handwritten note. He asked me not to search for him, and at the end he wrote, "Tell Peter that both dreams were true.""

"Yes," said Peter. "For many weeks we'd believed the first dream was precognitive, and had acted secretly on that belief, only to be faced with apparent evidence that it was not really prophetic. That fate was not as favorable to the Group's cause as we'd been given reason to think. Even apart from what I was forced to do to Jesse, I was in despair—"

"You, Peter?" Reiko asked incredulously, the others echoing his surprise.

"I was," Peter confessed. "If you're to understand what Ian and I planned in secret, you must now face facts that we've not wanted to face. I don't know how many of you have allowed yourselves to be conscious of these facts. Ian was increasingly worried about our future as his death approached, and discussed it with me. However, against one of the Group's most fundamental policies, we discouraged general awareness of the truth. We felt that as long as nothing could be done about it, no purpose would be served by spreading gloom. Some of you may have wondered why I've appeared less than eager to assume leadership—"

"Oh, no, Peter," said Reiko. But Kira, nodding, looked troubled. "I misjudged you," she said slowly. "It seems it's a heavier burden than I guessed."

"We've come to a crossroads," Peter said, "where to continue as we have in the past will mean our end. The Group has been growing, and for years we have known that it can't continue to grow safely. So far we've succeeded in hiding natural deaths through hacking, but the more there are, the riskier that becomes. Sooner or later the Hospital will remember a patient who hasn't been accounted for, and will check further than the database. Or someone will get suspicious about the healings, or the front groups, or even our ages, and will track us down. Once that starts, none of us are safe. We've lasted this long only because there's been no investigation."

"We all know that," said Hari, "but we put it aside. We're pledged to live past fear. There's no point in worrying over what can't be changed."

"I'd wondered, though," said Jesse. "Being from offworld,

I saw right off that what we do can't go on forever. Yet you all seemed so confident—"

"Your outside perspective was valid, Jesse," Peter said, "though I couldn't tell you so until we were ready to act."

"Was it why Ian considered me important, then?"

"One of the reasons. It was true that we needed an offworlder's evaluation. But the main consideration was the role you played in his dream." Peter paused, then went on, "Before I go into that, I must explain to everyone here what I've already told you and Carla. A threat now hangs over us that makes the problems of our existence virtually insurmountable. Friends, before long we are all going to be microchipped, as Jesse already has been."

Over exclamations of surprise and outrage, Peter continued, "The Hospital staff has been pushing for this, and has now succeeded in getting an election scheduled. The public will gladly vote it in—most people will welcome the idea of never for a moment having their heart condition and whereabouts unknown to the ambulance crews. The present concern over keeping track of potential criminals, which has been engineered by the Administration, will be the clincher. There's no chance that the measure won't pass."

"God, Peter," said Reiko. "How can we conceal hospices and healing houses if that happens? How can we die naturally and stay out of the Vaults when our own time comes?"

"We can't," said Peter bluntly. "We can't hold large meetings, either. The front group can't continue, and it's doubtful that we could train the few recruits we might find without it, even if we could continue working with neurofeedback—which won't be safe when heart rates are being monitored. And in any case, we can no longer conceal my friendship with people who come here. That means that I won't be allowed to handle their cases if any past crimes come to light, even if we break no laws in the future."

"The uproar over arson was engineered by the Administration?" Hari demanded. "How?"

"I have no proof beyond the fact that the press releases

were calculated to stir up fear and not much effort has been put forth toward solving the crime," replied Peter grimly. "But I wouldn't be surprised if those fires were started by someone on the inside. There was no intention of harming anyone, of course. All the houses were temporarily unoccupied except the one we were using in secret—and how could an arsonist have known that without access to their telemetry data? What's more, only a technically skilled person could have rigged the wiring, which is why they thought they could pin it on Jesse. When I hinted that I might suspect something, he was turned over to me immediately without examination by other psychiatrists who might have found him innocent, and Warick didn't interfere with the case as much I'd feared he would."

"That's what you were gambling on at the hearing?" Jesse asked.

"At the time I was simply desperate," Peter admitted, "but the reaction I got, then and later, made me realize Warick had more to hide than I'd sensed. Moreover, though only some of us on the Hospital staff know, the tampering with the wiring was done from outside, where it entered through the meter. That's why Ingrid didn't hear anyone enter the safe house. And it means an electrician's tools and knowledge were required."

"But Ian couldn't have done it that way," someone protested.

"No—and so whether or not Warick hired the arsonist, when he examined Ian he must have known he was lying. He may have rushed the execution to prevent anyone else aware of the details from hearing Ian's claim to have set the fire. The confession of intentional killing alone, after all, was enough to condemn him."

"Then why didn't he suspect that there was some connection between Ian and Jesse—that Ian lied about that, too?"

"Perhaps he did, but he wouldn't have pursued it; he'd have wanted to avoid an investigation."

"On the other hand," Kira said, "he may have thought Ian was simply trying to make sure of being judged calculating rather than insane. Ian was a neurologist under no illusions about the effects of psychiatric drugs. In his case, when he was already near death, avoiding treatment with them would be seen as ample motive for lying."

Jesse frowned. "Peter—Warick must be aware that *you* know Ian didn't start the fire. In fact, he must have realized when you examined me with truth serum that you knew I didn't start it."

"Yes. So I suspect that he won't cross me at all from now on, at least not until after the election. That may be why I was allowed to discharge you without a longer period of observation. Ian's confession cleared you of first-degree murder, but you're still considered sick."

"He may be simply giving you rope, hoping I'll provide an excuse to fire you."

"Possibly," Peter agreed. "But since you're not going to commit any more crimes, there's little he can accuse me of."

Concerned, Jesse bit back a reply that he knew this wasn't the time for. Peter was so overcome by shock and grief right now that he hadn't thought the situation through. It was all too likely that if his suspicion was on target, he would be silenced. This wasn't Earth; considering the prevalent attitude toward death in the colony, he might not need to worry about violence. But Warick would look for some way to discredit him.

"Every time one of us has been arrested, someone has died," Hari reflected. "First Ramón, then Valerie, and now Ian. Perhaps we were always deluding ourselves in hoping to continue indefinitely."

"Ian wasn't one to foster delusions," Reiko reminded him.

"Yet Peter's saying that if we go on we're bound to be caught. That we must give up our work and our expectation of an eventual peaceful death. That we can't even train new recruits to acquire our powers . . . so that in the long run, all we've accomplished will be wiped out. Isn't that so, Peter?"

"Yes, it is," Peter said gravely.

"Peter, you don't mean that," Kira declared. "The burden you must take on is very great, yes. But you have been under a tremendous strain since Jesse's arrest, and now you're further burdened by grief. This pessimism goes against all you have ever stood for. Your judgment is not reliable right now."

"I am judging as Ian did when he sacrificed himself for us," Peter replied. "He and I had agreed that when the time was ripe, I must say these things. But we did not give in to pessimism. In the dream we kept secret, you see, Ian saw us founding a new culture, not in this colony but on a world where we were free. A world where we could pass what we've gained on to children and grandchildren."

"We've all talked of that from time to time," Reiko said. "But we know, after all, that we couldn't live as we choose on *any* world. We might not be subject to arrest elsewhere—we wouldn't be tracked by microchips—but we couldn't raise children in our ways. We would always be a persecuted minority."

"Not," Peter said, "if we were to establish a colony of our own."

"Of course," said Kira. "That's always been the goal for future generations. Certainly he dreamed of it, in the sense of daydreaming, and no doubt in his nocturnal dreams, too; he spoke of it often enough. But it doesn't help our present situation."

"You misunderstand, Kira. Ian dreamed very vividly of us doing it personally, not in the future, but now."

"Well, but that's impossible," Hari stated. "We're too few to establish a colony. Besides, we learned long ago that there's no way for us to get to a new planet. Even if we could pay for passage, and were willing to face all the dangers and hardships of starting from scratch in the wilderness, we'd fail to meet the legal qualifications."

"Yes," Peter agreed. "But that was before fate sent us a Captain."

"One unemployed starship captain, at your service," Jesse said, matching what he took to be forced levity—and then, too late, he observed Peter's face. It was dead serious.

"At first Ian thought his dream was fantasy, mere wish fulfillment," Peter said, "for in it, a Fleet officer led us, and the few Fleet officers stationed here rarely mix with the public. Neither of us had ever met one. And then, several days later, I learned that you had been taken to the Hospital the very night the dream occurred. When I viewed your chart I was in awe of what I knew was too improbable to be mere coincidence. I showed a print of your file photo to Ian. He recognized your face. He knew you for the Captain who will take us to a new world."

55

JESSE FROZE. WAS that what his own dream had meant, if in fact it had been telepathic? Had the image of crossing space originated with Ian, rather than being drawn from his shipboard memories? *Oh Jesse,* he'd said, *I wish I could go where you are going....* But to take the Group to a new world would be impossible.

"Peter," he said quickly, "There's been some misunderstanding! I'm not that sort of Captain. Fleet wouldn't let me near a colonizer even if I were somehow reinstated with a clean record. I know freighters, not colony setup, and there's a big difference."

"As far as the technology's concerned, you could manage any starship, couldn't you? You could astrogate?"

"We don't have a starship," Jesse pointed out.

"We can get one. There'd have been nothing to gain by considering it without someone qualified to take command—but when you joined us, Ian instructed one of our contacts on Earth to check for colonizers available to charter. There's

a long waiting list, but we're a small party by colony standards, and old ships haven't enough room for the bigger
groups. We were lucky. There is an obsolete but still-com-
missioned ship available—if we move fast. The Group's combined funds can swing it with hacking to gain access to our
dead ancestors' principal, which is rightfully ours, and to
circumvent the restriction on spending our money offworld.
Ian and I sent in the application, and by supreme irony, we
received approval the day you were arrested. That was why
I was afraid that learning of your condemnation might kill
him."

Oh, God. It was true, then—Ian had sacrificed himself
for a false hope, not knowing enough to realize it couldn't
be done. "I don't think you understand how it works," Jesse
protested. "When you charter a colonizer, it comes with a
Captain and crew—they don't let you pick your own. It goes
to a world Fleet has already opened up. Since we're too few
to qualify for first world rights, our settlement would be
subject to the sovereignty of the original colony placed there.
We'd escape the Vaults and perhaps the worst of the health
laws, but as you've often said, Peter, the system on this
world is only a few steps beyond the trends everywhere.
We'd still need clandestine healing houses and hospices.
There'd be no chance of establishing anything approaching
a culture based on what we believe."

"I know that," Peter agreed. "Which is why we would
not let the crew sent by Fleet choose our site. They would,
after all, be considerably outnumbered, and legality has
never been of prime concern to us."

"But Fleet would send more ships. They would put
down any rebellion very quickly, just as they would if we
tried to settle elsewhere on Undine. Don't think there isn't
precedent."

"They could not send more ships," Peter declared, "if
they didn't know where we'd gone."

Jesse drew breath. "Hijack the ship in space, you mean?
Take it to an unopened world?" *You could astrogate,* Peter

had said. And he could, of course. There were many charted worlds that would not be considered worth opening for centuries. A colonizer would have complete charts on board. The chances of their being located on such a world were slim; Fleet wouldn't be likely to launch a costly search for an obsolete ship.

Such a plan was preposterous, and yet . . . it might not be hard to pull off. The crew wouldn't be expecting such a move from colonists and unlike a freighter or explorer crew, would not be armed—probably there wouldn't even be a fight. No harm need come to them. They could be put aboard a shuttle before the starship went into hyperdrive, and in hyperdrive, it would be past pursuit. Fleet would assume it had been lost in a miscalculated jump. As it very well might be, he thought grimly. Still, if Ian's dream had any validity, it would eventually land somewhere. . . .

As for operating the ship, the departure from Undine would be handled by the original crew. Once in space, there was no essential job other than the Captain's that he could not teach to bright people like Peter. Many in the Group had technical training. Some were experienced pilots, and, starting as his copilots, could learn to fly the orbit-to-ground shuttles needed for landing on the new world. Only the atmospheric portion of such flights required manual control.

But hijacking . . . it would mean lifelong exile to a penal colony if it failed, if they were caught attempting it. And he himself, as a renegade Fleet officer, would be charged with mutiny—which meant the death penalty, though he doubted if Peter knew that. There would be no possible defense.

Carla, sensing this thought, rose and faced Peter. "You *used* Jesse for this, from the beginning!" she accused. "From the very first day, when you put him through hell to make him hate the Meds. When you persuaded me to—" She broke off, not wanting him to hear it, but Jesse caught what was in her mind. Before he'd even left the Hospital, Peter had persuaded Carla to entrap him with her love.

"The speedup of his training, weeks of normal preparation bypassed—and all the talk about how it didn't really matter that he had no natural bent toward ESP or other psi skills—" She glared at him in fury. "You set him up!"

"It's for Jesse to decide," said Peter quietly. "I've never forced him; he has always been, and still is, free to say no."

"How can he say no, now? After what Ian did?"

Peter bowed his head. "That wasn't planned, of course. We assumed the choice would be Jesse's. It's true that now, saying no isn't really an option."

"It never was," said Carla bitterly. "He's in too deep; you knew he wouldn't leave the Group, yet wouldn't be respected if he refused the role you recruited him for. When you threw us together, when you pushed him so fast into committing himself in the Ritual, you put him in an impossible position."

"Carla." Jesse said, rising and drawing her to him. "All that's beside the point. I don't want to say no. I never would have wanted to."

She was close to tears again. "I couldn't bear it if this crazy scheme failed, as it probably would, and you were killed because of me."

"It wouldn't be because of anything you did. I'd have loved you anyway, Carla, whether we were thrown together or not. I'd have hated the Meds anyway, and the setup on this world. But I wouldn't have been able to marry you without the commitment. I wouldn't have gained the powers of my mind. What I've already had would be worth any danger that comes of it—but what we *could* have is worth more! Do you think I don't want a new world? A world where we could have kids, build a society free of this one's restrictions? Don't *you* want that? You've never shied from risk, after all—"

"But you've just now been given the chance to live again—"

"If it comes to the worst, I'd rather die for commandeering a starship than end up in the Vaults," he told her. "As far as that goes, I'd have chosen that risk over ferrying freighters till I was grounded by age. I was burned out, Carla—I was more than halfway to becoming an alcoholic! Have you forgotten?"

"No," she whispered. "Of course you have to be Captain. If there's any such thing as destiny, that's yours. I just hate the way Peter manipulated you."

"I hated it too," Peter said. "I pushed you harder than most trainees, Jesse—I had to find out, fast, whether you were strong enough to entrust with our lives. Your stalled career implied you might not be, yet it did seem as if fate had sent you. And you truly wanted to become one us."

"I did," Jesse agreed. "You know I did, Carla."

"We didn't tell you of our plan because we didn't want it to influence your decision," Peter explained. "Your psych profile showed you would favor the idea; we did not want you to serve as Captain and then find yourself forced to live the rest of your life among us without our full powers or a true commitment to our ways. Even after the Ritual, we dared not tell you—you'd become telepathic but weren't yet skilled enough to close your mind to the others. We didn't want to raise anyone's hopes until we were sure we could charter a ship. And in the meantime you were happy with your seaplane—"

Giving that up would be hard, Jesse realized. Much as he wanted to go back to space command, he would hate losing the freedom of the air. Barely more than an hour ago he'd envisioned a bright future island-hopping with Carla. On a raw planet with no imports, it would be generations before anyone would fly again.

"Then when you were arrested," Peter went on, "when I believed you would be destroyed, it seemed the end of everything. Ian and I had let ourselves face the truth, you see. We'd acknowledged that the Group can't survive here, and had seen a way out. I couldn't get back the acceptance I'd had before. And when Ian found out, he knew that what he'd worked for all his life couldn't outlast him unless he saved you."

"He trusted me," Jesse said, "but I'm not sure I can live up to his expectations. You know, don't you, that we'll be taking a hell of a chance whether or not we get away with the hijacking?"

"Our offworld agent hacked into Fleet's files," Peter said, smiling confidently. "Your technical skill is highly rated."

"Even so, calculating a jump to an unopened planet, charted maybe a century ago and off regular routes, isn't simple. Experienced astrogators can and do mess up."

"There's danger," Peter agreed. "But assuming that abandoning our commitment to the Group's goals isn't an option, it's no worse than what we'll inevitably face here."

"Well, we're not in danger of everyone being killed here, or having the whole Group sent to a penal colony." It was up to him, Jesse saw, to make sure that Peter's present emotional turmoil didn't overpower his grasp of reality.

Peter said soberly, "I meant no worse in terms of what matters most to us."

The others nodded. "If there's even a chance of having our own colony it's worth going for," Kira said. "I, for one, don't want to live with my every move tracked by the Net. I wouldn't even if I weren't doing anything illegal—not to mention the increased risk of being treated for mental illness if our past activities ever come to light."

"What's more, we may gain psi powers we've not tried to develop while forced to live with outsiders," Hari said, with fervor Jesse hadn't seen in him before. "We've barely scratched the surface of those known to exist. Free to use them openly—and with children who may inherit talent— who knows what we could become?"

"But won't it be risky," someone protested, "to foster those powers in a whole population, to establish them in the collective unconscious of its members from birth, instead of only in people who've been carefully selected?"

"It will," Peter admitted soberly. "But all human progress has involved danger, starting with the discovery of fire. For centuries, certain powers of the mind were confined to adepts who considered their wider dissemination too perilous to be permitted, and so little progress was made toward understanding them. Either universal possession of psi skills is a step forward or it's not. If it is, it's worth the inherent risk, just as advances in technology were worth risking misuse."

"And if it's not," Kira pointed out, "we'll have found out on a single world without affecting any others. Perhaps that's another reason why large-scale development of psi had to wait until interstellar colonization became possible. I don't doubt that it *is* an advance, but it may take a while before we learn to control it."

Risk, apart from the physical risks of colonization? Chilled, Jesse held back his questions. He had long suspected that the Group's experimentation with psi had gone beyond telepathy and healing, just as it had with altered states of consciousness not mentioned in his presence. But he sensed that Peter did not want to discuss this further. Merely reaching a new world would offer enough problems to occupy their full attention.

"We'll be making a start toward eventually influencing human history," Reiko mused. "We've been too scattered within society to have significant effect. To found a telepathic culture—I never imagined that could happen within my own lifetime."

"A colonizer doesn't have interstellar comm capability," Jesse said, frowning, "and without supply ships we can't produce the equipment to establish it. If we're isolated forever, what impact can we have on the rest of humanity?"

"Our friends on Earth will be told where we're headed," said Peter. "They will pass the secret on, so that in the future when our descendants are too numerous for Fleet to displace, contact can be initiated. The culture we've created may not be admired at first, but its mere existence will force scientists everywhere to acknowledge the reality of psi instead of sweeping the evidence under the rug. And ultimately, if we succeed in making our way of life work for new generations, it will spread."

"We've got to believe that, if we believe full use of emerging human abilities is important," declared Kira. "It can't be confined to one small group indefinitely—if what we've gained is real, if it's truly an aspect of evolution, it will affect our whole species."

But not while we're alive even if our colony thrives, thought Jesse. Will belief in a future we won't live to see be enough to sustain us on a remote planet, cut off from the rest of civilization?

"Settling a new world will mean extreme hardship," Peter warned, "in addition to the obvious danger." But a trace of his old sparkle had come back; plainly, he was eager to go. It was the only possible salvation for him, Jesse saw. Not only had Peter shared this plan with Ian, but even apart from the problem of the tracking chips, he'd lost faith in the way of the past. He could no longer endure his role at the Hospital, not after what it had just demanded of him and might demand again. If he could not lead the Group to a new world, he would be unable to lead it at all.

It was clear that neither Ian nor Peter had possessed any real grasp of the hazards of the venture or the magnitude of the odds against its success. They had been as sure that a competent Captain could get them to a suitable destination as were the clients who might charter his seaplane! And, Jesse decided, he wouldn't attempt to enlighten anyone beyond providing honest answers to questions. Any misgivings he might have, he would keep to himself. He owed the Group more than technical expertise. To its leaders, at least, he had become a symbol.

Somewhat reluctantly Peter turned to Jesse, saying, "It's only fair to tell you that our hacker cleaned up your AWOL record, as well as a notation about off-duty drinking that had put a ceiling on your advancement. You're now officially on leave. You could go back to Fleet if you wanted to. You might even be offered a promotion."

"To hell with that," Jesse said. "What would I want with a promotion in Fleet when I've been offered command of a colonizer?"

56

SILENTLY, THE PEOPLE in the Lodge rose and joined hands in a ring around the fireplace. Their minds, too, joined—not for conscious communication, but wordlessly—and Jesse sensed that this was another of the occasions when you were supposed to pray, or not pray, in your own way. For the first time since childhood, he prayed. He was too much in awe at the turns of fortune not to.

After a pause Peter said, "We're about to hold the most important gathering in the Group's history. I asked as many members as possible to come to the Island, not only for Ian's funeral, but because we need a quorum. A vote must be taken, although I don't expect it to be close. After that, there'll be no turning back. If there is any disagreement among you, let's hear it now."

No one spoke. "One more thing," Peter continued. "At the conclusion of tonight's ceremony, I will call on the Council—and you, Jesse—to renew our commitment in the Ritual. If we have not the strength to do so in this time of grief, we're not fit to lead in the difficult days ahead."

"You're asking a lot of yourself, Peter," Kira said. "Are you sure, considering the heavy stress you've been under this week and the unspeakable ordeal this morning—"

"Either I'm qualified to take Ian's place, or I'm not," Peter said. "We'll find out, won't we?"

Then Jesse knew that it was for Peter's sake that they must do this, rather than for their own recommitment. It was he who needed renewal, and only the paranormal power engendered by the Ritual—magnified many times by the unusually large group assembled—could give it to him. Furthermore, only in this way could he establish himself as leader in the Group's eyes. The others were already saddened by Ian's death; when they heard the details on the morning news, they would be bewildered. They were being asked to leave their homes, the material comforts they had always known, for a perilous trip in space, a trip that would end in raw wilderness where survival would be uncertain. Those who knew Peter loved and trusted him; still the many not present at the last Ritual needed to see him in the role that had always been Ian's.

And they also needed to see their Captain take part, Jesse realized. No doubt that was why his presence on the Island tonight had been considered important enough to justify the risk of tampering with the tracking system. The coming ordeal did not worry him. Against all hope he'd been given his life back—both lives! His new life with the Group, with Carla, and now his old life too, the youth when he'd dreamed of exploring new worlds in space. It was like being reborn. Any apprehension he might have felt about trusting his newly-healed hand to fire again was a small thing beside that.

They went out to the Lodge porch, where Peter, using a wireless microphone, said briefly, "We meet here tonight in sorrow and in joy. Sorrow not only for Ian's passing, but for the fact that his body can't be brought here to the Island he loved—cannot ever be buried in the sea." A murmur of dismay arose from the listeners, but he continued without elaboration. "Joy for Jesse's release from the destruction to which he had been condemned, and joy, too, in the hope he offers us for a better future. I will say more of this after the funeral ceremony."

The Council members went to the water's edge, where a boat had been prepared. They climbed aboard and beckoned to Jesse to join them, handing him an oar. As they pushed off into the gleaming bay, ripples caught the last light of the setting moon. On the beach behind them, the assembled people began to light candles.

It wasn't necessary to go far when no body was to be

buried; the anchor was dropped within voice range of the shore. Peter stood in the center of the boat, the others balancing its bow and stern. They too held candles, large ones fixed to buoyant bases, as had those who'd conducted the burial Jesse had observed. That had been the last night he'd been outside the Group—how many weeks ago? He was a different person now. It was hard to remember what being an outsider had felt like.

Peter began to speak words that even without the microphone would have carried across the water. They were formal, poetic words, which at points the others echoed, this ceremony evidently well-known and well-loved. Then, as the candles were put over the side to float away, the people on the shore began to sing. Peter's voice rose over the rest, clear and strong, and Jesse caught enough of the lyrics to join the chorus:

May the radiance of candles we light now amidst
  our tears
Fuel the rising flame within us to be passed on
  through the years.

As the song drew to a close, he saw Kira was crying. He knew Carla would be crying too, as were many, and his own eyes were wet.

They rowed back to shore and left the boat, moving to a beach fire that had been kindled near it. The mourners crowded around. Illumined by firelight, Peter addressed the gathering, saying, "We are here to honor Ian and to grieve for him. Tomorrow you will hear news of him from the media, not all of which is true. You all knew Ian, so I'll leave it to you to judge which part is true and which is not. For that which is true, you will weep. But know that Ian died as he did for a reason, so the falsehood you hear must not be contested. Say nothing in his defense to outsiders. Hold in your hearts the memory of what Ian was and what he stood for—and respect that memory by doing what he believed we must do, of which I'll now tell you."

Peter had been wise to put it to them at Ian's funeral, Jesse thought—and not only for the practical reason of having a quorum. Though uncontested leader, he had no claim to their obedience. Not only must the plan be accepted by vote, but they all would have to go along with it; the Group was barely large enough to form a viable colony. They must be willing to embark on a hazardous journey. They must abandon their careers and whatever families they had among outsiders. Furthermore, they must give up amenities they had never questioned and somehow learn to survive on an alien planet, with no more equipment than a colonizer routinely carried. Women young enough would have to bear children—not just a few but many, to increase the colony's population as rapidly as possible. Pledged to the Group though they were, it was a lot to ask of them, despite the coming restrictions they would face on Undine. Had they been given time to forget their emotional attachment to Ian, they might have been less easily convinced.

The people remained very quiet while Peter set forth the plan. Jesse could sense, however, what most were feeling. There was no doubt in them. Enthusiasm emerged triumphant over fear; many, after all, had long wished they could go into space. His friends had been fascinated by what he'd told them of it; he'd barely managed to make them stop talking about it when he wanted to forget Fleet. Now, he saw, it would be difficult to make them aware of the risks. And Peter did not seem to be trying very hard. Nor was he emphasizing the hardships—rather, he was using telepathic projection, as on the night of the firewalk, to make the venture seem pleasantly exciting. God, Jesse thought, am I right to go along with this without offering them fair warning?

The vote, taken by voice, was unanimous.

"We need one other vote," Peter went on. "With Ian gone there is a vacancy on the Council. Normally it would be filled later by secret ballot. However, we are about to put our lives into the hands of Jesse Sanders. In view of this and in accord with Ian's wish, I propose that he be elected to the Council now, by acclamation."

Jesse had not anticipated this, but he saw that it was fitting if he was to command in space. No one offered any objection. Somewhat dazed, he found he had—in less than a day—awakened not only to freedom and renewed captaincy but to an immediate share in responsibility for the Group's safety prior to departure. And departure might not be simple to arrange. The colonial government was unlikely to permit emigration; getting three hundred people onto a ship might prove even more difficult than hijacking it once they were aboard. He hoped he would prove equal to what was demanded of him.

"Relight your candles," Peter said in the hush that followed. "I ask you all to join us now in the Ritual, as we of the Council renew our commitment."

The five members took places before the fire, as equals rather than in the normal Ritual roles. There was already such heightened emotion among them, and among the onlookers, that no lengthy prelude would be needed. The upbeat Ritual music, amplified from the Lodge porch by remote control, was sufficient. Jesse felt himself slipping into altered consciousness, letting himself be overwhelmed by the feelings this day had stirred. Peter was right, he thought dreamily. This was a good time to do this. This was the climax they all needed.

Carla, in the front row of watchers, met his eyes and then his mind. She had recovered her balance and felt no fear for him, only love and pride. Peter, noticing, went to her and said, "Your strength too is needed, Carla. Will you be our torchbearer?"

She nodded assent, taking the unlit torch from him, and stepped forward, plunging it into the fire and then holding it steady, extended at waist level. Peter began the Ritual words: "Unfaced fear is the destroyer. We will acknowledge fear and accept it, we will go past it and live free. . . ."

The telepathic support of the onlookers was strong, tangible; Jesse found himself more sensitive to such projection than in the past. Perhaps, he now realized, he'd unconsciously perceived such support that last day in the Hospital, after he'd awakened from the dream. He knew that nothing could harm him while it continued. Into his mind came a vision of Ian . . . Ian, who had come to him telepathically when he most needed courage. Who had trusted him enough to die horribly so that he, Jesse, could take the Group to a new world. Ian: wise, unafraid, smiling—this vision was shared among them all. Each of them cherished the memory of casting aside fear when called on by Ian to touch fire. He too had done so with Ian, in the dream—just as he'd done it with Peter in reality and would now do it again. . . .

". . . We are stewards of a flame that will illuminate future generations. And we now seal our commitment with the symbol of the mind's power, which is fire." Peter thrust his hand into the flame before them. Almost simultaneously, the others followed: Kira, Hari, Reiko and finally Jesse himself. The moment was removed from time, would hold for eternity, although in fact less than thirty seconds passed before the torch dropped and he was staring at his unburned fingers.

A collective sigh rose from the assembled people as they extinguished the candle flames they too had touched. The music faded. Friends crowded around Jesse again, congratulating him, questioning him about the trip to come. It was a long time before they drifted away. Alone on the dark beach with Carla, he looked up at the stars. He wondered to which of them he was heading.

Part Six

57

JESSE TOOK CARLA'S hand and together they walked toward the Lodge. "We've got to go at sunrise," Carla said. "We'll be leaving this place forever. Let's take one more look inside, to keep in memory."

They stood by the fireplace gazing into the embers, hearts full of all that was past, the joys and the griefs, wondering how it would seem to look back on from a new world. Peter found them there. "I've saved beds for you," he said. "Best sleep while you can, since you'll have to be up before dawn."

They went with him to his private cottage, the one that had originally been Ian's, which Kira was also sharing. All the cottages and bunkrooms were full, people were camping on the ground—but not, Jesse thought, in public view. Telepathic sensitivity was still so heightened that there could be no doubt this night about what most couples were doing. He wondered, briefly, if it was seemly so soon after a funeral; but it was, after all, symbolic of new life despite Undine's suppression of that possibility. . . and life was what the Group affirmed. He decided that Ian would have approved.

Too high from the Ritual to sleep yet, the four of them talked in the cottage by lamplight. Jesse wished the night would go on and on. He wanted time to think, to absorb the momentous decisions of the past few hours, to hold Carla and not worry until tomorrow about his new responsibility. But there was no time. There were things he must say to Peter, because once he was gone from here it might be too late to say them.

"Peter," he began, "you told me my outside perspective is valuable—"

"Yes, very much so. I wanted you on the Council even before Ian advised me to propose your election. To establish a new colony—even to escape from this one—we'll need your courage and initiative, as well as your knowledge of Fleet policy."

"I think you also need my offworld slant on reality," Jesse said. "You remarked once that I'd seen too many action vids. But I've been on worlds where those vids aren't far-fetched. You haven't. Bad as the Med government is, there are things that don't often happen here. There's no violence to speak of. Kids prone to it are medicated, and the authorities stay on top without it, as a rule. But that doesn't mean they won't play rough when it serves their purpose. You say the Administration is responsible for the arsons—"

"Not collectively, except for stirring up public feeling. I suspect only Warick and whoever's working for him was involved in setting the fires—which weren't meant to harm anyone, at least not physically."

"They were meant to reinforce political power over people, Peter."

"Yes. Warick has an eye on the future; he intends to run for Administrator next year. Like the other Meds, he sincerely believes it's in people's best interests for their hearts to be monitored continuously. But he may envision more extensive use of the tracking data."

"And he's assumed the whistle-blowers, if any, could be labeled mentally ill. But you, Peter—he could hardly condemn you to treatment in your own psych ward. So what do you think he's going to do about you?"

"I don't see that there's much he can do."

"That's where you're mistaken. For starters, he can bug your office. You don't really believe he'll be held back by legalities such as doctor/patient privilege, do you? We were damned lucky he hadn't bugged it by the time you gave me the truth serum. Carla told me you said my having to report to you every week as an outpatient will give us a chance to discuss our plans in private. Forgive me, but I think that's naive."

Peter was silent. After a long pause he admitted, "I suppose it is."

"Another thing. You are Ian's heir, and Ian will be publicly denounced as a criminal. You think he won't watch your every move, hoping to discover a connection he can exploit? Ian owned the Island, and now you do. A lot of people have been coming here regularly. He won't wait for them to be microchipped before he puts it under surveillance."

Both Carla and Kira were staring at him in horrified dismay. "Jesse's right, Peter," Kira said. "We've been blinded by our past success. We're used to getting away with what's called murder; we've assumed that as long as none of us were given truth serum, only the discovery of a body would bring about an investigation. But if someone wants to discredit you, that no longer holds."

"They don't need evidence of actual crime," Jesse added. "Ian and I both admitted that we believed failure to prevent death isn't always an evil. That goes against the premise that ensures public support for the Med government. If Warick could say you're associated with others who share that belief, perhaps even without guessing that you really are, he could brand you as unreliable and throw you off the Hospital staff. So he will try to find something damaging in your private life. If his investigators look hard enough, they'll succeed. They might even learn that you're interested in the paranormal."

"Oh, God," said Carla. "They couldn't have been spying on us tonight, could they? No planes came over, but the Ritual could have been seen from a boat."

"What's worse, you explained the whole plan for our future through a wireless mike. That could have been picked up from a boat if they had the right equipment."

"I don't think so," Peter said. "The gathering might have been observed, but from a distance no one could guess what we were doing with the torch. A candlelight memorial for Ian at the lodge he owned would be considered natural. As for remote listening, the technology's not been imported to Undine; there's been no use for it. But Jesse's point is well taken. There can be no more Rituals or firewalks here, and certainly not burials."

"This is the last night on the Island for almost everyone, not just for me," Jesse said sadly. "You have to tell them in the morning before they go, Peter. Only a few of your known friends should spend offshifts at the Lodge. It should be put out that an open invitation was Ian's policy, not yours."

"I agree," said Kira. "It will be a blow to us all, yet it would have happened anyway if we were microchipped—and soon we'll be leaving this whole world."

"Dear God, what have I done?" murmured Peter. "It didn't occur to me that I was putting the Group in danger by what I insinuated—"

"You had no choice," Jesse declared. "They were about to give me truth serum, and that would have meant our immediate exposure. But be careful not to say anything more that suggests you're a threat."

He decided not to extend the warning any further. Peter, despite his wisdom concerning the mind's power, was an innocent. He still hadn't perceived that an official who resorted to serial arson for political reasons might be capable of arranging some sort of accident for a man he wanted to eliminate. If it were me, Jesse thought, I'd be damned thorough with my preflight inspections from now on. But that wasn't something Peter needed to hear on top of all he'd been through today.

"You and I can't talk freely in your office anymore," Carla

pointed out. "We'll have to rely on telepathy for anything secret, just as you and Jesse will."

"Yes. That's fine for sharing feelings and general ideas, but it's going to complicate the planning of our escape. Jesse and I can't meet anywhere that's not safe for him to be tracked to—and I can't be seen going to places he's known to be."

"I think I'm more of a telepath than before," Jesse reflected. "I never used to be good at it, except in bed with Carla. But because of what happened to me in the Hospital, I've . . . changed. Permanently, maybe. Tonight during the Ritual I noticed."

"Kira told me you and Carla were able to make sustained contact over a distance," Peter said. "I hadn't foreseen that. It's logical, I suppose, that suppressing the higher brain functions would free deeper ones from the psi filtering that limits the range of conscious telepathy. Yet the last time you and I were in touch, I noticed no change in you—"

"That was before Ian taught me how to do it," Jesse said.

Peter stared at him. "*Ian* taught you?"

"Yes, I'm sure he did, now that I know he was in the Hospital, though at the time I thought it was only a dream." He went on to describe what had happened in it. "I think he must have showed me snatches of his own dream, along with . . . other things. And at the end, he sent me to Carla. I called silently to her after I woke, and I *knew how*."

"In all the years he trained me, he never gave me that." Peter looked almost envious.

"Well, you weren't drugged, Peter. He probably couldn't have reached me if I hadn't been."

"But you reached Carla."

"Because we're closely bonded, and in any case *I* was still drugged. I wonder if maybe it isn't an altered state even Ian hadn't encountered before. Did they give him any kind of sedative?"

"Undoubtedly. He hated drugs, would never have taken anything voluntarily, but in the Hospital it's routine. He was an exceptionally powerful telepath to begin with; if he felt himself going into an unfamiliar state, he was strong enough to take advantage of it, and concern for you was uppermost in his thoughts, after all. Since your condition caused you to be receptive . . . the two of you may have made a discovery. An advance toward the goal the Group exists for, terrible though the circumstances were."

"Now that Carla and I have done it once, maybe we could again, even without my being medicated," Jesse said. "I've been told things are done in the lab that outsiders do only while stoned."

"Yes, in advanced training. There are mind-patterns you haven't been exposed to yet."

"Then if we could record this new pattern, others might be able to match it?"

"Perhaps. But I don't have the facilities in the Hospital; it would be too risky to run our software there. And you can't come here again."

"I'm here now," declared Jesse. "As you say, this is the sort of thing we exist for. The risks we take are meaningless if we throw away chances to pass on what we learn."

"It's a lot to ask of you, after all you've just been through," Peter replied, obviously tempted. "But if you're up to it—"

"Peter," Carla protested, "Jesse has to fly at dawn! To get into that state again he'd have to recall all the worst moments. It would wipe him out."

"Don't worry—I'm not about to risk losing our Captain in a seaplane accident. There are plenty of pilots here tonight and one of them can go with you when you leave. I can pick him up from Verge Island tomorrow; it will give me an excuse to go there so that Jesse and I can make specific plans for arranging the starship charter."

58

WITH KIRA TO handle the computer, they returned to the Lodge. For the last time Jesse went downstairs, through the storeroom and freezer compartment, into the hidden room where his introduction to the powers of mind had begun. He would miss it, he realized as Peter fitted the headpiece. They would, of course, take the lab equipment with them; it would be essential to new generations. But reassembling it might not be their top priority on a wilderness world.

Recalling how he'd felt while drugged would be grueling, he knew. Yet tonight he was past apprehension. The Ritual's afterglow would enhance their telepathic power, too. This was an ideal time to try it. Though perhaps, since he was high, it would be impossible to enter a state dependent on diminished mind . . . such a state was incompatible, after all. . . .

No. To his surprise, Jesse found that he knew something he had not known before, something even Peter had not known, and *should* know. . . .

"Peter," he said. "Go on dual with me! You have to experience this, not just record it as an observer. And besides, you and I might be able to establish a link we could use in an emergency—"

Kira broke in quickly, "Don't even think of it! Peter, you've been through far more than the rest of us today. There are limits to what you can endure; an experience of how Jesse felt while his mind was being destroyed is outside them."

"No, it's not," Jesse said. "The mental debility in itself, not just the long-distance telepathy, is an altered state like all the others. It's not harmful, Kira, not before there's brain damage—at least not to anyone with enough training to keep from involuntarily slipping back into it later on. It's . . . a tradeoff. No one would want to be stuck in that state permanently, but Peter needs to know it's not as bad as he's been assuming it is. He can't learn that from a recording, or even from ordinary telepathic sharing. We need dual feed-back from live minds to learn the other states, don't we?"

"Let me try it with you, then," Kira said. "Peter's not in shape for it, not now."

Peter had been standing transfixed as Jesse spoke. "God, I've been blind!" he said. "I suppose because nobody ever came out of the stupor before, and the patients I had to drug weren't trained to deal with altered states in the first place, I never looked for a positive side to it. I just took it for granted that it was wholly destructive."

"Yet other drugs, so-called recreational drugs, produce brain damage too, if taken often enough," Jesse said. "So it's just the same with psychiatric drugs. If we can sort out the useful effects and get them through volition instead of chemistry—"

"The catch in that," Peter said thoughtfully, "is that it was hell for you—I sensed that you *felt* your mind was dete-riorating. That you were in the process of losing it."

"Of course, because I'd been told that I would and I was scared stiff until Ian enlightened me. I suspect that's why he didn't even hint that I was going to be released. He wanted me to understand that no matter what happened, nothing could destroy my inner mind."

"He said as much to me many times," Peter admitted, "but I didn't grasp it. I felt so much guilt over what I was forced to do to people that I never put two and two together—not even though for years I've been helping mental patients out of unpleasant states they fell into spontaneously. I failed you, Jesse—"

"No," Jesse said. "If you hadn't kept contacting me tele-pathically, I wouldn't have been in shape to absorb what Ian gave me. The training alone wouldn't have been enough."

"All the same, I should have been better prepared. If I'd faced the fact that I might someday have to give that drug to a healthy person, I might have figured out its effects. Well, it's time I found out what it feels like."

"You're too stressed out to go on dual," Kira insisted.

"I was told on my first day here," Jesse said, "that being stressed out helps. That for a breakthrough it's best not to be in full control."

"Sure it is, with a qualified instructor as partner," said Kira grimly. "But you have never taken the lead role on dual before. If Peter gets into trouble, you'll both go down."

"If we do, you know how to deal with it," Peter told her, settling into the other chair and reaching for its headpiece. "But I'd hate to think I'm not capable of handing a state of consciousness that Ian considered harmless."

Resigned but not happy, Kira attached their sensors and went to the control booth. The lights came on, and then the feedback patterns on the wall. "They'll be crude," Peter warned, "because this state will be new to the software; Carla will have to reprogram the filters after we've had some experience with it. But they should be distinctive enough for matching."

Jesse lay back and deliberately strove to recall the hours of mental fog. All altered states, he knew, could be entered much faster and more easily after they had once been experienced. That was why what was learned in the lab could be applied to real life, and it was also why recurrent bad trips happened to outsiders even when they weren't on drugs. The pathways of the mind were indelible. He would never be quite the same person as before being medicated in the Hospital, any more than he was the same as he'd been before receiving lab training in pain control. The knowledge of how to reach the state medication had produced was somewhere within him, buried, but accessible.... He focused his eyes on the shifting pattern, letting his thoughts drift. It was getting hard to think ... it was as if a grey cloud was thickening in his mind.... He felt a stab of fear, but ignored it. There was nothing to fear. There was no need to think clearly for now ... his mind had other functions, with which thinking would interfere ... rational thought would suppress his other powers ... the power to reach Carla....

Carla?

I'm here. He was with her in the cottage, where she had remained waiting for contact. Through her eyes he saw the warm glow of candles. *I lighted them for proof we were in touch. I'll blow them out now. When you come back here, tell me what you saw.*

She in turn shared his sight of the neurofeedback. *I see the patterns, Jesse. Yours, and Peter's—he's on dual with you! That's more evidence—I didn't know he was going to go on dual.*

Carla . . . I've got to leave you and contact him. It's frightening at first. He's strong, still he shouldn't be alone.

You ought to be with him, Carla agreed. *You and I can do this anytime, now that we know how.*

Jesse broke off with her, calling out silently to Peter. They had communicated that way often before, of course; since they were in the same room, no new state was required for telepathy between them. But a link made now would be stronger. *Peter?* he probed.

Jesse! You were with Carla, I picked that up. I saw her blow out candles, through your eyes, I think, not directly. . . .

Their visual mind-patterns were identical; Peter's skill and experience in matching had thrown him quickly into the new state. Their consciousness merged, and Jesse became aware that Peter was experiencing not fear, but remorse . . . remorse not merely because he'd been inadequately prepared to help during Jesse's ordeal, but because he felt he had come close to losing faith in the Group's destiny.

But you didn't! Jesse protested. *Underneath, you never stopped believing that somehow Ian's dream would come true.*

I wish I could think so. He wanted me to believe . . . before he gave me the proof. The words didn't come like conversation; they formed in Jesse's own mind from what he sensed in Peter's. He knew he himself wasn't replying in words either, though only words would be recorded in his memory.

You believed. Otherwise, you'd have cancelled the application for the starship. It had been made in Peter's name, not Ian's; Ian wouldn't have had to know.

I never even thought of canceling it!

Exactly.

Peter's spirits lifted briefly, only to be engulfed as the dulling of his mental processes continued. *This ... to feel my mind slipping ... it's all my worst nightmares come true. Yet you endured it while believing it wouldn't end. ...*

I'm not sure I could have borne it indefinitely, Jesse admitted. *But I don't think I'd have died, which means I'd have known underneath I was still* myself, *even if Ian hadn't come. Otherwise my inner mind would have killed me, as Zeb's killed him. If we lost everything, we'd be brain-dead— by definition. There's something in us that persists through any state, as long are we're alive. ... Ian said that when we affirm the power of the mind, we're affirming that! That we've been saying it all along. ...*

His thoughts drifted, became hazy. The image of Ian formed again before his eyes, superimposed on the swirling patterns of light on the wall before them, and was shared so that he did not know whether it came from his mind, or from Peter's, or from somewhere else. And the patterns faded out as the image became less tenuous ... Ian was standing there, smiling, yet removed beyond any possibility of contact. He felt fresh sorrow in knowing that he would never again see Ian in real life, never feel the touch of his hand. His eyes blurred, and there was an ache deep inside him that was suddenly overpowering. He was losing control, could not fight the tears any longer ... he, Peter, was so tired ... he'd done all that need be done for now ... he could not bear further pain. ...

With a jerk, Jesse snapped back, brought his feedback pattern into clear focus, saw it shift and swirl into the familiar shapes and colors of normal consciousness. But Peter's did not shift. He turned his head and saw to his dismay that Peter was crying.

Kira! Jesse called out urgently. *Oh God, Kira, what have I done to him?*

She responded fast. *It's okay—just let him be. He needs to cry.*

Coming down from the control booth, Kira went to Peter and removed his headpiece. She stood silently beside him as he twisted in the reclined chair and buried his face against the headrest, making no attempt to hold back the sobs. After a while she whispered, "Help me get him into bed in the infirmary, Jesse."

Leaning heavily on Jesse, Peter went with them to the infirmary without speaking. Soon he slept, and Jesse realized Kira had sedated him telepathically.

She turned to Jesse. "I underestimated you," she said softly. "I knew this was likely to happen if he let go his rigid control of consciousness. I was afraid that if it did, you'd be sucked down with him and might panic, might cause him to try to help you when he wasn't in condition to do it. I didn't realize you'd acquired the strength to bring yourself back from a shared reaction as deep as the one Peter's going through."

"But what brought it on? What went wrong?"

"Nothing's wrong . . . except that though he's often said he's not superhuman, he asks as much of himself as if he were. Think, Jesse—he's been through weeks of strain, anticipating Ian's death and our coming danger while keeping the plan to save us secret; then your arrest and his belief that he'd be forced to destroy you; and finally the shock of Ian's sacrifice. Only this morning he watched while Ian was executed! He's loved Ian as he would have loved a father, yet he couldn't stop to grieve for him. He had to conduct the funeral and inspire the mourners to risk their lives traveling to an unknown destination in space. And on top of all that, he held the Ritual, which would have been demanding even without all that came before. He was overdue for a breakdown. Better now than later, when he'll have to take on the responsibility of leading our escape."

"So my telepathic image of Ian simply . . . triggered it?"

"Yes, though there's no knowing with which of you the image originated. You are both grieving, as are we all. But tears are normal, Jesse. Mourning isn't a weakness. And to have shared it beneath surface consciousness will bond the two of you. Peter needs that. He has many friends, but he was a crèche child, after all, and has recently lost his wife. No one except Ian has been truly close to him since Lesley died. I believe Ian intended you to become much more than our Captain."

Jesse nodded. "He sent Peter to me with a message that he trusted me *in all things*. Neither of us understood what it meant—though now I see he was counting on me to hold up long enough for his sacrifice not to be in vain."

"Yes. But I suspect the message was meant for Peter himself as much as for you. Ian knew he would need the support of an equal."

"I'm hardly that. There are a lot of Group members better qualified—"

"Leadership is lonely; you know that, don't you, from your past space command? As Captain you will have a unique relationship with Peter, one that his followers can't duplicate. As for the rest of the Council, I am an old woman; the only other man, Hari, is too absorbed by mystical aspects of psi to be concerned with practical affairs; and Reiko is focused mainly on scholarship. And besides, you are the only one among us with first-hand knowledge of the universe beyond Undine. So you see the responsibility has fallen on you, Jesse."

In time, he supposed, he would be up to it. But for now, all he wanted was to sleep with his arms around Carla.

59

SEVERAL DAYS LATER, Jesse went to Fleet's office at the spaceport. The likelihood that he would be tracked wasn't a problem, since it could be reasonably assumed that as a former officer he might be hoping to procure transport offworld. After confirming that he was indeed officially on leave, he changed his status to permanent retirement. Then he transferred his previously-untouched back pay and retirement accounts to Fleet as down payment on charter of the colonizer *Mayflower XI*.

"*Mayflower?*" asked Peter incredulously when they met later that day in a safe house. "Starships haven't been given that name since before Undine's founding! Is there a revival of sentiment for Earth's ancient history?"

"You knew it was going to be an old ship," Jesse said. "Didn't your contact mention its name?"

"No. And I hadn't realized quite *how* old."

"They don't wear out from age. This one established a brand new colony and spent a long time there waiting for it to get on its feet. And then it had to travel back the slow way to be refitted with the hyperdrive. It's transported a lot of emigrant groups since, but with larger and faster ships now coming off production lines, it's due to be decommissioned. That's the only reason we were able to get it."

"There's no question about its spaceworthiness, is there?"

"Oh, no. After all, its assigned crew's safety depends on that, and the Captain won't take it unless he's satisfied. Besides which, Fleet could be sued for far more than the charter fee if anything went wrong." Jesse did not mention that a normal crew included engineers who could repair the ship's drive in case of trouble, a capability he himself didn't possess. He must gamble on its smooth operation.

"Well, then, I'm glad to hear it's going to be decommissioned," Peter said. "I haven't been happy about stealing it—we've committed a lot of crimes, but so far grand larceny hasn't been among them. Yet they're not going to get it back, and we haven't the resources to buy a ship outright, even if we arrange to have our property on Undine transferred to Fleet after we're gone."

"They won't lose more than the scrap value," Jesse said. "But there's another problem with it, Peter."

"Something you didn't want Carla to hear." Jesse had contacted him, ostensibly to arrange for an outpatient visit, and made plain via a prearranged code that when they met to discuss what he'd learned of the ship, Peter should come alone.

"It's best if she doesn't," Jesse said, "You remember I told you that I had seen stasis units, the kind used in the early days on long trips, during Fleet training?"

"Yes, in a museum, I assumed."

"No. When old ships were refitted with the hyperdrive so that putting passengers in stasis was no longer necessary, the facilities weren't removed. And the *Mayflower* class was the last to have them."

"Good God. Are you saying there will be stasis vaults on our ship?"

"Yes. It might bother Carla to be aware of them, even though they're never going to be used."

"Surely they're not still in condition for use."

"As a matter of fact, they probably are. They didn't go to the trouble of tearing them out; trying to convert the deck to a hydroponics area wouldn't have been worth the cost, since converted ships are used only on short runs to established colonies and don't need a sustainable ecology. To tamper with their integration into the computer system would have meant totally replacing the ship's life-support AI. Besides, when the hyperdrive was new, many Captains viewed stasis facilities as good insurance against drive failure."

Peter frowned. "Are they going to be—visible?"

"No. All that part of the ship is sealed off from the passenger decks, and even from the ones those of you with crew duties will use. I'll have to inspect the whole ship myself, but nobody else needs to know the stasis deck is there, during the trip, at least."

"I think we had better leave it that way, then," said Peter. "Carla isn't the only one who'd be upset. Some of our people are having second thoughts about the relative risks in staying versus going, and the clincher is the thought of leaving stasis vaults behind forever."

"So I guessed. The truth will come out eventually, when we cannibalize the ship to build our colony. But then we can have a grand party and blow up what's left of them. There might even be an advantage to the symbolism."

"That's true," Peter agreed. "A lot of us have felt like blowing up the Vaults for years. To do it in fact, physically, will provide ideal closure."

They went on to discuss the rest of the information Jesse had been given at the spaceport. He had, of course, arranged for the ship as the representative of an approved group of colonists, not as an individual. Since obtaining the approval had required the first admission to anyone other than Ian's offworld friends that there *was* a Group, Ian and Peter had dared to apply only after their agent on Earth had determined that Fleet wouldn't contact the government. They'd had no need to worry. No colonial government was willing to let its population emigrate. Though League law guaranteed freedom of movement, there were various ways around that guarantee. Fleet, being in the business of providing ships for charter, knew better than to trigger them.

Nevertheless, some evidence of the group's actual existence had been required. "We gave them a password-protected Net address," Peter had told Jesse when they'd conferred in a miners' tavern on Verge Island. "It's reasonable that a persecuted religious order's private site couldn't be found through a public search."

"Persecuted religious order?"

"Well, there were only three choices on the application under reason for emigration," Peter had explained. "'Economic benefit' wouldn't make sense for a group as small as ours without capital for mining equipment, especially when we're leaving a colony where we're already rich. 'Political persecution' wouldn't be credible when Undine is known to have no political conflicts. So that left 'religious persecution.' Which is accurate, in a way—certainly it's a matter of conscience with us. There are plenty of small cults on Earth with views unlike those of the established religions."

"So what religion are we?" Jesse had inquired.

"The Stewards of the Flame—what else?"

"Well, it's apt, I suppose, even if a bit melodramatic." He hated to think how his former crewmates would have reacted to his announcement of such an affiliation; he'd found it hard to keep a straight face when transferring funds to Fleet in that name.

While Fleet did not care about violations of anti-emigration policies, it did object both to forced emigration and to the use of its ships as getaway flights for criminals. It took pains to ensure that no world could dump its undesirables into fledgling colonies. Thus background checks on all members of charter groups were required.

"That looks like a big stumbling block," Jesse said now, knowing the time had come to deal with the awkward details. "We don't want to be investigated by the local authorities."

"No, but fortunately Fleet just needs a password that will let them into police files on the local Net," Peter said. "Ian was assured that they don't require it to come through official channels."

"Do we know the password?" Jesse inquired.

"Certainly; as a staff psychiatrist I can access all the confidential files."

Then for once, it was a good thing that the police and the Hospital were one and the same. That would be convenient, since Fleet also required medical records. It did not want prospective colonists to die while aboard one of its ships, nor was it willing to take any chance of being stuck protecting a colony that proved too small and weak to survive on its own. Not only must all emigrants be healthy, but it was necessary for women of childbearing age to be certified fertile.

Jesse had not thought about this before. Gynecological records could be hacked where necessary, of course—but how many of the women who looked young actually were past menopause? How many had faked their birthdates in the files to conceal retarded aging?

"Slow aging extends to childbearing capability," Peter told him, "though it will mean using donor eggs—our older women's own stored ones have long since been relinquished to the Hospital's DNA bank. We won't have lab facilities for IVF after we leave the starship, so we'll freeze embryos to implant later. Susan, our gynecologist, is stockpiling supplies of the hormones we'll need to take with us."

"I'm not sure there's going to be time aboard the starship—for egg donation, I mean. Doesn't it depend on women's cycles?"

"Jesse, we have cryogenic storage facilities in the lab at the Lodge," Peter informed him. "Ian banked his sperm there years ago; one of our surgeons was able to retrieve it despite his implanted IVD. I wondered why he bothered, but now I suspect he had a premonition that it could someday be used. We'll begin banking eggs now—we won't wait until departure. Carla's already hacking the files of potential donors to make sure they're not called in for checkups after we've removed their contraceptive implants."

Fleet also required all prospective colonists to sign individual waivers acknowledging awareness of the risks they were assuming. This wouldn't be a problem, since they could do it via the Net, and privately Jesse was glad they would have to. It was one thing for people to agree to those risks when spellbound by Peter at Ian's funeral, but only a more objective decision could sustain them for what was to come. The waivers, to be sure, did not take into account the *real* perils: hijacking followed by isolation without the support of supply ships on a world that had not even been terraformed. But at least they were a step toward the abandonment of illusions.

The most pressing order of business was the selection of a planet. Actually, there were two to be chosen: the one the Group wanted to settle and the one it would officially be headed for. "We just have to make that one seem plausible to Fleet," Peter said. "Since we're not really going there, what kind of world it is won't matter."

"Like hell it won't," Jesse said. "If something goes wrong, if hijacking proves impossible and we're not caught trying it, we and our descendants will be spending our lives there." Peter was so hung up on Ian's dream, which he now considered virtually proven by events, that he was blocking this possibility out of his mind. That was okay. For a venture as risky as this, the leader must be a fanatic to inspire the others. But he himself could not ignore cold facts. He might never become Captain—and if he didn't, they'd be lucky to end up at the official destination.

Fleet had provided full descriptions of the planets open to them. All were already occupied, of course, and all were willing to accept immigrants who wished to retain aspects of their own culture. "Culture," however, did not include unorthodox ideas about health care. It was assumed that immigrants would not only arrive healthy but would respect local customs with regard to staying that way. Furthermore, most of these colonies were older than Undine's and more heavily populated. Somewhat to Peter's surprise, they did not have lush farmland free for the taking—immigrants were likely to become miners or factory workers. "That's to be expected," Jesse said. "You weren't thinking we could live anywhere else as we do here, were you? Undine is exceptional. It's rich in diamonds, which is why everyone has such a high standard of living. And don't forget the wealth that comes from the investments of ancestors in the Vaults. Our people are going to lose a lot that they take for granted, wherever we end up."

"I know that. We're going to arrive penniless in any case because all our funds will have gone toward chartering the ship. But somehow I hadn't stopped to picture what would happen if we were transported to an established colony where we might not be able to get the professional jobs most of us are used to. I've only thought about the hardships of settling a wilderness world where we'd eventually make use of our talents."

"Well, that risk is unavoidable, Peter. It's only fair for people to know about it—as they will, because the waivers they'll have to sign will include a description of the place they're supposedly en route to."

Peter nodded. "You're right, of course. Our willingness to accept risk must be unconditional. I'm too much of a visionary sometimes, I guess."

Frowning, Jesse persisted, "Maybe you need to pull a description of Fleet's penal colonies off the Net. There's more than one way the hijacking could fail."

"You've made your point. Let's just pick one of these back-up worlds, and then decide where we really want to go."

Seeing little difference between them, they chose the one that put least emphasis on excellence of health care facilities in its promotional blurb. Its name was Liberty, which suggested that its founders, at least, had had an acceptable scale of values.

With that out of the way, they began downloading pictures of unopened worlds from the Net's astronomical database. Ian and Peter had previously tried this, but had not known how to narrow the search to real possibilities. Hundreds of unopened worlds had been charted, but most of the suitable ones were ruled out by distance—the longer the jump, the greater the danger that a slight miscalculation would require a long trip in normal space to get close enough to orbit. The maximum length of such a trip would be limited by the onboard life support. Knowing the ship's specifications, Jesse was able to limit the search to destinations he'd be willing to try for.

The planet chosen must, of course, be habitable without terraforming. "I was surprised when I learned there are any such planets left," Peter said. "I'd have thought all those close enough would have been colonized long ago."

"That's not the basis on which they're chosen," Jesse explained. "A world's not worth the expense of opening unless it has minerals valuable enough to export. If it does have, terraforming is often cost-effective, just as it was on Undine. But a world already fit for farming that has no rich mineral deposits would be useful only to its colonists; they couldn't pay the cost of ongoing supply shipments. Since we won't be receiving supplies anyway, we can consider worlds normally ineligible for settlement."

Fascinated, they studied the images, some of which showed planets that were more or less Earthlike. "There was another factor in the early days of colonization," Jesse said. "At that time, environmentalism was politically dominant on Earth, and the form of it then popular held that planets with native lifeforms, even if not precursors of intelligent life, should be left alone. They were put off limits, as those that have primatoid species still are even though no signs of an ET civilization have ever been detected. So the worlds with terrestrial ecologies were bypassed, and by the time that attitude faded, terraforming technology was so well developed that there was no reason to prefer them."

"You're saying there might be *animals* on our world?" Peter, Jesse realized, had seen large animals only in vids. The Meds considered red meat unhealthy and Undine hadn't enough land area to grow feed for livestock, so none had been imported.

"There are likely to be. Dangerous animals, possibly," Jesse replied. He hoped not. Guns being taboo on Undine and game nonexistent, no one besides himself would have skills for dealing with predators. "These worlds haven't been thoroughly surveyed," he warned. "All we know about them is that their gravity, atmospheres and climates are within the habitable range, that their water is pure and their soil will support crops of Earth origin, and that the initial explorers encountered neither primatoids nor lethal microorganisms. Beyond that, we take our chances."

How could they choose? Ruling out those with gravity or rotation significantly unlike Undine's still left many possibilities. To pick the closest or most promising would invite discovery by Fleet. The only obvious ones to avoid, besides those without accessible metal deposits, were water worlds where local transportation would be difficult and on which, without solar power satellites, there would be no means of generating much power. The lives of the entire Group might depend on this decision, yet it would be like throwing dice when there wasn't enough information to base it on. . . .

Jesse clicked forward to the next image. He drew in his breath sharply. A familiar world, a golden world studded with sapphire seas . . . just as he had seen it with Ian, in the dream. It was real! *Ian showed me a real world. . . .*

"The world of his own dream?" Peter, picking up the thought, was awestricken.

"Perhaps. But could he have seen this picture, Peter?"

"He may have, later; he did look at some on the Net—after his dream, of course."

"For him to have seen this planet in it would mean clairvoyance across light-years of interstellar space!"

"Not necessarily. It could have been part of the precognition. He may have seen it in the same way that he saw us landing, through our eyes as we'll see it in the future."

"In that case we've already chosen it! Are we free to do anything else?"

"Precognition doesn't take away freedom. But since we don't want to change what he foresaw for us, let's stay on the safe side and help make it come true."

Jesse began downloading data about the planet, his mind still on the baffling question of what Ian had perceived. "You said he saw me in the dream before he met me, and later recognized my face. Was that precognition too, or did he see me clairvoyantly in real time, here on Undine?"

"He was never sure; remote viewing can show the future, and there's often no way to distinguish. But unless you wear your Fleet uniform on the new world, at least part of what he viewed must have been in real time before you were taken to the Hospital. In the bar, maybe."

Jesse's mind was whirling. "Peter . . . why did I pass out for a few moments in that bar? I never have figured it out; I hadn't drunk any more than I often had before. Was it fate, as you've been calling it—or did I somehow sense Ian's desire for me to stay? Were we in telepathic contact on an unconscious level before I was trained to recognize unspoken thought?"

"We'll never know, any more than we can be sure whether he saw this planet in his own dream via psi or showed it to you through recollection of the picture."

"It's a beautiful planet," Jesse said. "I don't think we could do better."

"Does it have a name?" Peter inquired.

"No—its star has only a catalog number. They don't name individual planets until they're opened for settlement."

"Well then," declared Peter, "from now on its name is Maclairn."

60

JESSE AND PETER did not attempt to meet secretly again. With Jesse being tracked, it was too dangerous. Jesse did not see Carla often, either. Reluctantly, they decided there was too much risk in her coming regularly to his apartment. They would have the rest of their lives to live together. A few weeks of separation was a small price to pay for making sure no suspicion would fall on Peter. And besides, he now could converse with her telepathically as she sat in a café near his building; he'd found that with practice this required less drastic alteration of consciousness than it had in the beginning.

He did see Kira, whose friendship could be explained by her having served as his nurse during his recovery. Through her as well as through Carla, the details of the plan were relayed to other members of the Group. Jesse's chief task was the selection and preparation of people for crew duties.

While in space, his role in the Group and Peter's would be reversed—Peter would be Executive Officer, although, lacking any experience with starships, his job would consist mainly of carrying out the Captain's orders. Carla would be in charge of dealing with the starship's computer. Kira, of course, would be medical officer, assisted by the other member physicians. Knowing more of the members than he did, she helped him pick those with qualifications for work in life support and communications. Since the former was AI-controlled and the latter consisted mainly of ensuring that no communication went out from the ship after they took it over, there would be little for them to do; but they needed to gain all the knowledge they could from the Net so as to be ready for emergencies.

An engineering team, headed by Kwame because of his power-plant experience, was also chosen. Though they could not hope to become knowledgeable enough to fix problems with the ship, once aboard they could begin learning how the equipment it carried could be used in building the colony. As for routine work such as meal preparation and cleanup, that would be rotated among all members not otherwise assigned, just as it would have been under Fleet command. Colonizers were not luxury liners; they didn't carry cooks or stewards.

One other team was assembled without Jesse's involvement: the remote viewers who, it was hoped, could provide valuable information when it came to choosing a landing site on Maclairn. "You need to be aware of this," Kira told him, "but Hari will take full responsibility for its implementation. Peter wants you to stay completely away from it. When he told me during your training that you were not to be exposed to remote viewing, I was puzzled; it's an easier psi skill to learn than some of the others and normally we do teach it to trainees. Once I knew you'd be taking us to a new world, though, I understood. We're dependent on your practical knowledge and experience as a control. Remote viewing is often useful, but it's inconsistent—it produces false information a fair percentage of the time. By comparing impressions from many of our most talented viewers, we can judge which ones are worth following up, whereas if you as Captain were to personally receive psi data about the planet's surface, you'd be tempted to rely on it. And that would be dangerous."

Jesse had not even heard of remote viewing except in connection with Ian's dream. "Do you mean to say people in the Group have been doing this all along—seeing things at a distance clairvoyantly?" he burst out in astonishment.

"Most of us have tried it from time to time. It's not very useful on Undine because there's nothing to see on the rest of this world—just sea and scattered islands, all alike, with no way to get feedback except from weather satellites. We've no need to spy on distant activities, which it was used for on Earth at times when an open-minded minority briefly overcame official skepticism."

"Did it work? Remote spying, I mean?"

"Yes, subject to the cautions I just mentioned. But tolerance of it never lasted long; its very success aroused people's underlying fear of psi, and led government officials who'd temporarily endorsed it to turn and run. They didn't *want* it to work, any more than you wanted to believe in the paranormal when you first came to us."

Somewhat dazed, Jesse protested, "Since we can gain information about Maclairn this way, Fleet could use it for exploration! If it's a known phenomenon on Earth—if there are even a few individuals willing to experiment—could they someday locate us?"

"Not unless they're orbiting our world. Controlled remote viewing isn't possible over interstellar distances. Though neither space nor time limits psi in principle, human minds have built-in filters that protect us from the infinite amount of input we'd receive if we had access to the whole universe."

But in dreams, Jesse thought . . . Ian might have crossed interstellar space in the dream, and in any case, he crossed time. . . .

While Jesse and Kira were planning the voyage, Reiko was designing the new colony, which as a historian and sociologist, she was well qualified to do. Of highest priority was the formation of committees from among experienced builders, farmers, and mining experts to coordinate the establishment of a settlement. Furthermore, there was the matter of government. At first, with only three hundred citizens, it would be run like a city government by the existing Council. But the Group's organization had never been formalized; now, it was necessary to write a charter to be discussed and voted on while the trip was underway. In addition, Reiko—with some input from Peter—began to draft the constitution that would shape the future society.

It was decided that until departure, Jesse should continue to fly, as for him to be unemployed might be considered cause for the Meds to question his stability. Though as a mental patient, he could now never qualify for a license to carry passengers for hire, he was permitted to carry cargo and in fact needed a source of income to keep them from wondering who was supporting him. So he kept on logging hours in the air, his feelings mixed at the thought that this phase of his life would soon end. Eager though he was for his coming space command, he would miss the rapture of flying out across the sea. Occasionally he flew over the Island from which he was now barred, looking wistfully down at it, wondering how it would feel to look back on it from another solar system.

The date *Mayflower XI* would arrive at Undine had been set by Fleet when the charter was confirmed by down payment of Jesse's legally-transferable funds. On the night before, all Group members would have to desert their jobs and relatives without notice and proceed to the spaceport. There had been a good deal of worry over how they were to get there; the bus that served the adjacent power plant ran infrequently, and for multiple cabs to be called would surely arouse questions. Fortunately, the road leading to it passed a public park on the outskirts of the city. This park could be

rented for private celebrations, and so Nathan and Liz—
who were both without families—had reserved it for a wedding reception that the Group planned to turn into an all-
night bash. Fleet had one passenger van, normally used to
transport crews on shore leave. During the night, it would
shuttle members in from the park. Once inside the port's
boundaries, there was no way they could be stopped. The
spaceport was Colonial League territory over which local
authorities had no jurisdiction.

Any property that people left behind, however, would
be confiscated by Undine's government. The Administration would be outraged by the loss of tax revenue that would
result from depletion of their dead ancestors' offworld accounts. Both those accounts and the Group members' own
would no doubt be frozen, which wasn't going to matter—by
that time there would be no funds left in them. The starship
would not load passengers until the full charter fee had been
paid. So the transfer of funds had to be carefully timed and
coordinated with the Group's contacts on Earth, who were
to perform the necessary hacking. A committee headed by
Xiang Li had been appointed to collect financial passwords
from individual Group members. All their liquid assets were
to be turned over; amounts above what was needed for the
charter fee would be earmarked for transfer to Fleet later,
as compensation for its loss of the ship. A clear warning had
been given that anybody who missed the departure, whether
accidentally or because of second thoughts, would probably
be arrested for tax evasion.

To be financially destitute would be no hardship for emigrants, since there would be no way to access offworld assets
from an isolated colony and cash would be meaningless there
for some time. The loss of personal possessions would be
more painful. Fleet had a strict limit on baggage—one duf-
fel bag per person, which was all that could be carried in
the rush to the spaceport anyway. That meant that except
for e-files, little trace of their former lives could be preserved.

The Group as a unit was entitled to ship just enough

freight to allow for some warm clothing not available on Undine—which would be brought from a colder world—and for the irreplaceable neurofeedback gear and cryonic bank. Most of the starship's cargo would be furnished by Fleet and was covered by the charter fee: all the equipment and supplies necessary to found a colony and support it for its first year, as well as seeds and embryos necessary to establish agriculture. Also included would be an electronic library covering the full range of Earth's accumulated knowledge. These things were not scheduled to be unloaded on Liberty. They were standard, sealed into detachable pods provided aboard all colonizers for emergency use in case a ship was lost. It had never occurred to Fleet that this policy might enable a party of colonists to get lost on purpose.

Removal of the lab equipment from the Island would be easy enough to accomplish, but its delivery to the spaceport presented a problem. Private export was not allowed, and though Fleet wouldn't report an illegal shipment, no Group member owned a truck and no trucking firm would accept unauthorized boxes. At least not openly. Peter, in desperation, concluded that the only solution lay in bribery, and put aside a sizeable amount of cash. But he dared not offer it far in advance, nor could the cryogenic container be maintained long with a portable power source. The boxes would have to be taken directly from his plane to the spaceport. So the lab would not be dismantled until shortly before departure.

Another reason for this was that Peter was doing some last-minute recruiting. There were three people in Hari's front group that he considered good candidates, plus several adolescent children of members. Ordinarily these potential recruits would not have been approached quite so soon, but Peter hated to leave them behind. One of the normal selection criteria was judgment of a person's ability to keep a lifelong secret from friends and family—and since this would no longer be a requirement, he decided to accept them despite relative immaturity. That meant bringing them one by one to the lab to be tested and then welcomed by the small number of Peter's friends he could still safely invite to the Island.

The worst of the problems confronting the Group was what to do about people currently receiving hospice care. No new patients had been accepted since the decision to leave had been made. There were three already living in safe houses, two of whom died during the ensuing weeks and were taken to the Island for burial despite the now-great risk. But one old black woman, a longtime Group member, was expected to linger. She was bedridden. There wasn't any way to transport her to the spaceport, and in any case, liftoff in a shuttle would kill her. Peter and Kira agonized over it, yet could see no answer. Finally, with less than a week remaining, she took matters into her own hands and called an ambulance. "I follow in Ian's footsteps," she wrote in the note she left, "just as I always have. They'll take care of me in the Hospital, and by the time I'm put into stasis, I won't know it's happening. The Group is about living, not dying. What matters is not how you die, but how you live on the new world." No member who visited her came away with dry eyes.

The departure date fell in the week before Undine's election. "A narrow escape," Kira said. "As soon as the votes are counted they'll start microchipping people; now that it's in the news, it's all too obvious that the public favors it. Peter says the Hospital staff will be the first victims. If someone's looking to discredit him, that could be disastrous—if he were brought in for questioning at the wrong moment, he might be held long enough to miss the ship. We're getting out just in time."

Jesse, as the only one with a legitimate excuse to contact Fleet openly, kept in touch with its office. *We've got a problem,* he told Peter telepathically during his final outpatient visit to the Hospital. *There'll be a freighter in orbit at the time we're scheduled to depart.*

What difference does that make?

A big one. Freighters don't call here frequently; the odds on it weren't great enough for me to worry about before. But freighters carry arms to protect their cargo from piracy. The crew we put into an unarmed shuttle can call ahead for help, and we'll be pursued until we go into hyperdrive. It gives us too narrow a window.

Does it take long to get into hyperdrive? Maybe I've seen too many action vids, but I assumed it was a fast process.

It's fast enough. The trouble is that I won't have access to the charts until we've gotten rid of the bridge crew. I can't go into hyperdrive without time to study them—God only knows where we'd end up.

Could we disable the comm equipment of the shuttle we put the crew in?

We could, but then their chance of survival wouldn't be large, Peter. Nobody will be expecting them, after all. They've got to be able to communicate with Undine to land here safely; if they can't even send an SOS they'll be shot out of the sky.

We don't want to get them killed, Peter agreed.

Seeing nothing that could be done about it, Jesse tried to put it out of his mind. The window would be narrow. He might get only a fast look at the charts. It had been many years since he'd calculated a jump not familiar to him in any case; this merely added one more complication. They could not give up the venture at this stage, so there was no point in worrying.

Yet he did worry. Not just about that, but about the incalculable number of things that could go wrong both before and after their arrival on the unknown world they now thought of as Maclairn. Natives of Undine had known nothing of physical hazards or hardships. Could courage alone ensure the survival of people whose lives had been as sheltered as theirs had?

It wasn't that he was personally afraid. What dismayed him was the responsibility—responsibility even for Peter, who was carrying the greatest burden and yet had too little experience to recognize the immensity of the perils confronting them. And for Carla ... he recalled, with a chill, the strong feeling in his dream that if he failed in what Ian expected of him, Carla would die....

She could not help knowing that he was troubled. It came through more in telepathic converse than it would have if they'd been together in the flesh. *Jesse*, she asked finally, *Is there something you're not telling me?*

Only that what we're getting into is more chancy than you know. Than anyone seems to know.

Is that what you think? Oh, Jesse, it's not like that.

You all act as if we were simply moving to a new island. Even Peter . . .

He's not as naive as he may seem. Do you suppose he didn't think it through for weeks before Ian died, before he ever decided to go through with it?

Of course he did, but he saw only what he wanted to see. The ideal. The vision worth striving for. And now, the goal for which Ian sacrificed himself. Not the dark side of it, the real possibility that we'll never reach that goal.

Have you forgotten the words of the Ritual, Jesse? None of us are unaware of the hazards—we're simply pledged to live beyond fear.

Yes. "Unfaced fear is the destroyer. We will acknowledge fear and accept it, we will go past it and live free." He *had* forgotten. The Ritual was a way of life, not simply a means of coping with the familiar risks of violating Undine's laws. Privately, they had all accepted the magnitude of the danger and were living as they had his first week on the Island, when he'd thought them young and carefree and had envied their ability to have fun. They believed the adventure *would* be fun, but not because they viewed it unrealistically....

It's like touching flame, Carla told him. *We just do it—and to be able to do it, we have to know we could be burned, and be willing. And the main reason we do it isn't to reach a goal. It's simply to be all we can be. We'd lose less by being burned than by turning away.*

Like touching flame. Suddenly Jesse's spirits soared. Putting your hand in flame was impossible—yet he had done it. His release from the Hospital had been impossible, yet he was free. Miracles did happen. But the key to them was that you had to be willing for them not to happen. You had to know that they might not, and still feel all right with what you were doing. Wasn't that what Peter had taught him in his very first feedback session? Wasn't it what Ian had conveyed in the dream? Ian must have known perfectly well that the chances of their reaching a new world and surviving there were not large. To assume that he and Peter, or for that matter other Group members, were hiding their heads in the sand did them injustice. He'd underestimated even Carla....

I'm sorry, he said silently. *Still, after all that's happened, I hadn't caught on. I was afraid for you when I didn't need to be.*

I was afraid for you, too, at first. Not for myself. It's easier to deal with fear for yourself than with fear for someone you love.

Yes . . . I never really loved anyone before loving you. Nor had he cared for friends the way he cared for Peter and Kira. He suddenly saw why the risks now seemed so worrisome.

61

ON THE NEXT-TO-LAST night before departure, Carla began to know something was wrong. It had begun that morning, when she had been scheduled to fly to the Island with Peter. It was the start of their offshift, and they'd planned to pack up the lab equipment and close the Lodge, from which everyone else had already departed. But Peter hadn't shown up. He hadn't answered his phone. Concerned, she'd called everyone she could think of, but he was nowhere to be found.

This was not like Peter—and in any case, there was

only one day left. To leave retrieval of the equipment until the very last minute was risky, to say the least; what if something went wrong with the undercover trucking arrangement he'd made? What if a freak storm came up and prevented flying? That was unlikely, to be sure, but still . . .

Peter had been acting strangely about the flight in any case. At first he hadn't intended to take her with him. "You need someone to help you," she'd insisted, knowing he had not asked anyone else and that the others weren't aware that another trip had to be made. "Besides, I want to check the software and records again. I know they're all in the datakeeper I downloaded them to, still I'd like to be the one to pack the computer."

"I'd just as soon go by myself, if you don't mind."

"I do mind." The loss of the neurofeedback software would be a major blow to the Group from which it would take years to recover. They were taking the lab computer with them, but she'd also stored the software on multiple backup devices. She dared not keep any of these in her apartment, much less carry them to work with her—they contained a complete history of the Group's discoveries and accomplishments as well as personal records showing mind-patterns of individual members, plus genetic and medical data she'd downloaded from the Hospital. All the copies were at the Lodge, as had been the normal policy. They would be taken directly to the spaceport with the other things. But she felt a need to watch over them personally except for the brief time the boxes were on the truck, and in fact she planned to carry one copy in her own duffle bag. Peter had too much else on his mind to give full attention to them.

"It won't be a pleasant trip, Carla," he'd said.

No, she supposed not. Saying goodbye to the Lodge would be hard on Peter; it held memories dating back to his first meeting with Ian during his college years. Being a crèche child, he'd never known any other real home. Everything important in his life had happened there, including his tragically-ended marriage as well as the friendships that mattered to him. "You need someone with you," she'd insisted. "You shouldn't have to go through it alone. And I have memories, too, after all."

So, reluctantly, he had agreed. And then, when the time came, he'd disappeared. She knew he hadn't gone alone because his plane was still moored in the city; that was the first thing she'd checked. By evening, she was frantic.

She was almost ready for bed when at last he phoned. "I was held up," he said shortly. "We'll go tomorrow morning. I've rescheduled the meeting with the trucker."

During the flight, he told her what had happened. It had started with one of the children. Only a few Group members had children—none below teenage—and luckily most of them happened to be home for their offshift. But there was one such couple on the alternate shift, which meant their son would, theoretically, be confined in the crèche on the night of departure. They had expected to hide him for two days instead of letting him go back there when the shift began. Unfortunately, one of his friends had shown up to walk to school with him, and it had been impossible for him to say he wasn't going.

From a crèche, there was just one conceivable escape. The boy, who was no fool and who had been let in on the secret, had done the only thing he could do—soon after arrival he'd feigned illness and had been taken to the treatment wing of the Hospital. The parents had then contacted Peter for help in getting him out. There wasn't any legitimate way to do it. The boy hadn't been aware that he should fake mental illness; he was in a medical ward over which Peter had no jurisdiction. Yet Peter was pledged to support fellow Group members and could hardly have asked them to abandon their son while they took off into space, even apart from the fact that the kid couldn't be trusted not to reveal their plans if pressed.

In the end, he had simply walked into the ward and smuggled the boy out in inconspicuous clothes, relying on Anne to suppress the alarm at the ID checkpoint. Which would have been okay, except that a search was initiated when he was found to be missing and Peter's presence in that ward had been noticed.

"God, Peter," said Carla. "They didn't suspect you?"

"No. They only thought I might have seen something. But I was questioned for a long time by Warick. The talk got onto . . . other things. I suppose a certain amount of unconscious telepathy goes on no matter how firmly I close my mind to specifics. He knew I was on edge. He jumped to the wrong conclusion as to why."

"Next week's election."

"Yes. He knows I'm bitterly opposed to the microchipping, and I couldn't deny it. I didn't give him any further indication of my suspicion about the arsons, but it was plain that he has a guilty conscience. There's little doubt in my mind that he was back of them, and he's afraid I'll go public with what he fears I've guessed."

"Oh, Peter." She felt a chill; Jesse's warning had impressed her deeply.

"Well, there's only today and tonight, and then I'll be out of his way for good." Peter frowned. "It was strange," he reflected. "Warick was hostile at first, made me feel my job might be in jeopardy—and then suddenly he was all smiles. In spite of the low opinion he's always had of me, he invited me home to dinner, and it wouldn't have been wise to refuse. That's why I didn't call till so late."

"Maybe he decided bribes would work better than threats."

"That's what I thought, but he didn't offer one. Perhaps he was buttering me up in preparation for a promotion that will depend on my cooperation."

"Peter . . . did you tell him you were going to the Island this offshift?"

"Yes. I hoped that might reassure him that I won't be around much before the election."

For some reason it made her uneasy. Though Jesse hadn't said anything about the possibility of tampering with the plane, she'd sensed that he was thinking it. But surely even the worst of the Meds weren't murderers. . . .

All the same, she was relieved when they arrived safely.

The dismantling and packing of the neurofeedback equipment and cryogenic bank took quite a while. Looking around the storeroom for padding materials, she came across the stock of imported candles used for the Ritual, and fit them in between the various wrapped items; there might be no way to make candles in the future. After everything was boxed and she had double-checked that the data back-ups were well protected, she started to clean up the leftover mess.

"Someone will eventually find this room," she pointed out. "The government will take over the Island, I suppose—" At Peter's look, she stopped, biting her tongue. Of course it was painful for him to think of the government seizing his beloved Lodge, even though he'd be long gone.

"Don't bother to pick up," he said. "It's not going to matter."

They carried the boxes down to the dock and loaded them into the plane, then went back to eat lunch. Most of the food had been removed earlier, but there were some imperishables left that no one had bothered to take. Neither of them had much appetite, but Peter could scarcely eat anything. His face was white. The emptiness of the Lodge so often filled with fun and laughter, the sunlight streaming into a deserted room, the cold fireplace . . . it was enough to depress anyone, Carla thought. Peter had been right; this was not pleasant.

"You'll need energy to fly," she said, looking at his untouched food.

"Take it with us. I can't get it down now, my head aches. I knew today would be hell, but I didn't think it was going to be this bad. Go back to the dock; I'll be along in a minute."

She complied. If he preferred to be alone with his bittersweet memories, he had a right to privacy. Hers had been dealt with the last time she'd been here, after Ian's funeral, when she had stood beside the fading fire with Jesse. Jesse, too, was making his last flight today, she remembered. He would perhaps fly over the Island once more before giving up his plane forever.

It was a long time before Peter joined her on the dock. She noticed as he approached that he seemed to be stumbling.

"Carla," he said. The hand that gripped hers was cold. "There's something I haven't told you. That I've known all along, but couldn't bear to tell anyone."

She waited, cold herself with a sense of deep foreboding.

"We can't let the government find the lab, Carla," he said. "Even though we've taken our records out, it's full of contraband. They would wonder where we got the infirmary equipment. They'd inform Fleet that we're criminals if they discovered it before the starship leaves orbit. Or they could trace it to the friends on Earth who smuggled it to us. Our offworld contacts would be arrested, would suffer for helping us—and those who know what we plan to do might be forced to reveal our destination."

"Oh, God. I never thought of that. But we can't prevent—" She broke off. Of course they could prevent it. There had long been a secret way to blow up the lab; that was common knowledge in the Group. It had been arranged years ago by a member with access to mining explosives. The blast would take the whole Lodge down. Peter had come here today not to close the Lodge, but to destroy it.

Carla put her arms around him, hugged him, and realized presently that she was holding him up. "Peter, it's okay," she whispered. "I know how much it will hurt. But think of what's ahead of us! Think of where we'll be tomorrow—the journey we've looked forward to so long." She was surprised to see him overcome to this extent. Painful though the act would be, he had always been so strong. . . .

To her horror, Peter collapsed at her feet. He was barely conscious.

She knelt beside him, feeling for a pulse. It was weak. This was not mere emotional distress; it was some kind of illness! But Peter was never ill. No one in the Group got sick; they could control their physiological responses well enough to prevent that. There were no infectious diseases on Undine anyway, and things like hidden heart problems were ruled out by the mandatory health checkups.

With her healer's senses, Carla probed Peter's body. She was not as adept at healing as Kira or Peter himself, but she'd had experience enough to know the basics. There was simply nothing wrong with him. It was as if he'd been drugged. . . .

Drugged. The dinner at the home of Dr. Warick, who was aware of his suspicion about the arsons. The wine, probably. It had to be that. He'd been given something with delayed action—something that would not affect him until late enough in the day not to endanger him while flying.

Warick didn't want to kill him. The aim was merely to keep him out of the way until after the election. But he couldn't stay semi-conscious as long as that . . . so a rescue must have been planned. He'd said he was going to the Island. They would send an air ambulance, keep him sick in the Hospital for as long as Warick chose.

Long enough for the starship to leave without him.

It would not wait for stragglers; that had been made plain. Anyone not at the spaceport by tomorrow noon when the last shuttle lifted would be left behind. Peter could not bear that! He couldn't endure abandonment on Undine even if it weren't that he'd be penniless and guilty of financial crimes which, if he was identified as the ringleader, might even lead to his execution.

And the Group probably couldn't survive without him, not on a raw new world where only the inspiration he could offer would keep them going. People with paranormal talents tended to be introverts. Ian had searched a long time before finding someone with both the gifts and the charisma required for leadership. Besides, Peter alone was qualified to provide the psychiatric help some individuals in the next generation—who, unlike their elders, wouldn't have been

selected for personal fitness to cope with emerging psi powers—might well need. Though this had not been openly discussed, Carla knew it worried him. The success of so small
a colony would depend on his ability to deal with potential
misusers of those powers.

She sat on the dock with his head in her lap, in despair
as to what to do. She could not revive him. If the drug had
affected only his body, she might have been able to, but it
had evidently been a psychiatric drug that crippled his brain
past the possibility of assisted self-healing. The best she
could do was ease the pain of his headache, which his own
mind was too debilitated to manage alone. If only she were
a pilot! She had handled the seaplane's controls occasionally when flying with Jesse, but she couldn't take off or land.
There was no way she could get Peter back to the city.

She dared not phone anyone. Warick would be expecting that. He would assume that whoever was with Peter
would phone for an ambulance. When that didn't happen,
he would have other phone messages to and from the Island monitored, guessing that Peter had caught on and had
told his friends. He might not be sure how soon the drug
would act. It was likely that he would wait, not send the
ambulance before trying to learn whether anyone knew—
wasn't it? If they came tonight, if Peter was taken to the
Hospital, there was no chance whatsoever of getting him
out by tomorrow morning.

But what chance was there anyway of reaching the spaceport? It was Peter's offshift; he wouldn't be missed at work
for days. No one in the Group would miss him in time to get
to the Island and back. Even Jesse wouldn't . . . Jesse would
be expecting them to come, waiting anxiously for them—
and he'd wait in vain.

For the first time it dawned on Carla that if she didn't
call someone, she too would be unable to reach the starship.
Jesse would go to the new world without her. They would
never see each other again.

He'd have to go, of course. Without a Captain, there

could be no new world. The Group would be taken to Liberty and be stuck there, destitute in a colony little better than Undine, for the rest of their lives. He wouldn't condemn them to that, hard though it would be for him to board the ship if she and Peter were not there. *Oh, Jesse,* she cried silently, *what shall I do? I can't bear not to go with you! I can't live if I'm left behind on this world! And there's no chance for Peter either if I just let time slip away—it's not as if I could get him aboard by giving up my own chance....*

Unless ... was it possible that Jesse would fly over? He might. He had planned to fly today, and might take a last look at the Island. He wouldn't land; seeing no reason to, he wouldn't let himself be tracked here even on this final day. But once he was overhead, telepathy might reach him. The distance wasn't much more than they'd been communicating over for days. It was a long shot, but he *might* come. . . .

She had a choice, then. Either she could call for help, ensuring her own freedom to get to the spaceport but eliminating Peter's, or she could wait with the very slim hope that Jesse might come unsummoned and save both of them. Carla bent her head in agony. It was an impossible choice. She couldn't give up Jesse! Yet she couldn't fail Peter, either—she couldn't face the idea of his waking in the Hospital and knowing that she'd betrayed him ... betrayed the Group. . . .

Oh, God. There *wasn't* a choice. To call might indeed betray the Group—for what if Warick gave Peter truth serum in order to find out how much he knew about the fires? That might have been his intent all along! And once he learned of their criminal activities, he'd have legal grounds to stop the emigration. So at all costs she must prevent rescue by the Meds until enough time had passed for the starship to get away.

If they came, could she hide Peter somehow? He wasn't suffering, though he was unable to talk and was apparently unaware of anything around him. She should move him off the dock anyway, or at least get blankets to cover him; it was going to get chilly as dusk came on. And there was the matter of destroying the lab. That had to be done before she left here, and if an ambulance came she wouldn't have opportunity. Besides, after the building exploded maybe they could hide in the ruins; maybe a rescue crew would assume they were dead and not search immediately. Carla eased Peter's head gently out of her lap and got to her feet, starting back along the dock toward the Lodge. She knew where the hot switch was. It would be safest to do it now, after gathering up whatever items they might need.

No, Carla! No, come back! She turned. It was as if he had shouted aloud. But he wasn't conscious enough for telepathy, at least he hadn't been. *I won't leave you for more than a few minutes,* she thought, not expecting him to respond.

Carla! You mustn't go! Get back down beside me! Suddenly she remembered the mind-pattern Peter had learned from Jesse—the altered state for enhanced telepathic communication. A drug had triggered it for Jesse, maybe even for Ian; perhaps that had happened to Peter, too. Especially since he'd already experienced it on dual. She turned, took several steps toward him, wondering if in his weakened condition he was afraid to be alone even briefly.

You don't understand! I've already set the timer . . . we should be airborne by now!

The blast threw her down flat. The dock rocked beneath her, making waves that splashed over its edge rail. Carla clutched Peter's arm while behind them, what had been Maclairn Lodge collapsed and erupted into a fountain of smoke and flame.

62

JESSE WASN'T FREE to fly until late afternoon. There had been all kinds of little details to attend to, plans to confirm with Kira, instructions to go over with his prospective crew and hijacking team. He was less hesitant about face-to-face contacts now that there wasn't time left for the authorities tracking him to question his movements. He might even have risked a meeting with Peter, had he not known that Peter and Carla had gone to the Island. In addition, he'd had to visit the Fleet office once more to make sure that the starship really was expected to arrive tomorrow. A change in schedule after the passengers were at the spaceport would be disastrous.

So it was almost sunset by the time he reached his mooring, and it was, he knew, foolish to fly at all. But it was the last time—probably the last time in his life, except for orbit-to-ground trips. And certainly his last look at the sea. Undine's huge, brilliant moon would be full this evening. He could not resist the chance for one final flight.

He did not intend to go as far as the Island. It would be dark by the time he got there, and he couldn't see much of it by moonlight. He wanted to remember it as a green jewel set in the blue expanse of ocean, rimmed with white shore . . . the rocky shore where he and Carla had walked and swum and once even made love. . . .

Carla. They would be together after tonight! They would never again be separated as they'd been these past weeks, when only their minds had been able to meet. Not that it wasn't wonderful that they *could* meet and converse while apart, not that they wouldn't still do it sometimes . . . he could almost hear her speaking to him now. Was she back in the city, or would Peter's plane, returning, pass his in the air? Almost without knowing it, he had set a course for the Island after all, though he'd be turning back long before he reached it. He must go to the park in time for Nathan and Liz's midnight wedding, be among the first to be shuttled to the spaceport. He knew he would not feel safe until he was within its boundaries. Nor would the others until they saw him there—after all, they couldn't get to a new world without him, and if some emergency should delay him at the last minute . . .

He should not be in the air even now. It was tempting

fate. As the sun slid below the horizon Jesse banked and turned, heading the plane back to the city.

Almost immediately, his tension grew. Something was wrong. He couldn't define what was bothering him, but it was more than distress at the thought that within a few minutes he would have to land for the last time and walk away from the plane that had brought him so much joy. Nerves, he thought with chagrin. Awe of the tremendous responsibility he was about to assume, mingled with the excitement of its being imminent. Did he, underneath, dread stealing the starship? Were his years of loyalty to Fleet so ingrained in him as that?

The closer he got to the city, the more agitated Jesse became. He longed to be going in the opposite direction. But that was crazy! Yes, he had been happy on the Island, but that was hardly cause to shrink from the return to space he was looking forward to. That Peter had dreamed of so long, and relied on him for . . . he could almost hear Peter saying, *Jesse, Jesse, you've got to help us, we can't get there without you . . . perhaps no one can get there. . . .* And Carla, too, calling out to him—*Jesse! You're the only hope we have. . . .* Well, he was on his way. Why did he imagine they'd beg for his help? They knew everything was set for tomorrow; the uncertainty, the risk of discovery, was almost over. He was fully committed to becoming their Captain. They knew they could trust him, as Ian had.

Ian's face suddenly loomed before him. *Jesse, listen! Listen to Peter, to Carla. . . . Go to Carla. . . .* Jesse shook himself back to reality. This would not do. He must not slide into some altered state of consciousness, dreaming of Ian, while he was flying a plane. It would be worse than disastrous for him to go down in it the night before he was due to lead the Group offworld. What had come over him? His growing paranormal sensitivity had never intruded on daily life before. He had, in fact, been assured that he was not the type in whom it could overwhelm practical matters.

He had veered off course; he could hardly see straight.

The image of Ian filled his vision. *Listen! Don't shut them out . . . they need you . . . they are trying to reach you!* Peter, too, seemed in the plane with him, as close as he had been while on dual when they'd shared the memory of drug-enhanced telepathy. Peter, normally so strong, was again the weaker partner—he must help him, for no one else could. . . . Then Carla called out to him again, and Jesse, instinctively, switched on the autopilot just in time to prevent falling into a dive. *Jesse, I love you, come to me, come now, or we'll be forever apart. . . .*

This was insane. More even than he had in the Hospital, Jesse doubted the clarity of his own mind. It was natural enough to be nervous in advance of the coming events— natural, he supposed, for his unconscious mind to suggest presence of the people he loved and knew were counting on him. It was not natural for apprehension about tomorrow to interfere with his control of a plane. He wouldn't have lasted long in Fleet if he'd been susceptible to that sort of thing, nor would he be much good as Captain if he'd gained paranormal talents at the cost of his technical skills.

He struggled to keep a firm hold on himself. It was dusk now; the plane was flying level on autopilot, but soon he would be close enough to the city to start watching for air traffic. A sense of impending doom hung over him. He should land quickly; that was the only safe course—and yet he still wanted to turn around and head back toward the Island. To do that would take him away from Carla. It didn't make sense.

Jesse! Please, oh please, Jesse—I can't bear to lose you, I want so much to go with you to the new world. . . . It was as clear as if she were outside his apartment, as if he were not imagining it at all.

Carla? Where are you?

We're on the Island . . . Peter and I are on the Island . . . Peter can't fly. . . .

Was it possible that this could be real?

All reason told Jesse it couldn't be. If they were on the

Island, they were much too far away to reach him telepathically even if he were in the state for enhanced reception—and surely he was not. He had struggled to stay in normal consciousness. The very fact that he was thinking of them as on the Island proved that the voices came from his own unconscious mind.

And yet, it didn't feel like hallucination. It felt like true communication.

He would be a fool to listen to it. They were probably safe in the city by now, and would worry if they tried to contact him and failed. If he was late getting to the park tonight they would surely worry, yet he couldn't get to the Island and back before the wedding. Furthermore, he was still being tracked. If he went there now, he'd be in the air so late that to be flying for practice would look suspicious. For all he knew, there could be a programmed alert that would trigger his arrest.

Besides, he hadn't taken time to get the plane recharged tonight. He hadn't expected to go far enough to need a full charge. On the way back he would have to put in to the recharging station on Verge Island, which might not be open until morning. If it wasn't, he'd be unable to reach the spaceport much before the noon deadline.

Jesse, Jesse, we need you . . . we need you on the Island. If you don't come the plan may fail. . . . Peter this time, with an intensity that before, had come only with altered consciousness. How could Peter have mastered the new mind-pattern after just one dual session, despite never having experienced it while drugged? Was he in the Lodge, using feedback? Jesse wondered.

Not in the Lodge. The Lodge is gone, it burned. . . .

Startled, Jesse became aware of incongruity. The Lodge burned? Such an idea as that would never have arisen from his own unconscious. It went against all his emotion about Undine, all the memories he wished to carry away with him. If he was thinking the Lodge had burned down, the concept must have come to him from somewhere else.

Peter and Carla had gone to the Island today. He could not be sure they had returned. What if they were in some kind of trouble? They'd have phoned for help, surely—there were many Group members with planes. If necessary, now that concealing their friendship with him no longer mattered, they could even have phoned *him*. They wouldn't need to use telepathy. Yet . . . how would he feel if they didn't show up at the park, and he'd suspected trouble without acting? How would he feel for the rest of his life if they missed the ship?

Always before he had depended on rationality. He could not function in daily life, let alone as a Captain, without it—and rationality told him that to go to the Island tonight would jeopardize everything the Group had worked for, perhaps even its very existence. If anything were to prevent his getting aboard the starship, it would mean the end of their hopes. And yet . . . what did the Group stand for, if not belief in the larger mind, the aspects of mind that weren't based on reason? What had he gained, if not trust in the part of him that was more than reason could explain?

Jesse . . . dearest Jesse . . . I love you—if you can't come to me, remember always that I love you. . . . It was Carla's mind touching his, as he had experienced it so many times when they'd shared not only their minds, but their bodies. To doubt it would be to deny the powers that the Group had awakened in him. Either his inner knowledge was true and important, or nothing was. He could not reject it, whatever the consequences might be.

Jesse turned the plane again, and headed back out to sea.

63

LONG BEFORE HE reached the Island Jesse saw its dull red glow, a beacon in the moonlight-silvered expanse of water. When he descended to circle, all that remained were stone ruins. The crises of my life are marked by fire, he thought as he touched down . . . the hearthfire where he'd first made love to Carla . . . the Ritual torch . . . the burning safe house . . . and now the embers of the Lodge. . . .

The fire had spread to the cottages, consuming them, and the Island's trees, too, had burned. The tide was low, and the beach shone white in the moonlight. It had been a buffer between the flames and the dock on which Carla and Peter were huddled together, shivering in the chill night air of autumn.

He had been in full contact with them for several minutes, since approaching within range of conversational telepathy, and already knew the basic facts of what had happened. As he taxied to the dock, Carla ran to meet him. Embracing her, sharing the despair and terror she had felt when she'd feared he would not come, Jesse was horrified at the knowledge of how close he'd been to losing her. To denying all that he had learned in the Group for the sake of what outsiders viewed as sanity. He held her close, wanting not to think of anything beyond.

But the time had come to be practical. They were not out of trouble yet. All three of them would miss the ship— the plan might even be exposed—unless he kept his head.

Peter sat propped against a piling; he could not stand, nor could he communicate telepathically on mundane matters. He was vaguely conscious of what went on; he had felt pain while watching the Lodge burn, agony when he realized that if taken to the Hospital he might be forced to reveal the Group's secrets. But he was very weak. His drugged mind was in a haze; for him to take part in decisions would be impossible. There was no knowing how soon whatever he'd been given would wear off.

"The worst of it is that I haven't enough of a charge to fly back," Jesse said. "We'll have to detour to Verge Island and probably wait there till morning. It doesn't leave us much time."

"Peter's plane is charged," said Carla, "and we've got to

use it in any case because of the boxes. There's not room for them in yours."

He had not thought about that. Peter's was a six-place plane, while his had only four seats—it could not hold three people along with the irreplaceable boxes of equipment. He supposed he could fly Peter's plane, which was otherwise similar to his own. Still, considering what he was going to have to do with it . . .

"The only trouble," Carla went on, "is that we've missed the connection with the trucker Peter bribed. Do you know how to get in touch with him?"

"Even if I did, he probably wouldn't be available on short notice. Anyway, we can't land Peter's plane in the city, Carla. They will track it and be waiting to meet it."

"Oh, God. I suppose they will." All planes had identifiable transponders; they weren't routinely monitored, but Warick would certainly have Peter's watched. "How are we going to get past them?"

"I see just one solution," Jesse said. "We've got to fly directly to the spaceport."

"But we can't land there either—there's no water."

"We can land. There won't be much left of the floats afterward, but Peter's not going to be using the plane again, after all."

"Put a floatplane down on dry land?"

"According to my flight manual it's been done on Earth. It would be less risky on grass or soft ground than on concrete, but we don't have a choice." He didn't look forward to doing it in a plane he had never handled before, carrying a heavier load than he was used to. But it would be better to crash than to let the starship depart without them.

Carla nodded. "We'd better get going, then."

"Not yet, not unless we hear an air ambulance coming. The last thing we want is to attract attention to the spaceport before all our people have gotten there. So we mustn't arrive before dawn."

"I suppose we should try to sleep for a few hours."

"In a while, maybe." Jesse pondered the thought that had just struck him. "There's another problem. Warick will send a crew to see what's happened here when we take off, since that's a move he won't be expecting from Peter—and official planes are much faster than ours. They'll find my plane moored at the dock while we're still airborne."

"Maybe they'll decide you flew past and saw the fire, and rescued him without having come on purpose."

"No, they won't. I'd have no reason to pass by late at night, and besides, why would I rescue him in his plane instead of my own? In any case, they'll realize that I'm with him. If they suspect conspiracy between us it will be too late to matter. But they may not; they may simply assume I was stalking him. They still believe I'm mentally ill and potentially violent. They may think he tried to fly and I took over when I found him weakened—that I may kill him because I hate him for drugging me in the Hospital."

"Well, let them think that. We'll be gone before they can do anything about it."

"They can force our plane down, Carla. Maybe hoping to save him from me—or maybe not. If Warick is planning to run for office, Peter's potentially a long-term threat. He might welcome a chance to eliminate him permanently and blame it on a mental patient."

"Oh, Jesse. Would he murder us, really?"

"I was right in fearing that he'd try something. I can't be sure he'll stop with drugging; he won't know you're aboard, after all. But for them to pick us up at sea would be just as bad—he'd have us in custody before the starship leaves orbit, and he'd surely use truth serum on me this time, even if not on Peter."

He felt Carla's surge of horrified dismay. "God help us," she whispered. "They'd uncover everything, even the facts about Zeb's death."

"I wouldn't let them pick me up," Jesse declared, "or Peter, either." He would sink the plane after getting Carla out, not to avoid permanent imprisonment in the psych ward, though he didn't believe he could face that a second time, but for the sake of the others. The ship would be recalled and three hundred people would be convicted of crimes— financial if not their earlier ones—if either he or Peter were given truth serum. That must not happen. The Group must escape to Liberty, even if he could not take them to a new world.

Carla clutched his hand with icy fingers, needing to hear no verbal elaboration. In a small voice she said, "They wouldn't need to find your plane. The tracking system already shows you're on the Island."

"An ambulance would be here by now if they were monitoring me in real time. I'm not a high priority case; they won't check routine tracking data before morning unless they have some reason to suspect that I'm with Peter."

"So if we go in your plane, we'll be safe? But the neurofeedback equipment . . . the cryogenic bank—"

"Are too important to give up. Besides, mine would have to be charged. I have a better idea. Let's cut the tracking chip out of me and throw it into the ruins to make them think I died in the explosion."

"How can we? We don't have a knife—I don't think we can salvage anything that used to be in the infirmary."

"I've got one." Jesse pulled a small well-wrapped blade from his pocket.

"What do you carry that for?" Carla asked, mystified. "Wherever did you get it?"

"Kira gave it to me," he replied shortly. This was not the time to point out that you couldn't hijack a ship without displaying a weapon of some kind, even if you didn't intend to kill anybody. This morning Kira had provided surgical scalpels from the healing house for the members of the take-over team; she was carrying one herself.

"It's not sterile," Carla noted, "but Kira can check tomorrow to make sure there's no infection. You're sure you want me to do this?"

"I'll be glad to be rid of the damned tracking device just as a matter of principle," Jesse said. He removed his shirt and lay prone on the dock while Carla probed with her healer's sense. The chip was small but there was a faint scar to guide her to its exact position between his shoulder blades; she had seen it in bed just after his release from the Hospital. She now used a flashlight from the plane to locate it, and without flinching, thrust the scalpel into his flesh, of necessity cutting out more than the tiny chip itself. *It won't hurt unless you let it*, he remembered—Kira had told him that, the night Peter had cut his arm, and it was true. The mind-pattern for pain control came easily to him now. He was even able to control his own bleeding.

Carla stayed down beside him, cuddling against him, as she healed the wound. After a few minutes he turned onto his back and gazed at the stars. With her free hand Carla reached out to Peter, so that the three of them were in contact, sharing a deep, semi-conscious awareness of all that was behind them, all that lay ahead.

They tried not to look at the desolation of the smoldering Island. Yet the emotions it stirred were too fresh to be shut out. Jesse knew that inside, Peter was mourning, would continue to mourn until he reached a new world. *It's all right, Peter,* he declared silently, slipping into the mind-pattern they'd entered during their last time on dual. *Ian would say it's fitting for it to end in fire ... fire is our symbol, isn't it? First the hearthfire within the Lodge, lighting the flame of the torch—and then spreading ... spreading until our old life is consumed and we go on, carrying that flame into a better one....*

Yes. He did say something like that, when he came to tell me I should reach out to you.... It was as before: no words were formed, yet only with words could the projected concepts be registered in memory.

Was he with you, too?

Not literally, not as a ghost. Departed spirits, if they exist, surely wouldn't stick around one small planet when there's a whole universe accessible! The notion that they would is the flaw in legends of ghosts on Earth.

How did we see him, then? It was more than remembering.

Everyone's unconscious mind contains some image, some concrete symbol, that emerges as a source of deep wisdom— wisdom that comes from beyond the limits set by space or time. In my mind, and I think in yours, it takes Ian's form.

And from now on I'll trust it, Jesse thought. "Whatever doubts I may have had about the validity of what we're doing, they're gone," he told Carla. "Before tonight I wanted a new colony; I knew we had to escape from Undine. But for us to give up all the concrete benefits of civilization, for ourselves and for generations to come—I was willing, yet I didn't see what more than freedom we stand to gain. Now—"

"There's so much, so much beyond what most of us guessed, that we have to learn," she agreed. "Telepathy over all those miles . . . and if that's possible, there must be other powers we've only begun to control. If our kids grow up in a world that fosters such powers, who knows what they'll be able to do?"

We're just beginning, came Peter's wordless thought. *And you, Jesse—you are the proof Ian and I always hoped for. If you, an outsider without natural paranormal gifts, have begun to tap these powers, then someday they can be attained by many . . . by our children and by the whole culture we establish. . . .* He drifted off into unconsciousness, letting go of all worry about the coming day.

With Carla's hand warm in his, Jesse gazed up into star-studded darkness. "My sister and her friends had it wrong," he mused. "They were always talking about some mythical past age, Atlantis or something, claiming civilization had fallen instead of risen. That was what I never could buy. Human abilities grow, they don't decline. I couldn't see why if the paranormal was real, they'd be looking back instead of ahead."

"Well, that's a universal attitude," Carla said, "expressed in the Garden of Eden myth, too. People have always sensed the existence of advanced human abilities, and a few have even gained paranormal ones. But they're frightening, as you know, and to think of their use as uncharted territory is even more scary than to imagine that something lost is merely being regained. A metaphorical tie with the past is comforting."

"She—my sister—claimed to *remember*," Jesse recalled. "She said she could remember past lives. Of course I thought that was crazy. But could the so-called memories really have come from her unconscious mind, like Ian's precognition in reverse, maybe?"

"Probably. That's one of the mysteries for which we don't have a full answer. We don't favor the reincarnation idea, at least not in the sense of returning to Earth, because as Peter just told you, it's unbelievable that if souls survive death they're tied to one particular planet. I mean, if you died, Jesse, would you be reincarnated on Earth where you were born, or on Undine, or Maclairn—or somewhere else you've never been in this life?"

"Wherever you were, I hope. But otherwise, I'd prefer someplace new."

"Exactly. What are the odds that a person would have successive lives in the same or related societies—especially if there are nonhuman civilizations in solar systems we haven't discovered? To say biological form determines spiritual destiny is a contradiction in terms. Yet people like your sister do sometimes have knowledge of the past that they couldn't have gotten through normal channels. We suspect it's unconscious telepathy, like so much else that orthodox science can't explain. It would have to be some kind of ESP anyway, after all, since transmission of such data obviously isn't physical. And psi communication across time with your former self is a lot less likely than contact with another person."

"But why does it seem like memory if it happened to someone else?" Jesse wondered.

"Lots of things are interpreted by the conscious mind as

memory, even childhood events that never happened at all—ask Peter sometime. He encounters that often with his patients. And on Earth in different eras, it's been common to remember talking with the gods or being abducted by aliens. Those aren't mere imaginings, they're metaphors from the collective unconscious. The human mind actually perceives them as memory; the brain hasn't any other way of processing them."

"Greg once told me that the collective unconscious doesn't extend from world to world. That the metaphors meaningful on Earth don't emerge here. Does that mean nobody born in this colony has such memories?"

"Not of past lives. That in itself is evidence against a simplistic form of reincarnation, because we in the Group do experiment with the kinds of altered states in which people on Earth perceive them." Carla hesitated. "We have other metaphorical perceptions, but maybe this isn't the time for me to describe them to you."

No, it certainly wasn't, Jesse thought. He still was uneasy about altered states unlike those he'd been taught to deal with, and Carla knew it. "Metaphorical perceptions" was, he suspected, a euphemism for "hallucinations." He was aware that much that went on in the Group had been kept from him. In the years ahead on the new world he would have to face up to whatever he'd been deemed unready for; but right now, getting there—managing as Captain to get everyone there—was more than enough to worry about.

Still . . . he had seen Ian tonight, and it had seemed as real as if Ian were actually present. And if that hadn't happened, he might not have come to the Island. . . .

The stars dissolved into the dark and for an hour or two, Jesse slept. When he woke the moon was near the horizon. His wound fully healed, he took the bloodstained cloth containing the microchip to the Lodge ruins and threw it into the deepest hole he could see. Tomorrow the Meds would search for his body, but by then it wouldn't matter that they'd fail to find it.

With Carla's help he got Peter into the copilot's seat, where he could keep an eye on his condition during flight. Carla, after helping to untie the mooring lines, squeezed into one of the back seats among the boxes. Without further discussion, Jesse powered up the plane and taxied out into the bay for takeoff. His last sight of the place showed him the blue seaplane that was his no longer, floating calmly in the moonlight; at least he would be spared the ordeal of crumpling its floats in a crash landing. As they rose above the Island, he did not look back.

After moonset, he flew on in the dark, on autopilot in both the literal and the figurative sense. He was past the point of decision, now. What was coming would come. He felt good about it.

It was dawn by the time they reached the city. As he flew over the shoreline, he could see that there was indeed an ambulance parked at the pier near which Peter's plane was normally moored. The men standing next to it looked up, staring, as the plane headed inland. "Carla, check the park and the road past it!" Jesse said. "Make sure nobody's still there." Within moments he was over the park, and she reported that it was deserted. Everyone who belonged at the spaceport must have reached it by now.

His first approach was too high. At the last moment he pulled up to go around again, and Peter was jolted into sudden awareness. The drug was wearing off. "Where are we?" he asked groggily, and then, seeing the ground beyond the window, he yelled. "God, Jesse! We're too low! We're over land!"

"I know," Jesse said. "Close your eyes, Peter. Pretend you're still dreaming." *And for God's sake don't touch the controls!* he added silently.

The ground rushed up to meet them. Perhaps, Jesse thought, it was just as well that he'd never landed a lightplane with wheels—he wouldn't miss the feel of a runway under them. He hauled back on the yoke, raising the nose just in time. The plane hit the concrete hard, bounced, and then sank with a loud crunch as its floats folded beneath it. But it was intact. Its passengers and cargo were intact. And they were now forever free of the Meds' authority.

64

MANY SHUTTLE TRIPS were needed to get more than three hundred passengers aboard the starship. Jesse, as the only one among them who had previously experienced the effects of liftoff and of weightlessness, had told those he'd personally talked to what to expect, and the word had been passed around. Spacesickness was not a problem since all members of the Group knew how to control physical reactions. The Fleet officers in charge of boarding were a bit surprised that the preventative shots offered were uniformly turned down, and even more surprised that there proved to be no need for sick bags. Everyone was in an exuberant mood. Even Peter, who rested for a while under Kira's healing care while his head cleared and therefore waited for the last departure, was fully enough recovered to enjoy the flight.

Jesse went aloft in the first shuttle to lift after his arrival at the spaceport, wanting as much time as possible to inspect the starship. *Mayflower XI* normally carried more passengers than it now held, so the quarters into which the Group settled were not cramped. He and Carla chose a cabin large enough to accommodate staff meetings after he became Captain. The dining hall would be a tight fit, since the ship's original design had assumed passengers would eat in shifts during the relatively short time they weren't in stasis, but the committee decided that the advantages of community gatherings would be worth some crowding during meals.

The crew's mess was separate, and had its own galley— unlike the officers of liners, those of colonizers did not socialize with passengers at dinner. Thus Jesse knew that once the ship left orbit, the entire crew, except for the watch officer on the bridge, would be together in one place at mealtime. It was not a large crew. The operation of the starship was fully automated; the crew, apart from the Captain and medical officer, had little to do except in emergencies. The main difference between a freighter and a passenger ship was redundancy for extra safety.

Of course, had this been a large colonizer officially intended to establish the first colony on an unopened world, there would have been staff officers trained in the skills needed for such an undertaking. The ship would have remained in orbit while they assisted the colonists in the building of their settlement. But *Mayflower XI* had been chartered merely to provide transportation to the existing colony on Liberty. The trip was, from the crew's standpoint, a mere milk run.

Jesse became familiar with the ship's layout by introducing himself as a retired Captain to the first officer he encountered. A message soon came from Captain Quinn, saying that he would be pleased to personally escort Captain Sanders on a courtesy tour of the sections normally off-limits to passengers. Jesse accepted thankfully, feeling a good deal of chagrin over the fact that he was about to betray the man's hospitality. Quinn was friendly; before long Jesse realized that he was as bored with routine trips as he himself had been, and was happy at the prospect of having someone new to talk to along on this one.

After visiting the various work areas of the ship, they paused before a sealed hatch. "What's in there?" Jesse asked.

"A relic of the past," Quinn replied. "That's the companionway to the stasis deck left over from when this ship was young, before the hyperdrive was installed. It was incredible what colonists were willing to undergo in those days— think of the courage it must have taken to climb into those boxes and be rendered unconscious, with no guarantee that they'd ever wake up. We don't give our predecessors enough credit. It's too bad that Fleet has so little regard for historical preservation. The ship's to be decommissioned after this run, and I don't suppose they'll save it as a museum even though it's the last one in existence."

Jesse nodded, but did not comment. "The units are still in prime condition," Quinn went on. "The AI has maintained them automatically. Do you want to look them over?"

"Well," said Jesse, "I saw some years ago in training, and I've seen similar units on Undine."

"Oh, yes," Quinn reflected. "I've heard they preserve dead bodies in stasis there, that the population views it as immortality. If so, I'm surprised that your people are willing to give it up."

"We're eager to leave stasis behind us," Jesse replied. "It's more or less the root of our disagreement with Undine's government—we don't think of immortality that way."

"That's understandable. I can see how it might lead to religious objections. You'll be better off on Liberty. They're tolerant even of oddball religions there. That is—I didn't mean—" Quinn reddened visibly. Jesse sympathized with him; it was evident that he was wondering how a former Fleet officer happened to have hooked up with a local cult called Stewards of the Flame that was emigrating to escape religious persecution. Deciding this wasn't a safe line of speculation, he moved on past the entrance to the stasis deck and hurried to change the subject.

"I'd like to see the bridge," he said. "That is, when we've left orbit and you have time on your hands before the jump. Incidentally, when is the jump scheduled?"

"Midnight, local time, which is what we'll be running on as long as we're in normal space. You'll be welcome on the bridge anytime after we break orbit. I'll send an aide to escort you—would you like to eat dinner with us? My crew and I would enjoy hearing about your travels."

Jesse agreed, inwardly dismayed at the shortness of the time between dinner and midnight. Quinn had evidently calculated the planned jump ahead of time and was allowing barely more than the minimum safe distance from the planet before going into hyperdrive. So they'd get just one chance to overpower the crew. What was worse, they wouldn't be as far from Undine as he had hoped when they sent the Fleet officers back in the shuttle. It would be dangerous to keep them onboard after the takeover—he was counting on the shock factor to make them leave. Yet he would have only a few hours to study the charts and plot a new course before they'd be back in the armed freighter.

After alerting Peter, who by this time had completely recovered his normal vitality and was ready to brief the hijack team, Jesse went to his cabin. Despite having slept little the night before, he was too tense to rest even with the help of Carla's soothing touch and the skills he'd been taught for quieting his mind. In due course a young officer knocked. "Captain Quinn presents his compliments, and asks if you'd like to visit the bridge now, sir," she said.

Jesse accompanied her, focusing on control of his heart rate. After a full and careful inspection of the bridge, hoping that his questions hadn't seemed overly naive on the part of an experienced Captain, he went with Captain Quinn to the crew mess, leaving the woman officer on watch. The rest of the crew was already there. Having glanced at the manifest on the bridge, Jesse knew by counting that all hands were present. Dinner was served informally; once it was on the table, no one remained in the galley. Jesse toyed with his food, having little appetite for it.

He did not have to wait long. Conversation had barely started when the passageway hatch slid open and Peter burst in, accompanied by Greg and Kwame, who, being among Jesse's oldest friends, he had chosen for the role. All three carried bared knives. Kwame walked quickly past the table to guard the galley entrance against attempts at escape.

Jesse rose, pulling out his own knife, and addressed Quinn. "I'm sorry," he said, "but you see, we've never had any intention of going to Liberty. There's nothing you can do to change our minds—there are more of us, armed, in the passageway."

Quinn was momentarily silenced by astonishment. Overcoming it, he tried logic. "This is insane," he said. "Armed or not, you can't force us to alter course, and even if you could, no world would accept you. If you try to land you'll be boarded in orbit and taken directly to a penal colony, all of you."

"I suppose so," agreed Jesse, "except that where we're going, there won't be anybody on hand to welcome us."

"If you think we can reach an unopened world, let alone survive there—"

"Don't worry about your survival—*you* are not going anywhere except back to Undine. Fleet will arrange passage for you from there, I'm sure."

Peter said, "Now if you'll all come along to the shuttle bay, you'll be perfectly safe. All we want is for you to leave us."

Nobody moved. Quinn turned to Jesse and said incredulously, "Do you mean to say you are going to attempt a jump yourself, with an untrained crew?"

"I've had plenty of experience jumping freighters, and this ship is roughly the same class. The AI will control it anyway—as you know, the crew's needed only to handle emergencies. We're gambling on not having one."

"The ship's not fully stocked with consumables," an officer warned. "Just a reasonable safety margin over what's needed to get your party to Liberty."

"That has no bearing on the length of the jump we can make," Jesse said. "I'm not planning to hang around long in normal space." Inwardly he was dismayed. It did increase the need for precision in his jump calculation—and besides, where else had Fleet cut corners for what was meant to be *Mayflower XI*'s final run?

"You're a decent man," Quinn protested, "and your people don't strike me as violent. Those knives are for show. You won't use them."

Without comment, Peter moved forward and slashed the nearest officer's arm from elbow to wrist, allowing the blood to flow freely. Greg, simultaneously, grabbed Quinn and gripped him, holding a knife to his throat. "The sooner you get to the shuttle bay, the sooner we can let a medical officer treat that wound," Jesse said. "We won't hurt anyone else unless we have to—but we do outnumber you, after all. You don't have much choice. A ship due for decommissioning isn't worth the risk of your lives."

This being true, the subdued crew proceeded to the shuttle bay, herded by more knife-bearing Group members. The wounded officer kept looking at his arm, surprised that it didn't seem to be bleeding as much as it had at first. He showed no sign of being in great pain. But Greg's knife remained at Quinn's throat, and the others weren't willing to chance what they assumed he might do with it. They boarded the designated shuttle without resisting.

Jesse and Greg—along with Captain Quinn, still at knifepoint—were the last aboard. "Okay," Jesse said. "Get on the comm and order your watch officer down here."

"She won't desert the bridge—there are standing orders not to leave it unattended."

"She will if she doesn't want to see her Captain's throat cut. The shuttle's comm has video capability, doesn't it?"

"If she sees what's happening here, she'll report it to Fleet—there's a freighter still orbiting Undine. It's armed, and it will reach you before you're far enough out to jump."

Jesse knew this all too well. No report would go out from *Mayflower XI*, however. Because there'd been no reason for the crew to expect communication before approaching Liberty, the comm room had been left unmanned during the meal, set to divert any incoming signals to the bridge. "We disabled the long-range transmitters while you were at dinner," he said. "If you think I'm bluffing, try them and see."

Quinn had no reason not to do so; he hoped it was indeed a bluff. He talked to the watch officer. Presently she arrived at the shuttle, white-faced, confessing as she boarded that her attempt to reach Undine's spaceport had not been acknowledged. At the back of Jesse's mind something nagged at him, some sense of an exchange between this woman and Quinn. But he hadn't time to figure out what it was.

Backing toward the hatch, he announced, "You have five minutes to seal your locks. The air will then be evacuated from the bay, and the outer doors will be opened. This area will not be repressurized. I suggest that you depart before we jump—I assume you know what will happen to the shuttle if you fail to get clear."

"We'll leave," Quinn agreed, "but only to report you from space. When we do, you'll be pursued."

"We've left the shuttle just enough transmission capability to send an SOS from low orbit," Jesse informed him. "No long-range voice communication. You won't be able to tell Fleet about us until you're close enough to the freighter to match with it. By then, we'll be in hyperspace."

"No, you won't. You won't be able to jump. Think twice, Sanders—you may be retired, but your oath to Fleet is still in force and commandeering a ship is mutiny. Back off now and you might get by with prison. If you go through with it, you'll be executed. Don't be a fool—" He broke off, staring at Kira, who had just appeared at the hatch. Clearly he had not expected to see a grandmotherly hijacker.

"You were right about one thing," Jesse said. "We never intended to harm you. Dr. Tarinov, will you do something about this officer's arm?"

Kira stepped forward and took hold of the man's arm, which under Peter's control had stopped bleeding entirely. She pressed the wound closed. "Hold onto it," she told him. "I can't stay with you till it's healed, but I've gotten it started. You will be okay in a few minutes if you don't panic."

Jesse and the others left the shuttle, watching with relief as behind them, its hatch closed. They hurried out of the bay and after the promised five minutes, depressurized it.

By the time Jesse reached the bridge, the shuttle was gone.

65

IN EXULTATION, JESSE and Peter hugged each other. "We
did it!" Peter exclaimed. "All the time I've believed we could,
it was theory. I know you looked at it from the practical
standpoint, Jess, and you thought it would work. But it never
felt *real*—"

"It's not real until we've jumped," Jesse said. "Better
save the celebration." He pushed on the hatch to the bridge,
finding that it did not slide easily. Strange, it had seemed
to move with a touch when he'd visited with Quinn this
morning. He pushed harder—and then stood back in dismay. "God," he said. "It's locked."

"Locked?" Peter pushed too, with no more success.

"The watch officer must have set it to seal when she
left," Jesse said. "That's why Quinn was so sure we couldn't
jump." Such a possibility hadn't occurred to him. Crew compartments on freighters didn't lock. But, he now realized,
on a passenger ship there would be a way to keep unauthorized people out of the bridge.

Peter, grasping the seriousness of the situation, drew
breath. "There's a keypad," he observed. "We'll never crack
the code! Can we find a laser and cut our way in?"

"Not without risking fatal damage to the control console."

"Jesse—are we defeated after all? By *this*?"

"Maybe not. There's probably a voice lock, too, for faster
access. If so, it's computer-controlled. There might even be
a direct computer override—the designers' intent was to keep
casual meddlers out, not security experts."

Peter nodded. "I'll get Carla."

The computer room was separate from the bridge, and
unlocked; the officer in charge had simply logged off when
he went to dinner. Carla, with long hacking experience, had
anticipated that finding a usable password would be time-
consuming but not impossible; in advance, she had questioned Jesse at length about terms likely to be used as

backdoor passwords by Fleet programmers. Again, they wouldn't have been trying to secure against experts. There wasn't anything worth an expert's effort aboard a colonizer, and it had never been thought that emigrants would attempt to take it over. "Don't worry," she told Jesse calmly. "I'll get in sooner or later."

"It had better be sooner," Jesse warned. "We have only the time it will take that shuttle to reach Undine's orbit and send the freighter in pursuit. That's just a matter of hours—and I need time to calculate the jump after I see the charts."

"How can they overtake us?" Peter protested. "Surely a freighter's not faster than a colonizer."

"It's faster than this one—we're an old, obsolete ship, remember. When the hyperdrive was installed the main drive wasn't replaced. Besides," Jesse added grimly, "we're not cruising at top speed, and I can't do anything about that until I'm on the bridge."

As Carla turned to her task, Peter took Jesse aside. "What Captain Quinn said about mutiny—was that true?"

"Yes," Jesse admitted. "If the League didn't have a harsh law, a lot of the small explorer ships would turn to smuggling instead of coming back to report rich finds."

"You've known all along that they'd execute you if they caught you?"

"Of course. Carla knows, too—she sensed it from my mind when you first proposed hijacking. That's why she balked initially."

"She knows your life depends directly on her finding a password and figuring out how to override the lock within the next few hours."

"I wish to God she didn't. It will make it hard on her if she fails."

"Jess . . . I've been—insensitive. Oblivious to everything but the vision, the ideal Ian and I had of a world that could be as we wanted it to be. That overrode everything, all the demands I made of the others, what I persuaded them to give up ... and you, Jess, even your life, when it's turned out that I owe you mine—"

"You don't owe me anything. You pulled me out of the black hole I'd sunk into, showed me what I could be. As for last night, if I hadn't had to use psi in a crisis I might never have seen why what we're doing is more than a matter of gaining our own freedom." Reflectively, Jesse went on, "Kira told me long ago—she said that to become all we can be, we must risk being totally destroyed. I didn't fully understand, then. Now I know that the vision's more important than anything we may lose by reaching for it."

"But vision's not enough. We need practical good sense, like yours."

"Which has let us down at the moment," Jesse said grimly. "I'm the one who should have foreseen a lock on the bridge. It was pure negligence on my part not to."

"Was it? If you had, we might not have attempted to take over," Peter argued. "We might never have left Undine. So maybe it was fate that kept you from it—"

"Or Ian's ghostly influence," Jesse said, trying to smile.

"Don't make light of it," urged Peter. "I know you don't share my confidence in fate, but Ian knew *something*. When he was dying, he knew something he wouldn't tell me. I've felt since then that he may have planted it deep in my mind—"

"Well, I hope the password's somehow been planted in Carla's mind," Jesse said, "because I guess I do trust fate when it comes down to the wire." It was believable that he would be executed, but not that the whole Group would spend the rest of their lives in a penal colony. Oh God, Jesse thought, that just can't happen. . . .

It took them several hours of trial and error to come up with the backdoor password, which proved to be derived from a common phrase any Fleet officer would know. After that, it took more time to discover how to program voices into the command system and add Jesse's as the new Captain. Before then, they'd found that the star charts could be accessed directly from the computer room on a monitor separate from the one Carla was using. So, by the time the bridge hatch yielded to him, he had already located Maclairn's star and gotten a head start on calculation of the jump.

Peter returned to passenger quarters to brief the others, and reluctantly, Carla went with him, knowing the Captain must focus totally on the job at hand. Jesse settled himself before the bridge control console, finding it virtually identical to those of freighters—it had, of course, been modernized when the ship was retrofitted with the new drive. The first priority was to increase their speed. That done, he brought up the appropriate chart on the big video screen. They were by now at a safe distance from Undine to go into hyperdrive. He had only to triple-check the data, run the figures through in pre-command mode rather than as the mere simulation they'd been considered when entered from a programmer's console. It was important not to rush into a virgin jump, one that unlike jumps between settled worlds, had never before been made.

"Jesse!" Erik, who had been stationed in the comm room to listen for incoming traffic, spoke urgently through the intercom. "They're hailing us."

Already? The shuttle was relatively slow compared to *Mayflower XI*; he had expected a bit more leeway. The freighter must have begun pursuit at full speed almost instantly after being alerted. "Put it on speakers," he ordered.

"*Mayflower XI*, we have matched with you," announced a commanding voice. "We are armed; you cannot break away. Prepare for boarding."

"Fleet freighter, we read you," said Jesse. "Don't attempt to board. We won't open our inner hatch."

"I repeat, we are armed. Our shuttle crew is suited and will enter your airlock. They'll blast the inner hatch if necessary. We'll give you five minutes to get your personnel into sealed compartments."

Jesse focused frantically on the calculations in front of him. If he jumped too close to Maclairn's star, they might collide with it; too far, and the normal-space journey required to reach their planet would be too long. He was not ready! They had lost too many hours. There wasn't enough time left to be sure. . . .

"*Mayflower XI,* acknowledge please. In four minutes we will blast your hatch if you fail to open it."

If the ship was boarded, it would mean a prison planet; they would never again set foot on any other. "Get your shuttle clear, Fleet freighter!" he warned. "We are about to jump. You don't want it matched with us when we jump."

"You're bluffing. You can't jump; we know you're locked out of the bridge."

Jesse switched the pickup to visual mode. "I'm in command of the bridge, as you can see if you're close enough to be using short-range comm. I will jump in three minutes. Get clear."

To treat this as a bluff would be suicidal—no shuttle pilot would be fool enough to stay in position to be sucked into hyperspace. Jesse was confident that the pursuers hadn't done so. But if he didn't jump at the time he'd stated, they would be back. There was no choice. He must go with the figures he had, even though he was not wholly sure of them.

His fingers found the switches to press, familiar as if he'd last flown a starship yesterday instead of in what seemed like a former life. Committing the ship to the care of providence, he jumped.

The stars on the viewscreen above the console blinked out, replaced by blackness. The ship was, in this instant, nowhere—literally nowhere in relation to stars or worlds. *The moment of truth,* Jesse thought. It had always been an exhilarating moment for him, the high point in the tedium of his Fleet captaincy. He knew now, for the first time, that it was like an altered state of consciousness. A mind-pattern in which all the reference points of ordinary life were irrelevant, swept away, so that there was only a formless void from which you would emerge into a clean new beginning.

It never worked out that way, of course. You came back to the same troubles or boredom you'd left behind, to fellow-voyagers who hadn't been aware that they were in hyperspace at all. There was no way to detect it within the ship except through instrument readings. People who were used to it did not even feel awe at the knowledge that they'd crossed hundreds of light years within a span of time that was scarcely measurable. The long part of the trip was yet to come, the days or weeks it might take to approach the new star in normal space and orbit the chosen planet. . . .

"Is the freighter still pursuing us?" came Erik's voice.

"No. We're now in a different part of the galaxy," Jesse replied. He turned to the instruments and began checking to make sure that it was the right part.

Two hours later, when Peter came looking for him, he was still checking.

"Isn't it time for me to take the watch, Jess?" Peter asked. "You're long overdue for a break. I assume we're back in normal space and proceeding as planned—"

"I'm afraid not," Jesse admitted, wondering how he was going to say what had to be said. "I had to jump in a hurry. We're a lot farther out than we should be."

"Not at Maclairn's star?" Peter exclaimed in dismay.

"We didn't aim to be *at* it," Jesse said. "We wouldn't want to fall into the star itself. Since I couldn't recheck the figures I leaned toward caution in my estimate of the approximation. Our position when we emerged into normal space wasn't quite what I expected."

"You can correct the course, can't you?"

"Oh, yes—I've done that. We're on course."

"Well, then, we'll get there eventually," Peter said with relief. "For a moment you had me worried, Jess."

"We'll get there," Jesse agreed with pain. "But our life support will run out before we do."

66

HE WENT OVER the figures with Peter, who though ignorant of astrogation and starship provisioning, had enough flying experience to know that computations don't lie. Nevertheless, it took awhile to bring him to the realization that the outcome was already determined. At the rate their life support was being consumed, they would not live to reach Maclairn—or any world.

Jesse himself found it hard to grasp. Despite awareness of the risk, he had not really believed that he would miscalculate. They had all trusted him . . . Ian had trusted him. And he had failed them. He'd been Captain for only a few hours, and he had condemned them to an ordeal far worse than any of them could have anticipated. How could he break it to them, command them, when it was his fault?

"There's no point in telling you not to blame yourself," Peter said, "because you're the sort of man who will. But the rest of us won't blame you, Jess. You did what you had to do. It was just bad luck that you were forced to act too fast."

"It's going to be hell telling people what has to happen," Jesse said, head bent in anguish. "It's the Captain's job, and I'll do it if you think that's wise. But they'll take the news better from you."

"The news that we're going to die? I can handle that," Peter assured him. "It may seem worse to us than it would to outsiders, since we in the Group have expected lengthened lives. But we're not idiots. Everyone has known underneath that we might not make it."

"That's not what I meant," said Jesse, realizing with shock that the alternative had not occurred to Peter. "We don't necessarily have to die. There's a chance we can come through this."

Peter stared at him. "I thought you said all worlds are out of range."

"Of our normal life support, yes. But there's the option we didn't tell the others about."

"Option?" Peter seemed genuinely puzzled.

"This ship still has stasis facilities," Jesse reminded him.

"Oh, my God."

"Had you forgotten?"

"I hadn't forgotten they are here—but Jess, you don't seriously think we could use them."

"Of course. They haven't been used for a very long time, but the AI system hasn't been tampered with. It diverts life support from the passenger quarters onto the stasis deck. Quinn told me it has been maintained, and I've checked it out with the computer; quite possibly it's functional. I'm not saying there's any guarantee we'll survive stasis, but the odds are a damn sight better than our chance of staying alive if we don't try it—which is zero."

"Oh, Jess. Our people wouldn't go voluntarily into stasis if the odds of revival were 100 percent. They would rather die, literally."

"Some would, maybe—but would they condemn the others? It won't work unless we all do it. If even a few refused and kept using up life support, it would run out too soon; then those in stasis would surely die there."

"Which is exactly why I can't propose such an option. The people who'd go along with it would become victims of the rest."

"Peter," Jesse said in dismay. "You of all people know that doing the hard thing generally pays off."

"It's more complicated than that, Jess. I've led you and others to do hard things—but not without support. You're relatively new to our ways and you still don't grasp the part unconscious telepathy plays in influencing what people do. Take my word for it, neither you nor anyone else could have done what you did in training without a lot of backing."

"You provided that backing. You can do it again."

"Not by myself, or even with the help of a small minority." Peter sighed. "As I told you in the beginning, we're not supermen. Our abilities are built on what those before us have undergone. Not just on the knowledge that they got through it, but on their presence, their psychic encouragement. That's why we hoped to establish our own culture, after all—why we've wanted our kids to grow up in an environment that supports the development of our psi skills."

"It doesn't take skill to go into stasis. Plenty of colonists did it, even on this very ship! There would be no colony on Undine if your forebears hadn't done it."

"But the telepathic backing of their contemporaries influenced them, just as it determined the way different societies on Earth—going back to ancient times—varied in what was routinely accepted versus what was viewed as beyond the pale. There were cultures in which cannibalism was common, yet you won't find anyone on Earth today who'd eat human flesh. And you won't find many among us fugitives from Undine's vaults willing to climb into stasis units just like the ones we've escaped from, even with the theoretical expectation of someday waking."

"Are you speaking for yourself, Peter?"

"No. I'd do it. I wouldn't find it easy, but I would do it—I'd even go first if I thought others would follow. But they wouldn't. The unconscious telepathic pressure from the majority, you see, would work against it instead of supplying encouragement."

"Then you're saying nothing the Group has achieved can be salvaged. That Ian's vision meant nothing, and we're all going to die to no purpose."

"Yes, I am, Jess," Peter said with sadness. "The Group has always believed in accepting death when the time comes. None of us ever envisioned facing it in quite this way . . . slowly, while our bodies are still strong and our minds are young, knowing that only a few secretly-transmitted records of what we've worked toward will survive us. But we can resign ourselves to it. We gambled and we lost."

"Damn it, Peter, I know you're a fatalist in the sense of

believing in fate, but you don't usually let that keep you from inspiring people to act."

"Nothing I might say to the Group could overcome a shared phobia as strong as this one." Peter had aged in the last hour, Jesse saw; he no longer seemed young and vital, and that was due not to fear of his own death, but to despair over the futility of what was past. "Foolish and tragic though it is," he maintained, "the majority couldn't face the very real possibility of dying in stasis—which existed even when it was routinely used on starships. They'd choose to wait and die naturally when our life support's exhausted."

Jesse was silent for several minutes, pondering. Finally he said, "I can't let that happen. I'm Captain of this ship, and I'm responsible for more than three hundred lives. I'll do what I have to do to save them."

"You have no power to save them," Peter said wearily. "The sooner you accept that, the sooner you can focus on getting us through what will be very difficult final days. There are decisions to be made about rationing, for instance—"

"I'm Captain," Jesse repeated. "In space the Captain has absolute authority. I will give the command for stasis—and if necessary I will enforce it."

"Enforce it? There's no way you can do that."

"But there is. For all you know about human nature, Peter, in some ways you're damned naive. Force of the kind common most places was suppressed on Undine. Guns couldn't be imported and I don't suppose you've ever seen one. But freighter command requires ability to defend the cargo, after all. The Captain's locker on any starship contains sidearms, and I'm experienced in the use of them."

Peter stared at him. "God, Jesse! You're not serious!"

"Of course I am. I know that for you it's a taboo, one of the kind that depends on the culture a person grows up in. But you, personally, are able to overcome that sort of conditioning. You're capable of judging between two evils and deciding which of them you'd rather have prevail."

"Put that way ... I can't argue with you. But it won't work, Jess. Our people aren't going believe you'd shoot them if they refuse to obey your orders. They know and admire you, and unlike the Fleet crew we threatened, they're sensitive enough to your mind to grasp your underlying intent."

"Are they? Or will they unconsciously block that sensitivity, as you're evidently blocking it now?" At Peter's gasp of shock Jesse added, "I wouldn't point a gun I didn't intend to fire, Peter. Consider this your first lesson in how to handle a gun."

"And are you going to hold a gun on Carla, then?" Peter demanded. "She won't get into a stasis unit voluntarily, you know; her phobia about them is stronger than anyone's. I suspect she'd prefer to be shot."

In anguish, Jesse bowed his head. "Which side are you on, Peter?" he demanded. "Do you want us to live, or not? If you do, you're going to have to help me, not make it impossible."

Peter did not answer. In turmoil, Jesse left him on watch and went alone to inspect the stasis deck. The sealed hatch opened to his voice. He descended the companionway to the anteroom, turned on the power, and entered the chamber. It looked just like the vaults in the Hospital. Most others in the Group had, like himself, served briefly as vault attendants; there would be no difficulty in operating the equipment. Although there was no way to test it and certainly no assurance that it would function throughout the time they would have to hibernate, everything appeared to be in working order.

But, he realized with dismay, there was one physical difference, a large difference, between what the Group would face and what the early colonists on this ship had experienced. When stasis had been used for long-term space travel, passengers had been sedated by trusted medical personnel before being put into the units. They had not gotten in by themselves. Now, on *Mayflower XI*, there was no supply of suitable sedatives. People would have to literally climb into what looked like coffins—might well prove to be coffins—and let the lids be closed before lowered metabolism could render them unconscious. It was all too probable that some of them might balk.

What was he going to do? He could not let everyone die when there was a chance of survival! Would ordering them to comply at gunpoint work—or would some really prefer to be shot? Would it be justifiable to shoot those who preferred it in order to save the rest? But, he thought in agony, if he started that, he would have to carry it through, and what if one of them was Carla?

Peter was leader of the Group. It would be easy to let him make the decision he'd seemed to believe was his. But that was not how it worked in space. The responsibility was the Captain's, whether he actively assumed it or not. Even if he proved unequal to it. Even if his miscalculation led to a slow, agonizing death for all aboard. Falling into Maclairn's star would have been better than that, Jesse thought despairingly. At least they'd have died instantly.

He sat for a long time, hunched over with his back against the anteroom's bulkhead, seeing no answer yet unwilling to give up hope. If they were to act, it must be soon. It would be no good having regrets once the life support resources dropped below the level that would permit stasis to be followed by reawakening. Furthermore, enough time must be allowed after waking for establishing an orbit around Maclairn and for the many shuttle trips that would be needed to get everyone to its surface; it would be worse to die within sight of their new world than never to have reached it.

Finally, reluctantly, Jesse went to his cabin. By the clock it was nearly morning; he would need a few hours of sleep to get through the demanding day to come. But in the cabin he would have to face Carla. She would want to make love, and if they did that, if they entered the enhanced telepathic state sex engendered, he could not prevent her from perceiving the truth. He'd hidden the existence of the shipboard stasis vaults so far because he'd felt no personal emotion about them . . . though on an unconscious level he must have shared *her* emotion, despite her resolute suppression of the memory that haunted her. Now, there was no way he could keep them out of his mind.

She was asleep when he entered; he left the light off and tried to undress soundlessly, hoping she would stay asleep. But of course she didn't. His desperation intruded into her dream. Carla sat up, not needing to see his face to know his anguish. "There's something wrong," she said, without uncertainty. "Tell me, Jesse."

He sat on the bed and drew her into his arms. "I can't tell you," he whispered. "It's too hard a thing to say."

"Then let me into your mind! Come to bed and show me, if you can't put into words." She threw off the sheet and pulled him down; he kissed her, but forced himself to hold back.

"Carla, we mustn't do this. If we do, you'll learn something you don't want to know."

"Jesse! How could I not want to know whatever's troubling you? Didn't I share the very worst with you, when you were condemned, when we believed your mind would be destroyed? Don't shut me out."

"The problem isn't just mine. It affects *you*—and everyone."

"Is the ship in danger, then?"

"Yes, Carla," he admitted.

"Well, are you going to keep that to yourself forever? Or are you planning to let me find out when you tell the whole Group? Isn't the Captain's wife entitled to advance notice?"

She did have a right, he realized. She would have to know eventually, and to find out this way, through their love, would be easier for her than to hear a general announcement. It was himself he was trying to protect, not her—if their minds merged he would share her shock and terror as intensely as her physical response. So be it. Perhaps he could give her some comfort, for a short while, at least. Anyway, this might be the last time. . . .

The last time. He had not thought of it that way before, but if they went into stasis and failed to wake, this would be the last time they ever made love. Oh God, they could not die like that—shut away from each other, alone in the dark, encased in steel boxes with the AI doing horrible things to their bodies, trapped there forever.... He must not let Carla find out that he'd ever considered it. Resolutely he thrust it from his thoughts and buried his face between her breasts, trying not to think at all as his perceptions and hers began to blend.

They joined, lost at first in the rapture of mutual sensations. But he could not feel his usual pleasure in them. Against his will, the image of the vaults welled up again—the vaults as he had just seen them ... row upon row of racked units, translucent covers darkened so that whether they contained bodies wasn't apparent.... In shock, he withdrew from her, but it was too late; they were both too aroused for the telepathic bond to weaken. Carla, confused, shrank as if from her old nightmare, the execution of Ramón. *I'm sorry, I'm sorry, I thought it wouldn't come back....* Then as she sensed more and cried out, panic overtook him, and she saw, in the nearest unit, her own face.

She jerked away from him, screaming.

As their shared consciousness shattered, Jesse knew with dismay that not all the fear had been Carla's. Though she'd pushed him over the brink, part of that fear was his own ... fear for her, but also for himself. The units *had* looked like coffins. He was no more eager to seal himself into a thing like that than anybody else. In horror he recalled the blue-faced body in the Hospital vault's unit that had failed, the one he'd helped to transfer ... what if he died in stasis and Carla did not, what if she woke to see his unrevivable corpse, knowing they were doomed after all since without him to pilot, they could not get to the surface of Maclairn? Or the other way around, what if he was forced to open the vaults and found many such corpses, hers among them?

Even if they all survived stasis, it might prove to be for nothing. Was it even possible that he alone, the only one capable of flying a shuttle, could make enough round trips in quick succession to get three hundred people off the starship before the meager life support that would remain ran out? If not, he was asking many to face a futile ordeal. . . .

He pulled Carla toward him again and held her, caressing her trembling body. Her mind was shut tight against him now. Neither of them spoke. After a while he began to shiver and pulled a blanket over them. Eventually she retreated into sleep, but Jesse could not. He lay wakeful beside her until morning.

67

BY THIS TIME tomorrow it would be too late, Jesse thought despairingly. He was Captain, he was responsible for over three hundred lives, yet he was powerless to sway the Group toward the one slim possibility of survival. He was no longer even sure that he himself was capable of doing what he must ask of them. Still, he must offer them the choice. He could not allow Peter to make it for them by default.

Carla was very calm. She knew everything, of course; telepathy takes less time than speech. She had grasped the whole truth in a flash, though not all consciously, and had processed it as she slept. They rose and dressed, saying little.

As he started to leave the cabin, Carla reached for his hand. "I'm not afraid to die, Jesse," she said. "That's what the Group has always stood for, isn't it—not fearing death?"

"But we might live, Carla!" Jesse said. "We might wake up within sight of a new world!"

"No," she said sadly. "Peter was right when he told you we can't do that."

There was a knock on the door and Jesse opened it to Peter. "Kwame has the watch," he said. "I've filled the rest of the Council in, and there's no question about how things will go. But as a member, you have a right to speak before we vote. Can we meet here, now?" He frowned, his eyes on Carla.

"She knows," Jesse said shortly. "We slept together."

"Then I assume she's confirmed what I told you."

"Yes."

"If the Council's going to meet, I'll get out of the way," Carla said, straightening the bed cover.

"No—stay, Carla!" Jesse pleaded. "You and I didn't talk. You sensed only the worst of it." To Peter he said, "I'd just inspected the stasis deck. It was vivid in my mind, and I—panicked. Do you suppose I don't know how hard it would be to—" He broke off, telling himself that it was only for Carla's sake that he avoided spelling it out.

Kira came in with Hari and Reiko. Before seating herself at the table, she embraced him. "Jesse, dear," she said, "we all know the hell you're going through. If there were any possible way we could support you, we would—and it's our own lives at stake too, after all. But we couldn't save them by proposing a plan we know people won't accept. We would only make things worse for those who'd want to follow it."

"My God, Kira. Are you so sure the rest won't listen to reason? I'm scared, too—more than I thought I would be. But that's no excuse for throwing away our only chance to live."

"There's more to it than simply being scared. Isn't that right, Carla?"

Carla nodded. To Jesse she said, "I'm sorry. I wish I were as strong as you are. But you—you came from Fleet, where such things seem natural. For us it's different."

"It is," Peter agreed, "and it's not a matter of strength or weakness. You see, Jesse, we're all afraid of *something,* deep down where we may not ever find it. And when we learn to overcome our more troublesome fears, we project the emotion we suppress onto that deep fear, that phobia, so that it becomes a symbol of all the rest. That's the price we pay for our freedom from them. In the Group, the maintenance of bodies in stasis is that symbol. And because we do live free from other fears, it's an exceptionally powerful one. It stands for everything we strive to resist."

"Yes," declared Jesse, anger suddenly rising in him. "That's exactly what it is—a symbol. No more than that! It matters to *us,* the living, not to those who die. There is life and there is death—there's no in between. Maybe something comes after and maybe it doesn't, but either way, what happens to dead bodies isn't going to change it."

"Then why have we been risking arrest all these years to keep bodies out of the Vaults?" Carla protested.

"Because it does matter to us. Because a society that worships mere flesh is built on false values, and can't ever move beyond that stage to empowering the mind. But we're beyond it ourselves, after all. Surely you don't think that if we die in stasis we'll be trapped in our bodies somehow— like the old tales of ghosts that can't go to their rest because they're not properly buried."

"I don't know what I believe," she whispered. "I just know I can't die the way Ramón and Ian did. I can't let *you* die that way."

"Carla—Ian died in stasis so that we could get to a new world! Considering that he did it to save me, shouldn't I be willing to do the same? Shouldn't all of us? Aren't we betraying him if we refuse to even risk the kind of death he accepted for our sake?"

All five of them froze, staring at him. "Dear God," said Kira. "I hadn't thought of it like that."

"Neither had I," Peter confessed. "I've been too wrapped up in how the others would feel to grasp what his sacrifice implies. In the light of it, of course we should follow his example—I'd do so gladly if it could accomplish anything. But I still see no way to persuade everybody. Much as our people loved Ian, they don't all have his courage—"

Ian . . . once again Jesse was overcome by memory of the dream in which Ian had come to him. The foreboding he'd felt at its end, the knowledge that Ian depended on him, the Group depended on him, that if he gave in to pressure or fear or despair, Carla would die. . . . Had that, like the rest, been drawn from Ian's prescient intuition? Would inability to get people into stasis, not miscalculation of the jump, be his true failure? Ian had given no clue as to how to win them over . . . or had he?

Suddenly, Jesse was hit by a flash of illumination. "Peter," he burst out, "what was it he said to you, his mysterious last words?"

"'You never really understood,'" Peter recalled, "'And for the Group's sake I couldn't tell you. But know that this won't matter in the end.'"

"You never understood that the Vaults *always were* a symbol," Jesse said. "Ian never thought stasis was in itself worse than other forms of burial! But he couldn't tell you that, because a symbol was what the Group needed. He turned the Vaults into a symbol in the first place in order to create the Group."

Slowly, thoughtfully, Peter admitted, "That might be true."

"And when he said 'this won't matter,'" Jesse continued, "he wasn't referring to our carrying on after his execution, as we all assumed. He meant that dying in stasis wouldn't matter to *him,* or to any of us, compared to other ways we might die. He believed what I just said, that it matters only to the living."

Peter paced across the cabin, his back to the Council table, drawing on memories. At last he turned to the others. "I was blind," he said, awestricken. "I had to be, to lead the Group without hypocrisy. He knew it would fall apart if we stopped caring about the burial of bodies. That's why he didn't let me sense his meaning telepathically."

Jesse drew a deep breath. "Forgive me, Peter," he said, "but you still are blind if you don't see the flaw in what you've been telling me. Our people have a phobia about stasis, you say. Sure—but isn't that precisely why we have to confront it? Doesn't the pledge in the Ritual demand it of us? You made me confront everything I was ever afraid of, step by step, and presumably you did the same with everybody. What was it all for, if we end up refusing to face the one thing that might give us a chance to survive?"

Peter, visibly shaken, spoke in a low voice. "I was too close to it," he said. "Ian gave us symbols, he taught us methods of empowerment, and they worked—I knew enough about psychology to make them work. But I never had to innovate—never had to go beyond the bounds of the one narrow culture we were trapped in. It's taken an offworlder to show me the limits I've set."

"Those methods still can work," Jesse said. "I don't know how to do it, but *you* do—you know how to arouse the powers that make us able to do things we think aren't possible. God, Peter—we walk on fire, put our hands in fire! Carla said that centuries ago on Earth, a charismatic leader could teach crowds of total novices to firewalk in a few hours' time! So don't tell me you can't get people into some sort of altered state that enables them to enter stasis units, phobia or no phobia."

"You have a point, Jesse," Kira said. "Appeals to reason wouldn't work. An altered state would be needed—even, I think, by you and me. Although," she added, "I guess in the old days, when they sedated passengers, somebody had to be the last one in, alone and fully conscious."

"I think that was the Captain's job," Jesse said. "It still is." He hadn't previously given thought to this, but it was glaringly obvious, even, he saw, to Carla, who sat quietly on the bed, white-faced at the turn of the discussion. The last person to go in would have no telepathic support from anyone. . . .

"We wouldn't want sedation even if we had drugs," Hari pointed out. "Our way of dealing with fear depends on full volitional control, after all. And our people are trained in it. It should not be impossible to use one of the states with which they're already experienced."

"You're right, of course," Peter agreed. "But practically speaking, we don't have the means to induce it. I could get one or two people at a time into a suitable state any number of ways. It could be done easily with hypnosis—or we could even set up the neurofeedback equipment and do it with mind-patterns. But a mass induction is another matter. The only area large enough to hold the Group is nowhere near the stasis deck. People brought to the point of such things as walking on fire don't go off and do it by themselves, away from supporters."

"Are we assuming there's not enough time to prepare people individually, then?" asked Reiko.

"Our time's running out," Jesse replied. "Every hour we continue to use normal life support increases the odds of our dying aboard the ship." Ironically, as the others were starting to consider the alternative, he himself was becoming more aware of its impossibility. His idea of forcing people into stasis at gunpoint would not work, he saw—not because it wouldn't be justifiable, but because, as Hari had said, the Group's freedom from fear was attained only through volition. Members were trained, and pledged, to resist pressure. Any attempt to compel someone would bring about more resistance than it would overcome.

"It's almost too bad that going into stasis isn't painful," Kira was saying. "If it were, people's attention would be on attaining immunity to pain, a state they all know how to get into. They wouldn't have time to be afraid."

"Well, yes," said Peter. "That's the principle behind a lot of what we do. But it can't help us with this. Even if we held the Ritual to bring people into that state—"

"Couldn't we do that?" Reiko suggested. "The shared high from the Ritual lasts long enough to get people into stasis without panicking."

Peter shook his head. "The Ritual requires stronger emotion than personal fear. A novice is emotionally aroused by the demand for commitment, while the onlookers not only renew their own, but take responsibility for that novice's safety. At Ian's funeral, when we held it with a large group, we were all feeling intense grief. And on top of these emotions, everyone who joins in the Ritual *wants* to participate—there is always desire. We couldn't pull it off with people merely repelled by something they wanted to avoid."

"We couldn't hold the Ritual anyway," said Hari. "We don't have a torch or candles."

"Yes, we do," Carla told him. "I packed the candles with the lab equipment because we might not be able to make any on the new world."

Jesse's mind was still on Ian. "Peter," he ventured, "when Ian first had the dream about us establishing our own colony, how did he know it was precognitive?"

"For one thing, he'd had them before, dreams of equivalent clarity that came true," Peter said. "The reason he believed this one, though, was because he had it the night you arrived on Undine. That was why we felt fate had sent you to us."

"Well, then, don't we know we're going to get to that colony—which we can't do without going into stasis?"

"No. They don't *all* come true. Precognition can be overridden by events."

"If that's so, he would have tried to do everything possible to foresee the events that might override it. He would have learned all the details he could about the plans you and he were making."

"I'm sure he did," Peter agreed.

"And yet you told me the agent who found out about this ship didn't tell you its name. That struck me as odd—any notation of its availability would have included the name and class. Did the report come to your computer, or Ian's?"

"To his. I was working full time besides going to the Lodge. Ian was at home, so he handled the offworld communication."

Kira, intrigued, said, "What are you getting at, Jesse?"

Jesse turned to her. "You said when Ian died that it was strange they executed him. That because he was so old and already dying, they should have shown more mercy."

"That's true," she said. "They couldn't have freed him after a confession of aggravated murder, but Undine's authorities aren't intentionally cruel. They could easily have waited a week or two and put him into stasis after he died. Even if Warick wanted to rush it, the others should have objected—and in any case, if he'd let Peter consult a lawyer, a stay pending exemption could have been obtained."

"I think," Jesse said, "that perhaps he *requested* not to be exempted. That he guessed we might have to go into stasis, and was trying to send us a signal."

The others, startled, gasped in dismay. "How could he have guessed?" Reiko asked. "Are you saying he had another dream about space?"

"That's possible," said Peter thoughtfully. "But even if he didn't, he was well aware that astrogating to an unopened world would be a risky undertaking."

"It's no secret that *Mayflower* class ships have operational stasis vaults," Jesse went on. "Ian surely would have known it; he would have investigated the ship he was told we'd be getting. But he didn't tell you, Peter—just as he didn't tell you what his last words meant."

"He couldn't," Peter agreed. "To bring up their former use in space travel would have jeopardized the symbol he knew we'd need as long as we remained on Undine."

"Then, when he confessed to murder in order to save me," Jesse went on, "he saw a way to show us he wasn't afraid of dying in stasis. And he asked you to be with him at the end, knowing you'd tell us he wasn't afraid—even if we never figured out any more. But if we *have* figured it out, it helps, doesn't it? To believe he went into stasis voluntarily while he was still alive?"

"Oh yes," said Kira. "The mere possibility that he did will help those who fear underneath that stasis interferes with what comes after death. They know Ian wouldn't have accepted it so calmly if he believed it does."

Slowly, Peter said, "I remember, now . . . feelings I had

during those last minutes with Ian. He had far greater paranormal powers than the rest of us; it's possible that he communicated more than he wanted me to be aware of then. I think perhaps he believed that he shouldn't spell it out for us—that only by facing our greatest fear could we become fit founders of a new culture."

"But he was taking a chance that you wouldn't ask people to face it."

"Not really. It's possible, Jesse, that when he told you he trusted you, he didn't mean only to command a starship, or even to serve on the Council."

"To do what, then?" Besides what Kira had said about supporting Peter. . . .

"To question symbols we might cling to too long, and to see what he had to hide from me. He came to you telepathically in a dream, after all. He may have planted something in your mind as well as in mine."

"Yes," Jesse agreed. "I realized, just a few minutes ago, that perhaps he had."

"When he found that he could, it all must have fallen into place for him," Peter said softly. "His own two dreams, his concern for our future, and then after our despair over your condemnation, the chance to help us survive that wouldn't have existed if you hadn't been arrested . . . he must have been awed by that strange pattern, just as I am now."

Carla, who had listened with increasing absorption, rose and came to Jesse, resting her hands on his shoulders. "How could I not trust you as much as Ian did, when I love you so?" she murmured. "He gave his life to make you Captain! He relied on you to do whatever it took to make his dream come true."

"Whether we go into stasis is not a matter for the Council to vote on," Peter said. "We were wrong to assume it's up to us. Ian placed our lives in Jesse's hands, knowing full well that in space, the Captain commands. If we're to die, it is for Jesse to decide how it will happen. As Executive Officer, my role is merely to see that his orders are carried out."

Moved to tears, Jesse said, "Personally I'll consider it an honor to die as Ian died, if it comes to that. But I believe it won't. I'm sure *he* believed we're going to live."

"An honor," Peter reflected. "Yes—yes, it would be that for us all. And on that—on our love for him, our desire to give no less than he did toward our goal, our realization that he entered stasis willingly—we can build the Ritual."

68

TO THE FULL Group, assembled on his command, Jesse explained the facts of their situation. He informed them of how long the ship's life support would last. But he said nothing about the option of stasis. "That must be revealed telepathically," Peter had warned. "I've already told some people—those whose support I can count on, who will help us spread confidence when the moment comes. The rest mustn't think about it in their normal state of mind. Our only hope of overcoming resistance lies in not letting it start."

Peter stood when Jesse had finished speaking. "The Captain has told you that we're going to die," he said. "Yet there is a chance we may not, and to understand that chance, we must look deeper than our fear, deeper than we have ever needed to look before. To perceive it, we must hold the Ritual."

He paused. There were a few teenagers and novice members present who must not observe the climax, lest foreknowledge interfere when the time came for their own rites. For them, blindfolds were provided by Kira; the telepathic ambience of the gathering would be sufficient to carry them along. Then Peter continued, "We must commit ourselves fully to the power of the Ritual, reserving no trace of worry or doubt. Is there anyone here who is not willing to do this?"

No one objected. They were already spellbound, having been offered unlooked-for hope of reprieve from certain death. Jesse knew that this was the greatest test Peter had ever faced, ever imagined that he would face. If he could not arouse the group's psi power and hold all minds to the perspective he presented, there would be no reprieve. He would not get a second chance.

The other Council members, too, would share responsibility, Jesse himself no less than the rest. "There are only a few of us to muster the courage of over three hundred people," Peter had told them. "So remember what's required to gain use of paranormal skills." *To gain true volitional control, you must be wholly, unreservedly willing to lose control—to let what comes, come, with full consent to the consequences,* Jesse recalled. He must not try to project telepathically by means of willpower; willpower would not work any better than it did for suppressing panic. He must be willing to let go, willing to let his unconscious mind decide the outcome. He must focus only on his belief in what they must do.

Then to the Council Peter had said, "We will hold our hands in fire longer than usual, not only to gain time for strong telepathic projection, but because power comes from risk. It goes without saying that if any of us were to panic or withdraw, it would break the spell among the watchers. It would be better to be burned than to fail them. If we've learned anything about volitional control these past years, let's use it now, when our lives depend on it."

Candles were passed out to the people, then lit. It occurred to Jesse that all those flames were using up oxygen, but what the hell—this was what it would take to keep from using the rest of it up. Carla, again serving as torchbearer, came forward holding a makeshift torch of candles bound to a rod. As he ignited it, Peter began to speak.

He spoke of Ian, of how they'd followed Ian through the many years of the Group's existence. Of how they'd loved him. Of his sacrifice in confessing to a crime of which he was innocent for their sake, paying a terrible penalty to give them the chance to seek a new world. Of how he'd dreamed of that world and believed they would reach it. There were tears in the eyes of most listeners by the time Peter began the formal words, the words Ian himself had spoken at the Ritual commitment of each and every one of them: "Unfaced fear is the destroyer. We will acknowledge fear and accept it, we will go past it and live free. . . ."

As he thrust his hand into the flame, Peter said, "We know now that Ian did not fear stasis. He died in stasis willingly—and if we too must die, let it be as he did. Fate has honored us by giving us that choice."

Quickly, Jesse and the other Council members placed their hands on Peter's as he continued, "But fate may also allow us to live. Those who want to live as Ian lived, at the risk of dying as he died, touch now the flame of life to seal your commitment."

The emotional force of the appeal was magnified as the watching participants passed fingers through the flames of three hundred candles. In that moment, knowledge of what they must do was spread wordlessly. Jesse sensed a greater melding of minds than he had ever felt. He became one with the Group, aware of the Group's faith in life. Once again he saw Ian as he'd appeared in the dream, with the torch between them, his hand clasping Ian's in fire, and then he was walking with Ian toward the world of Maclairn, golden against a backdrop of stars, as perhaps all now could see it through his eyes. And he was high, they were all high . . . the death sentence had been no more than a brief nightmare . . . they would dream again, dream of entrapment in stasis, but they would awaken to found a new world. . . .

He wasn't aware that his flesh was burning until Peter withdrew from the flame and the torch was lowered. Dropping his hand, Jesse saw to his surprise that it was red and blistered. Peter had intended this, he realized, seeing that it was true of them all. Controlling the pain of the burns would keep them in altered consciousness, keep them able to support the people who must now go, still entranced, to what mere minutes ago would have seemed an unthinkable ordeal.

Still holding their lighted candles, people left a few at a time for the stasis deck, escorted by Reiko and met by Kira and Hari. With Peter and Carla, Jesse stayed on the passenger deck, maintaining the telepathic high among the others, until the last of them had gone and the ship had been secured.

He had set the master stasis timer and sealed the bridge earlier. There'd have been no point in leaving a watch crew awake even if resources had been sufficient, since there was no one qualified to repair problems in any case. Either the starship would get them to Maclairn, or it wouldn't. Either the life-support AI would maintain their bodies in stasis and wake them in due course, or it wouldn't. Having no means of control over these things, he did not concern himself with them. He would entrust the ship and himself to whatever it was that Peter called fate.

The high from the Ritual still sustained them when they reached the stasis chamber, though their burns were already nearly healed. All the others had been sealed into units except Kira. They stripped quickly and placed their folded clothes in the storage compartments of the adjacent units reserved for them; then Jesse helped her into hers. "One way or another, we'll wake to a new world," she said, smiling and evidently at peace. Grasping her meaning, Jesse became aware that although this had never been his own faith, it was now a part of the merged knowledge, so that he could not be sure whether it had come telepathically into his mind or had risen from his own unconscious depths.

"I'll go last," Peter said, "since I'm the strongest telepathically."

"No," said Jesse. "It's the Captain's place to go last."

Peter nodded. "Okay. Carla?"

"I'd rather go closest to Jesse."

"That's wise," he agreed, getting into his own unit. Just before he closed the lid he said to her, "Ian must have told Ramón the truth, you know. He was with him at the end, as I was with Ian." And to both of them, "There's something I didn't mention that I learned then. There will be a brief moment awake in the unit, and then for a short while, I think, altered consciousness. Ian and I were in contact during that time—as we now know happens in other mind-impaired states, the prelude to stasis enhanced his telepathic power. That was why I was sure he had no fear. You may experience this with me; I don't know. But I believe you'll have contact with each other."

Jesse held Carla tightly as the translucent cover slid shut and the unit swung into the rack. In their minds, Peter's thought was clear. *What fools we all were to feel terror! What happens to mere bodies does not matter. The important things aren't touched by that. . . .*

"It's time, Carla," Jesse said gently. "The sooner we get it over with, the sooner we'll find ourselves near our new world."

"I know. I'm not afraid anymore, just so you're with me." She clung to him and they kissed, a long, passionate kiss. Then he opened a unit for her and helped her in. She looked up at him, eyes dark and luminous but not anguished, dark hair framing her pale face. "I'll see you in a little while, Jesse," she said, and pressed the switch for the lid.

He did not wait for the automatic racking, but got quickly into his own unit, fumbling with the controls in his hurry to go under as fast as possible. He could hear her calling in his mind, and feared she might lose consciousness before his, too, became enhanced. Or would they, somewhere in the deepest recess of their being, continue to share?

And then he was in darkness, oblivious to what the AI was doing to him, aware only of Carla as their minds merged. He saw her not in the unit but on the Island, as on the day of his Ritual commitment, the day they had made love joyously by the shore. She stood on the rocks with bay mists swirling around her; he moved forward to her, floating free of his body, free of all fear or grief, and he took her hand. *I love you, Carla,* he said and heard her answer, *I love you, Jesse,* as love enveloped them . . . and there was nothing more than that to say, because nothing mattered now except the love.

Afterword

Healthcare technology has advanced rapidly since I wrote this story in 2005. In some respects the story is dated—for example, it's no longer credible that implanted heart monitors would be viewed as an innovative violation of privacy by people living in the era of starships, since these are now already in use (although they surely would be unacceptable if made compulsory).

But in other respects the story is more timely than ever. The worldwide response to COVID-19 has shown the scope of government control that the public will accept in the name of health. Who would have thought that people would tolerate being told they could not leave their homes, go to church, meet friends, hold private weddings or funerals, or even gather with their extended families under their own roofs without being raided by the police? Certainly COVID-19 did make it necessary to restrict large public gatherings, but in my opinion the extent to which private actions were forbidden in some areas was less justifiable. In any case, the lack of widespread protest demonstrates that when curtailment of freedom is related to health, there's no limit to what people will stand for. The dictatorship ruled by medical authority in the story—which is supported by the colony's voters—goes only one step further; and I'm afraid it's less of an exaggeration than it may have seemed when the book was first published.

One other point about the book needs comment, as some readers have said that they agree, or disagree, that people should rely on mind-body healing rather than technological medicine. I never intended the novel to be interpreted an applicable in that respect to people of today. On the contrary, the characters in the story learn to banish sickness and pain only through the use of futuristic training technology that we do not possess, with the aid of a telepathic instructor—an option not available in our era. The point is not that technological medicine should be avoided, but that no form of medical care should be imposed by dictatorial laws, and that for people to give up their civil liberties out of concern for their health is a sad mistake.

ORIGINAL 2007 AFTERWORD, AS UPDATED IN 2019

We are closer than you may think to the things described in this story—both the bad and the good. When in 2005 I came to revise a draft of portions written years earlier, I discovered that some of my imaginings were no longer science fiction. For links to my detailed discussion of these topics and more, go to the Opinion section of my website, which was updated and expanded in June, 2019. It includes lists of articles and reliable books about them.

By 2007 when this book was first published, Antabuse implants were already in use for the treatment of alcoholism. Some patients voluntarily seek them.

Toilets that can measure health parameters and transfer the data to a home network have been on the market in Japan since 2005. More advanced features are on the horizon; according to an article in the *New York Times* for October 8, 2002, a Matsushita engineer explained, "You may think a toilet is just a toilet, but we would like to make a toilet a home health measuring center. We are going to install in a toilet devices to measure weight, fat, blood pressure, heart beat, urine sugar, albumin and blood inurine.' The results would be sent from the toilet to a doctor by an Internet-capable cellular phone built into the toilet. . . . But some civil libertarians are having nightmares about 'smart toilets' running amok, e-mailing highly personal information hither and yon."

Soon after the book's publication I learned that considerable research on remote health monitoring was being done, and an article about it in *Nursing Homes* declared, "Users must be willing to trade some degree of privacy for an added sense of security." By now, in 2019, monitoring technology has become big business. Before long it will be routinely used by most if not all medical facilities and the concept of personal privacy concerning one's body functions will be history. For more detail on this, see the Remote Monitoring page at my website..

Implanted heart monitors were undergoing clinical tests as early as 2001. An article in the May 4 issue of *EE Times* reported, "Ultimately, engineers say they can foresee a day when an implanted heart monitor will detect a problem and call an ambulance, all while the patient lies sleeping." It quoted a representative of Medtronic, Inc. who said, "We'd like to believe that someday a pacemaker could send a signal directly to a satellite. When it comes to this kind of patient management, we'd like to believe the sky's the limit."

None of this is to say that there aren't valid uses for remote monitoring technologies or that they may not be beneficial to people who choose them, such as those who find it difficult or expensive to travel to medical offices, or who might be enabled to stay out of nursing homes. But it is a short step from choice to compulsion once the government and the public come to believe that health considerations trump all other human values.

As for passive implanted microchips that merely refer to a medical database, these were approved by the FDA in 2004. Some people are eagerly getting them, although there are others who view them as the Biblical "mark of the beast" (Revelation 13: 16–17). Though there have been proposals to implant them in immigrants, the homeless, and all members of the military, voluntary acceptance of them seems likely to overshadow such uses—already thousands of people in Europe are using implants in place of cash and credit cards. Whereas an implantable GPS-enabled chip that could be used for tracking is not yet available, developers are working on it; to the dismay of privacy experts and countless bloggers, a wearable prototype was unveiled in 2000.

In 2006 New York began checking the blood sugar levels of residents with diabetes by requiring medical labs to report test results to the city—the first time any American government has monitored individuals with a non-contagious disease. The program is justified by its supporters on grounds that money and lives could be saved through intervention in the care of those whose diabetes is poorly controlled. As an article in the *New York Sun* commented, "This new diabetes regulation is, in short, a harbinger of more intrusive legislation to come—all in the name of 'public health.'"

The involuntary treatment of persons deemed mentally ill is not a new issue, and there is a huge amount of information about it on the Web and elsewhere; so here I will simply say that my portrayal of it in the story is, if anything, less appalling than the reality. Any opponent of tyranny who remains under the impression that it's okay to impose what's "best" for sick people on them by force would do well to investigate the horrific effects of psychiatric drugs, and ponder the implications of compulsion for health care in general.

While the maintenance of dead bodies on machines was an intentionally-exaggerated aspect of the story, it is closer to reality than I knew when I imagined it, at least with respect to people in the process of dying. More and more concerns are being raised about the medical prolongation of death, which few people would choose for themselves if they were aware of what happens in hospitals to the terminally ill who are no longer competent to decide. I learned to my dismay that some are consigned to LTACs (long-term acute care facilities), described by Dr. Jessica Ritter in her book *Extreme Measures* as "a factory environment where body after silent body [lies] in adjacent rooms, machines churning away." Their relatives consent to this, just as the majority of the public in the story supported the Vaults. Where would the line be drawn if our technology were further advanced?

On the bright side, in December 2005—several months after this novel was completed and many years after the first draft of Part Two was written—the Proceedings of the National Academy of Science published a paper describing research in which people have been taught to control pain perception through real-time functional MRI brain scanning. Neurofeedback of a less advanced type is now common, and a number of major books have appeared on the new science of neuroplasticity, So it appears that what I envisioned for the future may someday come true.

The influence of the mind on biochemistry—and the physical effect of psychological stress—is by now a well-researched field of knowledge and many excellent books for laypeople deal with it. This is the science underlying traditional alternative and/or spiritual healing practices, most of which have a foundation in fact however metaphorical the explanations they offer for their success. Unfortunately, in the twenty-first century we lack methods for fully utilizing this knowledge. The story is not meant to suggest that all conventional medical treatment could be abandoned by the average person living today.

The so-called "paranormal" powers in the story are exaggerated only with respect to the characters' conscious control over them. These abilities, with the exception of fire immunity and rapid healing, have been confirmed by a vast amount of scientific evidence, albeit evidence that is ignored by too many orthodox scientists. (And even fire handling—as distinguished from fire-walking, which is common—is occasionally practiced by small religious groups today, apart from the many historical reports that may or may not be true.) For a Web list of many excellent books on psi by scientific researchers and other respected authors, please visit my website's detailed background pages for this book.

The most optimistic development of the past few years is the growing concern on the part of doctors and other healthcare professionals about medical over-treatment. Hopefully, the trend toward unnecessary and sometimes-detrimental treatment is beginning to reverse. For a long list of recent nonfiction books and articles on this subject by physicians, investigative journalists and others, please visit the Overtreatment page at my website.

Despite the bitter struggles in Congress over the issue of how to reform the nation's health care system, nobody on either side of the debate has recognized the root of its problems—which is that society can never afford to provide medical care for everyone who really needs it as long as so much unnecessary—and often even harmful—treatment is given to those who do not. Often such treatment is not advised by doctors, but is the result of patients' demands. If public attitudes toward unessential health care don't change, I fear that we will be all too likely to end up with a system like the one in the story.

Sylvia Engdahl, June 2021

About the Author

SYLVIA ENGDAHL is the author of eleven science fiction novels. Six of them are Young Adult books that are also enjoyed by adults, all of which were originally published by Atheneum and have been republished, in both hardcover and paperback, by different publishers in the twenty-first century. The one for which she is best known, *Enchantress from the Stars*, was a Newbery Honor book in 1971, winner of the 1990 Phoenix Award of the Children's Literature Association, and a finalist for the 2002 Book Sense Book of the Year in the Rediscovery category. Her trilogy *Children of the Star* was reissued in a single volume as adult science fiction.

Her five most recent novels, a duology and a trilogy, are not YA books and are not appropriate for middle-school readers, but will be enjoyed by the many adult fans of her work. In addition, she has issued an updated and expanded edition of her nonfiction book *The Planet-Girded Suns: Our Forebears' Firm Belief in Inhabited Exoplanets* (first published by Atheneum in 1974 with a different subtitle) as well as three ebooks of collected essays.

Between 1957 and 1967 Engdahl was a computer programmer and Computer Systems Specialist for the SAGE Air Defense System. Most recently she has worked as a freelance editor of nonfiction anthologies for high schools. Now retired, she lives in Eugene, Oregon, and welcomes visitors to her website www.sylviaengdahl.com, which contains many of her essays, including those dealing with her long-term advocacy of space colonization.